Critical acclaim for Caro Fraser

'With such a sparkling debut, we may, with any luck be seeing the entrance of a new freshly minted John Mortimer'   *Daily Mail*

'A Mary Wesleyan tale of upper-middle-class snobbery, ambition . . . and love . . . Fraser writes with fluent flair'   *Sunday Telegraph*

'Fraser writes with panache, exuberance and humour, and never leaves the reader too long waiting for the next twist'   *The Times*

'There's never a dull moment: [a] brilliantly constructed plot. Fraser engages her readers quickly and never lets go'   *Tatler*

'Prepare to be seduced by this masterful tale of love, duplicity and ambition . . . Exciting, funny and sad, this is one hell of a racy read'
Company

'Gossip and intrigue from this former lawyer who uses the British legal system as the backdrop to her chilling tale . . . twists and turns to the very end'   *Woman's Journal*

'A witty, polished mirror of the profession's outward gloss and hidden foibles . . . Rumpole, eat your heart out'   *She*

'As compulsive as ever, combining an impressive grasp of the law with credible characters and a page-turning plot. And you thought lawyers were blooodthirsty boors'   *Cosmopolitan*

Caro Fraser was educated in Glasgow and the Isle of Man, before attending Watford School of Art. After graduating, she worked for three years as an advertising copywriter, then read law at King's College, London. She was called to the Bar of Middle Temple in 1979 and worked as a shipping lawyer, before turning to writing. Caro Fraser has been writing full-time for the last eight years. She is married to a solicitor and has four children.

By the same author

The Pupil
The Trustees
Judicial Whispers
An Inheritance
An Immoral Code
Beyond Forgiveness

A Hallowed Place

CARO FRASER

PHŒNIX

A PHOENIX PAPERBACK

First published in Great Britain by Orion in 1999
This paperback edition published in 2000 by Phoenix,
an imprint of Orion Books Ltd,
Orion House, 5 Upper St Martin's Lane,
London WC2H 9EA

A CIP catalogue record for this book
is available from the British Library.

ISBN 0 75381 090 5

Printed and bound in Great Britain by
Clays Ltd, St Ives plc

Chapter one

During the long vacation, that fallow summer period falling between the end of the Trinity Term and the beginning of the Michaelmas Term, the Inns of Court in the City of London fall into a drowse. The air barely lifts the leaves of the lofty plane trees, the lanes and courtyards lie quiet and warm, trodden only by the occasional barrister or clerk. The judges have shed their wigs and gowns, and the courts are hushed and still. In the days before the reign of that misunderstood and much-maligned lord chancellor, Lord MacKay, the Rules of the Supreme Court stated that 'time does not run' during the long vacation. This 'running of time' refers to the time limits within which lawyers, in the conduct of litigation, are required to progress the various stages of their case. The notion of its suspension aptly captures the air of torpor and inactivity which hangs about the City in the dog days. As though, in the geriatric world of the law, it ever managed anything above a reluctant shuffle. Nowadays, of course, under brisk new rules designed to encourage lawyers to prosecute the affairs of their clients as diligently as at any other time of the year, it is stated that time *does* run in the long vacation. But, in truth, nothing has changed much. Extensions to time limits are sought and granted, and if time runs anywhere, it is in Tuscan villas and on sun-kissed tropical beaches, where barristers and solicitors take their hard-earned rest. The City slumbers throughout August, until the lawyers return in September, rested and refreshed, sporting sun-bleached hair and rich tans, which sit strangely with pin-stripes and Turnbull & Asser shirts, better suited to wintry wine bar pallors.

It was at the end of one of these fading days of late summer that several of the members of 5 Caper Court, one of the most illustrious and renowned sets of commercial chambers in the Temple, congregated in a snug corner of El Vino's to enjoy a glass of wine. Beyond the propped-open doorway of the wine bar the late-afternoon sky hung blue and balmy above the roar of Fleet Street traffic.

'My wig's taken on this strange smell recently,' said David Liphook, taking another swig of his wine and frowning.

'Smell? What kind of smell?' asked Anthony Cross, reaching over for another smoked salmon sandwich.

'I don't know . . . A sort of musty, not very pleasant smell,' replied David. 'I thought one's wig was meant to last a lifetime. At this rate I may have to chuck it and get a new one. I had a look at the prices in Ede and Ravenscroft, and they're simply frightening.'

At this there was a general guffaw, and David, a stocky, blond man in his early thirties, glanced round resentfully. 'Well, they are! I'm not *that* tight, but they are, you know.' For a barrister whose practice probably earned him in the region of two hundred thousand a year, after tax, it struck the others that the price of a new wig wouldn't make a great dent in his finances. But David, an eligible young London bachelor with a Ferrari to care for, and extravagant tastes in wine, food and women to husband, was thrifty when it came to life's little things.

'Which parsimonious reflection,' murmured William Cooper, looking up from his *Times* crossword, 'forcibly reminds us all that it's your shout. Get another bottle in, David.'

David sighed, got up, and went to the thronged bar to order another bottle of Chablis. Coming back, he set the bottle down and remarked, 'I don't see why we need the bloody things, anyway. Wigs, I mean. They're archaic, they're uncomfortable, and they look ridiculous.'

William groaned. 'You've been reading articles in the *Guardian* about bringing the bar up to date, haven't you? You really shouldn't look at that paper. You're far too impressionable. Anyway, blame the criminal fraternity – they're all in favour of them. They did a poll of defendants in criminal cases a while back and ninety per cent of them said they didn't feel that they were getting the real thing if their brief didn't have a wig.'

'I'm personally all in favour of wigs,' remarked Anthony. 'They're part of the uniform. They help the general public identify you in court. And they lend a certain authority.'

A large man in his sixties, ruddy-faced, his bulky body straining the broad chalk-stripe of his dark three-piece suit, came in through the back door from Clifford Court.

'Cameron,' said William, 'pull up a chair.' He motioned to a passing waitress to bring another glass.

Cameron Renshaw subsided into a chair, puffing a little.

'I disagree with you entirely,' went on David. 'I think the public are quite capable of working out who's who in court without the benefit of a piece of horsehair. As for lending authority, I'd say they do the opposite. They're a relic from a bygone age. Besides which, they're bad PR. This wig and gown business just serves to distance the public, and perpetuates the myth that barristers are a pompous élite.'

'That's a myth, is it?' murmured William from the depths of his crossword.

'Not this bloody nonsense about wigs again,' snorted Cameron, sipping gratefully on the glass of wine which Anthony had poured for him. 'Do you know, this old chestnut comes up once a decade. By the time you're my age, you're sick to death of the thing.' Shifting his bulk in his chair, he lifted his plump chin slightly and ran a finger along his salt-and-pepper moustache. Cameron was the head of chambers at 5 Caper Court and the younger members waited respectfully for his own views on the matter. 'The fact is, they're part of the theatre. Just as a policeman has his uniform, so we have ours. And judges have theirs. British people like their barristers to look the way they do. And the judiciary. It sets us apart.'

'That's just my point,' said David. 'It creates an artificial barrier between the public and us. It distorts their perception of us as real people. Why can't we do as American lawyers do and just wear ordinary clothes, without these distinctions of dress? I think it's all nonsense.'

'Just because your wig pongs and you've got to get a new one,' observed William.

'It's more than that,' replied David. 'Our judiciary look like complete fools, too. I mean, look at that ridiculous charade at the State Opening of Parliament. Silk tights, buckled shoes, full-bottomed wigs. Absolutely ludicrous. Much better to have the kind of rig you see judges wearing in Italian or French courts.'

'That lot? They all look like clerics. The day we start importing any of the habits of our continental counterparts will be the end for this country,' snorted Cameron. 'Anyway, look upon it as a form of protection. There are more than a few judges on the criminal bench who are quite glad of the fact that nobody recognises them with their wigs off, at the end of the day.'

'You have a point there,' agreed Anthony. He glanced up and smiled at the pretty, auburn-haired young woman who had just joined them, and the others murmured in greeting. Camilla Lawrence was the newest tenant at 5 Caper Court, and its first woman member. When she had first joined chambers as a pupil fifteen months before, she had been a gauche bluestocking, fresh from Oxford and Bar school, brimming with ambition and ineptness. During her time in chambers she had matured into a quietly confident young woman, with a mind just as incisive as any of the men with whom she worked. The others knew of the relationship which had grown up between her and Anthony, but the matter was never referred to. It did not encroach upon their work, and in public they behaved towards one another as they did towards all their colleagues, with candour and friendly insolence.

She sat down and chucked a copy of the *Evening Standard* on to the table. David poured a glass of wine and passed it to her. 'Thanks,' she said, then nodded towards the paper. 'I take it that none of you has seen this yet?'

'What?' asked David, reaching for the paper.

Camilla smiled. 'Page five. A profile of one Leo Davies, top commercial silk and, if I remember correctly, the possessor of steely blue eyes and a courtroom manner as cold as it is courteous.'

'Let's have a look.' William lost interest in his *Times* and leaned over David's shoulder as he thumbed through the pages.

'Oh, listen to this,' said David, and began to read aloud, grinning. ' "The world of the commercial Bar is not renowned for its excitement. It doesn't generally produce headline-grabbing cases or celebrity lawyers. But over the past few days the media have gradually been discovering a new legal superstar in the person of Leo Davies QC. Davies, a charismatic, suave figure, with the kind of good looks not normally associated with middle-aged lawyers, is the barrister who has been conducting the cross-examination of Giannis Kapriakis, the London-based Greek shipping tycoon accused of masterminding a massive fraud involving the sale of metal futures. A member of 5 Caper Court, one of the most prestigious sets of commercial chambers in London, Mr Davies possesses a subtle, infinitely courteous technique, plus the ability to pierce through veils of prevarication with the most devastating and beautifully timed of questions. Although the case has attracted considerable media attention from the outset, Mr Davies has rapidly become its star turn. His steely blue eyes and chiselled features seem to be as much of an attraction for the members of the public gallery as his renowned forensic skills. He is one of the superbreed of commercial litigators, with enormous earning power, and is respected and well liked amongst his fellow barristers. Little is known about his private life, however, except that he is divorced and lives alone in London, and perhaps this enigmatic aspect adds to the fascination. Watching him in court number five today, one couldn't help feeling that behind the professional façade there is ultimately something cold and lonely about this most ambitious and highly regarded of QCs." '

'Extraordinary,' remarked William, as David laid the paper open on the table. Almost two-thirds of the page had been devoted to the article, which included a full-length photo of Leo Davies striding out of the law courts.

'They do a lot of this kind of thing these days,' said David. 'Especially if the case is high-profile. But even so, you don't expect them to pick on the commercial Bar.'

'It's because he's so good-looking,' said Camilla. 'He's got –' All eyes turned towards her and she hesitated, embarrassed.

'Got what?' asked David.

Camilla smiled. 'Well, he's got sex appeal, I suppose. I mean,' she went on hastily, 'he's a handsome, highly paid, successful QC, involved in one of the biggest City frauds in years, and the papers and the public perceive that as very sexy. After all, they've even managed to hype up old George Carman in that way, haven't they?'

Cameron shook his head. 'It's utterly beyond me why the newspapers these days have to turn everyone into a celebrity. Fifteen minutes' worth of fame.' Cameron paused, musing, then glanced up. 'That was that Andy Warhol chap, wasn't it?' He looked rather pleased with himself. 'Well, I don't think it does much good for the dignity of the profession, to have our QCs written up like soap stars. I can't imagine Leo will like it very much.'

6

Camilla glanced at Anthony, who had said nothing so far. 'What do you think Leo will make of it?'

Anthony picked up the paper and gazed at Leo's familiar, handsome, unsmiling features. 'I don't know. To be honest with you, I don't know what Leo thinks about anything, these days.'

Fifteen minutes later Anthony left the wine bar and walked back to Caper Court. He was seeing his father later that evening and wanted to go pick up a few papers from chambers beforehand. It was, he realised with a flash of guilt, a relief to be doing something on his own, even if it was just a drink with Chay. Since the start of their relationship last Christmas, he and Camilla had seen one another almost every evening. On top of a working day spent in the same chambers, though not necessarily in each other's company, things occasionally felt claustrophobic.

Pushing open the door of 5 Caper Court, Anthony was surprised to see Henry, the head clerk, still beavering away in his shirt-sleeves at one of the word processors. Henry was a slight, amiable young man in his early thirties, who had been unexpectedly catapulted to his position of responsibility two years before when the old head clerk had retired.

'Still here, Henry? It's gone seven.'

'Just chasing up a few fee notes. Otherwise you lot give me an ear-bashing, don't you?' He pointed to a sheaf of papers lying in one of the baskets. 'Those came in for you from Mr Poulson's chambers after you'd left.'

'They can wait till tomorrow. Anyone about?'

'Mr Davies came back just after half-five and he's still up there. That fraud case has him at it every night. Which reminds me –' Henry fished around on the desk for a copy of the *Evening Standard* and handed it to Anthony, folded open at page five. 'You seen that?' He grinned.

Anthony took the paper and smiled. 'Yes, someone had a

7

copy in El Vino's. Haven't had a chance to read it properly, though.'

'You can hold on to my copy, if you want,' said Henry.

'Thanks.' Anthony looked curiously at Henry. 'By the way, forgive the personal nature of the enquiry, Henry, but – is that a moustache you're growing?'

Henry flushed slightly. 'Yes, it is, as a matter of fact. Just an experiment. You know, by way of a change.' He fingered the sparse bristles of his three-day-old moustache nervously, his breeziness suddenly gone. Did it look messy? he wondered. He had hoped it would have been a bit fuller by now. It annoyed him that Anthony hadn't been certain what it was.

'Well, very nice,' said Anthony. 'I've never tried either myself. Beard or moustache, I mean. Good luck.' He turned and went slowly up the narrow wooden staircase to his room, reading as he went.

On the first landing he paused to finish the article, then glanced towards Leo's door. Had Leo seen it yet? Anthony longed to go in and show it to him, but the last thing Leo probably wanted was to be interrupted on such a trivial pretext. Anthony glanced down again at the photo. It was a face he had seen every working day for the last five years. Even so, the unexpected sight of it in the newspaper in El Vino's had caused his heart to give a little lurch. Absurd, but true. Leo had always had that effect on him. His smile, the faint Welsh lilt to his voice, the arrogant glance of his blue eyes. When Anthony had first begun at 5 Caper Court as a raw, nervous pupil, he had liked to think of Leo, the great Leo Davies, as his friend. But it was a friendship whose intensity seemed, over the months and years, to wax and wane according to Leo's emotional caprices, which were beyond Anthony's understanding. He rarely thought back to the time when Leo had tried to seduce him and he had almost reciprocated. The incident seemed to belong to another age. But there were still occasions now when the chemistry between them was so intense and perfect that it left Anthony confused and troubled. Not that they had spent much time together recently. That was partly to do with Camilla, and partly due to the fact that Leo seemed to be in one of his reclusive cycles, when he would retreat into his work and the others in chambers would see little of him. Time to break that, thought Anthony. He knocked lightly on Leo's door and looked in.

Leo was sitting at his desk in his shirt-sleeves, writing. He glanced briefly over his half-moon spectacles at Anthony, then continued with his work. Undeterred by Leo's silence, Anthony went in, closing the door behind him, and sat down in a chair opposite Leo's desk.

After a few moments Leo laid down his pen and sat back.

'How's it going?' asked Anthony, breaking the silence.

Leo gave a tired smile. 'Not badly. Kapriakis is all over the place. Every time he opens his mouth to answer a question his solicitors are almost galvanised with panic.' He sat forward again, yawning. 'I should be finished by tomorrow.'

'Well, it's certainly turned you into a bit of a celebrity, this case,' said Anthony. He chucked the copy of the *Evening Standard* on to the desk. Leo drew it towards him and unfolded it. 'Oh, God.' He sat back and perused the pages briefly, then shook his head. 'I can't understand why they bother.'

'Because you're a star. Enigmatic, charismatic, brilliant, all that bollocks.' Anthony got up. 'Listen, have you got an hour to spare this evening? I'm seeing my father tonight for a drink and he says he'd very much like to meet you.'

'Me? Why?' asked Leo in mild surprise.

'He's in the process of setting up some kind of gallery or museum, and I rather think he's trying to find people who'd be prepared to act as trustees. For God's sake, say no now, if it doesn't appeal to you.'

'Hmm.' Leo considered. 'I'm not sure about becoming a trustee of anything, but it would be interesting to meet your

9

father. He seems to be the king of the modern art world these days, doesn't he?'

Anthony grimaced. He had always thought it something of a fluke that his father had risen from anonymous, hippie-like inertia in a squat in Islington to his present status as darling of the post-modernists. Anthony could see no intrinsic merit whatsoever in what he regarded as Chay's pretentious pieces of voluminous abstract art. In the days when Chay had been on the dole, doing nothing more taxing than smoking the odd joint, eating vegetarian food and expounding his latest half-baked artistic theory, the teenage Anthony's attitude had veered between exasperation and embarrassment at having a father who behaved like a wayward adolescent. His parents were divorced and, living with his younger brother and his mother, he knew just how little effort his father made to contribute towards their upbringing. A few years ago fashion had turned its fickle face to smile upon Chay's works, and now he was successful and wealthy. For one who had always espoused a simple, frugal existence, he had adapted with remarkable ease to the possession of money, and led a life of some extravagance and style, with houses in New York, London and Milan. Anthony's attitude towards him since the change in his fortunes was a mixture of awe and cynical disbelief. Having no particular liking for or understanding of modern art, Anthony was convinced that Chay was part of an elaborate conspiracy to con the public and the art world, one which must, surely, eventually be discovered.

'That was once something of a mystery to me, until I paid a visit to the Saatchi gallery. Now I realise that if you tell enough people that something is art, eventually they'll believe it.'

'That's a bit hard,' replied Leo. 'I really think your father's work is excellent. I'd buy some, if only it weren't so highly priced. It's also rather – well . . . big. It calls for greater space than I could afford to be properly appreciated.'

Anthony shook his head. 'I must be missing something. Anyway, I'm glad you want to come along. I've just got to collect some papers, then we can leave. Give me ten minutes.'

Anthony went out, and Leo picked up the newspaper, turned to the article and began to read. When he had finished it he stood up and walked to the window, looking down on the courtyard. Why should he care what a trivial newspaper article said of him? No doubt it had all been designed to be largely flattering. Whoever wrote it had clearly enjoyed developing that picture of him as brilliant, but cold and aloof. Yet Leo felt faintly troubled. Cold? He had never thought of himself as a cold person. In fact, he sometimes thought that his capacity to love was excessive, that he unduly craved intimacy and affection. But this inner truth was at odds with the image he presented to the world, so the world, as represented by the pages of the *Evening Standard*, was perhaps entitled to regard him as chilly and remote. His loves, his passions, were all concealed, clandestine. Times might be changing, the things one did in one's personal life might be regarded with greater tolerance, even in a tight-knit, censorious community such as the Bar, but from the very first he had always sought to hide his sexual ambivalence, to keep his life away from work as private as possible. His marriage, which had lasted scarcely a year, had been his only public demonstration of affection and that had been largely a sham, designed to allay rumours about his dubious past at a time when he was anxious to take silk. Nothing good had come of it, except for his son, Oliver, and even he was presently the subject of an acrimonious custody dispute. So why should he be surprised if the world chose to regard him as remote and lonely? God knows, that was certainly the way he felt these days.

'Okay,' said Anthony, reappearing in the doorway. 'Shall we go?'

Leo slipped on his jacket and tidied his papers away, and

together they walked out into Caper Court in the late-August sunshine. In Fleet Street they hailed a taxi.

'So,' said Anthony, 'tell me why you've been such a reclusive figure these past few months. I've hardly had so much as a game of squash out of you.' Leo said nothing, merely glanced out of the cab window. 'I haven't done anything, have I?' added Anthony.

Leo shrugged. 'All the enforced intimacy of the Lloyd's Names case must have got to me. Besides, we've both been away over the long vacation. And since I came back, I've been caught up in this fraud case.'

There was a brief silence.

'Has it anything to do with Camilla?'

'In what sense?'

'Oh, come on, Leo. I think you know what I mean. I know you dislike her.'

'You're wrong. I don't dislike her. She's an extremely able lawyer. She's a credit to chambers. I only wish we had more female tenants. It does no good to be as weighted as we are in the other direction. In fact, it's a point I particularly wish to raise at the next chambers meeting.'

Anthony gave a short laugh. 'There's always Sarah.'

'God, Sarah.' Leo sighed, then added sardonically, 'She's quite another thing altogether.'

'We're getting off the point,' said Anthony.

Leo took out and lit a small cigar, then tugged down the window of the cab. 'Anthony, there is no point. Camilla doesn't come into it.' He turned to look at the younger man. 'It's been a difficult few months. I've been finding the divorce thing harder than I expected. Not so much to do with Rachel, but being away from Oliver.'

There was a pause. 'You miss him,' said Anthony.

'Jesus, yes,' said Leo. He smoked for a few seconds in silence, then added dryly, 'There are even times when I wonder whether I shouldn't try patching things up with Rachel, just to have him back.'

12

Anthony hesitated. 'I thought she was living with Charles Beecham?'

Leo shrugged. 'I suspect she turned to him because she wanted someone to comfort her. I have the feeling that if I really wanted her to, she'd come back.' Leo's tone was matter-of-fact.

'Why don't you ask her, then?' retorted Anthony sharply. He knew Rachel well, was fond of her, and the arrogance of Leo's attitude angered him more than a little.

Leo drew on his cigar. 'Because I have no wish to behave dishonestly. And that's what it would take.'

'But it's still something you think about?'

Leo's inscrutable blue eyes met Anthony's. 'I still think about many things. It doesn't mean I'm going to do anything about them.'

'Here we are,' said Anthony, as the taxi drew up outside a chic, but unobtrusive galleria-cum-wine bar, where trendy salads, wine and coffee were served at steel-topped tables, among photographs, paintings and sculptures by aspiring young artists.

They found Chay sitting at a table with a drink and a newspaper. Anthony introduced Leo and the two men shook hands. Chay Cross was a lean, tall man with pebble glasses, whose scalp was shaved to steely stubble against the ravages of incipient baldness. He was dressed in fashionable Comme des Garçons trousers, a Paul Smith shirt and jacket, and tennis shoes, and a Gauloise dangled from his thin fingers. He and Anthony, in his dark pin-stripe suit and sober tie, struck a curious contrast. Perhaps, mused Leo, as Chay ordered drinks, Anthony's dogged and ambitious pursuit of a career at the Bar, in the face of considerable financial odds, had been a form of rebellion against his father's bohemian image. These father–son relationships could hold strange dynamics. He wondered how he and Oliver would regard one another in twenty years or so.

Drinks were bought, and after a few minutes of small talk

13

Anthony brought up the subject of Chay's latest project. 'I've told Leo about the museum, but only in outline. You can fill him in on the details.'

Chay shoved his glasses enthusiastically a little higher up the bridge of his nose. 'It's a project I've been thinking about for some time. What London needs is a proper museum of modern art and I intend to establish one. I've bought an old brewery in Shoreditch and we're in the process of renovating it, turning the space into galleries, that kind of thing. Anthony's dealing with the legal side of the trust, and we're hoping to get some lottery money to help with finance. Of course, that means satisfying all kinds of criteria, but that's in hand. I have a vision of something really dynamic, exhibiting everything from sculpture to video art, installation pieces . . . Are you a fan of video installations?' He looked questioningly at Leo.

Leo hesitated fractionally before replying, 'To be honest, it's not a medium I've encountered very often. I've seen the kind of thing you mean, but my taste is rather more for sculpture and paintings.'

Chay nodded. 'Just wait until you see some of the things that are being produced. I attended a completely groundbreaking exhibition in Helsinki three months ago, called Monumenta. There were some fantastic ideas on display. Matthew Barney was exhibiting. You've heard of Matthew Barney – no? He's American, the absolute king of video installations.' Chay's eyes gleamed with enthusiasm as he leaned forward to expound. 'In one room there were tapes playing which showed him cramponing naked across the gallery's walls and ceilings, with an ice-pick inserted in his rectum. Fantastic. All to do with social neurosis and the artist's responses to the confines of his environment.'

Anthony took a quick swallow of his drink and glanced at Leo, whose expression was totally impassive.

'Then you moved on to another room,' continued Chay, 'which was filled with great piles of fetishistic rubber items, and there were screens showing Barney being pursued across the car-park of the gallery by members of the Royal Highland Fusiliers, then climbing naked up the car-park's lift shaft. That piece was to do with the homo-erotic appeal of men in kilts, underlining the fundamental dichotomy between the freedom of the individual and the threat of social-group force.' Chay picked the olive out of his drink and munched it.

After a pause, Leo said politely, 'It sounds – interesting. So your museum is going to be devoted to that sort of thing?'

'No.' Chay waved a thin, dismissive hand. 'No, those would be specialist, satellite exhibits. To get funding, we need a collection policy. I want to put together a core collection of the very best modern art – Koons, Kiefer, Boltanski. That's where we'll need the help of government funding, though one of our trustees, Lord Stockeld, has already given us very generous support. And we're doing quite a bit of private fund-raising. Then with that kind of solid foundation, we can give exhibition space to really promising new talent, using all kinds of media. So far we have six trustees and now we need one more. It needs an odd number, you see.'

Anthony's glance met Leo's and he smiled faintly. 'Which is where you come in.'

'Why don't you become a trustee?' Leo asked Anthony.

'In the first place, I don't know anything about modern art. And in the second, nobody knows me from Adam. They don't write profiles about *me* in the *Evening Standard*. Chay needs people of prominence to give the project the right image. You're a QC, you're the great Leo Davies. That's why Chay wants you.'

'He's right,' agreed Chay. 'Anthony's talked quite a lot about you, that you're interested in modern art, and it seemed to me you'd be just the kind of person we need. Someone from the legal world would be a great help.'

'Who are the other trustees?' asked Leo.

'Well, let's see. There's Tony Gear, the MP for Shad Thames, Melissa Angelicos, Derek Harvey –'

'The art critic?'

Chay nodded. 'We thought of asking Brian Sewell, but . . .'

'No,' said Leo, smiling. 'I think the ice-pick might have finished him off.' He frowned. 'Who's Melissa Angelicos? The name sounds familiar.'

'She's the presenter of the late-night arts forum on Channel Four,' said Anthony. 'Something Space.'

'*Open Space*. I know the one,' said Leo. 'Leggy blonde with a nervous manner. Who else?'

'Then there's Lord Stockeld, the publisher, whom I mentioned before, Graham Amery –'

'The chairman of Barrett's Bank?'

'That's the one. And then there's myself, of course.' Chay studied Leo's face. 'So – what do you think?'

Leo hesitated for a few seconds as he pondered the offer. Why not? Helping to get a new museum of modern art off the ground was an attractive idea, given his own enthusiasm for the subject, and from what Chay had said the role of trustee wouldn't be too demanding. He needed a new interest, something that took him socially beyond the cloistered confines of the Temple. His world seemed to have grown narrow of late. Time to change that.

Leo smiled. 'All right. Fine. I'd be happy to do it.'

'Excellent,' said Chay. 'Let's have another drink.'

An hour later Leo left Anthony and Chay, and took a taxi back to his flat in Belgravia. It was a good address, and the place was smart and well appointed, but Leo didn't regard it as a proper home. It had simply been the first decent place that he had seen after the hasty sale of the Hampstead house in which he, Rachel and Oliver had lived all too briefly. The place had none of the character of the little mews house in Knightsbridge in which he had lived as a bachelor. He had been happy there. Just over two years ago, but it seemed a lifetime away. True, there was still the safe haven of the house in Oxfordshire, but even the weekends there seemed lonely, in a way which they had never done in the days of his bachelorhood. He didn't go down there often.

Leo slipped off his jacket, loosened his tie, wandered into the bedroom and lay down on the bed. It was only half past nine, but already his mind and body felt tired. Since the break-up with Rachel, a strange lassitude seemed to have settled upon his spirit, like a mild depression. He couldn't understand it. When she had left him he had thought – apart from the issue of Oliver – that it hardly mattered, that he would simply revert to his former hedonistic, self-indulgent life-style. But months had passed and still Leo felt as though he were in some kind of limbo. It was as if the person he had once been now no longer existed. The invitations, the social life of the days before his marriage, had almost dried up. Things had changed and moved on in just a short space of time, leaving him behind. I'm middle-aged, thought Leo, rubbing his hands over his face. There wasn't even the consolation of Anthony. He was too bound up with Camilla now.

Leo lay for a long time gazing at the ceiling, reflecting. Perhaps the *Evening Standard* was right. Perhaps his life was cold and lonely. Perhaps it was going to be that way for ever.

Chapter two

Sarah Colman woke and turned to look at the clock by her bed. Twenty past eight. Maybe she should have set the alarm. Today was her first day as David Liphook's pupil and technically she should show up at 5 Caper Court for nine o'clock. Still . . . She yawned and stretched like a cat. David wouldn't mind if she was a little late. A 'Tim Nice-But-Dim' sort if ever she had seen one. Maybe not so dim, of course, but probably fairly easy to handle. She smiled to herself. The money wasn't bad, either. On top of Daddy's allowance, it made life even more comfortable. She only hoped David wouldn't work her too hard. That was the trouble with being a pupil at a place like 5 Caper Court. It was such a shit-hot set that everybody supposed you must be brimming with ambition and zeal. Sarah wasn't sure about any of that.

She swung herself out of bed and slipped on the robe lying on the end of her bed. Pulling back the curtains, she gazed out at the blue sky. It was going to be another warm day. She picked up a hairbrush from her dressing-table and sauntered through to the kitchen, where her flat mate, Lou, was already dressed and making coffee.

She glanced up at Sarah. 'Morning. Cup of coffee?'

'If there's one going,' said Sarah, and sat down at the kitchen table, yawning again.

Lou poured out the coffee, paused to tie back her dark hair, then brought the mugs over to the table. 'Aren't you going to be rather late, if you don't get going? It *is* your first day.'

Sarah flicked idly through the pages of the *Guardian*. 'Yes, I will be, I suppose. I'm sure nobody's much going to mind.'

'I don't know how you get away with it,' murmured Lou, and sat down opposite Sarah.

Sarah smiled up at her. 'Practice. Instinct. Charm. Anyway, you can talk. I thought you had a presentation this morning?'

'It's not till ten. I've ordered a cab for half-nine.'

'Good. I'll share it with you.'

'That means you won't get to chambers till nearly ten! That's pushing it a bit, Sarah, even for you.'

'Lou, the Bar is a more relaxed place than the world of corporate finance. You lot may have to grind away from seven till seven most days, but we barristers don't. At least, I don't intend to. I'm starting as I mean to go on.' Sarah took a sip of her coffee, picked up her hairbrush, then sat back and began brushing her blonde hair with lazy, even strokes. 'Besides, it's not as though I'm some trembling novice who hasn't any idea of what she's doing. I know half the people there. Some quite intimately, I might add.' She smiled.

'Really, what does that mean?' enquired Lou, avid for any kind of confidence or piece of gossip.

'Well, let's see ... there's Anthony, for one. Anthony Cross. He and I had a bit of a thing for a while. But that was when I was living on my own. I don't think you met him.' Sarah brushed a fine curtain of hair across her eyes and fingered it. 'Very much your type, though. Tall, dark, very sexy. A bit buttoned-up. You go for the anally retentive City type, don't you?'

'Thanks,' said Lou.

'Well, you know – a bit of pin-stripe really turns you on, doesn't it?' Sarah laughed. 'Does nothing for me.'

'Why did you go out with him, then?'

'Oh, I thought there might be more to him. But he turned out to be just another boring barrister.'

'So you dumped him?'

Sarah paused in her brushing and her eyes darkened momentarily. She didn't like to recall the humiliation she had received at Anthony's hands. Nor the fact that he had then taken up with that drip Camilla shortly thereafter. 'It was more a mutual thing. We agreed to call it a day.'

Lou sipped her coffee. 'So – who else?'

'Well, my pupilmaster, obviously. David Liphook. And there's a man called William something – I've met him a few times socially, and he was on the pupillage committee. Bit of a cold fish. Oh, and there's a girl there that I was at Oxford with. Camilla Lawrence. Very brainy. Boringly so. She used to be quite pink-faced and eager when she was at LMH, but she seems to have calmed down a bit since then. And then –' Sarah parted her lips and gave a little sigh '– and then there's Leo Davies.' She looked away, musing, flicking her hair back over her shoulder with one hand.

'Leo Davies ... I know that name,' said Lou, frowning. 'Isn't he the chap who's doing the big fraud case at the moment?'

'Very possibly,' said Sarah. 'I don't pay too much attention to the law unless I really have to.'

'There was a piece about him in the *Standard* last night. And a picture. *Very* attractive, even for forty-something.' She gazed curiously at Sarah. 'So – what's the story there?'

'Darling, it might not be entirely discreet of me to tell you, not if he's becoming such a prominent figure.'

'Oh, come on! Don't be so tantalising. Tell me. You know I'm –'

'Yes, the very soul of discretion.' Sarah laughed and put down her hairbrush. She leaned her chin on her hands. 'We go back a few years, actually. I met him through friends at a party. I'd just come down from Oxford and was stuck for something to do. And somewhere to live. Daddy wasn't quite as generous in those days, and I didn't really fancy spending all summer living with my parents. So – when Leo mentioned that he had a job going, I volunteered.'

'A job? What kind of job?' asked Lou, intrigued.

Sarah arched her eyebrows. 'Oh – he had a house in Oxfordshire, and he said he needed a housekeeper. You know, someone to look after the place, cook when he came down at weekends with his friends. Leo had lots of friends . . .' There was a silence. Sarah traced the rim of her coffee cup with one finger. 'And there was one special friend. A young man, staying in the house.'

'What? A lover, d'you mean?'

'Mmm. Sort of. Though that implies some sort of sentimental attachment, and there certainly wasn't any of that. A very dirty little boy indeed was James. Quite pretty, too, before he became a junkie. Anyway, Leo had installed him there and I don't think he entirely trusted him. So he put me in charge.'

'So . . . he paid you to look after the house and keep an eye on his boyfriend?'

Sarah smiled. 'There were other duties of a rather more personal nature, of course, but I regarded those more as pleasure than business.' She sipped her coffee. 'Certain things I would happily have done free – for Leo.'

'I think', Lou said slowly, 'that I get the picture.'

'It was a wonderful summer,' said Sarah with a sigh. 'But all good things come to an end. Leo realised if anyone found out about it that it wouldn't do his image much good – he was applying for silk at that time – and we parted amicably. So you see, I think of most of the people in chambers as friends already.'

Lou got up and took her mug to the sink. 'Frankly, I think I'd prefer to be starting somewhere where nobody knew anything about me. Especially not my lurid past. Too much baggage, if you ask me.'

Sarah stretched luxuriantly, letting the loose sleeves of her robe slip down her bare arms. 'That depends on whether you're prepared to turn it all to your own advantage, darling. Now, I must go and have my shower, so that I'm ready in time for your taxi.'

While Sarah was making her leisurely way into chambers for her first day as a pupil, work was already well under way at 5 Caper Court.

As Leo came into the clerks' room to pick up his mail before going over to court, David Liphook accosted him. 'Leo, you know that award that was handed down last month against those Greek scrap-metal merchants?'

'That Vourlides lot? I know them well.'

'Well, Bill Tate has just rung to say that they're contesting the arbitrators' award on the grounds that the arbitrators misconducted themselves and that Ken Lightman was guilty of bias. Can you believe it?'

Leo grinned. 'That bunch will try anything. They once tried to have me removed from a case on the grounds that I was in the pay of the Turkish government.' He glanced at the two sizeable piles of documents and books ranged next to David. 'Where are you off to with that lot?'

'I've got an arbitration. Which is why I suggested to my new pupil that today might be a good day to start her pupillage. Thought it would be interesting for her to see something through from scratch. And useful to me. Not,' he added, glancing at his watch, 'that it's going to be particularly useful unless she shows up in the next ten minutes. I'm going to be hauling this lot in and out of taxis myself, at this rate.'

'Ah, yes – your new pupil. Sir Vivian Colman's daughter, if I'm not much mistaken?'

'That's right. Do you know her?'

Leo hesitated. 'I've met her a few times. I think you'll find most people have.' He could hardly tell David just exactly how well he knew Sarah, or just how much havoc her exasperating behaviour had wrought in his life. 'Yes, Felicity?' Leo glanced over at Felicity, the junior clerk, who was waggling her hand to attract his attention.

'Sorry to interrupt, Mr Davies. It's Fred Fenton for you. Says he needs a quick word.'

'All right. Put him through to the waiting room. I'll take it there.'

Felicity came over to where David stood drumming his fingers. 'You look like a man who's been stood up, Mr Liphook,' said Felicity, leaning her elbows on the counter and making even more of her already ample cleavage. She was a pretty, bubbly type, an East Ender with a sharp wit who had been a clerk for only a year. Under Henry's tutelage, she was developing into a thorough professional, with a naturally maternal care for the interests of the barristers in chambers.

'I don't much care for being kept waiting around by my pupil, to be honest. I'd heard that having one can be more trouble than it's worth. Still, at the time, taking her on seemed like a good idea.'

'What's she like, then?' asked Felicity. 'Be nice to have a few more women around here.'

David shrugged. 'Very pleasant.'

'Nice looking?'

'Oh, definitely.'

Felicity sighed. 'I thought she might be.' She nodded towards the window. 'There's your cab. What do you want me to do with this Miss Colman when she gets here? Send her on?'

'No. Yes.' David glanced at his watch again. 'Yes. She should be able to find MFB under her own steam – just give her the address. It's a bloody nuisance. I was relying on someone to help with all this.' David began to pick up bundles and stuff them under one arm.

'Ta-ta,' said Felicity.

Leo reappeared from the waiting room just as Cameron Renshaw lumbered downstairs.

'Leo, can you do something for me?' asked Cameron.

'Depends what it is,' said Leo. 'I'm due in court in ten minutes.'

'Just a minute of your time. The thing is, I've got those people from the Lincoln's Inn Estates Committee coming over late today about the new chambers we've been looking at. The ones in New Square.'

'Oh. Yes,' said Leo flatly. He wasn't exactly keen on this idea of moving out of Caper Court to larger premises.

'Well, I don't want to put them off, but I need to see my doctor, and it turns out that the only time he can fit me in is around half-four this afternoon. After that he's off to some golfing holiday in Portugal and won't be back for three weeks.' Cameron dropped his voice. 'Between you and me, I don't think I can wait three weeks. I've been having these stomach pains all summer. I'm frankly not feeling quite the thing. I haven't been able to keep anything down for two days, and I really think I have to do something about it.'

'God, I'm sorry to hear that,' said Leo. Come to think of it, he did think old Cameron had been looking a bit yellow round the gills the past few days. And was it his imagination, or hadn't he lost a bit of weight? With a fellow of Cameron's size, it was hard to tell, but he certainly didn't seem his old Falstaffian self.

'So I wondered if you'd mind seeing these people for me.'

'Yes, of course I will. What time are they coming?'

'Around five.'

'Fine. I'll be back well before then. Anyway, I'd better dash.'

Leo hurried out of the door and collided with Sarah as she was coming up the steps.

'Morning, Leo,' said Sarah. 'Shouldn't run at your age, you know. Not dignified.'

Leo sighed. Exasperating as he found her, he couldn't help thinking how pretty and professional she looked in her immaculately cut black suit and white silk blouse, her blonde hair neatly tied back. The very picture of a demure young barrister. If only the world knew the true Sarah. 'Thank you for that piece of advice. Now let me give *you* one. It's not a good idea to keep your pupilmaster hanging about on your very first day. It creates a bad impression. And in your case, impression is everything. Don't get the idea that dear David is a soft touch. He may seem that way, but when it comes to business, he's all business. Goodbye.'

'See you later.' Sarah turned, smiling, as Leo hurried down the steps. 'Isn't it nice that we're going to be seeing so much of one another from now on?'

'Bliss,' murmured Leo as he strode up Middle Temple Lane.

Felicity looked up from her desk as Sarah came into the reception area. 'Can I help you?' she asked.

'I'm Sarah Colman. Mr Liphook's pupil. I'm starting today.'

'Oh, yes! Hello – I'm Felicity. I'm the junior clerk.' They shook hands, appraising one another. 'I'm afraid Mr Liphook's left. He's got an arbitration today. I think he was expecting you a bit earlier.'

Sarah did her best to look anxious and contrite. 'I know. I feel dreadful about being so late. The trains were all over the place.'

'Oh, well, not to worry. I'm sure you couldn't help it.'

Sarah's expression flickered slightly at this. She didn't much like the mumsy, patronising tone. Nor the implied criticism. A junior clerk was only a jumped-up office girl, after all. One with appalling taste in clothes at that. Low-cut jumpers and short skirts were pretty vulgar, even if you did have the figure for them. Still, since she was playing the part of the anxious-to-please pupil, she'd better keep up the front. 'No. It would happen on my first day, of all days, though.'

'Well, he's only just left. If you set off now, you'll probably get there before they start. It's at the arbitration centre at More Fisher Brown, near Spitalfields. You can get a bus on Fleet Street to take you up to Liverpool Street. I'll write down the address.' She scribbled it down.

'Thanks,' said Sarah, taking the piece of paper from Felicity. 'I only hope I'm not too late.'

She hurried out into the warm September sunshine, then dropped her pace to a saunter once she was out of Caper Court. A boring old arbitration was the last thing she felt like doing. She'd have preferred to sit and drink coffee in David's room and read a newspaper, or skive off to Middle Temple Common Room. Still, one had to show willing. As for a bus, sod that. She'd take a taxi.

Sarah arrived at the arbitration with minutes to spare and managed to fake a breathless apology to David.

'Don't worry,' said David, who had promised himself earlier in the taxi that he would take a stern, frosty line with her, but now found himself unable to in the face of her exceptional prettiness and charm. She had certainly caught the attention, too, of the other men seated round the large oval table. Sarah realised she was the only woman present, and at this her confidence lifted. 'Here,' said David in an undertone, passing her a pristine counsel's notebook. 'Just take notes and try to keep up with what's going on. I was going to explain the case to you beforehand, but I'm afraid we haven't got time.'

At that moment the arbitrator glanced across at David. 'I think we're all ready now, Mr Liphook.'

'Thank you.' David stood up. 'Good morning. In this case I appear for the plaintiffs, and my learned friend, Mr Gilmore, for the defendants. The matters in dispute arise from the issue in Hamburg of two bills of lading dated 18 April and 23

June 1997 for the carriage of containers of sugar from Hamburg and Bremerhaven to Dubai and Mina Qaboos . . .'

Sarah started diligently to note down the main points as David spoke, then after fifteen minutes she began to wonder why she was bothering. This was his case, after all, so he must know what was going on. Why should she go to the trouble of noting down what he was saying? There might be some point if the other side's barrister were talking, but this was just a waste of time. She put down her pen and yawned, then glanced idly at each man seated round the table, trying to assess if there was anything particularly attractive about any of them. Deciding there was not, she picked up her pen again and doodled covertly until tea was brought in. She ate four digestive biscuits and drank her tea, then sat, restless and bored, until lunch-time.

'Well, are you managing to follow what's going on?' asked David, when they broke for lunch.

Sarah gave a thin smile. 'Sort of. How long do you think it will last?'

'We should be finished by the end of the day.' He riffled quickly through his papers. 'Look, I wonder if you could do something over lunch for me. Beddoes and I – that's our solicitor, by the way, Paul Beddoes.' David glanced round. 'Oh, he's talking at the moment. I'll introduce you later. Anyway, we have to have a meeting over lunch with the client. We need to get these documents copied. They're communications between the master and the shore that didn't reach us till this morning, so none of the arbitrators has copies. I'll need – let me see . . . six copies. Can you manage that?'

'Sure,' said Sarah. David handed her the documents. 'Where can I get it done?'

'Ask down at reception. There'll be a photocopier some-where.' David glanced at his watch. 'See you back here at two.'

Sarah left the arbitration room and eventually found a

photocopier in the lobby. She stood drumming her finger-nails as the machine ate and fed, ate and fed the slim stack of papers.

'Sarah – hello! What are you doing here?'

Sarah turned. A tall, chubby man with wavy brown hair and a suit in the very broadest chalk-stripe stood grinning at her.

'Oh, hello, Teddy,' said Sarah. 'I'm having fun – what d'you think?' The photocopier chugged out the last sheaves of paper and Sarah stacked them all neatly together. 'Actually, I'm on the first day of my pupillage and already I'm being treated like slave labour.' Teddy was a solicitor, someone she had run into on regular occasions on her social circuit.

'Come and have lunch with me, then. I've just put in three hours of honest graft, and could do with something.'

'All right,' said Sarah. 'Anything's better than hanging around here.' She picked up the bundles of documents and they left.

'Oh, Teddy, not another,' said Sarah, as Teddy returned from the bar with two large glasses of white wine. Before them lay the remnants of a plate of avocado-and-bacon sandwiches. The wine bar was thronged with City lunchers. 'In fact, I shouldn't have had that first one. I'll fall asleep this afternoon. Honestly, arbitrations are so boring. At least, this one is.' She took a quick sip of the second glass and glanced at Teddy's watch. 'Is that the time? I'll have to go. I'm meant to be back at two and it's five to already. Listen, it's been lovely. I'll buy you lunch in return some time. You finish my wine. Bye.' Sarah, slightly pink from the wine, kissed Teddy quickly on both cheeks and left.

With a sigh, Teddy sat down and scoffed the remaining sandwiches, finished his wine and flipped through his copy of *The Times*. It was only when he got up to go that he noticed the neat stack of documents, lying where Sarah had left them.

The arbitration was reconvening just as Sarah got back. She slipped breathlessly into her seat and quickly retied her hair, which had come loose. The atmosphere, in contrast to the conviviality of the wine bar, was sombre and businesslike, the only sounds the rustle of paper and the mild hum of serious, muted conversation as everyone prepared to resume.

David came into the room and gave her a quick smile. 'Did you manage to get those documents done?' he asked, as he sat down next to her.

Recollection hit her like a shock. 'Oh, shit,' she said, and put her hand to her mouth. The word rang in the air with unexpected clarity. Heads lifted, conversation ceased. David stared at her.

'I'll be back in a minute,' she muttered and fled from the room. There was a surprised silence and the eyes of all the men in the room turned to David.

'Are we ready to recommence, Mr Liphook?' asked the arbitrator.

Pink with embarrassment, David hesitated, half rose to his feet. 'Gentlemen, I had intended to introduce some further correspondence between the master and the Bremerhaven agents, which came to us only this morning. However –' David rustled among his notes '– may I in the meantime move to another point, and that is the questions of the contractual status of the bills of lading at German law . . .'

Sarah sped back to the wine bar. It was emptying now, the tables littered with discarded glasses and empty sandwich plates, a noisy group of brokers still laughing and smoking by the bar. She cursed herself. She had thought this pupillage was going to be a breeze, that she was going to manage David beautifully and not put a foot wrong, and still get away without doing too much hard work, and already it was going haywire. Well, it was her own fault. Praying inwardly, she scanned the floor by the table where she and Teddy had been sitting. Nothing. Her heart sank. But who would want to walk off with some boring shipping documents? She hurried to the bar, where the barman was uncorking yet another bottle for the brokers.

'Excuse me, I was in here ten or fifteen minutes ago and I left some papers on the floor by the table just over there, by the window –'

Without changing expression, the barman bent slightly and pulled out from beneath the counter Sarah's bundle of documents. 'Young man said you'd left them, and that you might be back for them. Lucky, ain't you?'

'God, yes,' breathed Sarah. 'Thank you.'

Clutching the documents, she sped back to the arbitration centre. In the lobby, she stabbed at the lift buttons and leaned against the wall, trying to recover her breath. She was still panting when she reached the doors of the arbitration room. She could hear David's voice droning away, so she gave herself a couple of minutes to compose herself. Then she went in as unobtrusively as possible and slid into her seat, laying the bundle of photocopied documents on the table before her.

David paused and glanced down at her. She met his eye, and it was stony and expressionless. He suddenly looked much older than she had ever thought him before. Then he went on, 'This may be a convenient point to return to the matter of what was said by the agents to the master at Bremerhaven. As I indicated earlier, further correspondence has come to light and we now have copies of these exchanges.' David picked up the photocopies. 'I do apologise for the delay.' And he began to pass round the documents. Sarah sat with downcast eyes, feeling ignominious. It was not a familiar feeling and it was distinctly unpleasant. Well, she would just have to put a brave face on it when they got back to chambers. She suddenly remembered Leo's words to her on the steps outside chambers, and wished she'd got up early this morning and had just gone to a sandwich bar for lunch.

In the taxi on the way back, David was too busy talking over the arbitration with Paul Beddoes to pay Sarah much attention. To add to her humiliation, when she had been introduced to Beddoes, who was an attractive man with a preoccupied manner, she had tried to flirt mildly with him. But Beddoes clearly regarded David's new pupil as someone of no significance whatsoever, no matter how pretty, and he had snubbed her.

After dropping Beddoes off at his office, they carried on to the Temple. David took a small tape recorder from his pocket and began to dictate some notes. Sarah sat in silence. This had to be just a means of ignoring her. What could he have to dictate that couldn't wait till they got back to chambers? The cab pulled up, and David handed her a pile of books and papers. She stood on the pavement while he paid the cab, then they walked together across the road and down Middle Temple Lane.

Despite her anger and humiliation, Sarah knew that she should say something. 'I'm very sorry about the photo-copies,' she said. In an effort to make her voice contrite, she merely sounded cold and ungracious. Sensing this, she added, 'I had lunch with a friend and left them behind.'

'I see,' said David. They passed through the archway, and he stopped and turned to her. 'Do you realise that those were original documents, and very important ones at that? If you'd lost them, it could have jeopardised our entire case. What the hell would I have been able to say to our clients, or to Beddoes?'

'Well, I didn't lose them, did I? And I've said I'm sorry.' God, this was awful. She felt like a naughty schoolgirl.

David sighed and scratched his head. He didn't much like

playing the stern pupilmaster. Besides, when he thought back to the various social occasions on which he'd met Sarah – even fancied her at one point – it made him feel awkward. Maybe he shouldn't have leaned on the pupillage committee to select her. Still, she was here now and they'd both have to make the best of it. 'Right. Well, let's get this lot back to chambers.' They carried on walking. 'The thing is, you have to understand that this is for real. If you're going to be a barrister, you have to take it seriously. Everything. You can't afford to be careless.'

They went into chambers and through reception. Felicity greeted them cheerfully as David picked up his mail. Sarah ignored her. She didn't much care for Felicity's easygoing cockiness. In fact, she decided she didn't much care for Felicity. Still smarting from her mortification, she followed David up to his room.

'Just put them over there,' he said. Sarah piled the books on the side of his desk. He pointed to a desk on the other side of the room. 'That's yours. I'm sorry it's a bit cramped.'

Sarah smiled and shrugged. 'It's fine. Thank you.'

David shuffled through some of the papers on his window-sill and drew out a slim brief, tied with pink ribbon. He handed it to Sarah, his expression neutral, businesslike. He was no fool, and the events of the day had made him see that Sarah hoped to base this relationship on all those wine bar and drinks party encounters of the past. He was determined not to let that happen.

'Right,' said David, 'here's something for you to be getting on with. Barge being towed through South African waters. Bowline snaps, barge is lost, stranded somewhere between the Congo and Cape Town. Our clients are the owners of the tug, the plaintiffs are the barge owners. The contract is a BIMCO Towcon – ever come across one of those? No? Well, now's your chance to make its closely printed acquaintance. In this case it contains a clause conferring exclusive English jurisdiction over all disputes. The plaintiffs have issued a writ *in rem* against our clients in the South African courts, and I want you to tell me whether you think we can obtain an injunction preventing the defendants from pursuing the action in South Africa.' He handed Sarah the brief. Sarah took it, her face expressionless. 'I'd like something by the end of tomorrow afternoon, please. The clients are coming in for a con on Friday.'

At five forty Sarah was still in Middle Temple library, with books piled around her. She was in despair. She'd read the towing contract from back to front several times, and still she didn't have a clue. They hadn't covered anything like this at all at Bar school. It was a nightmare. She put down her pen and laid the side of her head down on her notebook, and stared out of the window at the buildings opposite.

Anthony was on his way out of the library when he saw her. He didn't recognise her at first, his attention merely arrested by the shining spill of blonde hair as she rested her head on her book. Then he realised who it was. He hesitated. The brief affair which he and Sarah had had just under a year ago had ended acrimoniously. They still acknowledged one another when they met, but Anthony hadn't exactly been happy at the news that she was to join chambers. He went over to the counter to sign out the book he was borrowing, then glanced back. She had lifted her head now and was writing. Hell, he thought, we've got to co-exist, so I might as well be friendly. He went back over to the table where she was working. 'You shouldn't work too hard. It's past half-five, you know.'

Sarah looked up, startled, and met his gaze. Her expression was open, unprepared for the sight of him, and, for a dizzying instant, Anthony experienced again the sexual charge which he had felt on first meeting her months before. 'Hi,' she said uncertainly. Normally any acknowledgement of Anthony was cold and grudging, but she was too surprised, and too weary and fed up, to bother. She sighed and looked back at her book.

Anthony was caught off guard. Where was the cool, assured Sarah that he knew of old, with her self-possessed and faintly mocking smile? 'You don't sound too happy,' he said tentatively, half expecting a rebuff.

But she merely shrugged and laid down her pen. 'David's given me this to do.' She pushed the papers towards Anthony and he picked them up. 'It's the first day of my pupillage, and he's given me something I can barely understand. Bastard.' She leaned her head on one hand.

Anthony sat down opposite and began to go through the papers. As he read, he glanced up once, quickly scanning her features, thinking how oddly vulnerable she appeared. Never, in all the few short weeks they had been together, had she been anything but sharp, assured, on top of things. There was something disturbingly new and touching about her. 'It's not as complex as it looks. These different forms are just basic contracts. Look –' he came round to her side of the table and sat down next to her, flipping over the pages of the contract '– here's the relevant clause. Clause 25, the jurisdiction clause. Now –' he glanced around at the books she had taken off the shelves '– none of these is going to help you much. We need a copy of the White Book. Hold on.'

Sarah watched as he went to fetch a copy. It had been true, what she had said to Lou that morning. He was just another boring barrister. But still better looking than most of them. And, Leo apart, the best in bed. The sudden recollection of their love-making aroused a faint, surprising flare of desire in her. He was still seeing Camilla – that much she knew. But might it not make life in chambers more amusing if she were to try and seduce him away from her? That kind of game could be played out slowly, deliciously, over quite a long time. Great fun. Sarah loved games, mind games, flirtations, bluffs, betrayals. It was what had first attracted her to Leo. And vice versa. The odds, of course, would be stacked against her, since the word was that Anthony was quite smitten, but Sarah liked long odds. Well, it was certainly something to think about. If she handled it delicately, there could be no risk of outright rejection or humiliation.

Anthony came back with a large white volume entitled *The Rules and Orders of the Supreme Court of Justice*, and sat down next to Sarah, leafing through it. 'I think you'll find you want order eleven. Anyway, it's a good place to start.' He was aware, as Sarah leaned over to share the book with him, of the subtle smell of her, familiar, sensual. He tried to ignore its effect upon him and moved slightly away to pick up the brief. 'Let's have a look at the terms of this clause. "This Agreement shall be construed in accordance with and governed by English law. Any dispute or difference which may arise out of or in connection with this Agreement or the services to be performed hereunder shall be referred to the High Court of Justice in London ..."'

She glanced at him as he read, and smiled to herself.

Chapter three

Two weeks later, Leo received a call at work from Rachel, his ex-wife. It was some time since they had spoken. The relationship had naturally been difficult following the initial break-up, but at least they had communicated. Since she had moved in with Charles Beecham, however, and the divorce proceedings had ground properly into action, a new, bitter element had entered into affairs. As part of the arrangements for custody of Oliver, who was now sixteen months old, Leo had asked to have him every other weekend. Rachel was opposed to the idea. The negotiations of their respective solicitors appeared only to have made the issue more acrimonious. As things stood, Leo was surprised that Rachel should call him.

After a fractional pause, he told Felicity to put her through.

'Leo?' Rachel's voice held its familiar hesitancy.

'Hello, Rachel,' said Leo. 'How are you?' His tone was neutral, belying his feelings. It was odd, but a call from her now could arouse more emotion in him than he had ever felt towards her during their brief marriage. All of that was entirely to do with Oliver.

'I'm well, thank you.' She was polite, almost chilly. There was a brief pause. Leo waited. 'I've been thinking – perhaps we should meet some time,' said Rachel at last. 'I feel it might be useful.'

'Really?' Leo's tone was derisory. He felt instantly annoyed at allowing himself to be provoked into this childish retort, but he couldn't help it. He thought he heard

Rachel sigh faintly, and when she spoke it was as though she was determined not to let him goad her.

'I don't think we're getting very far through the solicitors. I feel it might help if we were to get together and talk some things through.'

Leo resisted his inclination to turn down this overture. In truth, he agreed with her. Besides, this fraud case had left him no time to visit Oliver. Now that it was over, he wanted to arrange to see him. It wouldn't help if he behaved antagonistically towards Rachel now.

'Very well,' he said. 'When do you suggest?'

'I thought maybe this evening after work – if you're not too busy.'

'I suppose I can manage that.'

'I have to see some clients in the West End later this afternoon. Why don't we meet at that pub in Knightsbridge that we used to go to?'

'The Griffin?' It was a small, tucked-away pub near the mews house in which Leo had once lived.

'Yes. That's the one. I don't really know anywhere else. About six thirty?'

'Fine. I'll see you then.'

When he put the phone down, he realised how tense the call had left him. God, he was a mess where Rachel was concerned. Would it be different if she were not the mother of his child? He supposed so. After everything that had happened, he should be glad to be rid of her. He had never loved her, had only married her to further his career. He should be feeling relief that she was someone else's responsibility, and that he could return to his own life. But it hadn't worked like that. Somehow the knowledge that she was living in a contented threesome with Oliver and Charles Beecham – Beecham, of all people, a man whom he liked, genuinely liked, and with whom he had even once been slightly in love – mocked his own solitary existence, rendering his single life no longer the enviable thing it had once been. People now thought of him as lonely – look at that bloody piece in the *Standard*, a complete stranger making a guess, and guessing right.

He sighed. Time. It was simply a matter of time. Once they got this wretched divorce sorted out, and a sensible arrangement in place for him to see Oliver, then he could start living again. Maybe seeing Rachel this evening would speed up that process.

On his way out at six, Leo bumped into Roderick Hayter, a fellow member of chambers some six years his senior.

'How did the course go?' Leo asked Roderick, who had spent the previous seven days closeted in a hotel in Weybridge with several other lawyers, training to become a recorder, as part of the recognised route to the High Court bench.

'Very interesting, in fact. I recommend it.'

Leo grinned. 'I'm not sure that becoming a High Court judge is quite my style.'

'Leo,' said Roderick, 'I gather Cameron asked you to speak to the Lincoln's Inn people about the lease on that set of chambers?'

'Yes, he did. He had to see his doctor. Actually, I've been wondering where he was. I don't think I've seen him since then.'

Roderick sighed. 'That's something I need to speak to you about – that and the business of the chambers in New Square. Have you got a moment?'

'Sorry – I'm meeting someone.' He paused. 'What about lunch tomorrow?'

'Fine. See you about one-ish.'

Leo left and walked down to where his car was parked near King's Bench Walk. The Indian summer was fading now, a slight chill touched the early-evening air, and the first drift of fallen leaves scuttered across the cobblestones. He found himself brooding over the impending possibility of the move to Lincoln's Inn. Another thing to add to the uncertainties of his life. He had worked as a barrister in the Temple for twenty-four years, and Caper Court was more of a real home to him than anywhere else he knew. It was his comfort, his haven. The idea of moving now to an entirely new set of chambers at the other end of Chancery Lane was like a threat to the last vestiges of his stability. Cameron Renshaw, he knew, didn't relish the prospect of change, but in the end he would probably go along with Roderick and Jeremy Vine, the other two most senior members of chambers, who had originally mooted the idea of moving. Roderick was of the view that in the present building chambers had no room to expand, and Jeremy – well, Jeremy, pompous bastard, just liked the idea of more gracious, spacious surroundings, big rooms, state-of-the-art technology, a smart reception area. If Jeremy had his way, chambers would have all the artifice and pseudo-glamour of a big firm of City solicitors. That was the last thing Leo wanted. He liked the cosy, old-fashioned rooms of 5 Caper Court, the narrow wooden staircases, the old oak doors. Certainly it had its inconveniences, and even he had to admit that the old building wouldn't be able to contain them in a few years' time, but still the idea of moving to Lincoln's Inn was anathema. There must, Leo decided, as he drove towards Knightsbridge, be some way round the problem. And he was determined to find it.

Rachel sat in a corner of the little pub, watching the door. On her knee rested a copy of the tabloid which she had picked up from the bar. She had scarcely read a line of it. Each time the door opened she looked up, her heart ready to contract at the sight of Leo. The arrival of every newcomer confounded her prepared expectation of him; she had seen him come through that door often before, was ready for the look of him, the quick movements, the light glancing off his silver hair, the restless, handsome features. When she had first met him, she had always thought how Leo's presence seemed to fill a room, eclipsing everyone else in it.

Five minutes later he arrived. He looked a little older than when she had last seen him, his face tired and drawn, his expression restless, impatient. But still Leo. Enough to make her forget momentarily about everything else in her life.

He glanced over to the corner and saw her, nodded in acknowledgement. The sight of her was wearyingly familiar, the pale, beautiful face, the dark hair drawn smoothly back, slim hands cupped nervously round whatever drink she had bought herself. How was it that those features, whose delicacy he had once found touching, now possessed the power to irritate him so? She was the least smug person he knew, yet there was about her a complacency, a patient rectitude which could madden him.

'What are you drinking?' he asked, standing before her, hands in pockets. She could see a small muscle working in his jaw.

'Oh –' she glanced down at her glass '– this is just a tonic water. I'll have some white wine, thanks.'

He nodded and went to the bar.

When he brought the drinks over, she had put the newspaper to one side. He sat down opposite, lifted his glass and murmured, 'Cheers.'

They drank, then a brief silence ensued.

'How's Oliver?' said Leo at last.

'He's well.' Rachel nodded. Then she smiled, enthusiasm melting the tension in her expression. 'Wonderful, in fact. I got him some new shoes last weekend and he talks about them all the time.'

Leo gave a little smile. 'What does he say?'

'Oh, you know ... "Shoes. My shoes." Things like that. Nothing ... nothing complicated.' Her smile faded.

'I'd like to see him,' said Leo. 'I've been involved in something of a heavy case, so I haven't had much time.'

40

'I know. The fraud thing. I saw the piece about you in the *Standard*.'

'Oh?' his heart dropped slightly. He didn't want to think about the nuggets of truth contained within that article, and what impression they had made on her.

'It made you appear –'

'What?'

Rachel looked down at her drink, twisting it between her fingers. 'Dashing, for want of a better word. I can see why they ran the piece. I suppose sex appeal is a commodity that's in short supply at the commercial Bar.' She looked up at him, and with a pang of feeling realised that she would never stop wanting him. She was conditioned to want him, to respond to the look in his eyes, his smile, that restless way of drumming his fingers when mildly embarrassed. He was doing it now. Her mind moved to Charles. Dear, kind, loving, exasperating Charles. Charles made her feel safe, which was more than she could ever have said of Leo. Was it a kind of betrayal, to feel this way about someone who had deceived you, mistreated you, broken your miserable heart? Perhaps, but there was some dark, inner part of her that belonged to Leo, no matter what he did. In the end, it had only been an instinct for survival, the practical, reasoning part of her nature, which had made her leave him. Love had many different faces. There was the uncomplicated, grateful love she felt for Charles. And then there was Leo.

'Anyway,' said Leo, 'we didn't come here to talk about me. Tell me what it is you want to say.'

She glanced down at her hands. 'I wanted to see if we couldn't come to some agreement about Oliver. You know that what you suggested in terms of access is completely impracticable –'

'Why? Why shouldn't I have him every other weekend? He's my son, for God's sake.'

Rachel sighed. 'He's too little. He's still too little. He hasn't seen you for four weeks –'

41

'That's not my fault. I told you I've been tied up with this case.'

'Leo, I know that. All I'm trying to say is that it would be very disruptive for him to be taken away from me for two days every fortnight. He's too young to understand what's going on. He'd miss me.'

'It's not as though he doesn't know me. I *am* his father. And how am I supposed to build any kind of a relationship with him unless I see him regularly?'

'No one's saying you shouldn't see him regularly. I want that, too. It just seems more sensible if you were to come to Bath to see him. You could take him out –'

'Rachel, you're missing the point. I want him with me. I want him to have his own room, to have breakfast with me, to do things together. I don't just want to visit him in Charles Beecham's house –'

'That's what this is about, isn't it?' Rachel interrupted.

'What?'

'It's about Charles. You're jealous of him, whether because of me or because of Oliver, I don't know, but –'

Leo threw back his head and laughed. 'Christ, Rachel, you can't get anything right, can you?' She gazed at him. 'I'm not jealous of Charles Beecham. If I'm jealous of anyone, it's of you. This may surprise you – though God knows it shouldn't, given what you know of me – but I was in love with dear Charles for some months before I discovered that I was quite mistaken about his proclivities. So please don't imagine that I wish I were in his bed. Not with you in it, at any rate.'

He had seen it before, the way the blood drained from her cheeks, leaving her looking even paler than usual. But never before had he seen this much coldness and pain in her eyes. When she spoke, her breathing was rapid, her voice little above a hard whisper. 'You are an out-and-out bastard, Leo – did you know that?'

Leo drained the remains of his Scotch. 'I think I recall

telling you something along those lines before you married me.'

There was a silence. When Rachel spoke again, she managed to keep her tone even and controlled. 'I suppose I should thank you for reminding me of one very good reason why I shouldn't let Oliver come and stay with you. I don't really want him being exposed to your various boyfriends, or your unpleasant life-style.'

This threw Leo momentarily. 'That's rubbish, Rachel, and you know it. Oliver is more important to me than anyone else in the world. Do you really think I would be so stupid? I just want to have him with me, to be a father to him, to give him a home he can come to.'

'I don't think I want him coming to your kind of home, Leo. And if your solicitor tries to push this one, I may just find myself having to dredge up a few unpleasant truths about your past to show how unfit you would be to have custody of any child.'

'Stop it, Rachel,' muttered Leo. He wished he'd never said anything about Charles. Why did he have this need to wound her, when it only went against his own interests? 'You're being utterly bloody unreasonable.'

'Really? Frankly, I hoped we might be able to have a civilised conversation about our son and what's best for him. You don't seem to care about that.'

'Christ, Rachel, I do care.' He leaned forward suddenly. 'Don't punish me. I just want to be with him.'

Rachel dropped her gaze from his. Why did he have this effect on her? Hating him only seemed to make it worse. And how passionately he felt about this – much more than he ever had about her. 'Leo, we can't resolve this. Not now. I thought we could. But we can't.'

'I want to see him.' His blue eyes looked steadily into hers.

'Then come down on Sunday. You can take him out for the day.'

'What about the rest? What about having him at weekends?'

She shook her head. 'You know I won't agree to that. Not until he's older.'

'By the time he's older he'll probably be calling Charles Beecham daddy. I'm not prepared to wait until then.'

Rachel looked away. 'I'm not going to discuss it any more, Leo.'

Leo pushed his chair back sharply and stood up. 'Sod all this mediation and counselling. If you won't agree, I'm going to instruct my solicitor to fight it.'

She said nothing, merely sat with her head bowed over her drink as Leo left the pub.

Leo drove off, cursing himself for his indiscretion about Charles. Why had he told her? There had been no need. It had simply made things worse. He had wounded her pride, antagonised her, reminded her yet again that she was not, never had been, what he wanted. Maybe he had needed to hurt her. Maybe the very fact that she had all the winning cards had made him want to goad her. Whatever the reason, it had done him no good. It had simply given her more ammunition, provided her with further reasons for not letting Oliver stay with him. Not that she believed in her heart that those reasons had any foundation.

He swore between his teeth and ground the gears as he pulled away from the traffic lights. A light rain had started to fall and dusk was drawing in. The fading light and the dismal dampness of the streets depressed his spirits even further. What was there to do with the rest of the evening? Go back to Belgravia, eat supper alone, go through some papers. He found he couldn't even listen to music any more. It gave him none of the old solace. There were people whom he could call, of course, parties he could go to. But his heart wouldn't be in it. All those bright, bubbling egos, the chatter, the laughter, the watching and calculating. No, he wanted none of that. As he drew up at the next set of traffic lights, Leo glanced along the row of cafés and shops, and suddenly recognised one of them as the place to which Anthony had taken him to meet Chay. He had liked that bar – or gallery or café, whatever it was meant to be. It had had an exuberance and stylishness that had appealed to him. Just the kind of thing he needed to cheer himself up. He recalled seeing some rather pretty sculptures. Maybe he should drop in and have a look.

He drove once round the block before finding a parking space, then walked back through the drizzle, stopping at a news-stand to purchase a copy of *Vanity Fair* to while away the time. He noticed as he went in that it was called the Galleria Flore. At this early hour the place was half empty. Leo picked a table in a far corner, where most of the sculptures and paintings were exhibited, and ordered a coffee, thinking as he did so that he didn't remember the waiter from last time. He was sure he would have done. He was young, in his early twenties. His hair was reddish gold, his face slight, heart-shaped, eyes wide and beautiful. Leo could not tell their colour. He watched the boy's rapid, graceful movements as he negotiated the steel-topped tables. Leo could see that, for all his slightness, his body was spare and muscular. The waiter must have noticed Leo studying him and he gave him a covert, curious look as he set down the coffee. Leo saw that his eyes were light hazel, flecked with gold, like a cat's. He found the glance charming, heart-stopping. He smiled, and the boy smiled back warily, then left. Leo watched him for a few seconds, then, with a faint sigh, turned to his magazine. After twenty minutes or so he grew bored and chucked it to one side, glancing up at the exhibits around him. The paintings were all largely derivative, lazy, but in some he glimpsed possibilities. He did not think there was anything he would care to buy.

'Excuse me – would you like something to eat? We've got

an early-supper menu.' Leo glanced round. The young waiter had materialised at his side, holding out a menu.

Leo hesitated. He hadn't meant to eat here, but he might as well. 'Thank you,' he said. The boy sped away. Leo glanced down at the menu, then, after a few seconds, lifted his eyes. The boy was standing at the bar, fiddling with some glasses, watching him. Their eyes met and the boy looked away. After a few moments he came back to Leo's table, and produced a notebook and pen. He looked enquiringly at Leo.

'I'll have the Eggs Benedict,' said Leo, 'and – let's see . . .' He looked up at the young waiter. 'Some wine. Is there anything you specially recommend in the way of reds?'

The boy hesitated. 'I don't really know much about wine, I'm afraid. But I can ask –'

Leo shook his head. 'Don't worry. I merely wondered. I'll have a half-bottle of the Morgon.'

The boy nodded and scribbled, giving Leo leisure to scrutinise his features, the small, rather petulant mouth, the light frown of concentration which drew his brows together. He was altogether lovely, quite unconscious of the effect he produced. Leo felt that familiar slipping sensation in his heart. Beauty of any kind touched him deeply, but this young man stirred more erotic depths. Leo watched as he moved away, still writing. God, he was sublime. Leo was suddenly filled with a desire to talk to him, to get to know him.

When the boy returned with the food and wine, Leo indicated a picture on the wall just above his table. 'I've just been studying this, and I'm not sure whether I like it or not. What do you think?'

With an expression of surprise that slightly widened his hazel eyes, the boy looked up at the painting. Leo was pleased to see that he did not merely glance at it, but studied it properly, his mouth tightening in a line as he concentrated, considering. 'I like it,' he said at last. 'I'd say the style owes rather a lot to Diebenkorn, but it's still pretty good. I like all

46

those variegated planes.' He looked at Leo, his expression inscrutable.

Leo was both amused and taken aback. 'You're familiar with Richard Diebenkorn's work?' he asked.

The boy smiled. 'Actually, to be honest with you, that's my painting. So I'm not a fair judge.'

Leo raised his eyebrows, intrigued. 'Well, I'm glad I didn't express a firm view at the outset, in that case. That could have been embarrassing.' He looked back at the picture. 'Actually, I do like it.' He glanced round the Galleria. 'You have other things here. That –' he gestured towards another canvas '– is yours, if I'm not mistaken.'

The boy nodded. 'I didn't think my style was that unique. I always think of myself as just another boring abstract expressionist.' There was a pause, and the boy said, 'Enjoy your meal,' and moved away.

At the end of his meal Leo lit a small cigar and sat over his wine, brooding upon the dilemma of Oliver. He'd have to ring his solicitor tomorrow, get her to lodge whatever application it was to try and get to see him on his own on a regular basis. It was years since he'd so much as cast a glance in the direction of family law, didn't have a clue on what basis they made their decisions in these matters. Was it genuine, Rachel's threat to rake up his past if he took the matter to court? One could never be sure with her. He sighed and glanced up as the young waiter returned to take his plate away.

'Would you like coffee?'

'Thanks, yes,' said Leo. The boy slipped the plate on to his tray and poured the remains of Leo's wine into his glass. 'Do you sell much of your work?' asked Leo, settling back in his chair, studying the boy with pleasure.

He shook his head. 'Not really. London's crawling with would-be artists. The market's a bit saturated. Still, it's what I like to do, and working here pays the bills.' He gave Leo a

47

candid smile. 'I don't think I'll ever make a living as an artist.'

'What you need,' said Leo, 'is a return to the old-fashioned system of patronage. Someone with enough money to pay you and promote your work.'

'My work's probably not worth it.'

'But maybe you are,' said Leo gently. He drew on his cigar, watching the boy. 'What's your name?'

'Joshua.' His expression as he looked at Leo was somehow more intent, as though Leo's words had made an intimate connection. 'Joshua Spencer.'

'A good name for an artist. I'm Leo Davies.' He held out a hand, and the boy shook it. It did something strange to Leo's heart, just to feel those young, strong fingers in his.

'You were in here a couple of weeks ago,' said Joshua. Surprised, pleased, Leo nodded. 'With Chay Cross – that's why I remember.' Leo gave a rueful little smile. The innocent tactlessness of the young. But if Joshua had been here that night, Leo was astonished that he should have not seen and remembered him. 'He comes in here quite often,' added Joshua.

'I work with his son,' said Leo. 'We're barristers.'

'Oh. Right.' Joshua nodded, preparing to move away.

'I meant what I said,' murmured Leo. 'About patronage. Every young artist should have some sort of – protection.' Joshua's eyes met his, and Leo knew instantly that he had found his wavelength. It was unmissable. Was the boy gay? How could he look the way he did and not be? 'I'd like us to get together some time, to talk about your work. Maybe I could help you.'

This was the moment. If he wanted, Joshua could just walk away. But instead he held Leo's gaze and said, 'I'd like that.'

'Tonight?' asked Leo. 'When do you finish?'

Joshua shook his head and glanced quickly in the direction of the bar, as though embarrassed or guilty. 'Not tonight. Maybe tomorrow. I finish around eleven.'

Oh, Lord, thought Leo. Late nights weren't much his thing any more. Still, this boy had to be worth it. 'Fine.' He smiled and nodded. 'You can bring the bill with the coffee.'

When Leo left the Galleria Flore, it was with a new sense of pleasure and anticipation. He had no illusions. There was no reason to suppose that the young man found him attractive, though Leo didn't regard himself as quite past it at forty-five, but he had detected a spark of interest there. Maybe it was mercenary. Maybe it was intellectual. He would find out. Joshua Spencer, whom he had met only this evening, wanted to spend some time with him and that was a start.

Charles Beecham glanced up as Rachel came into the kitchen. 'Hello. I wasn't expecting you this early.' He leaned sideways from the sink where he was peeling potatoes and kissed her. He was a tall, rangy man, with greying blond hair and features which, though now a little worn, still possessed enough boyish charm to captivate countless female viewers of his popular historical television documentaries. 'How did it go?'

'Don't ask,' sighed Rachel. 'Just the same old Leo, as obstinate and unreasonable as ever.'

'I have to say', said Charles, shaking his head, 'that that's not the Leo Davies I recall. When I knew him he was persuasive, adaptable, thoroughly reasonable and utterly charming.'

'You only have that slant on him because he was so successful for you and the other Lloyd's Names,' remarked Rachel, subsiding into a chair and slipping off her shoes.

'True, he did save me from financial disaster. For which I am eternally grateful.'

'I don't deny that Leo can be all the things you think he is. But where Oliver is concerned, it's like talking to a brick wall. He can't see how unreasonable it is to want to have him to himself every other weekend. Anyway –' she leaned back and unfastened her hair, running her slender fingers through it a couple of times '– the best he can do now is try to get the court to grant him the access he wants. I'm certainly not going to. Which reminds me, I did say he could come down on Sunday and take Oliver out for the day.'

'That's fine. Give us an excuse to go into Bath and have lunch together, just the two of us. We don't often get the chance.' Charles wiped his hands on a cloth and pulled up a chair next to hers. He leaned across, cupping her face in his hands, and kissed her softly.

'Perhaps that doesn't appeal to me as much as it does to you,' muttered Rachel. She felt cross and tired. Seeing Leo had disturbed her. It was like reopening an old wound. That ache of loss, of having loved so much, the waste of it all. Still burning in her mind was the way it had felt when he touched her, the look of him. She could not, at that moment, respond to Charles in the slightest. It had never happened before, and she felt momentarily fearful. 'I'm sorry,' she added, glancing up at him. 'I didn't mean that the way it sounded. It's just that I don't want Oliver to go away every other weekend.'

Charles hesitated before he spoke. He had never expressed a view on the matter of access to Oliver, but had always secretly been rather in favour of Leo's projected arrangement. Oliver was a smashing little chap and all that, but a fairly noisy, demanding one, who did get in the way sometimes. It was Rachel whom Charles had wanted for himself from the very beginning, even though he did accept that the baby was part of the package. The idea that Oliver should spend every other weekend with his father seemed to Charles an excellent one. Forty-eight hours free of crying, or babbling, or high-chair rattling or spoon-banging. Sentences that could be finished. Sex that could last as long as they wanted, without Rachel freezing at every distant sound and saying, 'Was that Oliver?' Long, boozy lunches. Mornings when they could lie in. Walks that could be taken through the surrounding countryside without considering whether the terrain was suitable for Oliver's buggy. And, best of all, Rachel's full, undivided love and attention.

'Perhaps it would be good for Oliver,' he ventured. 'Getting to know his dad, and so forth. Male bonding.'

Rachel shot Charles a glance of irritation. 'He's one and a half, for heaven's sake, Charles.'

Charles shrugged. He wasn't going to rock the boat. 'He is indeed. And right at this minute he's fast asleep and I have you all to myself.' He drew Rachel towards him once more and began to kiss her again, but she pulled away.

'I'm sorry, Charles. I'm not in the mood right now. I think I'll go up and change, and look in on Oliver. I wish you could keep him awake in the evenings when I'm going to be a bit late. I do like to see him.'

Charles said nothing as she left the kitchen. He didn't think he could begin to explain to her how blissful it was when Oliver fell asleep and silence reigned. The last thing he intended to do was to prevent it happening, even for Rachel's sake.

Joshua was sitting with his friend, Damien, in a club they had gone to after Joshua got off work. It was one o'clock in the morning, and the place was still crowded and noisy. After a lull in the conversation, Joshua took a reflective pull on his bottle of beer and remarked, 'I met this man tonight.'

Damien grinned. 'Yeah?'

'No – nothing like that.' Joshua grinned too, then made a wry face. 'I mean, I reckon he's after it all right. In fact, definitely.' There was a pause. Joshua gazed thoughtfully at his beer. 'But he was different. He seemed interesting. Liked my paintings. Anyway, he wants to see me tomorrow night, have a bit of a talk.'

Damien sighed and took a drink of his own beer. 'They're all after one thing, mate. Just take the money and run. There's nothing interesting about any of them.'

51

'I don't know. This guy didn't seem like he was trying to pull me.'

'Course he was.' Damien glanced round impatiently, eyeing up a couple of girls at the end of the bar.

Joshua shrugged. 'Maybe. There was just something about him. Anyway, he looked like he had money. You could tell from his suit and everything.'

'Thinking of getting yourself a sugar-daddy, are you?' Damien grinned, glancing round at the girls again.

'I might,' said Joshua. 'You never know. I might.'

Chapter four

'Haven't lunched in hall for weeks,' remarked Roderick, as he and Leo strolled through Fountain Court the following day.

'I still put in the occasional appearance,' said Leo. 'The food's been getting slightly better of late, believe it or not.' They passed through the gloomy vestibule and into Middle Temple Hall, where the air was loud with conversation and the clatter of plates, and ambrosial with a smell akin to that of school dinners.

'The chicken,' remarked Roderick. 'That's the safest bet. That chilli con carne looks lethal.'

While Roderick ordered two plates of chicken casserole, Leo fetched a couple of half-pints of beer from the steward at the end of the hall, and they managed to find seats at one of the long wooden tables where they could talk in relative seclusion.

'So – you want to hear about the meeting with the Estates Committee?'

'That can wait,' said Roderick. 'I think we should talk first about Cameron. I'm afraid it's not good news. I spoke to Hilary a week ago.' Roderick's face was grim. 'After he saw his consultant, Cameron went for some tests.'

'And?'

Roderick paused and sighed. 'Apparently he has cancer of the liver.'

Leo put down his fork and pushed his plate away. 'Christ.'

'He'd had stomach pains for months, but just put it down to bad digestion. But when he started to lose weight, Hilary got worried and insisted he see someone.' Roderick sighed. 'There's nothing that can be done. There are transplants, of course, but I should imagine Cameron's too old.'

'How long has he got?'

'A matter of months. Of course, there's no question of him coming back to chambers.'

'No ... God, that's terrible news. Poor old man.' Leo felt shocked and upset. Cameron's cheerful, slightly eccentric character was part of the life of chambers. He had been there for years, ever since Leo had first started, an ebullient, reactionary presence whose untidiness and casual manner had exasperated countless judges, but whose incisive legal mind was beloved of solicitors and clients. Leo sat in silence for some moments, then said, 'That means we're without a head of chambers.'

'Quite. It's something that needs to be sorted out.'

'We can't – I mean, we can't do anything formal for a few months.' He looked questioningly at Roderick. 'Surely?'

'No,' agreed Roderick. 'It wouldn't be quite the thing. Not while Cameron's still ...'

'No.' He paused. 'We'll need an acting head of chambers till then. You're the obvious man.'

Roderick shrugged. 'I'm happy to stand in for a while. Depends on what the others say.'

'I'm sure everyone will agree. We can discuss it at the next chambers meeting. Lord, poor Hilary. I must go and see Cameron. Is he at home?'

'For the time being.' There was silence between the two men for a moment or two, then Roderick said, 'Anyway, you'd better tell me how the meeting with the Estates Committee went.'

'Oh, it was nothing much. They were simply outlining the structural alterations they're making to the building, room sizes, installing lifts, that kind of thing. They're completely renovating the place.' Leo rubbed his chin. 'Quite a few chambers have expressed interest, so there's no guarantee we'll be granted a lease.'

'I suppose that's true. The fact that Cameron is a member of Lincoln's Inn is obviously a help, plus the fact that he's a chum of the Estates Committee chairman, but if he's out of the picture ...'

Leo sighed. 'I don't see why we have to move so far afield. God, Lincoln's Inn ... It's not like the Temple. There's no sense of intimacy.'

'I know you're not keen on the idea, Leo, but the thing has to be faced. Five Caper Court is too small. Camilla shouldn't have to share with Gerald and Anthony's always complaining that he hasn't got enough room for large conferences. The clerks' room is bulging at the seams. There simply isn't anything suitable in the Temple. And it's not just to do with space. There's our image as well. We have to move with the times.'

'You're beginning to sound like Jeremy.'

'Like it or not, Leo, we have no option. If you can find another solution to the problem, we'll all willingly consider it.'

'I suppose I'm simply more of a creature of habit than I realised.'

'We all have to get used to change.' Instinctively, abruptly, Roderick asked, 'How's the divorce going?'

'It's going,' replied Leo. 'Decree nisi last July. Just tidying up the loose ends.'

'I'm sorry it came unstuck. I was surprised, I must say. Lovely girl.'

'Lovely,' agreed Leo. 'But it didn't surprise me. I wasn't cut out for marriage.' He glanced at his watch. 'Let's head back. I'm expecting some papers from Middleton Potts.'

On the way out, Leo and Roderick met Sarah crossing Caper Court from the cloisters.

'Hello,' she said, giving both a girlish smile.

'Hello,' replied Leo. 'Pupillage going well? Not interfering unduly with your social life, I trust?'

'No – but thanks for asking. I'm working quite hard, as a matter of fact.'

'How reassuring.' Leo held open the door of 5 Caper Court to let Sarah pass through and watched her as she went upstairs.

'What's she like, David's pupil? You seem to know her quite well.'

'I met her a few times before she came here. Her father's the Recorder of London.'

'Ah . . . *that* Colman.' Roderick nodded.

'As to her abilities, I have no idea. I've only ever encountered her on a social level.' As he said this, Leo could not help smiling at the inadequacy of this expression to sum up his numerous and very erotic sexual exploits with Sarah. A dangerous irritant she might be, but the sight of her neat bottom in its tight black skirt, the haughty way she had of flicking back her blonde hair, still had the capability to arouse him. Not that he had any intention of involving himself with a woman ever again. They wanted too much – too much time, affection and attention. Men, on the whole, were less demanding. As he considered this, Leo's thoughts turned to Joshua, whom he had arranged to see that night. Was he about to make a complete fool of himself? He might be entirely wrong about the boy. Maybe he should just forget the whole thing.

He sighed. 'Oh, Felicity – I'm expecting some papers from Andrew Donoghue. Have they arrived?' Felicity nodded and handed them to him. Leo noticed that she looked dispirited and was unusually quiet. 'Are you all right?' he asked. 'You don't seem your usual effervescent self.'

She gave a wan smile. 'Yeah, Mr Davies, I'm fine. Just hormones.'

'Mmm. Quite.' Leo unfolded the papers and began to scan them as he made his way up to his room.

How close to the truth that had been, thought Felicity. She felt dreadful, completely washed out, and she thought she knew why. Not that she'd had morning sickness or anything like that, but her boobs had been aching like hell, and – well, she just knew. She glanced over at her bag, in which lay the pregnancy tester she'd bought from Boots at lunch-time. It wasn't going to tell her anything she hadn't already guessed at. So why was she putting off doing it? Because as long as she didn't face up to it, there was still a little glimmer of hope that it was all a false alarm. She could cling to that. The bloody test would only turn it into a stark reality. 'Oh, come on,' she muttered suddenly to herself. 'Stop faffing about.'

'You talking to me?' asked Henry.

Felicity snatched up her bag and headed for the loo, leaving Henry looking baffled.

Five minutes later she was staring at it, gazing at the unmistakable blue line as though willing it not to be there. The instructions had even said you should use it first thing in the morning to get a clear result, but there could be nothing clearer than this. Of all pregnant women, Felicity felt she must be the most definitely pregnant ever. She closed her eyes and leaned back against the tiled wall. This was the last thing in the world she needed or wanted. Just when everything had started to go right for her, when she had a good job where she was really making headway, earning enough to keep her and Vince while he did his knowledge, and to put money by for the day when he would get his own black cab, this had to happen. What would Vince say? Not that she was going to tell him. Not yet. Maybe not ever. She thought back to her schooldays, to false alarms, to old wives' tales of drinking a bottle of gin in a hot bath, or jumping down six or seven stairs, or off a chair several times. And she knew in her heart that nothing like that would work for her. She couldn't even hope for a miscarriage. She wasn't built that way. Her own mum had fallen pregnant five times, worked through every pregnancy, dropped 'em like ripe fruit, no problems. She was the same. She was too robust, too clearly built by nature for childbearing for anything to go wrong.

She met her reflection in the mirror and saw that her eyes looked large with misery. She looked away. At that moment the door opened and Felicity quickly stuffed the tester into the sanitary disposal bin.

'Hi,' said Camilla. She glanced at Felicity. 'You all right?'

If it had been just two or three hours later, if she'd had time to come to terms with the discovery that she was really and truly pregnant, Felicity might have been able to keep up a front. But the shock was such that she found herself saying, 'I've just found out I'm pregnant.'

Camilla put her hand to her mouth. 'Oh, Felicity.' There was a silence, then Camilla said, 'I think I can tell from your expression that I'm not meant to say "congratulations".'

'Too bloody right you're not.' Without meaning to, Felicity began to cry, and Camilla put her arms around her and hugged her awkwardly.

'What are you going to do?'

'I don't know. I really don't know,' sobbed Felicity. After a few seconds the tears stopped. She sniffed, wiped her eyes and blotted at her running mascara with a tissue. 'You won't tell anyone in chambers, will you?'

'Of *course* I won't.'

'It's just – oh, God, it couldn't come at a worse time.' She shook her head. 'Still, I'm not the first woman in the world it's happened to. I've just got to sit down and think it through.'

'If there's anything I can do –' Camilla stopped, helpless. Of course, there was nothing she could do, except offer a shoulder to cry on. Felicity had to make her decisions on her own.

Felicity gave a watery smile. 'Yeah, thanks. I'd better be getting back.' And she slipped out.

A few moments later, as Camilla was making her way

back to her room, Henry called over to her, 'That was Freshfields on the phone. They were so impressed by the job you did for them in June that they thought you might like a three-week jaunt to Bermuda.'

'Three weeks!' Camilla looked astonished. 'What on earth for?'

'They want you to attend some long hearing they've got starting out there. I told Jane Rice you'd ring her back.'

'Right. I'll go and do it. When do they want me to go?'

'Next Monday. Don't worry. Apart from two things that I can move around, your diary's free.'

Camilla hurried back upstairs to her room. Three weeks in Bermuda. Not bad. And the fact that Freshfields liked her was a good sign. Passing Anthony's room, she knocked and put her head round. Anthony was busy arranging books on a shelf and smiled when he saw her.

'Guess what?' said Camilla, closing the door.

'Surprise me.'

'Freshfields want me to go to Bermuda for three weeks.'

'Three weeks? When?'

'Next week.'

'You jet-setter.' Anthony came over to her. 'I'm going to miss you,' he said and kissed her.

'I thought you might regard it as a welcome break,' replied Camilla, smiling and kissing him back. 'Don't you sometimes think we see too much of one other, working in the same chambers?'

'I don't think I could ever have too much of you. Why won't you just move in with me and put the thing on a forty-eight-hour basis?' It was something Anthony had first suggested a week ago and Camilla still wasn't sure how she felt about the idea. She gave a little sigh.

'Let's not talk about that now, Anthony. I'm not in the mood.'

'You never are.'

'Look . . . I promise we'll discuss it properly later.'

'When later?'

'Friday evening. Let's go out to dinner and discuss it then.'

'All right.' He put his arms around her and kissed her properly.

Leo came downstairs on his way out to a conference at 4 Essex Court. He paused outside Anthony's door. He had thought long and hard about Joshua, and had come to the conclusion that it was beyond his dignity and energy to pursue someone so young, no matter how desirable. If Anthony was free to go out for a drink, maybe dinner, then his evening would be better spent. He knocked lightly and opened the door.

Camilla was the first to see Leo. She pulled away from Anthony in embarrassment.

'I apologise for interrupting,' said Leo. His tone was lightly sardonic, but his face was unsmiling.

Anthony coughed, moving away from Camilla and going round to his desk. 'Not at all,' he replied.

Leo was astonished by how deeply affected he had been by the sight of Anthony kissing Camilla. He knew how many girlfriends Anthony had had, including Sarah, but for some reason the reality of Anthony's sexual intimacy with any woman had been, until this moment, non-existent. The pain it gave him was extraordinary.

Immediately aware of a tension between the two men that lay beyond mere embarrassment, Camilla excused herself. She brushed past Leo and left. Outside on the landing she hesitated for a few seconds, bemused and annoyed, then went down to her room.

'Sorry about that,' murmured Anthony.

'It's I who should apologise,' said Leo, his voice cold; he was still trying to come to terms with his own feelings, which seemed disproportionate to so trivial a matter.

'I think you already have,' responded Anthony, glancing at Leo with something like a challenge in his eyes and voice.

He understood only too well what Leo felt, and it angered him. There was no justification. And yet he understood.

After a pause of a few seconds Leo said, keeping his tone deliberately casual, 'I wondered if you felt like a drink after work.'

'I'm sorry,' said Anthony. 'I'm seeing Camilla this evening.'

Leo nodded. 'Of course.' He turned to go.

'Maybe some other time?' added Anthony.

'Yes, maybe some other time.'

The door closed. Anthony sighed and sat down slowly at his desk. A pattern seemed to be emerging where his relationships with other women and Leo were concerned. First there had been Julia, then Rachel, and now Camilla. Not that jealousy could explain what had happened with Rachel, after Leo had taken her away from him, knowing how in love with her Anthony had been. Leo had, after all, married her. But it seemed as though the friendship between himself and Leo could simply not flourish as long as Anthony was involved with any woman. The thing was ridiculous. Anthony stood up and turned to the window, thrusting his hands in his pockets. He saw Leo emerge below and watched him cross Caper Court on his way to his conference. He had waited at this same window just a few years ago in the simple hope of catching a glimpse of Leo, he had loved him so much. There had been a time when Anthony would have done anything for Leo. Almost anything. But that was the difference between them. He was not like Leo. He had never made love to a man in his life, had only once contemplated it ... Where would he and Leo be now, if he had allowed that to happen? It didn't bear thinking about. It hadn't happened, and his emotional life now was bound up with Camilla. If Leo couldn't handle that then it was Leo's problem, and there was nothing Anthony could do about it.

Leo crossed Middle Temple Lane and strode briskly into Essex Court. He had already decided that he would go to the

Galleria tonight after all. If there was no room for him in Anthony's life, then he would find someone else to amuse him. It had always worked in the past and he saw no reason why it should not do so now.

Joshua was sliding glasses into their racks above the bar when he saw Leo come in. It was a quarter to eleven and customers were thinning out. He gave Leo a half-smile. He hadn't really expected to see him. Leo hadn't struck him as the usual type, the type that he and Damien mildly despised, but whose money they would take in exchange for their sexual favours.

He came over to Leo's table. 'Can I get you a coffee?' asked Joshua.

Leo nodded. 'Thanks.' Joshua noticed that he wasn't wearing the pin-stripe suit of the night before, but was casually dressed in blue slacks and a lighter blue shirt open at the neck, a straw-coloured jacket slung over his shoulders. He looked younger, and Joshua suddenly realised how good-looking he was, for an old guy.

Leo watched as Joshua moved away to get his coffee, aware that his heart had begun to thud at the half-forgotten beauty of the young man. Each time, with every encounter, the thrill remained undiminished. Would there come a day when it would be hopeless, when he would be too old, too unattractive to inspire the kind of interest he saw in Joshua's eyes? Perhaps, but it had not come yet. Tonight, Leo felt, the balance was perfect.

Joshua brought the coffee. 'When do you finish?' asked Leo.

'About another fifteen minutes.' He hesitated, lingering. 'Where do you want to go? My place or yours?' He kept his voice low, but spoke casually.

Leo realised he was more surprised than he should have been by the baldness of the question. What else would Joshua assume Leo wanted? But Leo knew that he wanted more, much more, than merely a casual encounter with this beautiful young stranger.

He sat back, smiling. 'Joshua, when I said I wanted to talk to you, I meant it. Do you find that hard to believe?'

Something in Leo's eyes puzzled Joshua. Damien had said they were all the same, but this one was different. He had none of the pathetic, hopeful, predatory characteristics of the men who usually propositioned him. He was good-looking and assured, and he looked at Joshua with a mild, curious kindness which was new to Joshua.

Joshua shrugged. Then he smiled. The smile transformed his serene, rather languid features like cloud passing away from a landscape. 'I don't know,' he replied. 'Yes and no.'

Leo nodded. 'I shall sit here and drink my coffee. Then, if you like, we can go somewhere and talk. Just talk.'

Joshua moved away from the table.

Twenty minutes later they left the bar together. The proprietor scarcely glanced at Leo. What his bar staff did off duty was none of his business. Leo and Joshua stood on the pavement. A gust of night air made Joshua pull his thin jacket tight around him.

'My car's round the corner,' said Leo. 'We can go back to my place – or does that concern you?'

Joshua laughed and looked away. Where was this guy coming from? He shook his head, still smiling, and looked at Leo. 'No, that doesn't concern me.'

They walked down the darkened street together, not speaking, until they reached Leo's car.

'Wow. An Aston Martin DB7,' said Joshua in admiration. He nodded, surveying the lines of the car. 'Very nice.'

Leo unlocked the car and Joshua slid into the passenger seat. Leather interior, walnut dash. He'd never been in a car like this before. It had that special, subtle smell that belonged to expensive things. Joshua loved that smell. He loved the squashy, cop-a-load-of-this feel of the seat as he moved to buckle his belt. This thing was a dream. God, to drive this. He bet it did nought to sixty in about five seconds.

As they drew away from the kerb, Joshua said, 'So it's true what they say about barristers, then? That they earn a fortune?'

Leo smiled. 'Not all of us.' He pressed a button on the CD player and the gentle tones of Mahler filled the car.

Joshua gazed at Leo's lean profile, noticing the way the street lights silvered his hair. Yet he wasn't that old. 'But *you* do.'

Leo chuckled. 'Yes, I do.' He glanced at Joshua. In the half-light the boy's face was astonishingly beautiful, his expression open, interested.

'What kind of law do you do?'

'Commercial law. Shipping. Other people's money.'

'Doesn't sound very interesting.'

'You'd be surprised.' Leo drove smoothly through the traffic and into Sloane Street. 'Law is quite fascinating,' he remarked. 'It's part of every single person's life. It brings drama to everyone it touches, whether it's in the form of jury service, or a murder charge, or simply selling a house, or getting a parking ticket.'

'Or getting done for speeding. You ever been caught for that in this?'

'No. I'm very careful about that kind of thing.'

'Yeah, I suppose you have to be.' Joshua craned to look at the speedometer. 'What does it do?'

'A hundred and fifty-seven, if I recall rightly.'

'That's silly,' said Joshua.

'Yes, it is, isn't it?' They drew up outside the mansion block of flats. 'This is where I live,' said Leo.

'Right,' said Joshua, scanning the building.

They went upstairs to Leo's first-floor apartment in silence. Leo unlocked the door, and he and Joshua went in.

'This is beautiful,' said Joshua, following Leo through the

flat, gazing around him. 'You've got so much space. I wish I had this much space.'

'Would you like a drink?' asked Leo, going into the kitchen.

'Have you got any beer?'

'Beer,' said Leo. 'No. No, I'm afraid I don't.'

'I won't bother, then, thanks.'

Leo poured himself a Scotch and Joshua watched, fascinated, as Leo pressed the button on the ice dispenser on the fridge and chunks of ice fell into his glass.

'That's so cool,' said Joshua, admiring the dispenser. 'Wow, look, you can set it for crushed ice, too.'

'Or iced water.' Leo smiled, watching Joshua's face. He was a delight.

'Yeah.' Joshua gazed at the dispenser, then left the kitchen and went into the spacious drawing-room, turning his attention to the pictures on the walls. He studied them one by one, moving round the room, his fists still rammed into the pockets of his jacket. Leo sat down in an armchair, sipping his drink and watching Joshua, glad of the leisure to be able to follow the rhythms and movements of the boy's body while Joshua gazed at the pictures, unaware. He watched the way the light caught the reddish-gold glints in Joshua's hair, then wondered whether the boy had combed it since he had last seen him. It didn't look like it.

'You've got some nice stuff,' said Joshua approvingly. He pointed to a picture made up of a series of swathes of blue dissolving into one another. 'That's a Patrick Heron, isn't it?' He indicated another, larger canvas. 'And I recognise that style, but I don't know who it is.'

Leo got up and strolled over to look at the picture. 'That's by Martin Fuller. He was very big in the eighties. I bought that picture from the Austin Desmond Gallery before it collapsed.' He sipped his Scotch, letting his sleeve brush Joshua's, fiercely conscious of the proximity of the younger man, the physicality of him.

Joshua tilted his head, gazing at the picture. 'It's got a sort of sixties feeling about it.'

Leo gave a little smile, wondering what Joshua knew of the sixties. 'It should do. His work's very representative of ways of working in that era.'

'How do you mean?' asked Joshua, turning to look questioningly at him.

Leo wondered if the boy had any idea at all how his gaze stopped Leo's heart. The effect was such that he took a few seconds to answer. He looked back at the picture. 'Well, this way of building up his canvases with big blocks of brushwork. A bit reminiscent of de Kooning. He deals with the space before attempting to occupy it with figures. Formal structure first, emotional accent second. Characteristically sixties.'

Joshua nodded. 'You know a lot about it.'

'What about your painting?' asked Leo, going back to his chair. He felt that if he remained close to Joshua for much longer he would be unable to control the strength of his desire to reach out and touch him. 'Tell me about that. Tell me about yourself.'

Joshua left the pictures and sat down on a long sofa opposite Leo. 'My painting.' He laughed. 'It's a con, really. I can't paint. I did a year's foundation course at Goldsmiths' and that's about it.' He shrugged. 'I'm not saying I don't enjoy it. I've always liked painting and drawing, ever since I was a kid, but I don't rate myself. Still, since any old shit seems to sell these days, I keep on hoping. Look at Gilbert and George. They make a fortune. Maybe someday someone will look at my stuff and decide it's flavour of the month. That's the way it seems to happen. Talent doesn't seem to matter much these days.'

'That's a remarkably cynical point of view for someone of your age,' said Leo, dipping into his pocket for his cigar case. 'Still, you may have a point. What I think you're talking about is placement.' He took a small cigar from his pocket and lit it reflectively.

'Am I?' Joshua watched Leo, wondering. Here they were, the two of them, all cosy in his big Belgravia pad, talking away about art as though there was nothing else on the agenda. But there was, Joshua knew. He could tell, he could feel it, just something in the atmosphere when Leo had stood next to him. Your senses became attuned to it. So what was it to be? Just a one-night stand? There was something about Leo that told him things could be more worthwhile than that. The odd fifty quid here and there, you sometimes wondered if it was worth it. But this one. This one had serious money, and he seemed to be all alone. Everyone gets lonely, Joshua told himself. He glanced round the room again, waiting for Leo to speak. He thought of his bedsit in Earl's Court, the crummy toilet he shared with the two Australians across the landing, the racket from the street keeping everyone awake half the night, and compared it with the lovely silence of this apartment, the pictures, the furniture. Maybe he was wrong, but he had the feeling Leo was interested in him in more ways than one. There was a look in his eyes, a sort of – Joshua couldn't think of the word. A sort of look of understanding.

Leo's voice broke across his thoughts. 'Placement. Being exhibited in the right places, the good galleries. There's nothing like context to enhance the value of an artist's work.'

'You're right. It's how to get into those places. How do you do it?'

'There are ways.' Leo tipped the ash off his cigar into a large glass ashtray on the table at his side. 'Don't underrate yourself. Those paintings of yours that I saw are every bit as good as stuff that goes for thousands at galleries in Bruton Street and Bond Street.'

'Sure, tell me about it.' Joshua laughed.

There was a silence. Leo smoked. Joshua drummed one heel absently, staring round the room again.

'I could help you,' said Leo at last.

'Yeah?' Joshua glanced at him. 'Why would you want to do that?'

'Because I like you.' Their eyes met. 'But you know that, don't you?'

'Yes,' replied Joshua.

Leo lifted his cigar to his lips. 'Do you do this kind of thing often? Come to men's flats, I mean, men whom you've only just met, whom you don't know well?'

Joshua began to drum his heel again and looked away. 'Now and then.'

'What for?'

Was this some kind of game? Joshua wondered. He laughed uneasily, without humour. 'You know what for.'

'To talk?'

'Yeah, sure, to talk.' Joshua got up and began to pace around, looking again at the pictures.

'Joshua,' said Leo softly. Joshua turned and stared at him. 'Come here.'

There was silence for a few seconds. Joshua turned round. 'No,' he said, his voice thoughtful. 'You come here.'

Leo stubbed out his cigar, put down his glass and rose. He felt vulnerable, awkward, but he obeyed without hesitation. He came and stood before Joshua. When Joshua kissed him, Leo found it extraordinary. In most encounters it was he who had made the first move. But Joshua simply embraced him and kissed him for a long and exquisite moment.

For Joshua, Leo tasted of whisky and cigars. With a little slipping sensation in his heart, Joshua suddenly realised that he liked it. For the first time ever, he was enjoying what he was doing with another man. After a moment he drew away.

'That's what you wanted, isn't it?' There was no trace of anger in Joshua's voice. His eyes were fastened on Leo's, their faces close together. 'All this crap about wanting to talk.'

Leo felt entirely defenceless. 'Stay,' said Leo. 'Stay here tonight.' The touch of the younger man was intoxicating, shocking, in a way that Leo did not think he had ever experienced before. He felt beyond himself.

Joshua shook his head. His eyes did not leave Leo's. 'I can't,' he said, then shrugged. 'I'm sorry.' And with that, he turned and left the room. He walked unhurriedly, casually, as though it didn't much matter.

Leo heard the front door close. The silence seemed to press in on him from all sides. His senses felt totally numb. He sat down again. He had no idea why Joshua had left, or what had happened between them. But he knew with a sudden, dread knowledge that was like a pain in his heart, that he was hopelessly, completely infatuated.

Chapter five

Leo frowned in an effort of concentration as he went through his diary, checking items with Felicity. Thoughts of the night before, of Joshua, seemed to dominate everything.

'Summons for directions on the twenty-fourth ...' Leo flicked back a page, as an entry caught his eye. It was for this evening.

'What's this?'

Felicity craned over to peer at Leo's diary. '*Trustees meeting*. I dunno. I haven't got anything.'

Then he remembered. 'Oh, Lord – it's that thing with Anthony's father. I'd completely forgotten. No, you needn't worry about it. Anyway, see if you can change the date for that hearing on the fourth.'

'Okay.' Felicity scribbled briefly in her own diary, then left.

Leo leaned back in his chair, suddenly wishing that he hadn't agreed to become a trustee of Chay Cross's new museum. Right now, he didn't have much enthusiasm for it. Then again, it was a distraction. How he needed distractions these days. His thoughts returned ineluctably to Joshua, to the memory of his face, his body, his touch. His heart tightened with pain at the recollected sensuality of their encounter. He had no idea what he should do about the boy, about his feelings for him. Perhaps nothing. The boy had walked out. Simply, and against all indications, walked out. How could he pursue him, and still retain any vestige of pride? Yet the idea that he might not see him again was becoming unbearable.

With a sigh, Leo leaned forward once again and unwound the ribbon from a brief. He paused. For the first time in his life, it occurred to him that this was all he ever did. Unwind these faded lengths of ribbon from endless sheaves of paper, unfolding other people's dilemmas, absorbing them. He had never thought of it in this detached way. Slowly he fingered the ribbon. It had always been enough, until recently. Now the very point of his work seemed to escape him. Be careful, Leo, he told himself. Much more of this and you could be entirely lost.

Felicity went back down to the clerks' room, passing Camilla on the stairs. 'You all set for your Bermuda trip on Monday?' she asked Camilla.

'Just about. Have the travel agents sent the tickets?'

'Came first thing. Pop down later and we can go through your itinerary.'

'Okay.' Camilla paused, then added gently, 'How are you, by the way? I've been thinking about you, ever since the other day. Have you decided what you're going to do?'

Felicity hugged the diary against her chest. 'Not really.' She sighed. 'I haven't even told Vince yet.'

'Well, tell him and that way you can both decide.'

Felicity gave a wan smile. 'Yeah, right. Anyway, I'll see you later.' She carried on downstairs. All very well for Camilla to say that, but she didn't really understand the situation. Above all, she didn't know Vince.

Leo met Anthony on his way out of chambers at lunch-time. 'You haven't forgotten this evening, I hope,' said Anthony.

'No, but I would have if I hadn't put it in my diary,' replied Leo. 'Where is this place? I've forgotten that as well.'

'Shoreditch. I can give you directions, if you don't mind giving me a lift. I have to bring along the trust documents for everyone to sign.'

'Right.' Leo glanced in the direction of the door as Sarah came in from Caper Court.

She gave him a radiant smile. 'David says I can sit in with you on the case you have starting tomorrow. He hasn't got much for me to do for the next few days.'

'How utterly wonderful,' sighed Leo. 'Would you mind telling your pupilmaster that it would be kind of him to consult me, in future?'

'Oh, I told him I knew you wouldn't mind,' said Sarah. 'See you in the morning.' She gave Anthony a glance and a smile, too, then went upstairs.

Anthony followed her thoughtfully with his eyes. 'Do you think she had hopes of taking up a tenancy here?'

Leo sighed. 'Let's just live with the present, shall we? Where Miss Colman is concerned, one doesn't like to think too far ahead. See you tonight.'

That evening, in the two-bedroomed flat in New Cross, Felicity pressed the buttons on the microwave and watched as two portions of Marks & Spencer's pork in mustard sauce began to revolve slowly. 'Vince,' she said thoughtfully, 'how long d'you think it's going to take you to do your knowledge?'

'Hang on a bit,' said Vince, cracking open a can of beer, 'I only got me blue book from the Public Carriage Office the other day. There's fifty-six runs I've got to memorise.'

'I don't know why they call it the blue book when it's pink,' murmured Felicity. God, she felt tired. When she'd gone into the bedroom to change after work, it'd been all she could do to stop herself from snuggling under the duvet and just falling asleep there and then. 'But how long, d'you reckon?'

Vince shrugged. 'Depends on your ability, doesn't it? Just a question of keep goin' out on the bike, getting meself up to speed. There's a hell of a lot to learn. And they won't call me up for my first appearance for another six months at least.'

'But if you pass, say, in six months' time, you could start renting your own cab, earning proper money?' Felicity took two baked potatoes from the oven and put them on plates.

'No chance,' said Vince with a laugh. 'Nobody passes first go off. It's a lot tougher than it used to be. There was a time you could do it in nine months or so, but now it takes a good couple of years. Maybe three.'

Felicity slowly peeled back the Cellophane from the microwave meal. 'Two years?' She'd had the idea that Vince could be running his own black cab in a matter of months. She'd even planned ahead, saved, happy to think that he could use the savings to rent a cab once he'd passed his knowledge. But when he began to talk in terms of years . . . She spooned the pork out on to the plates. If she had this baby, how would they live? She was earning so well at the moment, more than she had ever imagined she could, and they both took it for granted. Vince had always sponged off her, but she didn't mind paying for everything for both of them if he was really serious about planning a means of making his own living in the long run. Doing the knowledge had been her idea, of course, but he'd taken it up with real enthusiasm. The notion of being a black cab driver appealed to Vince as having a certain amount of cred, and it meant that he would be his own boss. That was important, for Vince wasn't the kind of man who took kindly to working for anyone. So far he'd demonstrated a commendable seriousness of purpose, going up to the Public Carriage Office, doing the medical, getting his blue book, purchasing a second-hand motor bike to roar round the streets, memorising routes, street names and traffic systems. Felicity had paid for the bike, as she paid for everything, but the important thing was that Vince was undertaking something that could pay off. For Vince, that was a first. But she couldn't bank on it. She couldn't just give up work and have a baby, and wait for him to pass his knowledge. It might never happen.

Felicity brought their plates over and sat down. Vince held the can of beer over her empty glass. 'You fancy some?'

Felicity shook her head. 'No, thanks.'

'You all right?' asked Vince. 'You haven't had a drink in days. Not like you, is it?'

She smiled wanly. 'No. Maybe I'm coming down with something.' Why wouldn't she just come out with it, tell him and have done? Because she guessed what his reaction would be. She knew Vince too well. All man. He'd be delighted, proud, without even giving a thought to the future. Vince was a great believer in things working out for the best. He lived from day to day, like a child. And that was the thing. She'd have two children on her hands and an uncertain future. Once Vince knew, there would be no way out. There would be no question of an abortion. He'd close all the doors, heedlessly. But this was one door she had to keep open, for the present, at any rate. So she picked up her fork and ate, and said nothing.

'Just up here on the left,' said Anthony, as Leo drove slowly up the narrow cobbled street. 'There it is.' They pulled up outside what had once been a brewery, but was now to be the home of Chay's London Museum of Modern Art.

'It's quite a handsome building,' said Leo. 'What I can see of it.' The brewery was set back from the cobbled street behind high walls, in which were set heavy iron gates. 'Strange backwater, this, isn't it?' He got out of the car, locked it, and he and Anthony stood together on the pavement, gazing around.

'There are some very fine Georgian houses just round the corner from here,' remarked Anthony. 'I gather from my father that it's becoming something of an artists' haven. Anyway, he's found the right premises at the right address, so he's pretty pleased.' They passed through the iron gates and into a large cobbled courtyard, where a security guard was strolling. 'A functional building like this was just what he needed. Lots of space, good light.'

'It must be costing a fortune to do up,' said Leo.

'He's got a grant from English Heritage to restore the fabric of the building, so that's a start. And, of course, Lord Stockeld is chipping in a hefty sum to help fund the collection. The rest is all Chay's own money,' said Anthony. 'But, as he said, there's a good chance of lottery money once the trust is up and running.'

They went in through the large front door, which stood open. They found themselves in a small vestibule, and beyond they could hear the sound of voices. Passing along a short corridor, they emerged into a large, airy room, as high as the building itself, with a gallery running round.

Chay was at the far end, with three other people. He raised a hand in greeting when he saw Anthony and Leo. 'Good to see you. Leo, let me introduce a few of your co-trustees. Tony Gear, MP, Derek Harvey, Graham Amery. This is Leo Davies, who's going to add a bit of legal weight to the show. I'm afraid Lord Stockeld can't be with us this evening. He's in Frankfurt on business.'

Leo shook hands with each man in turn, he and Amery giving one another a brief grin of recognition. From what he could recall of the Barrett's Bank case a few years ago, Amery's dapper, slightly self-deprecating air masked a fiercely conscientious and industrious personality, and Leo wasn't surprised he had risen to become its chairman. Gear, in his mid-thirties, was some fifteen years Amery's junior, a short, rotund creature, with bright, ambitious eyes set in a clever, schoolboyish face, and floppy dark hair. He was dressed in a nondescript grey suit and suede shoes. Leo had trouble recalling whether he was Labour, Conservative or Lib Dem. Certainly his face and his faintly aggressive, gravelly voice were familiar from news soundbites. He was a regular spokesman on some issue or other, but Leo couldn't for the life of him remember what. Derek Harvey he recognised from the small, blurred black-and-white photograph which accompanied his column in one of the daily papers. He was taller than Leo had imagined, with curling grey hair and pouched, tired features, dressed in a long, shabby raincoat over jeans and a sweat-shirt.

'Quite a venture, this,' remarked Derek Harvey. 'Good location.' He gestured round the lofty room. 'This will be superb for large installation pieces.'

'I was just showing everyone round,' said Chay, 'while we wait for Melissa. She rang to say she's running late. Come through and I'll show you the area that I've got marked out for the video installations. I think you'll like it.'

Chay led them through a series of high-ceilinged areas. Work had begun on whitewashing the brick walls and on fitting lighting. The floors were still littered with the debris of builders and electricians, and as the group picked its way among planks, spools of flex and pots of paint, Chay kept up a running commentary on the functions of each individual area.

Eventually he glanced at his watch. 'I think we'd better make a start,' he said. 'Melissa didn't say how late she'd be.' He led them all through to a long, low-ceilinged meeting room, which still smelled of fresh varnish. An oval table stood in the centre, surrounded by chairs, and everyone sat down.

The meeting commenced in an orderly fashion. Chay, who was normally something of a laid-back individual, had been galvanised by enthusiasm for his project, and had set about organising matters with surprising efficiency. It helped that Anthony had been drafted in to act as secretary and general legal consultant. For this Leo was grateful; he hadn't wanted his own role in all this to be too onerous.

Chay opened the meeting with a little speech about the aims of the project, then Leo added his signature to the others on the trust documents and a general discussion began about the museum's collection policy. At this point

Melissa Angelicos arrived in a fluster of scarves, bags and papers, and the meeting ground to a temporary halt.

There was certainly something impressive about the woman, thought Leo, as he watched her murmur effusive apologies, darting smiles at each of them while introductions were made, settling herself into her chair with an exuberant flash of her long legs. Leo studied her covertly as Chay ran over the items which they had already discussed and Anthony produced the trust documents for her to sign. She was older than she appeared on television. Leo put her somewhere in her mid-forties. She possessed fine-boned, dramatic features, slightly coarsened by age, and a mane of ash-blonde hair which she wore carelessly pinned up. The slenderness of youth was toughening into wiry angularity in middle age, but Leo could see why men considered her attractive. Her movements were nervy and self-conscious, but her smile and general manner were charismatic, if a little hard.

No sooner had Chay explained that they were discussing the museum's collection policy than she launched into an enthusiastic endorsement of the work of a handful of young British artists recently exhibited at the Royal Academy and the Saatchi Gallery. 'There are some absolutely wonderful pieces we could obtain – sado-kitsch, you might call them. Totally transgressive. After all, any new museum of this kind must show generosity towards native young talent, and some of the work that's been shown is terribly exciting. Gayford's *Dwarf in Bondage*, for instance –'

Derek Harvey, who was sitting hunched over the table, still in his raincoat, interrupted her with a sigh. 'Melissa, the core collection can't concern itself with that kind of rubbish. If we're going to convince the powers-that-be to give us public funding to acquire new works, the museum has to demonstrate a collections policy that is sound, that is looking for established, serious work by well-known artists. It's not an exercise in promoting the kind of promiscuous, talentless work which your YBAs constantly produce, and which your television programme works so hard to sell. This museum is, I hope, about serious art.'

There was a brief, embarrassed silence. Leo was bemused. Clearly a certain hostility already existed between Ms Angelicos and Harvey. He wondered if Chay had been aware of it.

Chay scratched his designer stubble. 'There's something in what Derek says. I think for the core collection at least, we have to set our sights on well-established artists. People like Patrick Heron, Bill Woodrow, Warhol ... Works that the general public can feel safe with.'

Melissa laughed. It was a bright, scornful laugh with an icy edge. 'If safety is what this project is all about –'

Chay raised a hand. 'Safety isn't what it's all about. Perhaps I used the wrong word. What I mean is that we need established names to convince people that this is fundamentally a museum with a really prestigious collection of twentieth-century art. That way we can get funding to acquire more – more –' Chay groped in the air with thin fingers for the right word '– innovative, exciting work.'

'But, basically, what you're saying is that we have to take a philistine approach.'

Chay sighed. Leo smiled to himself, intrigued, and glanced across at Anthony, who was doodling on a piece of paper and looking bored.

'I don't think you can call my plans for the video installation philistine,' retorted Chay. 'I'm planning on bringing in some of the most ground-breaking work in years. Anyway, if you want to be confrontational, perhaps you can turn your attention to the open-space area. That really does need something ... transgressive to bring it alive.'

At this, Melissa looked interested. 'Open space? I didn't know we had one.'

'It's at the back, where the brewery lorries used to park to load up. Come on, I'll show you all before it gets dark.'

Chay led them all out to the back of the building and indicated a large concrete yard. 'This is all going to be broken up. I had no specific concept in mind, but it seemed to me that there must be some sort of interactive piece, an ongoing thing . . .' He gestured vaguely.

'Absolutely perfect,' said Melissa. 'I know a women's collective who create fantastic organic pieces, dealing in rootedness and estrangement. This kind of open space will be absolutely marvellous for them to work in.'

'Ask them to submit some ideas,' said Chay. 'We need it up and running in a matter of months.'

They went back inside and arranged themselves around the table once more.

'I was thinking about what Chay said earlier about the core collection,' said Leo. He hadn't spoken until now and Melissa glanced up. She had noticed on being introduced to him that he was a good-looking man, exceptionally so, but his City suit and apparently reserved demeanour set him, in her mind, among a certain unexciting type, rather like Graham Amery. She had assumed he might be Chay's accountant. 'A friend of mine in Paris tells me there may be a couple of good pieces by Anthony Caro coming on the market soon. We may be able to snap something up, if we move quickly enough.'

'Anthony Caro is just the kind of thing we're after,' said Chay enthusiastically. 'Is it an auction?'

'No,' said Leo, 'this would be private. I told him that I could discuss prices with him next week, if the museum is interested.'

'Absolutely,' said Chay. Derek Harvey murmured in agreement, nodding.

'Speaking of sculpture, I noticed that there's going to be an auction of some pieces by that brick fellow, Carl Andre,' said Tony Gear. 'Maybe that's something we should go for.'

Chay nodded. 'I'm thinking of employing a couple of junior staff in the next few weeks, people to whom we can delegate the business of actually purchasing works on the trust's behalf. What we need right now are suggestions for acquisitions, then we can make collective decisions as we go along.'

'Well, unless Derek is going to slap me down straight away –' Melissa shot Derek Harvey a cold glance '– we might like to consider obtaining a work by Damien Hirst. I know his agent very well.'

The meeting carried on for another half-hour or so and, apart from one more briefly abrasive exchange between Melissa and Derek, broke up amicably.

'Do you want a lift back?' Leo asked Anthony.

'No, that's all right. I'm going on for dinner with Chay. I'll see you tomorrow.'

Everyone made their way back through the gallery areas towards the main entrance. In the last and largest room, Leo stood for a few moments looking around him, studying the space and light.

Melissa Angelicos sauntered over in his direction, glancing around. 'Fantastic space, isn't it?' she remarked.

'I was just wondering,' replied Leo thoughtfully, 'whether it's big enough to take one of Thomas Schutte's installations. Something like that would make a very impressive centre-piece.'

Melissa looked at him appraisingly. 'You've seen his work?'

'I went to his exhibition in Düsseldorf last year. It was remarkable.' He turned to smile at her. Melissa, like most women on whom Leo smiled, felt instant pleasure and faint excitement. 'I have to confine my own collection of sculpture to rather more conveniently sized pieces, of course,' Leo added.

'You collect, do you?'

'On a modest scale. Mainly abstract works.'

They sauntered together to the door, talking about Leo's collection. Melissa glanced at him frequently as he talked, rearranging her initial impression. She was a woman whose interest in people, especially men, was easily quickened, particularly if they were attractive. And she found Leo attractive, decidedly so. Already her mind was leaping ahead to the possibilities. Age made her less subtle these days, more ready to engage. She had lived through so many relationships that she no longer considered or reflected. Each relationship was briefer than the one before, and each one left her harder, and hungrier.

By the time they came through the gates and into the darkening street, the others had gone.

'That the last of you?' asked the security guard.

'I think so,' replied Leo, glancing round. The guard nodded and clanged the gates together, then locked them.

Melissa peered at her watch and gave an anxious little sigh. 'God alone knows how I'm going to find a taxi around here. I suppose I'll just have to walk up to Liverpool Street.'

'Can I give you a lift somewhere?' Leo had no particular wish for Melissa's company. He had been around women long enough to recognise the faintly predatory atmosphere which was gathering. But he knew he had no choice.

'Well, I don't want to take you out of your way, but if you happened to be going anywhere near Kensington ... ?'

'I live in Belgravia,' said Leo, 'so it's no trouble.' Kensington was so close to Knightsbridge, so close to Joshua ... He could just drop in, on the off chance. The memory of the night before seemed to have grown more and more intense in the last couple of hours. He had thought about the boy on and off all through the meeting. But he shouldn't, he knew. He should not even consider compromising his dignity and pride for – for what? A mere boy. But such a boy.

Suddenly he realised that Melissa was saying something to him. 'I'm sorry, I didn't catch ...' Melissa repeated what she had said and Leo replied, 'No, not far. I parked just up here.'

The car, and Leo's preoccupied air as they drove off through the deserted, darkening streets of Shoreditch, gave

Melissa further cause for speculation. She fished around through a selection of opening remarks, then said brightly, 'You know, Leo, I can't quite place you in all of this. Chay did tell me at some point who all the trustees were and what they did, but I'm so busy these days that I forget everything. I know your name, but that's all.'

'I'm a barrister,' replied Leo. 'I'm in chambers with Chay's son, Anthony. Chay knew I liked modern art, and I think he thought having a lawyer on his team might help.' What if it was Joshua's night off? Already his mind and heart were living the possibility of disappointment. Or what if he were there, working, and simply ignored Leo? He had been over this countless times. There was no point. Either he should decide to go now, as soon as he'd dropped this woman off, or he should forget about the whole thing for good.

Melissa made a little face as she looked out at the passing streets. This wasn't exactly going to be easy, not if he was going to look so blank and speak so laconically. She turned back to him with a smile. 'A barrister! How very glamorous.'

He would go. That was it, the decision made. He should stop thinking about Joshua and concentrate on being polite to this woman. He caught her last remark and smiled, glancing at her. Better, thought Melissa, meeting his eyes briefly and thinking how very blue they were. Blue as a child's.

'Hardly,' replied Leo. 'You're the one with the glamorous job.'

She gave a modest laugh. 'Do you watch my programme?'

Leo nodded. 'Yes. It's good. I like it very much.'

'Sweet of you.'

'Though I sometimes think', went on Leo, 'that you concentrate very heavily on confrontational work.' He smiled reflectively. 'What a kind adjective. I really mean work that seems gratuitously offensive, purely there for its shock value.'

'I like what's new. I detest complacency. Anything that

82

shakes up the art world possesses merit for me. Serrano, the Chapman brothers ... Above all, I like to be excited.' She paused, glanced at him and dropped her voice slightly. 'Don't you like to be excited, Leo?'

Leo almost laughed. 'Oh, yes,' he replied. 'By art. By life.' He turned to look at her again, unsurprised by the sensuality of the gaze which met his. This could, he thought, turn out to be a tiresome thirty minute journey. As they drove, he managed to keep the conversation focused on the subject of Melissa's programme, deftly deflecting the occasional provocative remark, and wondered how long it would take her to get to the question of his marital status.

'I live just past those gardens at the end, the right-hand turning,' said Melissa. She sighed as though tired. 'My little haven of tranquillity at the end of the day. Silence if I want it. Music if I don't. Bliss. Living alone is one of the great pleasures in life, don't you think? Or do you go home to a life of happy domestic chaos?'

Leo took the right-hand turning. 'Which number?' he asked. 'Nine.'

The Aston Martin drew to a gentle halt outside Melissa's house. Leo left the engine running. He turned to her, to answer the question left hanging in the air. 'No. No domestic chaos, happy or otherwise. I live alone. My wife and I are in the process of divorcing.'

'I'm so sorry,' said Melissa, hardly even bothering to sound sincere.

Leo thought of Oliver. Tomorrow was Thursday. He still hadn't rung Rachel to make a firm arrangement about going to Bath to see him on Sunday. He pondered this briefly and Melissa took the silence which fell between them as potentially significant.

'It's still only nine thirty,' she said, after a moment. 'I haven't eaten yet. Would you like to come in for a drink? We could carry on our conversation about art and I could make us both some supper. Scrambled eggs and smoked salmon, if

I've got some salmon in the freezer –'

'I'm sorry. That's very kind, but I have an appointment. Someone I have to see.'

Melissa felt an unexpectedly strong pang of disappointment and jealousy. Some other woman, of course. Men like Leo always had a string of them. It suddenly seemed vitally important that he should not slip the net so easily.

She smiled and gave a little shrug. 'Just a drink, then. I'm sure you have ten minutes. It's not often I meet a stimulating man who doesn't make me feel threatened.'

Leo gave a little laugh of astonishment. 'Well, I'm glad of that. But really, I must say no. Maybe some other time.' He cursed inwardly – why had he said that? Because it was one of those things that simply slipped out.

She sighed lightly and opened the door, preparing to get out. 'Oh, well. As you say, some other time. Maybe after the next trustees meeting?'

The tone of enquiry was so direct that Leo was obliged to respond. 'That depends. We'll have to see.' He was damned if he was going to have his hand forced in this way. 'Goodnight.'

She startled him by leaning over and kissing him briefly and softly on his cheek, then she slipped out of the car and was gone. Her scent hung in the air and he sat for a moment trying to recall what it was. L'Air du Temps, that was it – one he had always rather disliked. Putting the car into gear, Leo drove off into the night in the direction of Knightsbridge.

As she mounted the steps to her flat and put the key in the lock, Melissa's mind was already working overtime on the matter of Leo Davies and the necessity of seducing him. The next trustees meeting might be weeks away and that was too long to wait. When Melissa got hungry, her appetites needed to be satisfied quickly. She smiled as she took off her coat and went to pour herself a drink. She liked projects. She liked plans. She always brought them to fruition. Always.

*

Leo parked round the corner from the Galleria and sat in the car for a moment or two. He felt uncharacteristically nervous. Rather than think about it any longer, he got out, locked the car and went into the Galleria. It was at its busiest and at first he couldn't see Joshua. Just as he was about to ask a passing waitress if it was his night off, Joshua came through the door leading from the kitchens. He saw Leo straight away, held his gaze for a moment, then went to the table he was serving. Leo stood at the bar, hesitant. He had been able to read nothing in Joshua's expression. Perhaps he was just going to ignore him. The girl behind the bar said something to him and Leo glanced at her. 'Sorry?'

'Would you like a drink?' she asked again. She had a strong Australian accent.

'Ah ... Yes. Yes. I'll have a Scotch, please. No ice.'

Joshua set the plates down in front of the customers, conscious of the sudden acceleration of his heartbeat. He had no idea whether he was glad to see Leo or not. Had he hoped he would come in tonight? Part of him had, another part had hoped he would just stay away. But he had guessed Leo would come. There he was now, leaning against the bar, cool as anything, having a drink. Waiting.

Joshua finished dealing with the customers and went over to Leo, his tray tucked under his arm. They looked at one another for a few significant seconds, then Leo, sipping his Scotch, asked, 'Do you mind my coming here?'

'No,' said Joshua.

Something tight within Leo loosened with relief. 'I had to know why you left the way you did. Last night ...'

Joshua swallowed and looked away, turning his head, gazing distractedly at the chattering customers. The way the light caught the skin of his throat, throwing the sinews into soft relief, made Leo's heart turn over.

'I can't talk about it here.'

'After work?'

Joshua didn't look at Leo. His expression was uncertain, almost unhappy. At last he nodded and said, 'All right.'

Leo finished what was left of his drink and left. Joshua stood by the bar for an uncertain moment. Maybe he should just try to get off early, not be there when Leo came back. But something told him that there would be no point in that, and that, if not tonight, Leo would be back another time.

For over an hour, Leo simply walked the streets. He hadn't eaten since lunch-time, but seeing Joshua again had taken away any appetite he might have had. He couldn't face the idea of sitting in a pub or a wine bar, of being with people. He was filled with restlessness and a sense of apprehension. Never in his life could he recall being so deeply, so painfully affected by another individual. He didn't even *know* the boy, for God's sake. They had had two conversations, Joshua had come back to his flat and they had kissed. That was the sum of it. At forty-five, Leo had long assumed himself to be above and beyond the kind of infatuation which seemed now to possess him, suffocating him. He walked and walked, thinking, counting the minutes until he could look upon Joshua again.

'Take the keys,' said Leo. They were sitting in the car outside Leo's flat. 'I've got a spare set. I want to put the car away. You go on up. It's number two, on the first floor. Help yourself to a beer. They're in the fridge.'

Joshua took the keys and unlocked the front door to the block of flats. He paused in the hush of the carpeted hallway and caught sight of his reflection in an oval gilt mirror. Christ, if one of the other residents came out now, they'd think he'd come to burgle the place. He went upstairs to Leo's flat and let himself in, fumbling for a light switch. He felt a little rush of pleasure at seeing the interior of the flat again. He really liked this place. In the fridge Joshua found a six-pack of Budweiser. There hadn't been any beers there the other night. Leo wasn't a beer drinker, Joshua could tell. So had he got this lot in on the assumption that he'd get Joshua back here again? Joshua decided he didn't care. He took one of the beers and went through to the drawing-room. He stood in the darkness by one of the long windows overlooking the street and gazed down, watching Leo walk up to the flat. He heard the front door open and close, then Leo's feet on the stairs. Leo always moved quickly, nimbly; that was something Joshua had noticed already.

Leo let himself in and came up the hallway, then stopped at the doorway of the drawing-room. He saw Joshua standing by the window, silhouetted in the glow from the street light outside.

'All alone in the dark,' said Leo.

'I was looking at the street,' said Joshua. 'It's so quiet. Where I live, it never stops, twenty-four hours a day. Restaurants, bars, music, people up and down the stairs all night. And the traffic. Then just when it goes a bit quiet, you get the bin lorries coming round about two in the morning. But here – it's so still. Civilised.'

Leo came across the room. He didn't switch on the light. 'You found a beer, I see.'

Joshua turned to look at him. Leo's face and hair were etched silver by the street light. 'You got them in just for me, didn't you?'

'Perhaps I happen to like beer,' replied Leo.

'Perhaps you do.' Joshua took a swig from the can. 'Then again, perhaps you hoped I'd come back here.'

'You're right. I did,' said Leo. 'I hoped it very much. But I wasn't sure, after the way you left last night.'

Joshua turned to look out at the street again. 'If you want to know why I left, I'll tell you.' He hesitated for several seconds, as though trying to find words, then went on, 'You know a bit about me. I can tell you do. You know I make a bit on the side going with blokes. I do it for the money, that's all.' Joshua was speaking rapidly. With his free hand he reached out and began to fiddle with a silken curtain tassel. 'The thing is, the more you do it, the easier it gets. That's not to say I ever liked it. I just tried not to think about it, really. But last night, I liked it when you touched me.' He turned to look candidly at Leo. 'Whatever happened was because I wanted it to.'

'And that worries you?'

'Yes. Well, no, not really . . . Look, to be honest, when you picked me up last night, I thought we would just come here, do the business, and that would be it. But then things got confusing . . .' He raked his fingers through his hair. 'I can't really explain it . . .'

Leo thought for a long moment before he spoke. 'Joshua, do you feel safe? Here, with me?'

'Safe?' Joshua echoed the question as he tested his feelings. Yes, he did feel safe. He felt reassured by Leo, by this place, by all the things around him. He suddenly thought that he would rather be here, in this flat, than anywhere else he could think of. He nodded. 'Yeah.'

'Then don't worry. Just stay and everything will be all right. I promise.'

Joshua said nothing. He liked the idea, the knowledge, that Leo was the kind of man who kept his promises.

Chapter six

Sarah was waiting for Leo in the clerks' room when he hurried in at a quarter to ten the following morning. 'You're cutting it fine,' she remarked.

'Thank you. I am aware of it. Hold these.' He thrust some papers at her and went to have a hurried conversation with Henry before heading out of chambers at a brisk walk, Sarah in his wake.

Henry glanced after them and remarked to Felicity, 'She's very free in the way she talks to him, for a pupil.'

'Yeah, I've noticed that.' Felicity looked up from the computer screen and glanced at her untasted cup of coffee. She felt hellish this morning. Even the smell of coffee nauseated her.

'Maybe they're having a little fling,' said Henry thoughtfully.

Felicity leaned back in her chair. 'Henry,' she sighed, 'I don't think girls are quite Mr Davies' type.'

Henry's jaw slackened. He turned to look at Felicity with such transparent astonishment that Felicity gave a little snort of laughter. There was something so dopey and sweet about Henry, sometimes.

'You never mean that!'

'What? That he's gay? Course I do. Hadn't you noticed?'

Henry said nothing. He stood thinking for a few seconds, then went back to sorting through the briefs in front of him. It was wrong in these days of tolerance and liberalism to feel disappointed, but somehow, after all the years he'd known Mr Davies, he couldn't help it.

*

Sarah tried to match Leo's pace as they crossed Fleet Street to the Law Courts. 'It must have been a particularly good night, to make you late for court,' she remarked. 'As I recall, you used to be quite scrupulous about not letting your private life interfere with work.'

'I got held up in the traffic,' replied Leo shortly. As they passed through security, he suddenly stopped and put his hand to the breast pocket of his jacket. 'Blast and bugger it!'

'What's the matter?' said Sarah.

'I've left my reading glasses in chambers. Look, give me these.' He took the papers Sarah was carrying. 'And run back to chambers for me. If they're not on my desk, they'll be in the top right-hand drawer. I'll see you in court.'

'Which one? I don't know which court we're in.'

'Look on the lists!' called Leo over his shoulder, as he trotted up the stairs to the robing room.

The morning had not started auspiciously, thought Leo, as he adjusted his bands and slipped on his wig. Because of Joshua he had overslept, and the face that stared back at him from the robing-room mirror was drawn and tired. He felt none of the euphoria and pleasure that usually came with the start of a love affair. Everything was too precarious. Looking down at Joshua sleeping in his bed, one arm thrown back, skin smooth and supple, his hair burnished and tangled, he had been acutely aware of the discrepancy in their ages. Three or four years ago he had thought of himself as still a relatively young man, but these days he felt distinctly middle-aged. He seemed to have acquired from nowhere the paraphernalia of reading glasses, stiff limbs, and an ex-wife and child. It was quite astonishing. Still, there was always the compensation of knowing that one's capacity for love remained, fresh and ageless. One could fall in love just as easily at forty-five as at twenty-five, and that, he now knew, his heart soaring at the recollection of Joshua, was what he had most certainly done. Leo picked up his papers and headed for the court room, hoping that Sarah would get a move on.

The morning continued badly. Sarah hadn't been able to find his glasses and Leo could only assume he must have left them at home. It meant he had to peer at the papers, and this made him feel awkward and interrupted the flow of his case. Added to which, they were before Mr Justice Dent, an irascible and pompous man whom Leo had long disliked, and who seemed determined that morning to pick holes in Leo's case.

'Mr Davies, you are not suggesting, are you, that an average adjustment is binding upon the cargo owners? I'm sure I need hardly remind you of the dictum of Lord Diplock in *Castle Insurance v Hong Kong Shipping*. The cargo owners are perfectly free to dispute the quantum of any contribution or claim attributed to their consignment by the average statement.'

'With respect, my Lord, I would submit that that is the position only in cases where there is no agreement to the contrary. In this case, it is my clients' contention that there was an agreement.'

'Well, Mr Davies, I can see no evidence of such agreement . . .' Mr Justice Dent began to sift through the papers as though to make his point, still talking. Endeavouring to listen patiently, Leo recalled with a sudden, irrelevant jolt that Joshua still had the spare set of keys to the flat. His mind ran quickly over the implications. In one sense it was good. It meant that Joshua might feel free to come and go, that he might still be there this evening. On the other hand, what did he know of the boy? He worked as a waiter, was a part-time prostitute and, for all Leo knew, he could get home this evening and find the place cleaned out. He doubted it, but it brought home to him the realisation that this affair with Joshua was fraught with uncertainties. '. . . And I'm afraid I must agree with Mr Glyn-Jones that one would normally expect such an agreement to be spelled out, as in the case of *Tharsis Sulphur & Copper Company v Loftus*, Mr Davies.'

With an effort, Leo dragged his attention back to what Dent was saying. *Tharsis Sulphur & Copper Company*? He wished this old bastard didn't have quite so much case law at his fingertips. One sometimes had the impression that he was expressly determined to make the case for the other side.

'Quite so, my Lord ...' Leo hesitated, trying to free his mind from thoughts of Joshua. There was a pause of several seconds, then he managed to find his way back to his argument. 'In this case, however, my Lord, I would submit that although there is no express agreement that the adjustment was to be binding, when the policy is considered in context, that is its clear effect.' He glanced up at Dent, who was surveying Leo with an expression of sour disfavour. Right, thought Leo, hitching his gown a little on his shoulders. Prepare to be convinced. He gave a sudden, dazzling smile, which had the effect of quite disconcerting Mr Justice Dent, and continued, 'Allow me to summarise my submissions as follows ...'

Sitting next to Leo, Sarah stifled a yawn and decided that she needn't take any notes. Leo appeared to know what he was doing. Instead, she let her mind wander to the matter of Anthony. It was most convenient that Camilla was going to be in Bermuda for a few weeks. That gave her ample time to put her little plan into action. As a mere idle amusement, it would be enjoyable to test the strength of Anthony's commitment to Camilla. Besides, she had no current lover and Anthony, as she recalled, was more than very good in bed. It was really a means of killing several birds with one stone. By destroying the perfect relationship between Anthony and Camilla, she would pay him back very nicely for having been crass enough to dump her once, and Camilla for having had the gall, two days ago, to ask her to fetch some books from the library. She might be merely a pupil, but Sarah didn't see why she had to take orders from someone like Camilla, who had been her inferior at Oxford in almost every way that Sarah could think of, except perhaps intellectually. And there was the additional pleasure, if things worked out, of having Anthony in her bed for a pleasant while. The whole exercise was something of a challenge. She had nothing to lose . . .

Suddenly Sarah became aware of Leo's fingers gently snapping in the direction of the books which lay in front of her. God, he must be referring to one of the authorities in his argument, and she hadn't a clue which one. Her face pinkening, she fumbled among the volumes, until Leo, murmuring 'Excuse me,' to Mr Justice Dent, leaned over and picked up one of the Chancery volumes and opened it where it was marked. Sarah noticed that he held it some distance from his eyes, then slowly drew it closer to focus before reading aloud from the pages. She smiled despite her own previous momentary embarrassment. There was something funny about seeing Leo, the brilliant advocate, the sexual conqueror, at a loss without his reading glasses.

By lunch-time, Leo was weary of the battle. He could tell that Dent wasn't going to accept his argument that a payment made on account couldn't subsequently be reclaimed if it were shown that nothing in fact was due. Well, he hardly blamed him. He didn't think much of it himself. He let out a long sigh as he and Sarah walked the echoing flagged corridors from the court room.

Sarah glanced up at him. 'I'm sorry I couldn't find the right volume. I'm afraid I wasn't really concentrating.'

Leo was mildly surprised that Sarah should demean herself so far as to offer an apology for anything. 'Forget it,' he murmured and stopped outside the robing room. 'Look, I've got a few phone calls to make in chambers. Would you mind picking me up some sandwiches and coffee, and bringing them to my room?'

'Okay.' Sarah left him and walked thoughtfully to the

women's robing room to take off her wig and gown. Something strange had occurred in the court room that morning. For the first time since she had known him, Sarah saw Leo in a new light. The quality of her feelings escaped her. They were beyond definition. It had to do with something small and simple, like the way Leo had difficulty in making out the words on the page. Maybe it was just pity. Poor old Leo. Still, it came to everyone, even the Leo Davies of this world. You couldn't stay young for ever. Alone in the robing room, Sarah looked into the mirror and smiled at her reflection.

'I know I've left it late,' said Leo. He had rung Rachel at work to discuss seeing Oliver that weekend. 'But if you didn't have anything special planned, I can't see what difference it makes. I'd really like to see him.'

'What were you thinking of doing?' asked Rachel dubiously. She knew it was wrong of her, but somehow, since their conversation in the pub, she didn't really like the idea of Oliver being away from her for a day, even with Leo.

'I don't know.' Leo hadn't given it proper thought. 'I might take him to Stanton. I haven't been there in a while.' This was the village not far from Oxford where Leo had a house, a beautiful old place in secluded grounds. He had owned it when Rachel first met him, and she felt a sudden pang at the memories she had of it. I was happy there, once, thought Rachel suddenly. It seemed odd, to think of Leo and Oliver there without her. An incomplete unit.

'I suppose I can't really say no,' she sighed.

'Why would you want to?' asked Leo abruptly.

'He's still so little, Leo . . .'

'Christ, Rachel, it's only for a day.' Leo passed a hand over his brow. A heavy morning in court after the late night before had given him a headache. Maybe Felicity had some Nurofen. 'How else am I supposed to spend time with him? I can't exactly come to Bath and make up a happy *ménage à trois* with you and Charles, can I?'

'Don't get so angry about it! I said you can see him. I was just explaining how I feel.'

'He's my son, too. I want to see him regularly. And if you won't –'

'Leo, stop it! I'm not going into that argument again! You can come down and pick him up on Sunday. I'll have everything ready. About ten.'

'Fine,' said Leo and hung up.

He sat with his face in his hands. It was the one area in his life where he felt defenceless. Oliver was something he could not shrug off. Not the way he had shrugged off Rachel. It was going to be an uphill battle to gain the kind of access to him that he wanted.

Sarah knocked lightly on the door and came in.

Leo looked up. 'Good girl,' he said, as she put down some sandwiches and a styrofoam cup of coffee. 'God, what a day. One damn thing after another.' He saw that Sarah still had her coffee and sandwiches in her hand, about to take them back to her own room. 'Stay, if you like,' said Leo. He had a sudden wish for company. Sarah, for all her devious, designing ways, and for all the danger implicit in the fact that she probably knew him better than anyone, was at least someone with whom he could relax.

'All right,' said Sarah. She sat down opposite Leo, and popped the lid of her coffee and took a sip. 'What's up – apart from this morning, I mean?'

'I have just been speaking to my dear, soon-to-be-ex wife,' said Leo. 'We are currently having a little wrangle over the amount of time I can spend with Oliver, our son.'

'Right,' said Sarah, not evincing much interest. She had never been able to understand how someone like Leo could get caught up in a mundane domestic situation. She had thought him above such average considerations. She remembered meeting Rachel at a party once and thinking she looked frigid. Had she been jealous of Rachel? Yes, possibly. There had been something galling in the fact that Rachel had, it seemed, managed to ground a free spirit such as Leo. Not that she, Sarah, had any intention of marrying anyone, ever, or doing anything as boring as having children.

She watched Leo open his sandwiches. 'I remembered you liked avocado and bacon.'

Leo laughed, in spite of his headache and his wretched morning. 'You used to make them for me at the house in Stanton.'

'Yes,' said Sarah. 'Afterwards.' It was true. She looked at Leo now, without embarrassment, and remembered all the times she'd had sex with him, wonderful and occasionally strange sex, and then making sandwiches afterwards. There had been James, too, of course. That had been a long, hot summer . . . What had happened to the Leo of those days?

'Mmm. Afterwards.' Leo gave Sarah a thoughtful glance and took a bite of his sandwich. They ate in companionable silence for a while, then Leo asked, 'What are you thinking about?'

Sarah sipped at her coffee. 'I was wondering why you ever got married.'

He stared at her for a few seconds. There was no point in dissembling where Sarah was concerned. And it would be a relief to tell someone the truth. 'If you really want to know, I got married as a means of advancement,' said Leo. 'Simple as that. You remember the business with James and the reporter from the *Sun*, all that stuff, don't you?' Sarah nodded. 'My entire private life seemed to be blowing up in my face just as I was on the point of taking silk. I thought I had to convince the powers-that-be that I was a nice, normal boy, just the kind of chap they wanted as a QC.'

'So you mean, marrying Rachel was an exercise in damage limitation?'

'Something like that. A cover of respectability. Besides, she was pregnant.'

Sarah snorted into her coffee. 'You wouldn't have married me if I'd got pregnant.'

'How very true,' murmured Leo. 'But then, what kind of respectability would you have afforded me?'

They both laughed. 'None,' admitted Sarah. 'Bastard.'

'Now,' said Leo, gathering up the sandwich wrapper and draining his coffee, 'leave me in peace to make some more phone calls. I'll see you back in court at two sharp. And this time, pay attention when I'm on my feet.'

As he came back from court later that afternoon, Leo met Roderick crossing Caper Court.

'Chap from the Estates Committee rang this afternoon,' said Roderick. 'Good news – though *you* won't necessarily like it. It seems they're quite keen for us to take up the lease on these new chambers. So much so, that they're offering to throw in free carpeting and shelving.'

'Why on earth should they do that?'

'Well, look at it from their point of view. We're a much better bet for the rent than some criminal set. Anyway, from where we stand, it makes the place an even more attractive proposition. I went up to have a look with Michael the other day. It's got much more promise than we thought at first, now that they're getting on with the renovations. The whole place is being completely gutted. We could be in there by the new year.'

Leo gave a wry smile. 'You'll never convince me.'

'I'm off to meet Stephen in the Devereaux for a swift drink. Care to join us?'

'Yes,' said Leo. 'I just want to drop these papers off and have a word with Anthony first.'

'I think you'll find he's already gone. I saw him leave with Camilla about ten minutes ago. Love's young dream, eh?'

'Quite,' said Leo, and went up the stairs to 5 Caper Court.

In his room he hesitated, then picked up the telephone and dialled the number of his Belgravia flat. At the other end the phone rang and rang, unanswered. Leo stood there for a full minute before putting the phone down at last. What had he expected? Why should he imagine that Joshua might still be there? None the less, after last night, he had hoped. He realised that the hope had been there at the back of his mind all day. What would he find when he got home? Perhaps he should go straight back now and discover the worst. Then it occurred to him, like a light breaking in his mind. Of course – Joshua had gone to work. In his relief at this simple realisation, Leo instinctively wanted there and then to call him at the Galleria, to hear Joshua's voice, to know that all was well. With a hand that trembled faintly with excitement, he picked up the phone again. He fumbled the card with the number on it from his jacket pocket and pressed the numbers.

'Hello, Galleria Flore?'

Leo recognised the voice of the Australian girl who worked behind the bar.

'Hello. I'd like to speak to Joshua.'

'Joshua? I don't think he's come in yet. Just a minute . . .' Leo could hear the sounds of muted conversation at the other end. His heart tightened within him as he waited. The Australian girl spoke again. 'Hello? The manager says Joshua isn't working here any more. He rang in before lunch and said he wouldn't be back.'

Leo felt a chill spread throughout his body. He couldn't lose him. Not now. God, not now. 'Did he leave a number? I mean, do you have a contact number for him, or his home address?'

The girl's voice drifted off as she spoke again to someone in the background. 'I'm sorry, that's all we know,' she said at last.

'I see. Thank you.' Leo put down the phone. It all slipped into place. Last night had meant nothing to Joshua. The boy had taken him for a complete fool. He must have woken up this morning, alone in the flat, had seen his chance to take what he could and chucked in his job so that Leo would never track him down. That was the end of it. Leo wondered what he would find when he got back. Or not find. Not that he cared. At that moment, Leo felt he would gladly have surrendered every last valuable possession for the assurance that he would see Joshua again, and have his love. But that was now the remotest hope possible.

Leo stood there for a few minutes, wondering if he should go straight home. What was the point? Joshua would have done whatever he wanted to by this time. He would see about getting the locks changed tomorrow. Right now, he would join Roderick and Stephen, and drown this fresh misery in a few whiskies.

Anthony and Camilla made their way along the riverside to the Blueprint Café, which Anthony had earmarked for dinner that evening.

'What time did you book for?' asked Camilla.

'I didn't book,' remarked Anthony. 'I didn't think we needed to.'

Camilla stopped in her tracks. 'Anthony, you are joking! It's a Friday night! Of *course* we needed to book. Now we've walked all this way for nothing.' She stared around the deserted street in exasperation. 'Why couldn't we have got a cab, anyway?'

'I thought it was going to be a nice evening,' replied Anthony, as a few large spots of rain began to fall. 'Besides, you don't know it's going to be fully booked. We might as well go and see.'

'And then find we have to walk all the way back in the rain. Why don't we just cut our losses and turn round now?'

They stood there for a few minutes, arguing in the now steady drizzle. Neither had an umbrella.

'Well, where else do you suggest we go?' said Anthony at last.

'I don't know. But there's no point in going to the Blueprint Café.'

'You don't know that.'

'Anthony, this is pathetic. I'm going back.' Camilla turned round and began to walk back along the street.

Anthony hurried after her. 'I'm sorry,' he said, putting a hand on her shoulder. 'Look, we'll find a cab and go somewhere where we *will* get a table.'

'To be honest,' sighed Camilla, 'I don't want to slog around looking for a restaurant. I'm too tired. Let's just go back to your place and order a take-away.'

Anthony shrugged. 'All right.' He felt slightly depressed. Camilla seemed to have been in a bad mood ever since they left chambers.

It took them twenty minutes to find a cab, and by the time they got back to Anthony's Kensington flat they were both wet through and short-tempered.

'Put this on,' said Anthony, chucking Camilla his terry-towelling bathrobe. Camilla got out of her wet clothes and snuggled into it. Once Anthony had changed out of his damp suit and made them both a drink, she was beginning to feel better. Still, at the back of her mind there lurked some small seed of annoyance. Maybe it was the pressure of work, or the thought of the Bermuda trip next week. She was feeling intensely nervous about that, even though she was confident she could handle the work.

'Come here,' said Anthony, pulling her towards him on the sofa.

She snuggled against him, wondering why the touch and warmth of him did not soothe her, as it usually did. 'I'm sorry,' she murmured.

'What for?'

'Being such a cow.'

'You're not. You never could be.' Anthony kissed her, slipping a hand inside the robe, stroking her breast, enjoying the familiar slow surge of desire.

'Anthony,' said Camilla, breaking gently away, 'I swear if I don't eat something soon I'm going to expire.'

'All right.' Anthony rose reluctantly and went to phone the local curry house. 'Fifteen minutes,' he said, returning from the phone. 'Think you can wait that long?'

'I'll have to,' murmured Camilla. She wished she could smile, be pleasant, feel happy.

'So,' said Anthony. He sat back down and put an arm around her, picking up his drink with the other. 'Have you thought any more about moving in on a permanent basis?'

Camilla sat up slightly, drawing her fingers through her auburn hair, wishing they didn't have to have this conversation. Not in her present mood. 'Yes, I have. And I'm not sure if it's such a good idea, really.' Her voice was unhappy.

'Oh, come on,' said Anthony gently. 'You can't live at home for ever. It's not as though your parents would disapprove. They know you spend half your time here, anyway.' He stroked some strands of hair away from her eyes. 'I really would like you to move in, you know. I love you and I want to be with you as much as I can.'

'Anthony, we're with each other all day. We work in the same chambers. Do you really think it would be healthy, spending so much time in one another's company?'

'I hardly see you throughout the day.'

'Yes, you do. Anyway, that's not quite the point. It might make things claustrophobic, the idea that we don't inhabit any space away from each other. I don't think you've thought it through.'

'I have. I want you to be here.'

'And that's another thing.' Camilla sat up properly, looking at him with a candid gaze. 'This is your place. Everything in it belongs to you. Don't you think that I haven't spent years dreaming of the time when I might be earning enough to find a place of my own, somewhere I could fill with my own things, make my own life? Apart from Oxford, I've never lived away from home. I don't necessarily want just to move from my parents' house into your place. I think I need to find my own independence before I make a commitment of that kind.'

'I see.' Anthony said nothing for a few seconds. 'I can understand your point of view, I suppose.'

He sounded so morose that she put her arms around his neck and drew him towards her. 'It's not because I don't love you. Please don't think that. I do – you know I do.'

'But not enough,' replied Anthony. 'If you really wanted to be with me, you wouldn't hesitate.'

'Nothing's ever that simple. I'm only twenty-three. There are things I want to do on my own.'

Anthony kissed her. 'What if –' He hesitated, wondering if this was what he meant, wanted to say. He decided it was. 'What if I asked you to marry me?'

Her eyes clouded. 'I'm sorry. I know you'll only say that I don't love you enough. But it's not that. I wouldn't marry you because I'm too young, and there's so much I want to do first. Besides, I'm not sure you mean it.'

'Maybe I don't. But I wish you'd give it a little more thought – about moving in, I mean. If it didn't work out, then you could always find a place of your own. But why not give it a try?'

'Look, I'm going abroad for three weeks on Monday. Maybe being away from you for that long will make me feel differently. I don't know. But why don't we wait and see?'

Anthony sighed. 'If you say so, It's just –' His eyes searched hers. 'It's just I miss you when you're not here. The nights you're not here.'

'Maybe we can work something out when I get back.' Something at the back of her mind told Camilla that even a separation would not change the truth of the things she had just said. 'Meanwhile, I think it's time you went to get that curry.'

*

Leo got home around nine. It was not his way to drink too much; he regularly and steadfastly stuck to his allotted two or three whiskies in any evening. But tonight he had drunk much more than that, leaving his car in the Temple and taking a taxi back. The uncharacteristic excess was due partly to the inevitable argument which erupted in the pub over the proposed move to Lincoln's Inn and partly to a desire, a longing, to blot out all thoughts of Joshua.

It couldn't have succeeded, Leo realised, as he paid the driver and stood, slightly unsteadily, looking up at the darkened windows of his flat. Alcohol might dull the pain of reality, but it couldn't remove it. He made his way slowly upstairs and put his key in the front door, uncertain what he would find on the other side. He flicked on a light in the hall and wandered into the drawing-room. Nothing was out of place. There were no bare patches on the walls in place of paintings, as he had half expected; all his pieces of sculpture stood where they had always done. The drinks cabinet was untouched. There was no evidence that anyone had been in the room that day.

In the kitchen, the only trace of occupation was a mug standing upside down on the draining-board. Leo had had nothing for breakfast that morning. Joshua must have made himself coffee or tea, then carefully washed and rinsed the mug. Leo picked it up and stared at it, tracing the rim with a maudlin finger. He flicked open the pedal bin; Joshua's crumpled beer can was the only thing in it. In the fridge the rest of the beers and what food there was lay untouched. Leo closed the fridge door and let out a long sigh.

He looked around for a few moments, thinking, then went into his bedroom. The big bed, where he had last night tasted such pleasure, was still unmade. Leo stared at the pillow where Joshua's head had rested, then traced with his eyes the folds of sheets where he had lain, naked. How could absence be so poignant as to possess as much force as any presence? He pulled open the drawer of the tall lacquer cabinet which

103

stood in one corner of the room and in which he habitually left loose money. The neat, thick fold of twenty-pound notes, which he had put there the other day, lay undisturbed.

He wanted nothing of me, thought Leo. Nothing at all. He realised that the whisky he had drunk had eaten away at his control and reserves of dispassion, and that he was on the verge of tears. He lay down on the sprawl of the unmade, empty bed and closed his eyes, listening to the silence of the flat and the steady beating of his own heart.

Chapter seven

It was hard to be sick quietly. Felicity groped upwards for the little radio that usually hung next to the shower and fumbled to switch it on, hoping that the sounds of Capital FM on a Saturday morning would drown the noise of her own retching. Why was this starting now? She reckoned she must be six weeks pregnant. She had thought that if you were going to get morning sickness, you got it from the word go. Clearly not. She stared dizzily at the white interior of the lavatory, then sat back. At the sound of Vince's feet outside she pulled herself to her feet and flushed the lavatory quickly.

Vince appeared in his boxer shorts, scratching his chest. 'Was that you throwin' up?' he asked conversationally.

Felicity nodded, giving him a pained little look and going to the sink to splash water on her mouth. 'It must have been that curry we had last night,' she said, patting her face with a towel.

Vince leaned against the door jamb. 'Na, can't have been. We both had the same and there's nothin' wrong with my insides.' He looked at Felicity speculatively as she brushed her teeth. Felicity studiously avoided his eye. Light dawned slowly. 'Here – are you pregnant? Is that what it is?' Felicity brushed her teeth harder and debated briefly within herself whether to try and deny it and talk her way out of it. One glance at Vince's face told her there was no point. She gave a little sigh and let him hug her. As she rubbed her face slowly against his bare muscled shoulder, she was aware of an inner sense of relief, tinged with fear.

'You are, aren't you? Aw, bloody brilliant!' He put an affectionate arm round her shoulder and gave her a squeeze, almost pulling her off balance. 'I thought your tits was looking a bit on the bouncy side these days. And you've been off your drink.' He pulled away and looked into her face. 'How come you never told me?'

'I've only just found out. I wanted to be certain.'

'Fantastic ...' he murmured proudly, and hugged her gently again.

'Vince,' she said, pulling away, 'it's not as though it's something we planned. I don't know why you're so pleased. Look, come through and have some coffee. I think we have to talk about this.'

Vince made coffee while Felicity sat at the kitchen table, shoulders slightly hunched, hardly listening as he talked. He'd be choosing names next. The horrible thing about morning sickness, she realised, was that, unlike ordinary sickness, you didn't feel better afterwards. Hadn't she read somewhere that you should try to eat something dry, like a cracker? What a disgusting thought. Vince put a mug of coffee in front of her and she shook her head. 'Vince,' she said, as he sat down opposite her with his coffee, 'stop going on as though everything's wonderful. I don't think you've thought any of this through.'

'What? Course I haven't. I've only just found out, haven't I? I'm reacting, aren't I? Anyway, what's to think through? You're having a baby, bingo.' He took a sip of his coffee. '*We're* having a baby. Fuckin' great.'

She sighed. 'I'm not so sure about that. I mean, it's not exactly an ideal time, is it? You're still doing your knowledge – and will be for the next two years, if what you said the other night is right. I'm just starting to earn really good money ... I mean, what's going to happen if I have to give up work?'

Vince shrugged. 'We'll manage. My mum did. So did

yours. It's only a job. You can always get another one, like when the kids start school, an' that.'

The kids. Vince had already painted the picture of her future. Not an ambitious man himself, content with enough money for booze and the most basic standard of living, he would be happy to see her life turn into the kind his own mother had led, and hers. Tied to the house, three or four kids to yell at and pick up after, washing, cooking, shopping, ironing, the days turning into months, the months to years. Occasional holidays, family celebrations, eventually the arrival of grandchildren. That would do for Vince. She studied him as he drank his coffee and wondered if he really had any idea of what she did all day. Probably not. He thought of the people in chambers as a ponced-up set of lawyers, nothing to do with him, just Fliss's bosses. If he thought about them too hard, his monumental chip would probably appear. By the same token, she guessed that his mind shied away from the thought that her job might in any way be important, valuable. Leaving aside the money she earned, he probably liked to think of her as a kind of secretary. In fact, he doubtless consoled himself with the notion that he could do Felicity's job any day, if he had a mind to.

'What if I don't want to give up my job?' she asked.

Vince looked up at her. 'Well, come on, girl, you can't have a baby *and* work. I mean, not straight away. Anyway, it won't be much fun for it all on its own. Gotta have another, to keep it company, like. A proper family.'

'Vince, Vince.' Felicity gave a small, despairing laugh.

'What?'

'Oh, I dunno . . . You talk like it's easy, like we'll be able to afford things, that everything will go on as before. But it won't. What are we going to do without my money?'

'Manage. I told you. It's just a matter of months.'

She thought for a moment. 'What would you say if I suggested that I go back to work after the baby's born and you look after it?' This was rather more hypothetical than anything else; Felicity was curious to know his reaction.

'What? Me?' He laughed. 'You are joking, aren't you? How could I do me knowledge and look after a baby? Strap 'im on the pillion, or something? I don't see it. Anyway, that's what mothers are for. Gotta have your mum.' He shook his head. 'I just can't believe it. Me, a dad.'

'Yeah,' sighed Felicity. 'You, a dad.'

Leo woke early on Saturday, his mind as tormented by thoughts of Joshua as when he had fallen asleep. He shaved, showered and dressed. He could eat nothing. He went out and drove to Earl's Court. There he parked and began to walk the streets. They were only beginning to come to life at nine o'clock. By lunch-time, when Leo was still walking, they were crowded. People spilled in and out of the tube station; the shops and supermarkets were teeming. Part of his mind was suspended in disbelief at what he was doing – the futility, the stupidity of it. But the other part was too filled with feeble hope to care, too busy scanning the faces, the random knots of young men passing by. The merest glimpse of hair the same colour as Joshua's set his heart racing. But nowhere, nowhere did he see the face he longed for. The hours drifted by, his heart and mind were sick and weary with it all, but still he looked and walked and hoped. What else could he do? All he knew was that Joshua lived in Earl's Court. That was as much as he had told Leo. And Earl's Court, of course, was thronged with itinerant young people, moving from job to job, bedsit to bedsit, country to country. What hope had he of finding him? None. None, he knew, none. But even the most minuscule possibility seemed, in Leo's state of mind, too precious to abandon.

By two thirty he gave up. Heartsore, hungry, savagely ashamed of himself, he drove to the Galleria where Joshua had worked. Maybe there was some chance . . . He ordered a ham and cheese croissant and coffee, eating and drinking mindlessly, his eyes moving to the door every time it opened. He had no idea why he was there. After a while he noticed the Australian girl behind the bar, polishing glasses. She was big, rather plain, wearing a shapeless black T-shirt, her hair tied back. Leo paid the bill and went to the bar. 'You had a boy called Joshua working here, I believe?'

She looked up, her expression indifferent. 'Yeah. For a few months. He left last week.'

'I need to find him. I'm a friend of his.'

'Yeah?' The girl shrugged. 'Can't help you. Sorry. I didn't know him that well.'

'Did he have any friends – people who used to come and see him here?' The girl looked infinitely bored, and Leo added, 'It's really very important that I find him.'

She began sliding the clean glasses into the rack above the bar. 'Well, he had this mate who used to come when we were closing up. They'd go off together. Damien, his name was.' She gave a little smirk at what she clearly thought was a daft name.

'Anything else? I mean, could I find this Damien?'

'All I know is that he worked at some art cinema. Camden, I think it was. Don't know the name. He sold tickets and coffee and stuff like that.'

'Thank you,' said Leo. 'Thank you.'

Leo left the Galleria and went to the nearest newsagent's and bought a copy of *Time Out*. In his car he riffled through the pages, conscious of a disproportionate nervous excitement. Camden, Camden . . . There was only one cinema that he could see listed – the Odeon. The girl had said an art cinema, though. Still, maybe she had made a mistake. Or maybe she had meant around the Camden area. That could include Hampstead, Swiss Cottage, even Islington. He glanced through the Hampstead listings. There were three that he could see, two of which looked more promising – the Everyman and Screen on the Hill. They were roughly what one might call art cinemas. A Pasolini double bill presumably ranked as art. There was the ABC, of course, and the Swiss Cottage Odeon, and the Screen on the Green in Islington. He would try them all.

Leo threw the magazine on to the passenger seat and started the car. As he checked in the rear-view mirror before pulling out, his own eyes looked back at him. For a moment he paused, appalled. What was he doing? What did he hope to gain from all this? Suppose he did track down this Damien. Was he likely to tell him where Joshua was? Leo had no idea. None at all. He only knew that he felt for the young man who had slipped in and out of his life something bordering on obsession. If there was the faintest hope that he might find him, just to talk to him and look at him, and perhaps persuade him to come back, then it was worth it. What else was he to do with his time, anyway?

There was no Damien to be found at any cinema. Leo tried them all. After drawing a final blank at the Swiss Cottage Odeon, he got back into his car and picked up the copy of *Time Out* again. Maybe the girl had got it wrong. Maybe the cinema was in another part of London altogether. He began to go through the listings, then stopped. He couldn't go on with this. It was more than pride and reason could bear. Defeated, Leo flung the magazine aside and drove home.

On his answering machine, Leo found three messages, all from Melissa Angelicos. The first had been left at twelve, inviting him to an impromptu dinner party she was having that evening. Short notice, she knew, and Leo was probably already busy, but if he could give her a call . . . The second had been left later in the afternoon, just calling to see if he had got her first message, she did so hope he could make it, waiting to hear from him, bye. The third, which had been left just shortly before Leo got in, was short. Melissa. Still hoping to see you. Call if you can.

Leo played back the messages as he mixed himself a drink, moving from drawing-room to kitchen and back again, the sound of her cultured, slightly rasping tones following him. How the hell had she got his home number? He had known the other night that she was attracted to him, but hadn't expected her to make her next move quite so quickly. At Melissa's age, perhaps you couldn't afford to hang around. He had no intention of going to her dinner party. Under other circumstances, and purely for the amusement value, he might have gone as a means of passing the evening and escaping thoughts. Melissa's friends were possibly worth meeting. But he had no wish to escape his thoughts, painful as they were. His feelings for Joshua were so deep and so new that he simply wished to contemplate them, to nurse them. He wasn't fit for company. Besides, he had no desire to give Ms Angelicos the slightest encouragement. Rude though it doubtless was, he didn't even intend to answer her calls.

Throughout the evening Leo sat watching television, drinking Scotch, the answerphone switched on. It rang three times. Each time the caller hung up and left no message. Perhaps it was Melissa, perhaps not. His heart gave a little flip of fear. What if it had been Joshua? But it couldn't have been. Joshua didn't know his number, had no means of finding it out. More depressed than he had felt in his life, Leo switched off the television and began to read, conscious of a dull, whisky-induced headache. He mustn't drink any more. He had told Rachel he would pick Oliver up around ten, so he would have to be up early.

Just before midnight the phone rang once more. Leo hesitated, about to cross the room and pick it up before the answering machine cut in. But he left it and went to bed.

Joshua put the phone down and crossed the lobby of the club to where Damien was waiting for him.

'I don't know why you keep ringing him. What's the point?'

Joshua shrugged. 'I don't know . . . feel a bit bad about the whole thing. Maybe I should have left him a note. I don't know what he expects.'

'I'd forget it, if I were you. That kind of thing is seriously bad news. I reckon you should try pulling some girl tonight. That'll take your mind off it.'

'Yeah, maybe you're right.' He put the piece of paper back in his pocket, the one on which he'd copied down Leo's phone number from the bill which he had come across when riffling through the contents of the hall table the morning before he'd left. What Damien said could be true. Maybe it was bad news. But he'd got nothing out of it. He'd thought he hadn't wanted anything – money, that is. Leo had plenty to spare, Joshua had seen that from going through his drawers. It was just that he couldn't get Leo out of his mind.

Melissa closed the door on the last of her dinner party guests and let the smile slip from her face. She sighed and slid on the chain bolt, then went back through to the dining-room, where the remains of the meal scattered the table and the air was pungent with cigar smoke. Melissa pulled back the curtains and opened a window, letting the air billow in. She stood there for a moment, breathing in the chilly freshness of it. He hadn't even rung back. Bastard. Something small and dark and very close to hatred crept from her soul and nestled next to all her mixed-up desires and hopes. She liked him. She liked him too much. And if he was going to let her down like this, then it was all going to get very painful. Of course, she had plenty of men friends. Friends were fine, in their way. But in Leo Davies she had detected something for which she longed, lusted. Now she had her sights fixed on him she could not let him elude her. It did not cross her mind for a moment that perhaps Leo had been out all day and all evening, or that he might be away for the weekend. In the scenario she had constructed he had become, from the first moment when he had cold-shouldered her, an object, a target, a being whose motives and strategies must be bound up with hers, in order to make the game worth playing. She was convinced he had received her messages and ignored them. The cold air made her shiver. She closed the window, drew the curtain again slowly, and went to pour herself a small brandy. Then she sat in an armchair, thinking, for a long time.

Rachel plucked Oliver from his high-chair, wiped jam from around his mouth with a damp flannel and set him down on the floor, where he staggered purposefully towards the back door. Outside, Charles was cutting back a tangle of overgrown clematis from an apple tree. Rachel watched as Oliver squatted down next to Charles and began to fill one of his tipper trucks with handfuls of gravel. She turned back to the heap of things which she had prepared for Oliver's day out, and checked through them. Baby car seat, juice, bib, banana just in case he got hungry and fretful before they got to Stanton, nappies, change of clothing . . . How long until she was packing pyjamas, too, and his velvet elephant that he took to bed? Perhaps sooner than she wished. Rachel knew Leo. When he wanted something he could be totally ruthless. He would fight for this shared-residence order. If he succeeded, Oliver would be away from her every other weekend. It wasn't that Rachel didn't want Leo to see Oliver regularly. Of course he should. But not every other weekend, while he was still so little. Rachel did not think she could bear for Oliver, who eclipsed everything else in her life, to be away so often. There seemed to be no room for compromise. The last thing she wanted was an acrimonious legal dispute, but it seemed there was no alternative. If she and Leo couldn't agree, they would just have to let a court do it for them.

At the faint sound of a car engine she glanced up and saw Leo's Aston Martin turning in through the gateway. Oliver stood up and began to run towards it, and as Rachel's heart leaped a little in fear, Charles loped after him and scooped him up. There had been no danger, Leo's car had already stopped, but the flicker of a few seconds' anxiety didn't help Rachel's already disturbed mood.

Leo sat behind the wheel for a moment, watching as Charles lifted a laughing Oliver on to his shoulders, where he sat, chubby legs dangling down over Charles's chest. He felt jealous. No question about it. Charles had an intimacy with Oliver that he could not have, not even with his own son. Well, perhaps that was his own fault, seeing the child so infrequently over the past few months, but he was going to change that. His solicitor was already seeing to it.

He got out of the car and came towards Charles, who suddenly looked faintly apologetic and lifted Oliver from his shoulders. Beecham, you're a tactless sod, Charles told himself. The two men shook hands, trying to appear at ease with one another, then Oliver, after a moment's hesitation, let Leo pick him up and kiss him.

'Rachel's inside, getting his stuff ready. Like equipping an overseas task force, so far as I can see,' said Charles. 'Want some coffee?'

Leo shook his head. 'I won't hang about, thanks.' Oliver wriggled out of his arms and headed for the house.

'Fair turn of speed on him,' remarked Charles, watching him. 'Four-minute-mile material, I'd say.'

'Not if he's anything like his father,' said Leo. Why had he said that, used that word? Was he trying to tell Charles something?

'Oh, I don't know,' replied Charles. 'As I recall, you're pretty nippy round a squash court.'

There was a brief, uneasy pause. The relationship, which had been so unforced and friendly just a year ago, had quite changed. Rachel put a distance between them. It had to be that way, thought Charles. Even though he hadn't exactly pinched Leo's wife, the situation was awkward. 'Right, come inside and get his gear,' he said. They walked towards the house, chatting about Charles's latest documentary to try to ease the vague tension.

Rachel stood in the kitchen, putting things methodically into Oliver's baby bag. Even the sight of his stupid car can do it to me, she thought. Indifference, that's what I want to feel. I want to look at him and feel nothing. She heard their voices as they approached the back door and turned to greet Leo with a polite smile, bracing herself for the tumbling sensation she always felt in her heart when she saw him.

Ten minutes later, as Charles stowed Oliver's things in the boot of the Aston Martin, Leo was struggling to put the baby seat in.

'Here, let me,' said Charles. 'It's a bit of a knack.' Leo stood back and watched as Charles expertly threaded belts and tightened straps. 'The thing goes round the front and then through, not the other way round. Had me completely baffled the day we first got it.' Just this casual reference made Leo feel marginalised. Charles and Rachel and Oliver were a happy little unit, one which he, Leo, by his mere presence today, was threatening to destabilise.

'What are you going to do with him?' asked Rachel. She stood a few feet away from the car watching operations, her arms folded. Leo had sensed from the moment he arrived the brittle state of her mood. He put it down to anxiety over Oliver's day out. It did not occur to him that her apparent aloofness was an attempt to stifle any betrayal of the feelings she still had for him. He was unaware that they existed. It had never been his habit to consult too closely the state of Rachel's mind or heart. She belonged to Charles now. 'Don't worry. I'm not going to smuggle him out of the country. I've got a hearing tomorrow.'

'Leo –'

He cut in, holding up an apologetic hand: 'Sorry. I'm going to take him to the house, make him some lunch and then, if the weather holds out, I thought he might like a ride on the narrow-gauge steam railway. Would you like that? A ride on

115

a train?' Leo asked Oliver, as he picked him up and put him gently into his car seat.

Gratifyingly, Oliver smiled and said 'train' three times.

As Leo searched for the straps, Charles stepped forward to help, but Leo said, 'Thanks – I can do it. I have got a little experience.'

Charles stepped back again. Poor bastard, he thought. What a rotten situation, having to come here and take his own son out for the day. He could see Rachel's point of view about Oliver's age, but it seemed to Charles it might be more sensible to let the child go to his father every other weekend. Might as well establish a regular relationship now. Better for Oliver. Better for Charles, too.

'What time will you be back?' asked Rachel. She stepped forward to stroke Oliver's hair and absently tuck down the label of his jumper.

'About half-six?'

Rachel nodded, bent to kiss Oliver, and Leo closed the car door. She watched with a small pain in her heart as they drove away.

'Cheer up,' said Charles, putting an arm around her. 'I'm taking you to lunch in a couple of hours. I've booked a very special place on the river. Then we have the whole afternoon to ourselves to do exactly as we like.'

'Are you glad?' she asked, unable to keep the resentment out of her voice. 'I mean, you seem relieved that he's gone off for the day.'

'I'm not glad,' replied Charles carefully. 'But it's only for a few hours.'

The tension within Rachel gave way and she began to cry. Charles held her against him, wondering. After a few moments he lifted her face to his and kissed her. 'We have two whole hours,' he murmured. 'And nothing to interrupt them. I suggest, unless you can think of anything better to do, that we go to bed. Unless, of course, you want to listen to

116

the omnibus edition of *The Archers*. Or do both at the same time.'

Rachel gave a little laugh through her tears and kissed him. 'Just you.'

When they made love, Rachel was conscious that she was searching her heart and mind for some elusive feeling. She badly wanted to be able to dwell on the wonderful fact that Charles loved her so generously and so completely, to let the comfort of that flood her and make her want him as much as he did her. But even as he entered her, and she gave a gasp of pleasure at the familiar sensation, Rachel knew that she wished, in spite of everything, that it could be Leo, and she had to fight the temptation to close her eyes and pretend that it was.

When they reached the house, Leo took Oliver out of his car seat and carried him and his belongings to the house. He hadn't been there since late spring, and the air was close and musty, despite the fact that Mrs Lee from the village came in every two weeks to water the plants and keep the place dusted. Leo went from room to room, opening windows. When he came back downstairs he found that Oliver had taken all the logs out of the log basket and was filling it with books from the lower shelves.

Scooping him up, Leo glanced round the room. There wasn't much damage Oliver could do to the room or himself, but there wasn't really anything for him to play with either. Although Leo had brought Oliver's high-chair from London, he hadn't thought to bring any of his toys. They would have to go into Oxford after lunch and see what they could find. He wanted there to be things here, familiar things, which Oliver would look forward to playing with, and which would make it a home for him, as much as the flat in London.

'Let's get the shopping out of the car and make you some lunch,' he said and kissed Oliver.

While Leo ate a ham sandwich and glanced through the *Sunday Times*, Oliver worked his way steadily through a plateful of bread and Marmite fingers. When he had eaten as many of these as he wanted, he rolled up the remaining three, mashed them between his fingers and dropped them over the side of his high-chair, glancing candidly at his father for his reaction. Leo sat watching him as he did this, marvelling as he always did at the texture of the boy's skin, the silkiness of his hair, and at his ability to spread food in all directions. There were glistening little lumps of mashed banana adhering to the floor and to the wall, where they had flown after Oliver had wrested the spoon from Leo's grasp while Leo tried to feed him. Leo hadn't realised that Oliver fed himself these days and clearly found his father's attempts to spoon stuff into his mouth pretty patronising and offensive. Leo went to the sink for a cloth, and as he came back Oliver began to batter the table of his high-chair with his beaker of juice, showering himself and Leo with sizeable splashes of baby Ribena. The expression of exuberant delight on his son's face made Leo laugh aloud, and at this Oliver began to laugh too and bang his beaker harder.

'Right, enough of that.' Leo took the beaker and guided it towards Oliver's mouth. As he watched the toddler drink, Leo realised that there was a quality to this time with Oliver that had not existed when he and Rachel had lived together. She had always been possessive of Oliver in a way which Leo had assumed was naturally maternal, but it had meant that Rachel did most things for Oliver. While he had not felt exactly excluded, Leo hadn't had the chance to spend sustained periods of time with the baby, doing everything for him as he was now. He liked this intimacy, the way that he and Oliver could concentrate on one another without any distractions.

As soon as he saw that Oliver had quenched his thirst and was about to embark on another bout of beaker battering, Leo took it away and wiped him comprehensively with the damp end of a towel. Then he released him from the high-chair and let him lurch into the living-room while Leo cleared up the mess of lunch.

In Oxford that afternoon they bought a little tractor which Oliver could sit on and push along with his feet, a cart filled with coloured building blocks, a very basic Thomas The Tank Engine train set, and a variety of little cars and farm and zoo animals. By the time he and Oliver had pootled up and down on the narrow-gauge steam railway, which Oliver loved to distraction, Leo realised that it was four thirty, and that he would barely have time to get him back to the house and give him tea before taking him home to Rachel.

After a messy meal of scrambled egg and toast, Oliver insisted on playing with each one of the toys which he and Leo had bought that afternoon. Leo had not the heart to refuse him, realising that he would actually rather capitulate to most of his son's demands than be subjected to the ear-splitting wailing which Oliver was capable of setting up when thwarted. At six o'clock, while Oliver, who was now grizzly with tiredness, pushed Thomas The Tank Engine round and round the plastic track for yet another time, Leo tried to call Rachel to say he would be late. There was no answer.

Clearly she and Charles had gone out for the afternoon and were late themselves. Fine. Oliver could play with his new toys until he dropped, which wouldn't be long now, and then he would take him back.

In the barn at the far end of the garden, Rachel and Charles were sorting books on to shelves. Charles had decided to turn the barn into a proper work place, and now that the builders had finished he was moving in the contents of his study, plus a new computer system.

'Was that the phone?' said Rachel, pausing with a book in hand.

'I don't know,' said Charles. 'I think I'm growing progressively deaf.'

'When is the phone line going to be installed here, anyway?'

'Tuesday, I hope. It's not going to be much of a work place without one.'

'Look, d'you mind if I leave you to it?' sighed Rachel. 'Oliver's going to be back in half an hour and I've got a few things to do in the house.'

Like wait for Oliver, thought Charles. All day she had been distracted, clearly occupied with thoughts of Oliver and what he was doing. 'No, off you go. I won't be much longer myself.'

Rachel went back up to the house, thinking, as she had done all day, of Leo and Oliver together, wondering if her desire to be with them both was born out of jealousy, or some other emotion.

The next hour and a half dragged by. Six thirty came and went, and still there was no sign of Oliver and Leo. Charles came back from the barn and found Rachel pacing round the kitchen in an agitated manner, and did his best to soothe her.

'But it's seven thirty! They were meant to be back an hour ago!' Rachel was close to tears.

'It is only an hour,' pointed out Charles. 'Leo was probably late back from wherever it was they went. He said something about a steam railway and they always take far longer than you think they will. He probably didn't realise where the time was going. A few hours go very quickly with a small child. Or slowly, depending. I mean –'

'Charles, stop babbling!' Rachel groaned and sat down at the kitchen table. 'Anything could have happened to them! An accident . . . Leo and those fast cars of his. God, I feel sick with worry.'

'Well, don't,' said Charles. He went over to the drinks cupboard. 'What I suggest is a large gin and tonic –'

'Charles, why does alcohol always have to be your answer to everything?' snapped Rachel.

Charles, a little hurt by this remark, but conscious of its essential truthfulness, poured himself a hefty slug of gin. 'I don't know,' he murmured. 'It just is. It always has been. Maybe I'm just lucky that way.' God, he hoped Leo would get the child here soon. Normally a man of placid, unruffled temperament, he found the atmosphere created by Rachel's tense fretting distinctly unsettling. He didn't feel he could decently switch on the television, or sit down and yawn over the Sunday papers, in case it looked callous in the face of Rachel's vision of Leo and Oliver splattered all over the M4. Charles was pacing round the kitchen with his drink, trying to think of something encouraging to say, when headlights gleamed in an arc across the kitchen and they heard the sound of a car drawing to a halt outside.

Rachel was on her feet in an instant and through the back door, before Charles had the chance to tell her to stay calm. He was about to follow her when he heard the beginnings of an angry tirade outside, thought better of it, sighed and sat down with his drink. It was nothing to do with him, anyway. Let them sort it out. He suddenly found himself remembering, quite unexpectedly, the cosy solitude of his house before he had met Rachel, the Sunday evenings of peace, with nothing more to do than go down to the pub . . .

Rachel came back angrily into the kitchen clutching a drowsy Oliver, Leo in her wake. 'You didn't even change him before you set off, did you? He's sodden! Honestly . . . I'm taking him straight upstairs to bed.'

She left the kitchen. Leo stood in the doorway, Oliver's baby bag in his hand.

'Hi,' said Charles, and raised his glass.

On the journey back to London, filled with late-Sunday depression, Leo had nothing to do but think. He thought, as usual these days, about himself. These last few months he had felt fragmented, with no cohesion to his life. The various roles he played had no connection. Now that his day with Oliver had come to an end, his thoughts began to drift back to Joshua. One was many things to different people. How could he be a good father to Oliver, and the lover of young men? It had never been Leo's way to impose any moral order on his life, and even now he would not admit of any contradiction in its various facets. It was a question of practicality. Loving Joshua, and young men like him, was simply an aspect of his life which he could not deny. The answer was to keep things separate. Rachel had touched a nerve when, during their argument in the pub about Oliver, she had raised the threat of bringing his personal life into question if he should pursue the matter of access. That worried him. He must be careful, very careful where Oliver was concerned. Not that there seemed to be any present scope for concern. Joshua had come into his life, wrought unlooked-for emotional havoc and left it. Perhaps just as well. At least it should be easier to get over such fresh, slight wounds. Better than the pain of a prolonged love affair. And yet that was what it should have been. He knew himself to be capable of such passion, and Joshua would have been, could have been ...

He decided he would think no more about it. Instead, he turned his mind to the call he intended to make later that evening, to a dealer friend in Copenhagen who might have some works of interest to the museum. Leo switched on some music and concentrated on driving and keeping his thoughts off Joshua.

As soon as he slipped his key in the front door and opened it, Leo saw the light from the living-room. He walked slowly, edgily, up the hall, not daring to allow the hope in his heart to expand. He stopped in the doorway.

Joshua glanced up and saw Leo standing there, looking tired, dressed in jeans and open-necked shirt, and a battered leather jacket that looked as though it had once been very expensive. Joshua noticed that there were small purple stains on Leo's shirt and that the faint stubble on his face was dark, in contrast to his hair. It made him look younger. He couldn't read the expression in Leo's eyes, so he just sat there, the book he had pulled from a shelf still in his lap, one leg hooked over the side of the armchair. Perhaps Leo didn't want him there. Perhaps that night had been all he wanted, and this was a mistake. Still, he had had to come back. Leo had played too much on his mind, kept invading his thoughts. He had wanted to be with him again, be in this place, in this quiet. To find out.

Leo closed his eyes briefly, as though very weary, then opened them again. 'Where did you go?' he asked. His voice was slightly hoarse. 'You do realise . . .'

'What?'

There was a silence. 'I thought I might never see you again.'

Joshua said nothing for a few seconds. The depth of feeling in Leo's voice, in those simple words, astounded him. He felt his own eyes brighten unexpectedly with tears and he looked away quickly. This wasn't what it was all about. 'Yeah, well . . . I'm sorry.' After a moment the wetness in his eyes cleared and he could look directly at Leo again.

Leo crossed the room to where Joshua sat and knelt down. He put his face in Joshua's lap and Joshua, astonished, uncertain, put out a hand to stroke Leo's head. Then Leo looked up, drew Joshua down to him and kissed him. 'Don't,' he said. 'Don't ever do that again.'

Some hours later, lying in bed, Leo asked, 'Do you have a friend called Damien?'

'Yes. How do you know?'

'The Australian girl at the Galleria told me. I went there when I was looking for you.'

'Looking for me?' Joshua lay with his chin propped on his hand, gazing at Leo.

Leo said nothing for a moment, tracing a line with his finger from Joshua's neck and down his shoulder. 'Where does he work?'

'Damien? The Ritzy Cinema, in Brixton.'

'Oh.'

'Why?'

Leo sighed and smiled. 'I was just curious.'

Chapter eight

Next morning Leo stood in the kitchen, tying his tie, watching Joshua flicking through the book of poetry he had taken from the shelf the night before.

Joshua looked up, feeling Leo's eyes upon him. 'I know what you want to say,' he said after a few seconds. 'You want to know if I'll be here tonight.'

Leo sat down, smoothing the corners of his collar. He reflected briefly on what Joshua had just said. It could have sounded arrogant, or unpleasantly triumphant, the words of one displaying his power. But Joshua had spoken gently, matter-of-factly. After a moment's consideration Leo said, 'I want you to be here tonight. I want you here every night.' Joshua's hazel eyes looked into his. 'You know how I feel about you. I can't bear any uncertainty. If you don't want to come and live with me, then say so now. I have to know.'

Joshua considered this, faintly amazed. If Leo wanted him here it meant he wanted to keep him. He would pay for things. Food, clothes, everything. When someone like Leo took you on, that was what it meant. You belonged. Did he want to belong to anyone? Joshua thought of the bedsit in Earl's Court. He thought of his mother, whom he hadn't seen in eighteen months, and of his stepfather, that bastard. There was no belonging there any more. What would it be like to share Leo's home and life? There was no point unless he could return Leo's feelings in some measure. Could he love Leo? He supposed he could, in whatever way Leo wanted. And there would be safety and affection, and a home. All for as long as he chose. That was the main thing. He could decide for himself how long it went on. Leo was in love with him, he could tell that. He might not ever have had this kind of a relationship with a man before, but he knew love when he saw it. This was his game all right. What had he to lose? Freedom, perhaps. Some people were unconditional and he guessed Leo was one of them. Yet there might be much to gain. Leo knew things, understood things about which Joshua wanted to learn – art, money, the ways of possession and influence. And he was generous. Were seedy, boring clubs, nights out with Damien and the occasional girl much of a sacrifice? Not in the short term . . .

'Why do you want me to live with you? Why can't you just see me now and then?' If he was honest, he supposed he asked this question just to torment Leo, and just to hear him say the thing Joshua wanted to hear.

'Because I love you. I want you. I want you to be there. You must know all that.'

Joshua did. He put out a hand to Leo's face. He liked this guy. More than liked him. Something about him turned Joshua on, and that was a start. 'Yeah. Okay.'

Leo kissed Joshua's hand. 'You can have your own room. Treat everything here as though it's yours.'

'Including you.'

Leo did not think he would ever feel so utterly besotted, so entirely and immediately happy, as at this moment. 'Including me.'

Leo's day in court passed smoothly, perfectly. He dealt with what was a difficult and complex case effortlessly, with a clarity of thought and swiftness of response which he had not found within himself for months. He felt charged, purposeful, and went back to chambers at the end of the afternoon glad in his heart and easy in his mind.

In the clerks' room he picked up his mail, paused to exchange brief banter with Henry about his moustache, then went up to his room, whistling.

Henry gazed thoughtfully after him. 'Haven't heard him whistle in chambers for months,' he remarked to Felicity. 'Not since Wales won the Five Nations. Sir Basil couldn't stand it.'

'What? Wales winning the Five Nations?'

'No, the whistling. That, and him taking the stairs two at a time. Not that he does much of that these days.'

'Getting on, I suppose. Still, nice to see him happy for a change.' She sighed. 'Wish I was.'

Henry glanced at her. 'What's up?' Henry had for some time nurtured an unrequited love for Felicity. He had once managed to kiss her in the back of a taxi after Felicity got drunk at a chambers Christmas party, but that was as far as it had gone. It was treated as a joke between them. He knew Felicity wasn't interested in him, except as a friend, but still he cared about her, and any suggestion that all was not well with her made him worry.

'Oh, nothing, Henry.' She smiled at the sight of his kind, anxious face. 'Nothing that time won't sort out.' She turned back to the papers in front of her. She might as well resign herself to the fact that her days at 5 Caper Court were numbered. In a few months she would be gone and it would be the end of her precious, wonderful job. She might have known it would be too good to last.

Leo left chambers at six and went to catch the train at Temple station, conscious of anxiety growing within him. He didn't think that Joshua would leave again, not after last night, but he couldn't be sure. He couldn't be sure of anything until he got home and was able to reassure himself. The journey to Sloane Square and the five-minute walk to his flat had never seemed longer. When he got in, he could hear music coming from the kitchen. His sense of relief was almost as great as that of the night before.

At the sound of the front door closing, Joshua stepped out into the hall. He was wearing jeans and a sweat-shirt, his feet bare, and in one hand he held a kitchen knife. He looked more cheerful than Leo had ever seen him. 'I brought my things over this afternoon. I put them in that bedroom at the back. And I bought some food. Just chicken and stuff. I thought I'd cook us some supper. And I got some wine, just something from Sainsbury's. It's in the fridge.' There was something new and pliant about Joshua's manner, less streetwise, more ingenuous. How Leo loved him.

Leo opened the fridge and glanced at the wine. Definitely not. He would put something else in later, after he had changed. 'That's kind of you, to think of supper. I had to wait for ever for a train. Bloody District line.'

'I thought you drove to work.' Joshua sounded faintly surprised.

'Not always. Only if I'm going in after the rush-hour.' Leo leaned back against the sink, happy to watch Joshua inexpertly cutting up a red pepper.

The evening was more companionable than Leo had expected. It was the first amount of time they had spent together that was not emotionally or physically charged. They simply ate and talked. Joshua listened while Leo talked about his past, about Wales and his mother, about the father he could not remember, and about Rachel and Oliver. He told Joshua about the room he had prepared for Oliver's eventual weekend visits. 'Rachel thinks he's too young to be staying away from her on a regular basis, but it's important to me that I build up a close relationship with him while he's still little. I know what it's like not to have a father.'

'We're a bit alike,' said Joshua. 'I'm an only child, and my dad walked out on us. But I was ten, so I remember him, of course – I mean, I still see him. Well, I used to. He moved to Halifax two years ago.' He sipped his wine. 'I really missed him when I was a teenager. That was when I wanted him around. Some days I felt like I hated him for leaving.'

'I know,' said Leo thoughtfully. 'That's why I want to be there for Oliver.' He glanced at Joshua. Having the boy living with him was going to complicate things, especially if Rachel found out. But what else could he have done? Feeling as he did, what else could he have done? Anyway, Joshua was here now. Thank God. 'Tell me more about yourself, about your family.'

Joshua gave a dismissive shrug. 'I haven't seen them since last Christmas. I left home the summer before, after I'd finished art school. I couldn't take all the rows with my stepfather. His name's Alan and he's a bastard, besides being a policeman. My mum met him about a year after my dad left. We used to get on all right when I was a kid, but then as I got older he tried to pull the big authoritarian act all the time. He used to try and make me look small in front of my friends. That was when I really started to hate him. Then when I wanted to go to art school, he made out that it was a soft thing to want to do, that it was a cop-out. My mum never thought it was. But he tried to discourage her from paying my tuition fees and stuff. He never shut up about what a waste of time it was. Still, she backed me up. Then when my friends from art school started coming round to the house, he'd have a go at them. Nothing direct, but sort of snide, insinuating remarks. He made a lot of the fact that he was in the police, sort of hinted that he could shop them if they were using drugs, stuff like that. They couldn't stand it, or him. We used to have really bad rows, and my mum would get all hysterical and upset. So I left. Got myself the bedsit in Earl's Court and the job at the Galleria. I'd ring Mum up now and again, of course, just so she knew I was all right, and then just before Christmas she said it would be nice if I came home for a few days. Well, I didn't really fancy spending Christmas in the bedsit and all my mates were going to be with their families, so I went. Biggest mistake of my life. Alan started off okay, but after he'd had a few drinks, he couldn't resist getting the needle in. So when I told him the police were a complete load of corrupt racists with a collective IQ of an average snooker score, he got really

129

rattled. He actually went for me, grabbed me. I don't think he'd have hit me, but poor old Mum was all over the place. I haven't been back since and I never intend going. Of course, the money's a bit of a problem, which is why I've done those things on the side. I didn't believe I could do it at first, but then ... Well, after a while it becomes easy money.' He stopped, faintly embarrassed.

Leo had been listening with interest, studying him, absorbed in the beauty of the boy, the movements of his face as he talked, the expressiveness of his hands. 'What about your art? How much does it mean to you? Are you ambitious, for instance?'

Joshua laughed. 'No, not really. I don't want much out of life, to be honest. I mean, I take what comes.' He leaned back in his chair, clasped his hands behind his head. 'I do like painting. It takes me out of myself. I suppose in a couple of years I might think of studying some more, turning it into a proper career, become a designer, something like that. But for the moment, I don't much care.'

Joshua's tone was nonchalant, but Leo knew from the pain in his eyes that leaving his family had been more traumatic than he had been prepared to admit. He tried to make it sound as though he had chosen his way of living, but Leo could see all too clearly that the boy was too broken, lonely and dispirited to make anything of his life at present. Maybe he could change that. Maybe with time and enough affection, Joshua could make something of himself. Leo desperately hoped that he could be the one to help him.

By the end of just one week, Joshua's presence in the flat seemed so perfectly right, and so necessary to Leo's well-being, that the past months had a nightmarish blankness when he looked back on them. His love for Joshua had sprung from nowhere, but became, with every day that passed, more settled and absolute. He did not question it, could find no motive for it, but simply accepted it. He knew that Joshua's feelings for him were of a different kind, but he hoped that, with time and patience, they would strengthen and deepen.

At Leo's suggestion, Joshua had set up an easel and paints in the back bedroom, and for some of the day he worked there. Leo didn't know what he did the rest of the time. He didn't ask. He was happy just to see him there each night, apparently content. Some evenings Joshua cooked, on others Leo took him out to restaurants. On Saturday, at the end of that first week, they went shopping and Leo bought him new clothes, and in the evening they went to the theatre, where Joshua sat a little restlessly through one of Tennessee Williams's less well-known plays, and then to dinner. Sitting in the Ivy, watching Joshua take it all in, the faces, the food, the wine, the novelty of his surroundings, Leo was reminded of the time, some years ago, when Anthony had first come to 5 Caper Court as a pupil. Leo had taken him under his wing, had loved him, wanting to teach and mould him, to turn him into the companion of his heart. It had never happened. Perhaps that would be possible with Joshua. With all the delusion of new and undisappointed love, he hoped and believed that it would be.

Sarah was careful to leave Anthony alone for the first week of Camilla's absence from chambers, but on the Monday morning of the second week she went to ask his advice about a piece of work she was doing for David concerning liability insurance, knowing that Anthony had a hearing coming up on that very same subject. She sat in his room as he explained the point, only half listening but making a show of intelligent interest and, as she gazed at him, idly pieced together the distinctly erotic events of the first time they had gone to bed together. Oddly enough, she had discovered that her decision to indulge in a bit of mischief-making had actually rekindled her old interest in Anthony and she found it hard to be with him without wanting to touch him, to

131

provoke some kind of sexual response in him. For the moment, though, she would keep her distance. There would be ample opportunity to test his powers of resistance over the days to come. With an effort, she drew her attention back to what Anthony was saying.

'. . . So the contractors would have to demonstrate a legal liability in damages in respect of the third-party claims. That's the main point. Does that help you?'

Sarah nodded and smiled. 'Yes, thanks very much. It's an interesting area of law. I like insurance work.'

'Good.' Anthony leaned back and tapped his teeth with a pencil, his eyes scanning Sarah's face, unconscious that he was subtly stimulating his own latent desire by dwelling too long on her mouth and the line of her throat tapering into the neck of her blouse. 'Actually, I have a hearing in the Court of Appeal tomorrow which might interest you. It's a case involving a cruise line trying to recover under their liability insurance for compensation paid out to passengers. It shouldn't last more than two or three days. Why don't you ask David if he'll let you sit in?'

'Yes, I will. And thanks for the help.' She went out, smiling a little smile.

Anthony sat for a few moments, fiddling with his pencil, thinking about Sarah. It was odd how relationships shifted and changed. He recalled first meeting her and the effect she'd had on him. That was history, though. They'd moved from an intense, brief affair to cold mutual dislike, and now that had given way to a friendly tolerance. She was a strange girl. You never knew if what you were getting was the genuine article. Looking back, he felt that perhaps the only times he had seen the true Sarah were when she lost her temper. She was someone you learned to be wary of. Then it suddenly occurred to him – Leo treated her that way. Cautiously, cynically. Anthony wondered why that was. According to Leo, theirs was just a nodding, social acquaintance. Another mystery, one he couldn't be bothered to ponder. He glanced at his watch and decided to go to the common room for tea.

As he passed the clerks' room Anthony caught sight of Leo, laughing about something with Felicity. Good to see that he'd cheered up recently. But Leo was like that, going into periods of reclusiveness, then emerging, brisk and happy.

'I'm just going for some tea. Coming?' he asked.

Leo glanced at his watch. 'Yes, why not?'

But at that moment Felicity, who had just answered the phone, said to him, 'Call for you, Mr Davies.'

'Who is it?'

'A Miss Angelicos. Says it's personal.'

Leo caught Anthony's eye and grimaced, then said to Felicity, 'I'll take it in my room. I'll see you in the common room in a minute,' he added to Anthony. There was no point in putting her off, thought Leo as he went upstairs. She'd only call again. Best to get it over with.

'Hello, Leo?' The affected huskiness of her voice, so effective on television, instantly annoyed Leo. Its tone suggested an intimacy which he by no means felt.

'Melissa,' he replied, trying to sound brisk, 'what can I do for you?'

'Actually, I'm calling for some professional advice. I have something of a legal problem.'

Good, at least he could deal with this on a business footing. 'I'm afraid,' he replied, 'that I can't take instructions directly from you on the phone. If you need my help, you'll have to go through a solicitor first.'

'Oh, no. No, I didn't mean that I need you to act for me. Nothing like that. No, I thought you might be able to put me in touch with someone who can help me. You see, my sister and I have been left some property in Italy under the will of an uncle of ours, and the lawyer who's handling the estate out there is simply disastrous. The whole thing is going to take for ever to sort out unless we do something on our own

133

initiative. I was wondering if you could give me the name of a good Italian lawyer.'

'I see. Yes – yes, of course I can. Hold on a moment.' Leo reached out for his address book. Thank God it was something straightforward. He didn't mind helping the woman out. 'Where is the estate being handled?'

'Genoa.'

'Right, let's see . . .' Leo leafed through the pages and gave her a name and number. Melissa noted them down.

'That's wonderful. Very kind of you.' She hesitated. 'Why don't you let me repay the favour by buying you a drink one evening this week?'

Oh, no, thought Leo. He wasn't going to be caught in that way. 'I'm sorry,' he replied, 'but I seem to be busy every evening this week.'

'Oh . . . Well, I'll see you at the next trustees meeting, in that case.'

'Yes. Anyway, glad I could be of help. Goodbye.'

Leo put the phone down. Had that just been a device, something to lead round to the suggestion of going for a drink? He had no idea. But it seemed on the evidence that she wasn't someone who gave up easily. He left his room and went to the common room to join Anthony for tea.

'Why on earth is Melissa Angelicos ringing you in chambers?' asked Anthony, as Leo pulled up a chair.

'She needed the name of a Genoese lawyer. Some problem with family property. I gave her Carlo Cigolini's details.'

'I didn't realise you and she were quite that chummy.'

'We're not. Although I rather think she'd like us to be. She's been coming on rather strong ever since that trustees meeting.'

'Ah, you've been exercising that fabulous charm of yours in an indiscriminate fashion. That's the problem. Try to keep it in check.'

'First of all she inveigled me into driving her home, then she invited me in for supper – which I declined, by the way –

134

and last weekend she called my home and left several messages about some dinner party she wanted me to go to.' Leo drank some of his tea. 'I didn't, of course. But I'd like to know how she got my home number.'

'Probably from Chay.'

'You think?' Leo mused on this. 'I suppose that's possible.'

There was a silence of a few seconds, then Anthony said, 'You seem to have recovered your spirits recently. Things going well?'

'Excellently,' replied Leo. 'You know that breach of contract case I told you about? The one where some Americans were meant to be supplying pipelines for an oil refinery and didn't?' Anthony nodded. 'Well, against insurmountable odds, I managed to persuade Langley this morning to stay the action in favour of Libyan jurisdiction.' Leo chuckled.

'Good God. The Americans must be apoplectic. They're not going to get very far in a Libyan court.'

'Well, quite. I do regard it as something of a triumph.' Leo suddenly thought of Joshua, and was instantly filled with an expansive happiness and the urge to tell someone about it. Anthony could be confided in. He would understand. 'Actually, it's not the only good thing that's happened recently –' Leo hesitated.

'What?'

Leo leaned forward in his chair, clasping his hands together. 'There's nobody else I could tell this to, without feeling and sounding incredibly foolish ... I've met someone. A young man. His name's Joshua.'

Anthony nodded, not quite sure how to respond to this, uncertain of what his own feelings were. On one level he was happy for Leo. Leo needed love like everybody else, and if he'd found it, good luck to him. But a relationship with any young man was bound to be precarious and he didn't want Leo to get hurt, or to make a fool of himself. And there was something more – he felt a tender little tension within him,

135

something like jealousy, at the idea that Leo should love someone the way he had once loved Anthony. 'I'm glad,' said Anthony at last. 'You seem to be happy.'

'Yes, I'm very happy. He's staying with me. After all the wretched business with Rachel, and all the hell of these last few months, I can't tell you how much it means to me.'

'How's it going? The divorce, I mean.' Anthony wanted to deflect the conversation away from Leo's new love. It was something he didn't want to contemplate.

Leo sat back. 'On the whole it's fairly amicable. But we're having something of a disagreement over my access to Oliver. I want to have him every other weekend and Rachel's completely opposed to the idea. Says he's too young.'

'What does your solicitor say?'

'She thinks it's perfectly reasonable that I should have him on that basis. He's not going to be eighteen months old for ever. It's just a question of getting a court to see it that way. She's lodged an application on my behalf for a defined residence order.'

'What does that involve? I didn't study much family law.'

'Oh, the court welfare officers come and interview me, take a look at the flat, see that it's a decent place for Oliver to stay. I don't anticipate much of a problem.'

'What about this new boyfriend of yours? I thought you said he was living with you. That might not go down too well.'

'Don't worry. I'll make sure he's not there when they come round.'

'But there's more to it than that, isn't there? I mean –' Anthony hesitated. Perhaps his interference was unwarranted. Leo could be pretty touchy. But as a friend, he had to say it. 'Well, it's more than just a question of appearances, surely? You have to ask yourself whether it's going to do Oliver any good, seeing his father living with whichever young man happens to be –'

'Anthony,' interrupted Leo, 'Joshua is not one of a string of lovers. I hope he's here to stay. And despite what you may think, I do have Oliver's best interests at heart.'

There was a brief, uncomfortable silence. 'How old is he?' asked Anthony at last. 'This Joshua.'

'Twenty.'

'Twenty.'

'For Christ's sake, Anthony,' said Leo abruptly, 'don't try to sit in judgment on me. You know nothing of the situation. His age doesn't matter.' Leo stood up. His manner had become chilly. 'I have to be getting back.'

After Leo had left, Anthony sat in the common room and stared at his hands. Did Leo really think he was going to find permanence with some twenty-year-old pick-up? Still, it wasn't any of his business. And maybe Leo was right. You shouldn't judge a situation you knew nothing about. He himself had been a mere twenty-two when he had fallen in love with Leo, and he had been as sure and devoted in his feelings as anyone could be. But he hadn't been prepared to become what Leo wanted. That was the difference. Maybe Joshua was what Leo needed and wanted, and vice versa. Somehow Anthony doubted it. He finished his tea and strolled back to chambers, wondering whether Camilla would ring that night. He had begun to find the evenings lonely and dull.

He met Sarah as he came into chambers.

'I asked David if I could sit in on that case you mentioned and he says it's fine.'

'Good,' said Anthony. 'I'll see you in the morning.'

Sarah sped lightly upstairs to her room. Things were about to become rather enjoyable.

When Leo got home that evening the flat was empty.

'Joshua?' Leo slung his coat over a chair and went quickly into Joshua's room. The little coil of tension within him eased. Joshua's belongings were still there. Leo loosened his tie and went into the kitchen to fix himself a drink. He sat

137

with the evening paper for half an hour, waiting, finding it hard to keep his attention fixed on what he was reading.

Joshua came in just after half past seven. He was wearing the Hermès jacket which Leo had bought him on Saturday, and his golden-brown hair was, for once, brushed, the tumble of curls pulled back in waves. It made the soft lines of his handsome face harder and more mature.

'Hi,' said Joshua. 'Been home long?'

'Half an hour,' said Leo. He felt tense. He realised that if Joshua had stayed out all evening, he would have been reduced to a miserable wreck. But it was not so for Joshua. The casualness of his tone when he spoke was completely unaffected. He couldn't really have cared one way or another whether Leo was in when he got back. It was in small moments like this that the balance of the relationship was clearly discernible, and Leo hated it. He wanted Joshua to care as much as he did and that was impossible.

Then he glanced across at the set of keys which Joshua had dropped on the work surface before opening the fridge to get himself a beer. They were the keys to the garage and to the Aston Martin.

'Where have you been?' Leo tried to keep his tone light.

'Just out and about.' Joshua cracked open his can of beer.

'In my car?'

Joshua turned to look directly at him. 'D'you mind?'

'Yes,' replied Leo quietly. 'As a matter of fact –' He took a deep breath, trying to contain his anger. 'Apart from the fact that it is a very expensive car, you're not insured to drive it. Didn't that cross your mind?'

'Sorry. Didn't realise it was such a big deal. Anyway, I was very careful, don't worry.'

'That's not the point!' Leo was about to give full rein to his anger, but he stopped. It was pointless. Joshua's thoughts and actions were those of a child. Leo could tell from the way Joshua had come in, from his very attitude, the new clothes he had on, that he'd been swanning around town, showing

138

off. Pretending that the car was his, feeling big, amusing himself. Well, he was young. Young people did that kind of thing. They were selfish and heedless. He would just have to make sure it didn't happen again.

'In future, you don't touch the Aston Martin. Understand? If you need a car to get about, I'll buy you one. Something more practical.'

'Christ, you're so patronising!' burst out Joshua. 'Treat everything here as though it's yours, you said. But when it comes to your car, that's off limits. Joshua's too young to be trusted. Why can't you just get me added on to the insurance?'

Leo sighed. The boy simply didn't get it. 'Joshua –' Leo put out a hand, but Joshua shrugged it off and stood up.

'I don't want to be treated like a child, Leo. I don't want to be here if it's not going to be on equal terms. I think I might as well just go and put my things together now.'

Leo's heart suddenly flooded with fear. This was the first time there had been any kind of altercation between them. This was a new side to Joshua. He hadn't realised that he could fly off the handle so easily, that his cheerful, easygoing nature masked this aspect of his personality, sullen and volatile all at once. 'Don't be stupid. Joshua –' Leo got up and went to him. 'This is absurd. I don't want to argue with you about a car, for God's sake. I can see you might need one. I just thought you might want something easier to handle, more practical.' Joshua looked at him woodenly. 'But don't talk about leaving. I need you. That's more important than anything.'

Joshua relented. It was too easy to make Leo afraid. He didn't really like doing it. Anyway, if there was a car in it . . . 'Okay. I'm sorry.' Joshua put his arms round Leo and held him.

On Tuesday morning, as he put together his papers before going over to court, Anthony felt mildly depressed. Camilla had called last night, but for some reason the conversation had been stilted, disappointing. It was hard to be affectionate at a distance, he supposed. But Camilla hadn't wanted to talk for as long as he did, was impatient to get away. How was it going to be when she got back?

Sarah put her head round the door and said cheerfully, 'Morning. Are you ready?'

'Yes,' said Anthony. 'I think I've got everything. Let's go.'

As the day in court progressed, Anthony's spirits began to lift and, in concentrating on the case, he forgot entirely about Camilla. He hadn't initially entertained much hope of this appeal succeeding but, to his surprise, the three Appeal Court judges seemed favourably disposed towards his argument.

'I must say I tend to agree with you in that respect, Mr Cross,' said Lord Justice Hazel. 'I don't see that the fact that there were additional underwriters involved in the 1995/6 year affects the right of set-off of the individual underwriters in respect of claim and counterclaim.' He glanced in mild enquiry at his fellow Lords of Appeal and Anthony was gratified to see Lord Justice Youell give a little shake of his head. Lord Justice Mildon looked slightly more thoughtful.

Sarah glanced up at Anthony, noting the expression of satisfaction which crossed his face. He was easy to read. His manner held a directness which was almost naïve. Leo was not dissimilar. Perhaps it was a result of living in this hothouse world of the Temple, this unique and claustrophobic little society. Barristers were loud in proclaiming that they lived in the real world, just like other people, but Sarah somehow doubted it. Shopping at Tesco's and going to the children's sports days did not amount to the real world. There was something exclusive and stultifying about the Inns of Court, something which drew you in, timeless, artificial, indescribable. To live and work in that world day after day was what shaped people like Anthony, regardless of what they might do in their spare time. This was their life.

And from the couple of months she had spent at 5 Caper Court, Sarah wasn't sure that it was a life which she wished to lead. Still, she would wait out her six months and then see what happened. In the meantime, she could while away the time in considering how to play her hand this evening. If she got the chance, that was.

By four o'clock, Anthony had still not completed his submissions and Lord Justice Youell interrupted him to confabulate briefly with his brethren. 'Mr Cross,' he said at last, 'I think we are all agreed that it would be desirable to dispose of this matter within two days, if possible, as Lord Justice Mildon has other commitments on Thursday. You are, as I take it, close to completing your submissions. May I suggest then, if everyone is agreeable, that we sit late this afternoon – say, until five o'clock, so that you may finish and we may then hear Mrs Shepherd first thing tomorrow morning?'

There was a general murmuring of agreement and Anthony ploughed on. Excellent, thought Sarah. More chance of having a drink with Anthony than if they were to finish at four, as usual.

By the end of the afternoon, as he gathered up his papers, Anthony felt exhausted. He had been on his feet for most of the day, but at least he had finished his submissions. Tomorrow he could just sit back and listen.

'Well done,' said Sarah. 'I think you deserve a drink after all that hard work. Let me buy you one.'

Anthony hesitated, glancing at his watch. There probably wasn't much point in going back to chambers now. 'All right. I'll see you downstairs in ten minutes.'

The wine bar in Chancery Lane was still relatively empty when they got there. Sarah, despite Anthony's gentlemanly protests, insisted on buying the wine. 'Let's sit in here,' she said, indicating a snug booth. 'It's going to be busy in half an hour and we won't be able to hear ourselves talk if we sit at a table.'

Anthony poured them each a glass of wine. Sarah unfastened her hair and gave her head a little shake to let it fall free around her shoulders. Then she took off her dark jacket and put it to one side, and began to unbutton the top few buttons of her high-necked blouse. She did all these things in the leisurely, detached fashion of someone merely relaxing after a long day, but the sensuality of every little movement was not lost on Anthony. He handed Sarah her glass, and she sighed and pushed her collar back, rubbing her fingers gently across her throat, aware that Anthony was watching as she did this.

'God, I hate this uniform. Anyway – cheers.' She took a sip of wine. 'Here's to victory in the Court of Appeal.'

'Yes – well, it went better than I'd expected.' Anthony drank his wine, wondering why he felt faintly awkward with Sarah. He couldn't really think of anything to talk about. There was something about sitting in this booth with her which reminded him of the first time they had gone out together, and recollections of that evening seemed to be crowding into his mind. He decided the safest topic was the case and so they talked about that for a while, then gossiped briefly about other members of chambers.

'How's Camilla getting on in Bermuda?' asked Sarah eventually.

'Fine, I think,' replied Anthony. 'I spoke to her last night. Though I suspect she's finding it quite stressful. But, then, working in foreign surroundings must be.'

'Mmm. She's very good, isn't she? Seems to get tons of work. I'm sure she'll do very well. She was always very conscientious when we were at Oxford together, as I recall. I was one of those people who spent all their time at parties, not turning up for tutorials, handing essays in late, but Camilla wasn't like that. She was very studious and it's paid off.' There was a pause, then Sarah added reflectively, 'I'm glad you're seeing one another. I mean, you and she are so well suited. You're the same kind of people.' She laughed, finished her wine and poured them both some more. 'Unlike you and I – God, we were disastrous!'

'Were we?' Anthony found the picture which Sarah was painting faintly disturbing. It made Camilla and himself sound like a couple of stuffy young fogeys, set apart from the exciting and irresponsible world which Sarah inhabited.

Sarah smiled and gazed directly at Anthony. She looked very pretty, he thought, with her hair round her face, her eyes very bright and mischievous. The looked spurred him to recollections of being with her, of how tantalising and sexy she could be, when she wasn't being bad-tempered and argumentative. 'A total disaster,' said Sarah firmly. 'As I recall, I was always trying to persuade you to stay at my place when all you wanted to do was go home and get a good night's sleep before work the next day. I wasn't good for you in the slightest. Unlike Camilla. I'll bet she always puts work before pleasure. Sensible girl.'

The truth of this rankled momentarily with Anthony. 'Oh, I don't know . . .' He tried to think with affection of Camilla's dependable, reserved personality. She wasn't at all as dull as Sarah was implying.

'I wish I could be like her,' sighed Sarah. There was something in the words which suggested that the last thing in the world Sarah wanted was to be like Camilla. 'But I'm not. So I might as well be happy with who I am.' She glanced at Anthony's glass. 'Drink up.' Anthony obediently finished his wine, and Sarah poured some more. 'I remember when I first realised that she was the one for you, actually.'

'Oh?' Anthony wasn't quite sure how they'd fallen into this line of conversation and wanted to change it, but didn't know how.

'It was at a party we went to. We'd had an argument before coming out – I don't think you wanted to go. Something like that. Anyway, Camilla arrived late, and I saw the way you looked at her.' Sarah smiled a little wistfully.

'Rubbish,' said Anthony. 'We didn't start going out together for months after that.'

Sarah smiled. 'I'm more perceptive than you think. Not that it matters. Even then I think it was becoming obvious that you and I were particularly bad news for one another.'

There was a pause, and Anthony found himself saying, 'Not in all respects.'

'No?'

Their eyes met, and suddenly Anthony was dizzyingly overwhelmed by memories of making love to Sarah, quite without wanting to be. He said nothing, dropping his glance to her parted lips.

'Anthony,' said Sarah softly, drawing on the intensity, the closeness of this moment of shared recollection, 'this has nothing to do with Camilla, or anything else.'

'What hasn't?'

She leaned forward and put her hand on the nape of his neck, drawing his head towards hers. He let her kiss him, his hand loosening its grip on the wineglass, his senses drowning in the pleasure of it.

He drew away. It had everything to with Camilla. He was serious about her. He couldn't just sit in wine bars and let Sarah do this, much as he might like it. The last thing he had expected at the end of a hard day in court was to find Sarah seducing him. 'That wasn't a good idea,' he said, his voice a little unsteady.

'No? You just said we weren't bad news for each other in all respects. And that was where we were very, very good . . . weren't we?' The table in the booth was narrow, and Sarah slipped a hand beneath it, running it swiftly along Anthony's thigh and up to his crotch.

'Jesus, Sarah –' Anthony glanced quickly round, and put his own hand beneath the table to pull Sarah's away, but instead, despite every good intention, found himself pressing her hand against his body and leaning forward to kiss her again urgently. They were almost entirely hidden from view in the booth.

Sarah pulled her mouth away from his for a moment, slightly breathless. 'I don't want to spoil anything between you and Camilla. I don't care about you and Camilla. She's a long way away and what we do isn't going to hurt anybody. I promise. I just want you. I just want you inside me again.' Anthony let out a small groan and searched for her mouth with his. What this woman could do to him . . . He felt totally irresponsible, overwhelmed by the feel of her, the taste of her. But she leaned away again, her voice no more than a whisper. 'Remember fucking me, Anthony? Remember . . . ?' Their mouths met again.

After a moment Anthony sat back. He felt as though he was going to explode. 'Let's get out of here.' They left the wine bar, found a taxi and went back to Sarah's.

A few hours later, Sarah lifted her head from the pillow. 'You've got a long day in court tomorrow. You should be going.' She smiled at Anthony and he stared expressionlessly into her eyes, then kissed her.

'This is a one-off. It's not going to happen again.'

Sarah laughed. 'What? Because of Camilla? Don't worry. I understand all about that.' She turned over, lifting one arm behind her head, watching as he dressed. 'Let's say it was just for old times' sake.'

Anthony buckled his belt and slipped on his jacket. 'I have to be going.'

Sarah rolled on to her stomach again and blew him a kiss. 'See you in court,' she said.

Just a one-off, Anthony assured himself, as he left Sarah's flat and began the short walk to the underground station. He knew he should never have gone back with her in the first place, but at the time he hadn't been able to help himself. God, it had been good. He went downstairs and stood on the gusty platform. But it had been madness, too. Madness.

Absolutely the first and last time. At the thought of Camilla, and his betrayal, he felt a horrible, sliding sense of guilt. Why hadn't he felt it two hours ago? Then, it had seemed the furthest thing from his mind. The train came in and Anthony got on and sat down. At least he could reassure himself that it was never going to happen again.

Chapter nine

The next morning, just after eleven o'clock, the computer system at 5 Caper Court decided to crash. Henry rang the engineers, who came round, inspected things, and said that it would take them three or four hours to get the system up and running again. At this, Felicity burst into tears.

'Hey, come on,' said Henry, gently leading her out of the clerks' room. A telephone began to ring. 'Answer that, will you, please, Robert?' called Henry to the post boy. He sat Felicity down in one of the armchairs in the waiting room and gave her a tissue. She sobbed for a few seconds, then stopped, sniffed and wiped her eyes, streaking the tissue with mascara.

'It's not that bad,' said Henry consolingly. 'I know you've got a lot of work to catch up on, but it'll wait.'

Felicity blew her nose. 'I know. I'm sorry. I'm in a bit of a state at the moment. I've a lot on my mind. That bloody system breaking down is the last thing I need.'

Henry put an awkward arm around her shoulders. 'There, there.' He thought for a moment, as Felicity carefully dabbed wet mascara from beneath her eyes. 'Listen, there's nothing much we can do around here till they've fixed the thing. Why don't you let me take you to lunch? That lot upstairs are always at it. We'll go out somewhere decent, then you can tell me all your troubles. Robert can answer the phones, or one of the girls.'

Felicity looked up miserably at Henry. 'All right,' she said. 'That would be nice. To tell you the truth, I'm starving.' But then, she was always starving these days.

*

Henry rang up and booked a table for two at a little Italian restaurant near Waterloo Bridge. He had never taken Felicity to lunch before. The sight of her in tears had made him feel protective and assertive all at once. He was accustomed to feeling something of a diminished personality in Felicity's company, especially when she was in either her customary high spirits or bad temper, but today he saw a new and vulnerable side to her, and it made him want to take charge. So he did.

'It was really nice of you to take me out like this,' said Felicity, after she had demolished a plate of spaghetti alle vongole and drunk a large glass of the house red wine. 'Though I probably shouldn't have had that wine.'

'Why not? Look at the state some of our lot come back in, if they've settled or won a case. Lunch till four, then straight off home in a taxi. Who says the Perrier brigade's taken over the City? No evidence of it in Caper Court. Anyway, red wine's meant to be good for you.'

Felicity smiled. 'Yeah, I know. Remember how chuffed Mr Renshaw was when he read that? He seemed to think that the more red wine he drank, the healthier he'd be.'

Henry began to laugh, then stopped when he saw that Felicity had, unexpectedly, begun to cry again. 'Hey,' he said gently. 'Come on, don't start that again. I thought you'd cheered up?'

'I had,' sniffed Felicity. 'But just thinking about poor Mr Renshaw and how ill he is ... I'm really going to miss him. And I'm going to miss all of you!' This trailed off into a small, subdued wail and more crying.

Henry stretched out his hand and Felicity gripped it, struggling to control her tears. 'What do you mean?' asked Henry, beginning to feel a little hollow inside. The idea of Felicity leaving 5 Caper Court was dreadful and unexpected. He'd resigned himself some time ago to the fact that he would never get anywhere with her, but at least he had the consolation that she would always be around, that he would see her and be with her every day in chambers. And now she was talking about missing everyone.

Felicity overcame her tears and once again resorted to dabbing and sniffing and nose-blowing. 'Sorry,' she said. 'I must look a complete mess. I don't seem to be able to stop myself crying these days. Anything brings it on. I suppose it's just my hormones.'

'What do you mean about missing everyone?' His hand still held hers.

Felicity heaved a deep, shaking sigh. 'I've got to tell you some time, Henry, I suppose. I'm pregnant. I'll have to give up my job at Caper Court in a few months.'

Henry drew his hand away and sat back, not sure what to say to this news. It wasn't something he'd ever anticipated. He knew she lived with Vince but, like a nicely brought-up boy from Chigwell, he tended to the view that people should get married before they had children.

'I see,' he said at last. 'Well, congratulations. It's a pity about your job. You were getting on so well. Really well. You've got Gerald Wren eating out of your hand.' Henry was referring to the clerk of the Commercial Court, a difficult and exasperating individual whom Felicity charmed with an ease envied by clerks from other chambers. She could wheedle the hearing dates she wanted from him with the merest smile. But Henry's remarks now had the effect of setting Felicity off again.

'Don't!' she implored Henry, her eyes brimming. This time she reached out and took Henry's hand, and Henry felt a hot little flush creeping up from below his collar and into his face. 'You don't understand. The last thing in the world I want is to give up my job,' she said passionately.

'But you must be happy about the baby?'

'No!' Felicity astonished herself as well as Henry. All the pent-up feelings of the last few weeks came spilling out. 'No, I'm not! I don't want a baby right now, but there's nothing I can do about it. Vince knows, and he's pleased, he wants to be a dad, and that's all there is to it.'

'You have choices, you know,' said Henry quietly. He wasn't in favour of abortion in principle, but he felt it was really up to women to make their own decisions.

'No, I don't, Henry. You don't understand. Now Vince knows, all the options are closed. If I had an abortion he'd kill me. Or he'd try,' she added. She remembered suddenly the time when Vince had hit her. He'd been drunk, which she supposed made a difference, but he hadn't even said he was sorry. He hadn't *been* sorry.

Henry stroked her fingers absently as he listened to this. 'I know you love him. But we're all capable of loving the wrong people for the wrong reasons. Is he really the fellow you want to have children with?'

Felicity stared at Henry. She suddenly imagined how it would be if she did go ahead and have an abortion. She would lie, she would try to tell Vince that she'd had a miscarriage, but he would know. In the way that Vince always found things out, he would find out. And he wouldn't just be angry. He'd go berserk. Yes, of course he would take it out on her physically, if he had a mind to. She could see it all too clearly. It was something she had shut out of her mind until this moment, until she looked into Henry's kind, earnest face and listened to what he was saying. Vince was capable of anything. Yet she loved him.

'I don't know,' said Felicity sadly. 'I just know that there's nothing I can do about the situation.'

'No, well ... It's not up to me to offer you advice. I wouldn't know, anyhow. But if I can help in any way – I mean, well ... I am your friend. I think you know how –' He hesitated, filled with embarrassment, wishing he could say these things smoothly. '– Well, that I care about you.'

Felicity gazed into his anxious brown eyes and couldn't help smiling. Oh, God, if he kept on being so sweet and nice to her, she was going to be off again. 'Henry, you *are* a real friend. I know that. Thank you. I know I can always count on you to look out for me.'

'Look,' said Henry suddenly. 'I may not be a hard man, your Vince could probably turn me inside out without getting his hair messed, but there's a lot to me. A lot more than you think.' His brief, desperate outburst came to a halt. Felicity glanced away, embarrassed. 'What I mean is –' Henry faltered. 'Vince should care more. About what you want. Any man should. I would.'

'Yeah. Well, not everyone sees things your way, Henry. Unfortunately.' She looked at him again and it suddenly struck her that Henry was a lot of things she wished Vince would be. The things about Vince that she'd fallen for in the first place, his irrepressible optimism and carefree attitude, his masculine ego and his laddish irresponsibility, began to lose their charm when the realities of life pressed in. Still, that was the way things were. 'Come on,' she said, 'we'd better be getting back, see if everything's up and running yet.'

'Right,' sighed Henry. The idea of Felicity leaving in a few months left him feeling blank and depressed, and the realisation that he was powerless to prevent it made it even worse. He paid the bill and they left.

All the computers were blinking and humming away happily when Felicity and Henry got back to chambers. Leo was on his way out, putting on his overcoat as he came downstairs.

'I'm going to Tunbridge Wells for the afternoon to see Cameron,' he told Henry. 'Don't expect me back. If Donoghue calls about that vessel under arrest at Manila, put him through to Simon. He knows all about it.'

'Righto,' said Henry.

As he drove out to Tunbridge Wells, Leo pondered the phone call which he had received that morning from Alison, his solicitor. She had told him that now that she had lodged the application for residence and contact in respect of Oliver, the next step would be an interview with the court welfare officers and a visit by them to inspect the Belgravia flat. That in itself wasn't a problem. There was a third small bedroom, which had been set aside for Oliver ever since Leo had taken the flat, and which was already furnished with a cot, a chest of drawers and some toys and books. What exception could any welfare worker take to the Belgravia flat of a QC who was pulling in several hundred grand a year? He felt confident that the court would grant his application and Alison shared that confidence. But, then, Alison didn't know about Joshua. Perhaps she ought to, but he couldn't bring himself to say anything. It gnawed at Leo's conscience. There was enough stuff in the papers about lesbians adopting children and gays fostering them – why should it make any difference to the court welfare people if he was living with another man? But Leo knew in his heart that it mattered. Which was why he hadn't told Alison and why he was afraid that Rachel might, without even knowing about Joshua, try to use Leo's past affairs with men to affect the court's decision. He was going to have to make very sure that Joshua was well out of the way when the welfare officers came to call, that there was no evidence of his presence in the flat.

And what then? If his application were to be granted, if Oliver came to stay every other weekend? How would that affect things with Joshua? So far he hadn't even mentioned anything of this to Joshua. Leo decided he would have to cross that bridge if and when he came to it, explain to Joshua that every other weekend he would be devoting all his time to Oliver. He had no idea how Joshua would react to that. What Leo feared most was indifference. He had not dared to look too far ahead where his relationship with Joshua was concerned. A small voice at the back of his mind told him that it couldn't last, that a twenty-year-old was bound to get bored, to take things for granted, to want other things to stimulate him. Fears such as these, in the face of the helpless love he felt for Joshua, prevented him from worrying about the situation with Oliver in two or three years' time. There might be no Joshua. The dreadfulness of that thought made Leo's heart tighten in his chest. He would do anything to keep him. Anything. But the most important thing was to conceal that fact from Joshua, to preserve the balance.

Cameron lived in a large, comfortable house on the fringes of Tunbridge Wells, set in a couple of acres of well tended garden fringed with mature trees. As he got out of his car, Leo was struck by the peacefulness of the bright autumn afternoon, the soft light spilling across the lawns and flowerbeds and the neat gravel driveway. Hilary Renshaw, who was weeding the borders around the front of the house, put down her tools, took off her gardening gloves and came across the lawn to greet Leo. She was wearing a tweed skirt and a twinset, and as he kissed her, Leo felt himself touched with melancholy. There was something so essentially English about it all, about Hilary's gardening gloves and her trug, the house set in its pleasant grounds, which brought home to Leo the loss of a normality which he would never know again, and had tasted only briefly with Rachel and Oliver. Even though he was dying, Cameron was doing it in the tranquillity of a life harmlessly spent, with his wife and family at hand. What could he, Leo, hope for in the years ahead? This sudden rush of feeling, knitted in with his earlier thoughts about Joshua, left him momentarily confused and unhappy.

'Cameron has been so looking forward to your visit, Leo,' said Hilary, leading him into the house. 'You're his first visitor this week. He can't see too many people, you know – he gets tired very quickly.'

'How is he?'

Hilary Renshaw sighed. 'There's no pretending about these things. I can't say – oh, Cameron's fine, he's doing very well. Not the usual things you would say. The fact is, Leo, he's dying. But –' she looked up at him, her eyes bright, tranquil '– he's not in any pain, and he manages to read a great deal. So – that's how Cameron is.' She led the way upstairs to Cameron's room.

As he followed her, Leo realised that the prospect of seeing Cameron made him uneasy, almost afraid. How did you sit and talk with someone when that knowledge hung there between you – that one of you was dying? How could anyone chat away normally in the face of that?

But the fear fell away as he went into the room and saw Cameron lying in bed, propped up against his pillows. His skin had a yellowish tinge and his big body had shrunk horribly since Leo had last seen him, but it was still Cameron and he looked cheerful, even delighted, at the sight of Leo. He put down the book he was reading and put up a bony, slow hand for Leo to shake.

'Good to see you. How's everyone getting along at number five? Give me all the gossip.'

'Would you like some tea, Leo?' asked Hilary.

'Please,' said Leo.

Hilary brought them both tea and biscuits, and Leo gave Cameron an account of the goings-on in chambers, making it as amusing as he possibly could.

'And what about the place in New Square? Any further developments?'

Leo told him about the Estate Committee's offer of free carpeting and shelving. 'Which just about clinches it for Jeremy, of course. Anything to save money.' Leo sighed. 'You know how I feel about the whole thing.'

'You like the Temple. We all do. But we can't stay stuck in Caper Court for ever. We're bulging at the seams.'

Leo noticed that Cameron still spoke of everyone in chambers as 'we' and was touched. It made no sense to think of Cameron as dying. As long as he was alive, here and now, he was still part of things. And would be until the very last breath left his body. That was clearly how Cameron saw it and why he wanted to hear about the world of which he still felt so much a part.

'I know all that,' said Leo. 'But I don't think you quite understand –' He stopped, looked down at his teacup. How could he explain to Cameron that the Temple was the nearest thing to a home he had ever known? For the rest of the members of chambers, home was a comfortable house in Pangbourne, or Woking, or Henley-on-Thames, with wife and children, neighbours, dogs and horses. For Leo, it was the cloisters and passageways, the cobbled squares, the halls and libraries, the narrow wooden staircases, the hushed courtyards and green gardens of the Temple. That was his world, the only one where he felt truly happy. It seemed a small enough matter, moving chambers from one side of Fleet Street to the other, but it was, for him, far larger than that.

He could not begin to say anything of this to Cameron. So instead, he hesitated and went on, 'I suppose we'll have a chambers meeting soon enough, to vote on it.'

'I understand Roderick's standing in while I'm away,' remarked Cameron. Again Leo noticed how Cameron spoke as though this was a purely temporary matter.

'Yes. He seemed a natural choice for acting head.' Leo drank the rest of his tea. 'I suppose he'll become head of chambers in due course.' Then he realised what he had said and was appalled. 'Christ, Cameron – I'm sorry ...'

Cameron waved a dismissive hand and smiled. 'Don't be a fool. I don't go around pretending all the time. I know I'm never coming back. Life goes on.' He looked away for a few seconds, then glanced back searchingly at Leo. 'If I had any say in it, y'know – which, naturally, I won't – you would be my first choice as head of chambers.'

Leo was momentarily astonished. 'I can't say it's something I've ever thought about,' he replied candidly. It was true. Part of the illusion of youth. Heads of chambers were people of gravitas, well into middle age, serious, responsible types. He'd never quite seen himself that way.

'Look, it needs someone with a bit of personality and authority. Someone who's well known and respected around the Temple and the City. It's as much a matter of good PR as anything else.'

'Roderick's all those things. Besides, he's my senior. So's Stephen Bishop, by a couple of years.'

Cameron waved a dismissive hand. 'Stephen's a non-starter. Nice man, good lawyer, but he has no status. It needs to be someone who has the respect of the junior members of chambers. As for Roderick, it's just a matter of time before he's appointed to the High Court.' Cameron leaned back against his pillows and closed his eyes, breathing slowly and deeply for a few seconds. Leo, faintly alarmed, wondered if he was all right. After a moment Cameron opened his eyes, his gaze weary and dull. 'I'm sorry, Leo. I forget how tired this wretched illness makes me.'

'I'd better be going,' said Leo. 'You must need some rest.' He rose and put his teacup aside. Once again Cameron stretched out his hand and Leo took it.

'Good to see you,' said Cameron. 'Very good indeed. Give my best to everyone, won't you? And think about what I said. You're a natural. I'd like to think of number five in your capable hands.'

Leo gave a small, deprecating shrug. 'You think more of me than I do of myself, old man.' He hesitated, then added, 'I'll try to drop in again. Goodbye, for the present.'

'Goodbye,' said Cameron.

As he went slowly downstairs to take his leave of Hilary, Leo knew in his heart that it was the last time he would ever see him.

When he arrived back in Belgravia it was only five o'clock and Leo wondered, as he parked the car, whether he would find Joshua in. The melancholy afternoon had lowered his spirits, and the drive back through crowded late-afternoon traffic had left him with a headache. He longed for a drink and Joshua's company.

Even as he climbed the carpeted stair to the flat, Leo could hear music coming from the flat, and when he opened the door the sound blasted out at him. In the background he could hear people laughing and talking in the drawing-room. Slowly, thoughtfully, Leo closed the door and took off his overcoat, trying to work out how to play the situation. His first instinct was to go straight in and turn the music down, but he resisted this. He walked down the hallway to the drawing-room door and glanced casually in, taking in the scene of some five or six youths variously draped around the room in chairs or on the floor, and said 'Hi,' as casually as he could. Everyone in the room stopped talking instantly.

Leo went into the kitchen and stood there for a few seconds, trying to gauge his feelings. Above all, he had a headache. He didn't want the incessant thump of that music in his home. Secondly, he felt angry at the invasion, but beyond that he also felt marginalised, middle-aged and helpless. Afraid. Afraid of angering Joshua, of estranging him. He, Leo Davies, who had never been afraid of any human being in his life. He rubbed a weary hand across his face, and at that moment the kitchen door opened and Joshua came in. Leo stood where he was, his back to the door, waiting for the touch of Joshua's hand on his shoulders, conciliatory, kind. That at least would help.

But Joshua brushed past him and went to the fridge. 'You're back early,' he said, taking out some beers. Leo was instantly aware that Joshua had somehow taken it upon himself to feel the disapproval that Leo had not even hinted at. The messages were all so subtle, the currents wonderfully underplayed. And the result was that Joshua felt resentful. He could sense it in the very way that Joshua closed the fridge door.

Leo sighed. 'Are they staying very long, your friends?' He

tried hard to ask the question carelessly, putting no edge on it, but as soon as he'd spoken he knew that it made no difference. Joshua would hear whatever he wanted to hear.

'Why? Are they a problem?'

'No, Joshua. They're not a problem . . .' Leo went to fill the kettle, deciding that he wanted a cup of tea rather than a drink. He watched as the water rose over the element, wondering how to negotiate this situation. 'The music is a bit loud, however –' He turned, the kettle in his hand. Joshua had left the kitchen. Anger flared instantly in him and he went into the drawing-room, walked straight to the music centre, almost tripping over the trainered feet of one of the youths, and turned the volume right down. He turned and left the room without a word, aware of the silence, the sullen eyes following him.

In the kitchen Leo made his tea, then sat at the kitchen table, drinking it and waiting. He half expected the volume of the music to creep up again, almost hoped that the sound of conversation and laughter might resume. But after a few moments he heard feet in the hallway and the front door opening, then closing. Still he waited for Joshua to come in, anticipating the inevitable tirade of resentful anger and wondering how best to defuse it. But the silence in the flat continued unbroken and it dawned upon Leo that Joshua had left with his friends. The faint relief he felt at first was quickly swallowed up by bitterness. He had wanted nothing more than to be alone with Joshua this evening. Slowly he got up from the kitchen table and went into the drawing-room. A few crumpled beer cans were scattered by the sofa and the reedy sound of whatever music they had been listening to still floated at a low volume from the music centre. Leo switched it off. Then he walked to the window and stood looking down, anticipating the long, painful hours to be endured until Joshua chose to come back.

Anthony's day had been an unsettling one. He had felt

ambivalent about seeing Sarah after what had happened the night before. Was she going to start behaving knowingly, flirtatiously? But Sarah merely smiled and said a cool 'good morning' to him before the morning's Appeal Court proceedings began, and scarcely looked at him thereafter. She was a model of efficient note-taking and strict concentration. Anthony had been considering taking her to lunch and explaining that what had happened the previous evening couldn't be allowed to reoccur, should never have happened in the first place. But Sarah disappeared at lunch-time before Anthony had the chance to say a word and he went off to the nearest sandwich bar alone, vaguely disgruntled.

The pattern in the afternoon was much the same. After lunch they exchanged a few brief remarks about the case before the proceedings recommenced, but there was nothing in Sarah's behaviour that reflected the passion of last night. If anything, although her manner was friendly, there was a faint distance in it that almost suggested she wished it hadn't happened, and that it was best not contemplated. Anthony sat, scarcely appreciating the growing disfavour with which the three Appeal Court judges were receiving the opposing side's arguments, and revolved these matters in his mind. He had no notion that the little currents of thought were exactly those which Sarah had deliberately set in motion. He glanced at her a couple of times, but she was apparently absorbed in the proceedings. Then he caught a very faint drift of the scent which she wore and was suddenly, erotically, reminded of making love to her. He leaned slightly, imperceptibly, closer to catch the smell again and relive the recollection, but Sarah made a quick movement as she made a note of something and he leaned away. He tried to analyse what was going on. Her manner today suggested that what had happened last night was the furthest thing from her mind. Perhaps it was. It came to him in a sudden, humiliating flash of thought that perhaps she hadn't even enjoyed it – although she had appeared to. Perhaps she had found it all repetitive and boring, but had kept up an appearance of pleasure because she was the one who had started it. Anthony was well aware, from things which Sarah had said and done in the past, that she considered him rather staid and unadventurous. Had she been laughing at him?

Anthony glanced at her again, the way her skirt rode up when she crossed her black-stockinged legs, her blonde hair shining soft and silky even in the dreary light of the court room. He disliked the idea that she should have dismissed him from her mind. Okay, last night had been a mistake, and unfair on Camilla, but still . . . Most men would expect some sort of – what? Acknowledgement? A subtle hint of recognition that something intimate had happened? He sighed and scratched his head beneath his wig, aware of the confusion of his thoughts and feelings. Glancing at the clock, he saw that it was a quarter to five. Mrs Shepherd, counsel for the other side, was drawing to a close. Anthony stifled a yawn as she sat down. Lord Justice Hazel leaned forward a little to address the court.

'Thank you, Mrs Shepherd. As we have sat late to finish these proceedings, I don't intend to detain everybody. Our decision will be communicated through the usual channels. As I understand this is a matter of mild urgency, we shall endeavour to deliver our judgment within the month. Thank you.' The three Appeal Judges rose and withdrew.

'Well, are you optimistic?' asked Sarah, as they gathered up their papers.

'Fairly. If body language is anything to go by.' They walked together to the door of the court room. 'By the way –' Anthony stopped and Sarah turned to look at him.

'Yes?'

'About last night.' He paused as a group of people passed close by them, waiting till they were out of earshot, then realised he had no idea what to say next.

'What about last night? Is your conscience troubling you? Do you feel the need to confess all to Camilla?'

Stung by the lightly mocking tone of her voice, Anthony replied, 'Frankly, I wish it had never happened.' At this Sarah merely laughed and began to walk away down the stone-flagged corridor. Anthony caught up with her. 'I simply meant that it wasn't fair on Camilla.'

She stopped and turned to look at him. 'Anthony, you and I have never seen eye to eye, morally. As far as I'm concerned, last night had nothing to do with Camilla. I don't know why you're so puritanical about everything. All right, she may be your girlfriend, but she's not here at the moment. You and I had a thing once, it didn't work out, but there were certain things about it that were good. Sex, for instance.' She shrugged. 'I've got no hang-ups about enjoying it while she's away. It doesn't go any further than that.'

'Well, you're right about one thing – we do see things differently, morally. I can't abuse someone's trust like that.'

Sarah smiled her foxy smile. 'In case you hadn't noticed, Anthony darling, you just did.' She turned and walked away down the corridor, and Anthony did not follow.

Leo spent part of the evening negotiating with a dealer in Paris regarding the Anthony Caro sculpture which he hoped to acquire for the museum, then ate a scrappy supper of avocado and ham while he went through notes for a case conference the following morning. As he did these things he made a conscious effort not to think of Joshua. He could not, he told himself, weaken to the point where he allowed all his thoughts and energies to be consumed by Joshua. That Saturday when he had trailed round Earl's Court and then half of north London in a futile attempt to track him down had been a nadir. He would not plumb those depths again. Yet, even as he told himself this, his eyes strayed again to his watch, his ears attuned for the opening and closing of the door downstairs and Joshua's footsteps approaching the flat.

The sound of the telephone breaking the silence made him jump. It was Chay, ringing with news of an unexpected benefactor for the museum, an individual named Anthea Cole who had amassed a formidable collection of modern art since the early seventies and who, on reading of Chay's venture, had decided to donate it in its entirety to the Shoreditch museum.

'She's a Tate trustee and a friend of Andrew Stockeld,' said Chay. 'It's a hell of a collection. Warhol, Bill Woodrow, Cindy Sherman ... She says we can just have our pick of what we want. It's an unbelievable piece of luck.'

Leo agreed, then told Chay about the Anthony Caro sculpture.

'Fantastic! I had no idea we'd be this far ahead so soon. At this rate we'll be open by Christmas. I'm going to arrange for us to have a look at what she's got in a week or so. In fact, I've been doing some thinking. It seems to me that we need a special committee to handle the acquisitions. To be honest with you, I asked Andrew Stockeld, Tony and Graham Amery to become trustees to lend the whole venture a bit of public credibility. They don't exactly know a lot about art. I'm heavily involved in getting the building fitted out, so I wondered if you'd mind teaming up with Melissa and Derek Harvey to take responsibility for deciding on the acquisitions? Subject to majority approval, of course.'

'I don't mind,' said Leo. 'I'm rather enjoying spending other people's money.'

'Excellent. I'll speak to Mrs Cole and find out when we can look at the collection. Half of it hasn't seen the light of day for twenty-odd years, because she hadn't room to house it. I'll call you when I've sorted something out.'

'Fine,' said Leo.

He hung up, sat for a moment listening to the silence, then picked up his pen and drew his notes for tomorrow's conference towards him.

At one o'clock, Leo stopped waiting and listening. He knocked back the remainder of his whisky nightcap and prepared to go to bed. Just as he was about to set his radio alarm for the next morning, the phone rang. Leo picked it up. He could hear nothing for a few seconds, then Joshua's voice said, 'Leo?'

'Where are you?' asked Leo. He almost added that it was past one in the morning, but in Joshua's world, that probably didn't mean very much.

'I'm in Brixton.' He sounded embarrassed and a little forlorn

'Right. Brixton.' Leo rubbed a hand across his tired face.

'We came to a club and I got split up from my friends. They must have gone off earlier. Anyway, I've missed the last train and there aren't any cabs around. I've been waiting ages. Plus I've run out of money.'

'I'll come and get you,' said Leo. 'Where are you?'

A few minutes later he was crossing the cobbled mews to the garage, thinking that he knew now how the fathers of teenage children felt.

Joshua was waiting on the corner of the main road when Leo pulled up. He got in, shivering a little, grateful for the warmth of the car, the sight of Leo. He was just about to embark upon an apology when Leo's voice cut across his.

'How come you've run out of money? What happened to the two hundred I gave you at the weekend?' Leo's irritation at being dragged out late at night had eclipsed his earlier relief at hearing Joshua's voice.

'I've spent it,' said Joshua.

There then followed a sullen argument over the amount of money which Joshua spent and the question of whom Joshua had been with at the club after he had got split up from his friends, and this then escalated into a blazing row, Joshua accusing Leo of possessiveness and paranoia, and Leo reproaching Joshua with selfishness and indolence. The whole thing degenerated into an exchange of violent abuse. By the time he screeched the car into the mews and brought it to a halt, Leo was shaking with emotion. He had never

163

argued with anyone so violently in his life. Joshua got out of the car, slamming the door and storming off. Leo rested his forehead on the steering wheel, waiting for his emotions to calm. After a few moments he put the car in the garage and went up to the flat. The front door was open. Joshua was in the living-room, the stereo turned up loud, slumped in an armchair.

Leo crossed the room and turned the music off, then poured himself a large Scotch. It was half past two, but this had to be resolved. He sat down opposite Joshua and tried to talk reasonably, to coax him out of his sullenness. But the argument blew up again, and Joshua went to his room and began to hurl belongings about. Leo sat in the drawing-room, listening, numb. Without thinking, he poured himself another drink, then went to Joshua's room. Joshua seemed determined to maintain the emotional temperature, but Leo managed to talk him down to a calmer level. They talked for a long while, Leo trying to sort out Joshua's resentments, to find ways round the problems. There had to be a *modus vivendi*. The only alternative was for Joshua to go, and Leo could not bear that.

'I understand what you say about dependence. I see all that. Look, I promised to get you a car. That's the first thing to sort out. I will. We'll do that at the weekend.' Joshua was lying back on his bed, one arm behind his head, his temper worn out, frayed into exhaustion. Leo, sitting on the edge of the bed and nursing his whisky glass, put out a hand to stroke the soft skin at the base of Joshua's throat. 'I don't want you to get the idea that you're not free to do as you please. But you must understand . . . It's very difficult, when you love someone, to accept that there are things they want to do without you.'

Joshua moved restlessly. 'Don't start that again. You know how it is. I can't just stop seeing my friends because I live here with you. I do –' The hesitation in Joshua's voice was like a trickle of ice in Leo's heart. 'I do love you, sort of . . .

but it's not as though we can do everything together. I mean, I'm only twenty ...' He rubbed his eyes like a tired small boy, and Leo was infinitely touched, infinitely hurt by the gesture and by all that his words implied.

'All right,' said Leo. 'I wish you could get all your socialising done in the day, when I'm at work, but I suppose I have to accept that you need evenings when you can see your friends. Just don't invite whole gangs of them back here without asking me first.' There was a brief silence, then Leo added, 'The other thing we should sort out is to find you some work.' Joshua seemed about to say something, possibly in protest, but Leo went on, 'There's this museum in Shoreditch. I know that Chay Cross could find you plenty to do. I'd like you to get involved in something that we can share.'

For a while there was silence. Leo looked down at the remains of the whisky in his glass. He shouldn't be drinking so much. But the tensions of the last two hours had been extraordinary. He had never known so volatile a relationship in his life, nor one where he felt so utterly powerless, so much in need. He put the glass on the floor and stood up, weary.

Joshua stretched out a hand to touch Leo's. 'All right. I don't mind doing something at the museum.' He paused. 'About the car –'

Leo looked down at the boy. He looked tired, pale, his reddish-gold hair a mess, hollows beneath his eyes. A greedy, beautiful child who threatened to suck the life out of Leo.

'Come to bed,' said Leo, deciding he didn't care what time it was, 'and we'll talk about it.'

Chapter ten

As Leo's brain began to break clear of the fog of sleep and hangover, he realised that the phone by the side of the bed had been trilling for some minutes, the sound etching itself into part of a dream. Joshua lay next to him, still fast asleep. Leo stretched out a groggy hand for the phone and his half-open eyes caught sight of the bedside clock. He registered the time in disbelief. Half past ten. The shock brought him fully awake as he fumbled for the receiver, almost dropping it. He had come to bed without setting his alarm and at that very moment he was supposed to be halfway through a case conference with Fred Fenton, the owner of a Greek shipping company, the head of their legal department and a representative from the UK P&I Club. He cursed himself inwardly, appalled at what had happened, trying to straighten his mind as he hauled himself out of bed.

'Mr Davies?' It was Felicity's voice. 'I've been trying your mobile, but it's switched off. I didn't think you'd still be at home –'

'That's all right. Listen, are Fred and the clients still there?'

'Yes, they've been here half an hour. I said you'd probably been held up, but I think they're getting a bit impatient.'

'Okay, listen, I want you to give them my abject apologies – *abject*, understand? Say I've had a bit of a domestic crisis, that I'm on my way. Twenty-five minutes at the outside.' Twenty, thought Leo, if I skip the shower and shave in the car. He flung down the phone and went to the wardrobe to pull out the first clean shirt he could find.

As he sat at the traffic lights, shaving inexpertly with a

cordless shaver which he hated and rarely used except in emergencies, Leo glanced in the mirror at his own gaunt face and slightly bloodshot eyes, and thought how awful he looked. The lights changed to green and the traffic began to move forward. Leo chucked the shaver to one side and passed a hand over his chin. Not good, but passable. Not having had a chance to shower was the worst thing. Everything about him, including his mental processes, felt grubby and sloppy. At least he'd remembered to scoop the case notes from the table before he left. Thank God he'd had the long hours of the previous evening to go through them.

Leo reached chambers just before eleven, made his apologies, and the conference got under way, tinged throughout with the heavy disapproval of the Greek shipping magnate and his legal minions. Leo did not enjoy it. He felt entirely at a disadvantage, bereft of his usual full control and easy charm. At the end of it he was completely washed out.

'Felicity, have we got any paracetamol?' he asked, turning in relief from seeing Fred and the clients out.

'Yeah, here you go, Mr Davies.' Felicity fished a packet out from her drawer and handed two to Leo.

'Thanks,' said Leo as he took them. 'And thanks, too, for holding the fort earlier.'

Felicity watched Leo as he wandered off in search of a glass of water.

'I've never in my life known Mr Davies to get in late for a con,' remarked Henry. 'He's always bang on the dot. Did he say what held him up?'

'The line I gave them was that he'd had some domestic problem to sort out. Deepest apologies, all that stuff. But when I rang him at home, I could tell he'd just woken up. He must really have shifted himself, to get here as fast as he did.'

'Yeah, he looks a bit rough. That's really not like him, you know.' Henry shook his head. 'Not like him at all.'

'Listen, Henry –' Felicity began, then paused.

'What?'

'You know what we talked about the other day at lunch?'

'Mmm.' Henry put down the files he was going through and gave her his full attention.

'I think I've come to a decision. Can you come for a drink after work tonight?'

'Yes. Of course I can.'

'Good. Thanks.' Felicity gave him a grateful smile and Henry turned back to his files with a full heart, happy that she should confide in him.

Anthony met Leo coming out of the kitchen with a glass of water. 'Heavy night?' he asked with a grin. Leo did look rough, worse than he'd ever seen him.

Leo sighed and popped the first of his pills. At least he could be honest with Anthony. 'You could say. My domestic life is rather fraught at the moment.' He swallowed the second of the tablets. 'So much so that I nearly missed a con this morning. Mr Theodoracopoulis of Navitas Shipping Lines, no less.'

Anthony was surprised. He had never known Leo to be less than entirely punctilious when it came to work. Nothing got in its way. Certainly not anything which might be described as 'domestic', which Anthony took to be a euphemism for Leo's private life.

'I know what you're thinking,' added Leo, catching Anthony's expression. 'Not the best person in the world to stand up.'

'No. Bad luck.' Anthony felt slightly at a loss.

'Still, I've only got some paper to shuffle around this afternoon, then I can get off home for an early night.'

Anthony shook his head. 'You've forgotten about this evening, haven't you?'

'What? I haven't even looked at my diary. Don't tell me –' Leo suddenly remembered. 'Oh, Lord. Friday. Our drinks evening. We're entertaining half the City, aren't we?'

'It just looks that way from the guest list. A variety of senior partners of commercial and shipping firms, and other serious movers and shakers.' Anthony looked at Leo's face with a certain amount of pity.

'Oh, God, oh, God, oh, God . . .' Leo leaned against the wall and drank the remains of his water. 'Roderick's away, so I've got to be there, haven't I?' He sighed. 'Bloody Jeremy and his PR drives. Still, it can't be helped.'

'No, I suppose not. Anyway, I have to get going,' said Anthony, glancing at his watch. 'See you this evening, then?'

'Yes,' replied Leo wearily. 'This evening.'

The rest of the day seemed unpleasantly out of kilter to Leo. He was in no state to concentrate properly on his work and recollections of the ghastly scenes with Joshua of the night before kept resurfacing. He hadn't known anything like it since his long-ago student days and the turbulence of his relationship with Christopher, when the potent mixture of late-night drinking and emotional upset sometimes gave the waking day an air of unreality. That was the way he felt now. It was absurd, he told himself. Life should not be this way at forty-five. If there was to be no serenity in his relationship with Joshua, how was he going to cope? This emotional roller-coaster was going to wear him out. Yet to lose Joshua was unthinkable. He gave colour and shape to Leo's entire existence. Everything else, except Oliver, seemed an irrelevance. To love so desperately could be, he knew, ultimately dangerous and destructive. But what could he do?

He stared down at the papers in front of him, his fingers idly winding the faded length of red tape. It was a case involving the purchase of 20,000 tonnes of commercial propane of Saudi Arabian origin f.o.b. one safe port Yanbu. So what? What the hell had propane, commercial or otherwise, got to do with his life? Never had his work seemed so mundane, of so little importance.

The phone rang and Leo picked it up. 'Alison Draper for

you,' said Henry's voice. His solicitor. There must have been some developments concerning Oliver.

'Put her through, please, Henry.' He waited. 'Alison? Hello. What news?'

'We had the directions hearing a couple of days ago and now we've got a timetable. The court welfare officers will be interviewing Rachel in the next couple of weeks, then you. They'll want to look at the flat and speak to you generally about Oliver.'

'Fine.' Leo drew his diary towards him. 'Any dates?'

'The date they've suggested is October the twenty-sixth. That's a Friday, three weeks from now.'

Leo flicked through the pages of his diary. 'I'm in court that morning, but the afternoon looks all right. I can tell my clerk to keep it free.'

'Fine. Let's pencil that in for the moment. I can confirm it later. How's everything else going?'

'It's going,' said Leo. He hesitated, wondering whether he shouldn't take the opportunity now to mention Joshua. Then he remembered what Alison had said about Rachel and the interview with the welfare officers. Could Rachel really be so vindictive as to bring up his past, try to make it work against him? Forget vindictive, he thought. Knowing Rachel, she might just do it anyway and justify it from the very purest of motives. The well-being of Oliver. Just supposing she did say something – it could make Joshua's presence in the flat potentially fatal. He decided to say nothing. 'To be honest, I just want to get this whole business sorted out as quickly as possible.'

'I know. Just remember, the welfare people are still in the business of mediating. They'll be trying to find some compromise between you and Rachel, without the matter going to a final hearing.'

Leo gave a sigh. 'I'm afraid the word compromise does not feature in my ex-wife's vocabulary these days. Anyway, thanks for keeping me up to date, Alison. I'll wait to hear from you.'

He put down the phone and swivelled round in his chair, gazing out across Caper Court, watching figures moving to and fro behind the windows of the chambers opposite, the watery autumn sun casting shadows on the old sundial set in the wall. Was that true? Was there really no possibility of shifting Rachel from her position? He thought back to their last encounter, when he had brought Oliver home late from his day out. She obviously hated Oliver being away from her for even a few hours. No wonder she considered a whole weekend – every other weekend, in fact – to be out of the question.

Leo got up and strolled to the window, brooding on this. What about Charles? He was clearly fond of Oliver, but he'd already served his time with small children some years ago. The idea of having every other weekend to himself and Rachel probably appealed to him. Besides, he was in a position to see things in a more detached fashion than Rachel. Ever since he and Charles had first met, Leo had been able to read Charles quite easily and he had detected, at their last meeting, that he had some sympathy with Leo's position. Perhaps the best strategy would be to speak to Charles and see if he couldn't persuade Rachel to give in. It was worth a try. And he'd be able to get some idea of Rachel's present frame of mind, gauge the likelihood of her saying adverse things about him to the welfare officers. Letting his gaze wander around the upper floors of the buildings surrounding the courtyard, Leo made a mental note to call Charles.

He found himself staring at the windows of Desmond Broadhurst's flat on the top floor of the chambers adjoining 5 Caper Court. He hadn't seen the old boy out and about for a few weeks. Broadhurst was an old friend, a former High Court judge from the days when High Court judges were allowed to stagger on for as long as they liked, or until their mental processes entirely decayed. Desmond and his wife had lived in that flat for as long as Leo could remember. Lettice Broadhurst had been a familiar sight of an evening in the Temple, walking their two Cairn terriers in their little tartan coats. She had died last winter, well into her eighties, and now Desmond lived in the flat alone. In the old days, Leo had quite often visited him there for the odd glass of whisky, keeping him up to date on the goings-on in the Temple, listening to his endless fund of hoary legal anecdotes. The Broadhursts had even given him a bed now and again when, for whatever reason, he had found himself still in the Temple late at night. Desmond was one of the reasons why he had no wish to leave the Temple. Leo realised with a little pang of guilt that he had called on him only once since Lettice had died. He should visit him soon.

In fact, thought Leo suddenly, glancing at his watch, there was no time like the present. Hardly an ulterior motive, but it would be useful if he could take a quick shower at Desmond's flat, before the drinks evening. It was something he had done occasionally in the past.

Leo went back to his desk and tied up the papers, then slipped on his jacket, went downstairs and crossed Caper Court to Number 7. The little painted legend on the board beneath the lists of names of barristers still read: *Fourth floor, Lord and Lady Broadhurst.* He went up the narrow wooden stairs to Desmond's flat and rang the bell. After what seemed an age, Desmond opened the door, a very small, wrinkled old man of gnomelike appearance, wearing carpet slippers and neatly dressed in a rather old pin-stripe suit, minus the jacket. He seemed immensely pleased to see Leo and ushered him in. When Leo explained his predicament and asked if he could have a shower, Desmond readily agreed.

'Help yourself to towels from the linen cupboard. You know where they are. I'll fix us both a drink in the meantime.'

When Leo emerged, feeling distinctly fresher and better

prepared for the next few hours, Desmond handed him a tumbler filled with a large amount of Scotch. After last night, the last thing that Leo felt like was whisky. He took only a small sip and nursed the rest. For an hour or so he and Desmond talked, mainly about matters relating to the Inn, Desmond with one of the little terriers on his lap. Gradually Leo felt a familiar peace descending on him. To listen to old Desmond, almost a figure of antiquity, talking in his quiet, wavering voice of this and that, while the autumn dusk gathered in the courtyard outside and the shades of the Inn drew about them, was a perfect kind of happiness.

'But you know, Leo, I find I have less and less contact with people in the Inn these days. All so much younger ... Everything moves faster and the faces are not the same. Since Lettice died I have been thinking of moving away, perhaps to Lincoln. My daughter lives there, you know.' Desmond sipped his whisky. 'This place is far too large for one old man and two small dogs.'

Leo glanced around. 'How big is the flat?' He really had no idea of the extent of the place.

'Why, haven't you ever seen? It takes up the entire floor. Let me show you.' And he took Leo round, showing him the couple of rooms which he himself inhabited, then leading him up the corridor, opening doors into unlit, unused rooms as he went, some furnished with old, dark pieces of furniture, others empty, uncarpeted. 'Of course, when we first took the flat we did a lot of entertaining, and we used the large dining-room, and this as an extra drawing-room. That was a guest bedroom ...' He opened another door. 'I can't remember if we ever used this room. Jonathan stayed with us sometimes, so perhaps it was his bedroom. I really can't remember. No idea what became of the bed ...'

They went back into Desmond's snug living-room and Leo glanced at his watch. 'That drinks party I told you about will be starting in ten minutes or so. I'd better be getting back.'

Desmond shook his head as he showed Leo to the door.

'Touting for business. Never done in my day. And you say you have a website? Well, I don't know what one of those is, but I hope it's good for business.'

'I'm not sure that it is, actually,' replied Leo with a smile. 'Thanks for the shower. I'll pop in again shortly.'

'Don't leave it too long,' said Desmond, raising a hand in farewell salute. 'I may be off to Lincoln before Christmas.'

Felicity and Henry went to the Devereaux after work, and Henry bought himself a pint of bitter and Felicity a pineapple juice. They sat in a corner, well away from the busy bar.

'So,' said Henry, 'what's this decision you've come to?'

Felicity heaved a long, deep sigh. 'I think it's the right one. In fact, I know it is. It sort of came to me the other night, after I'd been talking to my mum on the phone.'

'Have you told her, then?'

'No, but I will. I'll have to.' She looked up at Henry. 'I'm going to have the baby.'

Henry nodded, looking down thoughtfully at his pint, giving no outward sign of the odd pleasure and relief he felt. He had been unaware of his true feelings in the matter until now.

'It was only the other night that I began to think about it properly. The baby, I mean. The fact that it *is* a baby. Right up until then I'd just been thinking of being pregnant in terms of myself, like it was an obstacle, just something which had happened that wasn't convenient. But it's a lot more than that.'

Henry nodded. 'It is.' There was silence for a moment, then he added, 'I'm very pleased, if you want to know.'

'Of course I want to know – that's why we're here, now. Because I care about what you think.'

'Do you?' To hide his smile, Henry took another drink of his beer.

174

Felicity nodded. 'Anyway, I'm glad you think that it's the right decision.'

'I do. What about the job? Does it mean you'll have to leave chambers for good?' Whatever he thought about the rights and wrongs of Felicity's situation, that prospect was a bleak one. On any terms, he wanted Felicity around.

Felicity ran her fingers through her curly hair and sighed. 'Maybe I can work something out. There's nannies and things. Child-minders. I dunno. It's mainly a question of talking Vince round. He's a bloody chauvinist, my Vince. Maybe my mum would help out. She lives in Camberwell, not far away. I'll have to see . . .' She stared blankly at her pineapple juice, then a slow smile crept over her face. 'Anyway, the best thing is that I can feel happy about it now. Once you've made a decision like that, there's no point in being miserable any more. I'm having a baby. I can start planning. The only thing that worries me is the money.'

'You get paid during maternity leave, don't you?'

'Yeah, only a certain amount. And what if I can't sort things out? What if I can't arrange for someone to look after the baby and I have to give up the job entirely? Vince won't get his knowledge for another couple of years, and we've got to live.'

'He'll just have to get some work.'

'Yeah, try telling Vince that.' She stared moodily at her drink. 'You know, I really don't like fruit juice. Go and get us a white wine, Henry, to cheer us up.'

Leo, his best smile fixed firmly in place, manoeuvred his way through the evening, chatting to solicitors, laughing at jokes, making a few, conducting himself with his usual easy, polished charm. But his head ached and the mask he was wearing felt paper thin. Perhaps it was just a result of the late night and his earlier hangover, but never had he taken such a jaundiced view of the members of his own profession. Everything seemed hollow, horribly false. He listened to

Jeremy Vine's loud, plummy tones as he held forth to John Maskell, senior partner of one of the City's wealthiest legal practices. How hard Jeremy tried, how much he wanted to impress people. And yet what a stereotype he was, a parody of all the worst portrayals of barristers on stage and screen. As Leo glanced around, it suddenly seemed to him that everyone in the room was a fake, trying too hard, eager to please, to wheel and deal, to impress and to dominate. As he stared morosely at his drink, it suddenly occurred to him that he could retire tomorrow, chuck up the place in Belgravia, go and live in Stanton with Joshua. He was fed up with the idea of moving out of the Temple, fed up with change, with Cameron dying, with everything. But would Joshua want to go and live in rural Oxfordshire? Leo had no idea of what Joshua wanted, or where the whole thing was going. He looked up, preparing to mingle and do his social bit once more, and his eye caught Sarah's as she came across the room towards him. She gave him a wink, and he couldn't help smiling and winking back. No matter what little schemes and games she played, at least, out of all of them, Sarah was real. She recognised all this for the bullshit it was.

'You let the mask slip for a moment there,' said Sarah as she came up to him. Leo was momentarily astonished by the accuracy with which she had read him. 'Won't do, you know. All these lovely solicitors whose business you're supposed to be hungry for. You should be chatting them up.'

'Just taking a brief reality break,' said Leo and knocked back the remains of his Scotch. He hadn't meant to drink anything this evening, but the few sips of the drink which Desmond had poured for him earlier had given him a taste for it. Besides, it helped to take the edge off his misanthropic mood. Anything was better than being sober with this lot. In fact, he felt as though he could do with another.

'I thought you loved all this,' said Sarah, widening her eyes.

'Normally I can tolerate it. But lately –' He stopped, staring down at his empty glass. It wasn't the time and place to start unburdening his soul. Especially not to Sarah. She had a habit of putting personal information to all kinds of mischievous uses. At that moment a couple of people came over and greeted him, and Leo resumed his affable smile and began to make polite conversation.

Sarah stayed with them for a moment or two, then excused herself and made her way over to where Anthony was chatting to Brian Potter, a solicitor in his late twenties.

As he introduced Sarah, Anthony couldn't help noticing the look of interest in Brian's eyes. Every man looked at Sarah that way. He watched as Brian and Sarah conversed, and wondered if her body language was deliberate, or whether he was imagining it. She was half turned away from him, chatting and laughing with Brian, in a way which made Anthony feel mildly excluded. The manner in which she flicked her blonde hair back over her shoulders only heightened the illusion. Anthony was aware that he felt annoyed and tried to fathom the source of it. It was, he realised, that he still felt helplessly attracted to her, that making love the other night had rekindled something which he didn't want to feel. It was the attempt to suppress it that made him feel irritated.

A few moments later Jeremy came over with John Maskell and, annexing Anthony and drawing him over, introduced him to Maskell in a manner so patronising that it infuriated Anthony. Still, he smiled pleasantly and began to make the kind of deferential small talk appropriate to an illustrious senior partner. Glancing back at Brian and Sarah after a few moments, he saw that they appeared to have become very friendly in a short space of time, and was aware that he felt dismayed and a little jealous. He nodded and smiled while pretending to listen to something Jeremy was saying, and tried to think of Camilla. She seemed a very long way away indeed.

*

By the time it was nine thirty, people were beginning to leave in various states of inebriation. In an attempt to conquer his melancholia, Leo had drunk several Scotches on an empty stomach. Anthony realised, joining the group of people to whom Leo was talking, that Leo was a little drunk and being mildly aggressive. Since everyone else in the group seemed pissed, that didn't matter, but Anthony was surprised at Leo. He was usually careful to keep himself in full control.

Anthony waited for a lull in the conversation and drew him to one side. 'Hadn't you better steady on, Leo?' he said mildly. 'You've put away quite a lot this evening.'

The fact that Anthony was right, that Leo knew he had drunk more than he should have, only made Leo ill-tempered. 'Thank you, Anthony. At my age, I think I know my limit.' A little unsteadily, Leo took another swig at his glass, only to discover it empty. With a sigh, he set it down.

'Look,' said Anthony, 'have you – I mean, are there any problems? Anything you want to talk about?'

Leo looked at Anthony's anxious brown eyes, and felt a wretched sense of regret and loss. Why could it not have been Anthony, first and always? Why had it not worked out that way? There would have been a rightness about that, a kind of harmony which, he knew now, was never going to emerge with Joshua. Still, things were as they were. He was in love with Joshua, trapped by the force of his own emotions. Anthony couldn't help, even if he wanted to.

Leo shook his head. 'Thanks for asking.' He glanced at his watch. 'I've had enough of this lot. And yes, you're right, I've had too much to drink. See you in the morning.' Abruptly he left Anthony's side.

Sarah crossed the room with Brian. 'We were just talking about going to have something to eat,' said Sarah. Her expression was bright, almost playful. 'Do you want to join us?'

Anthony glanced from her face to Brian's. Brian quickly

relaxed the expression of faint disappointment which had crossed his face and added, 'Yes, why don't you?'

'All right,' said Anthony. 'Good idea.' They left Caper Court together. As they reached Fleet Street, Anthony saw Leo hailing a cab. He paused on the corner and watched with a sudden feeling of concern as Leo climbed in and the cab drove away. He hoped, without conviction, that Leo was happy in this new love of his.

As he climbed out of the cab and paid, Leo glanced up at the long first-floor window of the flat and saw the glow of light behind the curtains. Gratefully he hurried up the stairs. Coming back in the taxi Leo had realised that he'd hardly eaten anything all day and had decided he would take Joshua out for a late dinner. It would be intimate, happy, and everything would be as perfect as it had been in the beginning.

'Joshua?' called Leo, closing the front door. There was music coming from the drawing-room, but the volume was low, and he could hear no other voices. 'Joshua?' he repeated, glancing into the drawing-room as he drew his scarf from round his neck. The room was empty.

'Yeah?' called Joshua, appearing in the doorway of his bedroom.

Leo smiled. He still had his headache, but that didn't matter any more. Joshua looked more desirable than he had ever done, dressed in some new black trousers which Leo hadn't seen before, and a red silk Armani shirt, his golden hair newly washed and tied back, the way Leo liked it. Leo wanted to take him out and show him off to the world.

'You must have read my mind. Come on, I'm going to take you out to dinner. To make up for not ringing to say I'd be late.' He stepped forward to embrace Joshua, but Joshua had turned back into his room, bending to pick up a towel from the floor.

'You've been drinking,' Joshua remarked as he straightened up, turning to glance at Leo. There was nothing in his eyes. 'You really stink of Scotch.'

Leo felt momentarily humiliated, exposed. He shrugged, trying to maintain a dignity he did not feel. 'We had a few drinks in chambers with some solicitors.' He watched as Joshua moved around the room, straightening things, hanging up garments. In the corner by the window stood Joshua's easel and on it a canvas begun two weeks before, which Joshua had not touched since. Leo's mind flickered over the possible ways in which Joshua filled his days, but nothing seemed to possess any clear definition. 'Come on,' Leo said, trying to sound buoyant, sober. 'I haven't eaten all day and I feel like taking you somewhere special, showing you off.' He stepped closer to Joshua. 'What about trying –'

But Joshua interrupted him. 'I'm not a possession, you know, Leo.' Then he sighed. 'I'm sorry. It was just the way you said it – "show you off". Like I'm a pet, or something.' He hugged Leo briefly, kissed his cheek, then turned away. 'I can't come to dinner, I'm afraid. I promised some friends I'd go clubbing with them.'

Leo said nothing for a moment. It was as though a gulf had suddenly opened up between them. The offhand manner in which Joshua spoke was the worst thing. 'Come on, you can see them any time,' said Leo, trying to match Joshua's tone with a casualness he did not feel. 'We could have a talk about the kind of car you want,' he added quickly. How he despised himself as he said this. Did the desperation show? Was it apparent in his words, his manner?

Joshua shrugged. 'I promised. Anyway, you look as though you could do with an early night. Besides, I'm not hungry. Don't wait up. I won't be back until breakfast.' He picked up his jacket from where it lay on the bed and put it on, brushing past Leo on his way to the front door. 'By the way – I could do with fifty quid, if you've got it.' His voice was candid, unashamed.

Leo reached slowly into his pocket and drew out his wallet. He held out a handful of twenties. 'Here, take a hundred.'

Leo listened to the sound of the front door closing. He no longer felt hungry. Instead he poured himself a drink, then crossed the room and looked down from the long window, watching as Joshua crossed the darkened square and disappeared from sight.

Anthony, Sarah and Brian went to a restaurant in Chancery Lane. Dinner was brief. Brian, realising he could make no headway with Sarah and conscious also of certain tensions between Anthony and Sarah, left early.

Anthony polished off the remains of his wine and glanced at the empty bottle. 'One bottle never goes far between three people. Let's have another.' He gestured to the waiter. There was a silence between them until the waiter returned with the wine. 'I don't think Brian was particularly pleased when you invited me to dinner. I rather got the idea that he hoped it would just be a cosy twosome, you and him.'

Sarah shrugged. 'I wanted you to come,' she said. 'Anyway,' she added, 'you could have said no if you'd wanted to.'

'I was hungry.'

'Hmm.' She smiled and sipped her wine, regarding him over the rim of her glass with cat-like eyes.

He returned her gaze. God, she was unfathomable, infuriating and very sexy. He was getting a hard-on just looking at her across the table. 'I'll get the bill,' he said.

She watched as he paid. How predictable he was. Like all men, he imagined he was in control of things, without having the first idea of the ways in which he was being manipulated. She reached for her handbag and pulled out some money, handing it to Anthony. 'My share.'

'Put it away,' said Anthony. 'I earn more than you do. Besides, Brian left more than he needed to.'

They left the restaurant and walked together down to Temple tube station. They spoke very little during the walk and Anthony was careful not to touch Sarah or even brush against her. Contradictory thoughts and emotions plagued him.

As they reached the platform, a Richmond train was coming in. Sarah sighed and sat down on one of the platform seats. 'I'm going to wait for a Wimbledon train. It's a drag having to change at Earl's Court.' She yawned and glanced at Anthony. 'You can get this one, can't you?'

It was true. Any of the trains would take him to South Kensington, whereas Sarah was going to Fulham. He hesitated, then sat down on a seat next to her. 'I'll wait with you,' said Anthony. 'It is rather late, after all. I don't mind changing.' They watched in silence as the tube doors closed with a hiss and the train pulled out.

A Wimbledon train came in a few minutes later, and Anthony and Sarah got on. At ten thirty on a Friday evening the carriage was crowded and they had to stand. Sarah glanced idly around, apparently reading the ads, while Anthony stood close to her, feeding his longing for her by breathing in her scent, catching warm, small currents of movement from her body as the train jolted along. He counted the stops. As the train came into Earl's Court station, people surged and jostled towards the doors. Anthony half turned, willing himself to get off with the rest of the crowd, framing his farewell in his mind. Sarah turned to look at him and smiled. There was something so provocative in her eyes that Anthony found he couldn't move. Behind him he heard people getting off the train, then the doors closed.

'You've missed your stop,' said Sarah.

Anthony said nothing. Sarah turned her head away, still smiling.

*

Later, in Sarah's bed, he lay back with his eyes closed, luxuriating in the sensation of her mouth caressing his stomach, her hands upon him. He lifted his head, put out a hand and wound it into her hair, pulling her up gently so that she turned and looked at him. 'This is just about sex. Nothing else. In two weeks' time –'

'In two weeks' time you'll have rediscovered your conscience, I know.' Sarah drew his fingers from her hair, then moved up to lie in the crook of his arm. 'But in the meantime, there's no reason why we can't do this every night.' She kissed him, softly at first, then moving her tongue against his.

For the briefest of moments Anthony wondered how it was that every good resolution formed in his mind could be eclipsed in an instant by physical instincts so overwhelming that they left his mental processes standing. Then Sarah began to move her hands downwards over his body and he wondered no more.

Chapter eleven

Joshua came back at ten the following morning. When he saw Leo, who was up and dressed but looking haggard from the night before, he felt instant remorse. Although he was a careless, selfish young man, he was fond of Leo. Without having any proper understanding of the depth of Leo's feelings and the torment which he put him through, Joshua knew he'd been behaving badly recently and he resolved to be kinder. The implementation of this resolution was made easier by the fact that Leo wanted to take him out that afternoon and buy him a car. This raised spirits on both sides and by the end of the day Joshua was the owner of a red Golf convertible.

As the days went by, Joshua seemed to become a little more settled. Despite the fact of his new car, he now seemed to spend much of his days painting and was always there in the evenings when Leo got home, always in a good mood, and there seemed to be no threat of tantrums or moodiness.

One evening after dinner, Joshua went to his room and brought three canvases into the drawing-room to show Leo. As he studied them, Leo was aware of Joshua's anxious eyes on his face. He was both delighted and touched that the boy should care so much what he thought of his work.

'They're good,' said Leo at last. 'A little derivative, but then – what isn't?' He glanced up and caught Joshua's disgruntled expression. 'Don't worry. It's because you're so young. You still have to find your own voice.' He looked back at the canvases. 'But you are definitely good. You could sell these. I could help you.'

'I'd like that,' said Joshua slowly. 'But it seems . . . I don't know . . . It just seems like if they're good enough to sell, I shouldn't need any help, should I?'

Leo laughed. 'You've yet to become wise in the ways of the world, Joshua. Take help where you can. I just meant that I might be able to get these hung in the right kind of place. If you keep working and produce a few more, we might be able to get you an exhibition of your own.'

Joshua's face seemed illuminated by the possibilities he saw for himself. 'You reckon?'

'I don't see why not. Just keep working.'

Despite the apparent harmony of the atmosphere, however, the knowledge of Joshua's volatility, and of his own dependence, were always at the back of Leo's mind. Alcohol helped to blanket his anxieties, and he found himself drinking more. Every day he promised himself that he would cut down soon, but his new sense of insecurity where Joshua was concerned had subtly altered his personality to a state of general dependence.

Some days later, Chay rang Leo in chambers. 'Are you busy tomorrow night?' he asked. 'I've arranged for us to have a look at Anthea Cole's collection – you, me, Derek and Melissa. It's in a secure warehouse in Whitechapel.'

Leo pulled his diary across his desk and glanced at it. 'Fine,' he said. The diary checking was purely force of habit. He rarely arranged to do anything in the evenings these days. Time with Joshua was too precious. He hadn't played squash in well over a month. 'Would you mind if I brought someone along with me?' asked Leo. 'A young friend of mine. He's an artist presently in need of useful employment. I thought perhaps you could find some work for him at the museum.'

'I'm sure there's something he could do,' said Chay. 'It's getting to the point where we'll have to start drawing up lists of people to invite to the opening, get the media primed. He could probably be useful there.'

When he had finished talking to Chay, Leo looked down at the pages of his diary. He had intended to call Rachel last week and arrange to see Oliver, but hadn't done so. Keeping steady the delicate equilibrium between himself and Joshua had occupied all his attention. But he must arrange something for this weekend. He picked up the phone, about to call Rachel at work, then remembered his earlier intention of calling Charles about the custody business. Damn. He should have done it the day that Alison had called him. The welfare people might already have been to interview Rachel, and God alone knew what she'd said. He would ring him now and hope Charles might agree to help him.

Charles was not surprised to hear from Leo. He had imagined that Leo might try to enlist his support in the matter of Oliver, that he might see their past friendship as a way through.

Leo came straight to the point. 'I want to try and compromise this thing, Charles. I don't want it to go as far as a hearing. I hoped that you might be able to persuade Rachel to see the sense of it – always assuming that you're sympathetic to my position.'

Charles picked up his mug of tea and wandered across the room with it. 'Well, yes, I am, as a matter of fact.' From the window where he stood he could see Oliver staggering around beneath the horse-chestnut tree at the end of the garden, picking up conkers and handing them to Margaret, the nanny, whose coat pockets bulged with them. 'But it's not as though we haven't discussed it, you know, Leo. I've tried to make her see the advantages, I've said that I think it would be in Oliver's best interests to live with you for a few days every fortnight, but Rachel's not exactly open to persuasion where Oliver's concerned, I'm afraid. She's something of a possessive mother.' Was he being disloyal to Rachel in saying that? Perhaps this conversation was itself a form of disloyalty.

Leo sighed. 'Don't I know it. It's just that there's no point

186

in my trying to persuade her any further. I hoped you might be able to make her see sense.'

'I'll do what I can, of course, but I don't think there's a lot of room for manoeuvre.'

'No, probably not. Has she mentioned anything about the welfare officers coming to visit?'

'Funny you should say that – they're coming round tomorrow morning. Rachel's taking the morning off work and I intend to make myself extremely scarce. People like that terrify me.'

'I'm just worried –' Leo stopped, faintly embarrassed.

There was a pause, then Charles spoke. 'What? That Rachel's going to make reference to your sexual proclivities and put you in a bad light?'

'I'm grateful to you for putting it so succinctly and with such candour, Charles,' murmured Leo. 'Yes, that does worry me.'

'Well, frankly, I take the view that that's simply not cricket. I'll do my best to see that she doesn't do anything like that. I'll say something beforehand. But I don't intend to be there when she talks to them. This is her affair – and yours.'

'All right. Thanks. By the way – I wondered if I might take Oliver out on Sunday?'

'Sunday's not a good day. My sister and her husband are coming round to Sunday lunch. They've got a three-year-old daughter and Oliver is meant to be her date, as it were. Why not Saturday? You could have him for the whole day, he could stay the night with you, and you could bring him back in time for lunch on Sunday.' This seemed to Charles a perfectly inspirational idea. It gave Leo more time on his own with the kid, and he and Rachel could have a whole Saturday – including Saturday evening – all to themselves.

Leo considered this. What about Joshua? The idea of taking Oliver back to the Belgravia flat was not a happy one. Then it occurred to him that he could take him to Stanton instead. Joshua hadn't shown any particular signs of restlessness recently, but it might do them both good if Joshua spent Saturday night in London with his friends. And Leo could concentrate on Oliver without having to worry about keeping Joshua entertained and happy. He seemed to have to do a lot of that, and he wasn't sure that he was always entirely successful.

'That's an excellent idea. I haven't had him to stay the night yet. I'm sure he'd be all right. What about Rachel?'

'Don't worry. I'll square it with her. Consider it settled. What time will you pick him up on Saturday?' Charles was already considering booking lunch for two in Bath, at a restaurant where they didn't have high-chairs.

'I'll be down first thing,' said Leo. 'Around ten.'

No sooner had he put the phone down than it rang. It was Felicity. 'I've had Ross Barclay from Sinclair's on the phone. He wanted to speak to you but you were engaged.'

'What did he want?'

'He was chasing up an advice he'd been expecting from you at the beginning of last week. His clients are getting pretty shirty, apparently.'

Oh, God – it suddenly came back to him. The shredded steel scrap contract. Barclay's clients had wanted an early advice. How could he have forgotten it? He turned and rummaged on the shelf where he kept those briefs still awaiting attention, the receiver held to his ear. He could see no sign of it. 'Don't worry,' he said to Felicity. 'I'm on to it. I'll ring Barclay back.'

He put down the phone and stood up to begin an exhaustive search of the room, aware of his heart beating hard with apprehension. Not because of the brief – he could do it in an afternoon once he found it – but because this was not the kind of thing he had ever done before. Ever. He was exact in his habits, scrupulous in delivering work punctually and so organised as to be incapable of losing track of any piece of work. Or so he had thought. When he had exhausted all the possibilities, he stood behind his desk, hands on hips, staring round the ordered room. Unlike the rooms of the other members of chambers, Leo's was immaculately tidy, everything in its place. There were no heaps of files or bundles of paper, nowhere for a brief to get lost, to slip down behind something else. He thought back. The last few weeks seemed a muddle, work had taken secondary importance to Joshua. Where once his days had been landmarked by hearings, conferences and trial dates, now they were lit by the thought and fact of Joshua, the evenings possessing luminosity, the workday a grey jumble of routine events. When had that brief come in? He fought to regain his grip of events, his former clarity of thought. He had once prided himself on being able to keep mental stock of every piece of work, without recourse to his diary. It had come in on a Friday, he remembered, and he'd taken it home with the rest of his papers, intending to look at it over the weekend. Then when he got home he would have put it – where? He had no idea. He had no recollection of taking it out of the car and putting it anywhere in the flat. He would just have to search for it when he got home. But for the moment, he would have to ring Ross Barclay and stall him. It was going to be a demeaning and embarrassing exercise, one he had never performed in his life before. Until the advent of Joshua, Leo had not been a man to make excuses or apologies. Things had changed.

When Rachel came home, she was pleased to find Oliver still up, dressed in his Postman Pat sleepsuit and sweet-smelling from his bath. He was sitting on the rug in front of the television, a bottle of juice in his mouth, watching a Thomas The Tank Engine video. Charles was lying on the sofa, his glasses on the end of his nose, leafing through the *Guardian*. Rachel picked Oliver up and kissed him, detaching the bottle from his mouth.

'Charles, you know I don't like him to have bottles of juice. It's bad for his teeth.'

Charles looked up. 'Sorry. Margaret must have given it to him after his bath.'

'Well, would you speak to her about it, please?'

'Me?'

'You see more of her than I do. And I hope he hasn't just been watching videos all evening. I'd rather he was played with. He needs stimulation.'

'He's not the only one,' said Charles, putting down the paper and holding out his arms. 'Come here. You come in grumbling after a long day, and it's not good for you. Or me.'

Rachel put Oliver back on the floor and sank on to the sofa into Charles's arms, grateful for his tolerance, his good humour. She did go on at the poor man. He kissed her, stroking her dark hair, slipping his hands inside the coat she was still wearing.

'Oh, my wheels and coupling rods,' murmured Charles, as he caressed her.

'What?' laughed Rachel.

'It's what Henry says. At least, I think it's Henry. Possibly Gordon. Which is the big green one? Oliver would know. Anyway, it's what one of the engines says when he gets excited. Rather a good expression, don't you think?'

Rachel smiled, combing her hair with her fingers. 'Actually, I think Thomas The Tank Engine is sexist. Annie and Clarabel as the stupid, put-upon female trucks, all that stuff.'

'In art as in life. Or possibly not.' Charles stood up. 'I must check my casserole, like a good house husband, while you, career woman, can spend some quality time with your offspring.' He was halfway across the room when he remembered. 'By the way, Leo rang today.'

Rachel, who had gone to kneel next to Oliver, looked up quickly. She should be able to receive this news casually, she knew, but it never quite worked that way. 'What did he want?'

'Mainly to arrange to see Oliver at the weekend. I told him Sunday was out, so he's going to take him out on Saturday. I suggested he should keep him overnight.'

'What?'

'You know, spend some more time with his dad, give us a break. We can have all Saturday to ourselves. Leo will bring him back in time for lunch on Sunday.'

Rachel rose. 'Charles, you really have no right to arrange these things behind my back. And why did Leo call *you*? He should have spoken to me about it.'

Charles shrugged, beginning to get a sinking feeling. He might have known that Rachel wouldn't be happy about this. 'I don't know.' He paused. 'Well, I do actually. The reason he called me was to see if I couldn't try to persuade you to settle this custody thing. It seems daft to –'

Rachel dismissed this with a wave of her hand. 'I'm not interested in that. You know how I feel about it and I'm not prepared to budge. Leo's the one who's being unreasonable.'

Charles sighed. 'Well, anyway, that's why he rang, and then he mentioned the weekend.'

'He should speak to me. I'm Oliver's mother. I'm really cross with him.'

'Why? What difference does it make which one of us he arranges it with?'

'The difference is that I wouldn't have suggested that Oliver stay the night with him. I know Leo, I know the kind of company he's probably keeping and it's one of the reasons why I'm not prepared to let him have custody of Oliver on the terms he wants.'

Charles began to feel annoyed. 'Look, I know Leo, too. Not in the same way as you do, but he's a decent bloke. Whatever his private life is like, I don't think he's going to expose Oliver to anything – anything –' He hesitated, searching for the appropriate word.

'Oh, don't you? Well, it's not a chance that I'm prepared to take.'

'Oh, come on, Rachel, be fair. For all you know, Leo could be leading the life of a monk. And anyway, he has Oliver's best interests at heart. He loves him. You know that. You only have to see the way he behaves when he's with him. I don't know why you hold it against him, all this stuff in his past. What's it got to do with the amount of time he's allowed to see his son?'

'Everything, Charles. It has everything to do with it.'

'Well, I think you're being unfair. And by the way, if you mention any of it to the welfare people when they come round, I think it'll be a pretty poor show.'

At this, Rachel said nothing. Charles had hit a raw nerve. She was still in two minds about what she would say to the welfare officers about Leo. Part of her knew that everything Charles said was probably right, but another small, fearful part told her that she must take every advantage she could, unfair or otherwise, when it came to fighting Leo's custody application. She was still undecided.

Charles tried to read the expression on her face. 'You're not going to do that, are you? Not when you don't even know how things are with him these days?'

'I'm not sure. But one thing I am sure about is that Leo's not going to have Oliver on Saturday night. It's the thin end of the wedge.' She crossed the room and picked up the telephone.

When the phone rang in the Belgravia flat, Joshua was sitting idly on the sofa, flicking through the TV channels with the remote, wondering whether he hadn't been a good boy for long enough and whether he might not go out that evening with Damien. He stretched out a hand for the phone, turning the sound on the TV to mute. 'Hello?' He flicked the remote. The MTV channel came up and Joshua watched as Bjork sang and pranced soundlessly. 'No, sorry. He's not in yet. He's usually back around seven. Can I take a message?'

Bjork faded out and gave way to Prefab Sprout. 'Yeah, okay. I'll tell him when he comes in.' Joshua put down the phone and pressed the mute button to bring the volume back up.

Leo came into the flat and set down his briefcase. He picked up the mail from the hall table then went into the drawing-room.

Joshua glanced up. 'Someone rang for you just a moment ago. Rachel. Said could you call her back when you got in.'

Leo said nothing for a moment, wondering what Rachel had made of Joshua answering the phone. Damn, if only he'd been just five minutes earlier. He chucked his coat on a chair and went to pour himself a drink. Then he noticed the brief from Sinclair's sticking out from a pile of magazines. They were mainly Joshua's. Why couldn't the boy ever tidy up? Still, at least he had the brief. He'd look at it first thing in the morning. Leo pulled it out and went to put it in his briefcase.

Rachel put the phone down and went into the kitchen, where Charles, in his Wallace and Gromit apron, was attending to supper. She leaned against the door frame, her arms folded.

When Charles glanced at her he saw that her expression was oddly cold and triumphant. 'What? Why are you looking like that?' he asked.

'I just rang Leo's flat. And guess who answered?'

'Who?'

'Some young man. He said that Leo wasn't home yet, but that he usually got back about seven. Doesn't that imply more than just a passing acquaintance? It's obvious that Leo's got someone living with him. He had affairs with men when he was married to me and I don't see why he should change. Now do you believe me when I say I'm right to be concerned about the kind of life Leo leads and how it might affect Oliver?'

Charles gave a heavy sigh and shoved his casserole back into the oven. 'I suppose so.'

The phone rang and Rachel turned and disappeared into

193

the living-room to answer it. Charles could hear cold, clipped snatches of Rachel's voice and knew she was talking to Leo. Bang went Saturday night. Charles closed the oven. He felt fed up with the whole thing. After this, he decided, he was going to keep well out of it. No more trying to act as helpful intermediary. From now on, this was up to Leo and Rachel.

Leo slammed down the phone in his bedroom, infuriated by his brief conversation with Rachel. The main thrust of it had been that he couldn't have Oliver on Saturday night, but she hadn't been able to resist referring to Joshua as 'the young man of yours who answered the phone'. And she had been angry. Very angry. There was no hope now that she wouldn't say something to the welfare people.

He went back through to the drawing-room and poured himself another Scotch. Joshua, sensing Leo's mood, switched off the television. After a few seconds' silence he asked, 'Something up?' He didn't particularly want to know what had been said between Leo and Rachel to make Leo so upset, but he felt he should be doing his caring, sharing bit.

'It was my ex-wife,' said Leo. 'Just something to do with Oliver.' He sipped his drink. 'By the way, I won't be here on Saturday. I'm going to take Oliver out for the day. I'll probably spend Saturday night at Stanton.'

That was cool, thought Joshua. A night of freedom. 'Okay.'

Leo glanced at his watch. 'That's another thing – sorry, I should have rung to tell you – we're going to look at the collection that this woman Cole is letting the museum have this evening. Chay's arranged it. I thought I would take you along, introduce you to some people, see about getting you some work.'

Thanks for asking, thought Joshua, feeling a prickle of resentment. He debated briefly whether he should say to Leo that he was going out, sorry and all that, but decided against it. After all, he had agreed to do some work for the museum if it could be arranged, and it would just piss Leo off if he didn't go along this evening. Wouldn't do to piss off the old golden goose. There was always Saturday night. He would have the flat all to himself. That was worth thinking about. Anyway, if this thing didn't go on for too long this evening, maybe he could still go out. Leo couldn't expect him to stay in all the time. So he nodded and said, 'Fine.' He glanced at the glass in Leo's hand. 'That's the second drink you've had in ten minutes. You'd better let me drive us there.'

Leo put down the glass and smiled. He liked Joshua's rare flashes of concern, reproof. They made Leo feel wanted, protected. Every token of a balanced domestic arrangement, where each looked out for the other and the interests of both, was precious to him. 'All right,' he said. 'You drive.' Whatever the outcome of the custody dispute, there was still the consolation of Joshua. After a couple of Scotches, it was easy to feel completely secure and happy about all that.

It took Leo and Joshua some time to find the warehouse in Whitechapel and, when they arrived, Chay, Melissa and Derek Harvey were already waiting in the office with Mrs Cole, a diminutive figure dressed in black, wearing a vast, swirling cape and a close-fitting hat pulled down over her head. She gave an imperious, unsmiling little nod as Chay introduced them.

'We have to sign in,' said Chay, and handed Leo and Joshua name tags. A member of staff led the little party down through the warehouse. The air was cool and still from the climate control, and vast numbers of works of art were ranged round the storage space. They passed through a series of bolted doors, opened by pass keys, and eventually reached the viewing area. It was completely bare and starkly lit, the size of a small gallery. At Mrs Cole's clipped request, two white-gloved technicians lifted the first of the exhibits on to foam blocks and the viewing began.

Even as some of the finest pieces of contemporary art passed before her eyes, Melissa found she could barely concentrate. She had been keyed up to Leo's arrival, but the sight of Joshua had entirely thrown her. Why should he have some young man in tow? She had hoped that she might be able to persuade Leo to go for a drink with her after the viewing was over, to find some way of spending time alone with him. She had thought about him on and off for the past few weeks, hoping to devise some scheme for seeing him, but without success. Tonight had seemed to present the best possibility, but this Joshua person was – well, what was he? Covertly Melissa studied him as he stood, arms folded, close to Leo, watching as the paintings were put on view, remaining silent while Chay, Leo and Derek Harvey mur-muringly discussed each one. He was very young, she saw, and quite beautiful. The realisation of what Joshua might be to Leo suddenly hit her and she felt a pang of sheer disbelief. This could not possibly be Leo's lover. Every sense had told her, on the night he had driven her home, that he was a woman's man, nothing else. Joshua suddenly turned his head in her direction, possibly sensing her scrutiny, and she looked away, picking up the thread of the conversation, trying to concentrate on the works before her and offer her own views.

When the viewing was over, the party went back to the office to sign out. On the way up, Chay chatted to Joshua. 'Leo tells me you're interested in helping out at the museum. Says you know a bit about the kind of work we'll be exhibiting.'

Joshua nodded. 'Yes, I'm not working at the moment. Well, only on my paintings.'

'Okay. We're a bit short-staffed on the publicity side. Why don't you give my assistant at the museum a ring in the morning? Her name's Sandra. Here's her number. Then you can go along at the beginning of next week and see what she can find for you to do.'

'Thanks.'

Chay scribbled down the number on a piece of paper and Joshua took it.

196

Chay turned to speak to Mrs Cole and Joshua went over to Leo. 'Listen, I've talked to Chay and he thinks he can find some work for me. I'm going along to the museum next week.'

'Good.' Leo smiled warmly at Joshua. As soon as this was over they could drive back to Belgravia and spend the evening together. Evenings were the happiest, most complete times in Leo's day, when he could be with Joshua, eat with him, talk to him and make love to him. At such times he wanted nothing more from life.

'The thing is,' went on Joshua, 'I did tell Damien I'd see him for a drink tonight. Would you mind if I went off now? I've done the stuff with Chay and I don't really know these other people.'

For a few seconds Leo said nothing. Why, when Joshua made such an innocent request, did he feel as though his insides had been washed down with ice? Because he didn't want Joshua to need other people, or other interests. He wanted to be everything to Joshua. That was the reality. Masking all that he felt, Leo gave a shrug and said, 'Sure. I can get a cab back. I'll probably go for a drink with the rest of them, anyway.'

Joshua's relief was palpable. 'Great. I won't be late. See you.' He wondered whether he should kiss Leo goodbye, but decided against it.

Leo watched from the office window as Joshua went out into the night, pulling his car keys and his mobile phone from his pocket, already in another world where Leo did not belong.

Melissa, as she conversed with Anthea Cole about the collection, registered this brief exchange between Leo and Joshua even as she talked. She couldn't hear what was said, but her heart rose as she saw Joshua leave. She had gathered from Chay that the boy wanted some work at the museum, so that was probably all it was. He was just a friend whom Leo was helping out, probably someone's son. After a few moments she went over to Leo. 'I don't know about you, but I'm positively in need of a drink.'

Something in Leo's system had already kicked into alcoholic gear; he needed a drink, too, more than one to blunt the keen edge of his feelings of insecurity. It was the same every time that Joshua went away. Would he ever come back and, if he did, in what altered frame of mind? Everything was so fragile ... Yes, a couple of hours in the pub was just what he needed. Presumably the others would be joining them. 'Good idea. What about everyone else?'

But it turned out that Chay had other arrangements, and Derek had a deadline to meet and a column to finish. Anthea Cole, bidding them all goodnight, was on her way out to her chauffeur-driven car.

Melissa raised her shoulders in a helpless shrug. 'Oh dear, just you and me.'

Leo could do nothing. He had already said yes and the fact was, he didn't much care. The alternative was to go home and brood alone, pretending to fill up the waiting hours with trivia until Joshua came back. At least Melissa was company, someone to get moderately drunk with. She clearly had a thing about him, too, and that went for something. His self-esteem was such these days that it could do with a bit of shoring up.

They went round the corner to a pub and ordered drinks. Leo ordered doubles. The pub, set in a part of Whitechapel which was an up-and-coming artists' colony, was lively and noisy. After the first couple of drinks, Leo found he had reached a state of pleasant detachment. Melissa was amusing company, the practised flirtatiousness with which she had previously behaved now replaced by a light, unthreatening, casual tone. The persona was that of a woman with no pretensions about herself, prepared to say what she felt and damn the consequences. She told Leo about the highs and lows of her job in a self-deprecating way, and she had a rich store of gossip about semi-celebrities, which Leo enjoyed. He found it all undemanding stuff, rather like reading a tabloid newspaper while moderately stoned. He told her a little about his marriage and about Oliver. He deliberately tried not to think about Joshua.

Melissa gauged Leo's behaviour carefully. She was surprised by the amount he was drinking. Still, maybe it helped. The conversation was moving along nicely enough, but what was needed was something to create a climate of intimacy and she knew just the thing. Argument. Nothing like a bit of provocation, a bit of friction, to bring people together. She recalled some remarks he had made driving back on the first evening they had met and decided to capitalise on those. She began to enthuse about a recent exhibition of work by Serrano which she had seen in New York, describing the works in graphic detail, knowing that the grotesqueries would prove too much for Leo.

After a few moments they did. 'You're not seriously suggesting that that kind of studied perversity deserves the name of art, are you?' Leo put down his glass, banging it slightly harder than he had intended, so that the whisky slopped a little on to the table. 'It's depressing – this urge to outrage, to do anything to win attention, no matter how grotesque and depraved. How many extreme gestures does an artist have to make in order to be noticed, for God's sake?'

'Good art has to be dangerous,' observed Melissa, pleased with the warmth of Leo's response.

'Rubbish,' replied Leo. 'What you're talking about is an addiction to extremity. It's a natural corollary to the obsession with novelty. This desperate search to say or do something new. It's the worst kind of cultural huckstering and it's bad for artists. You of all people must see that. What kind of message does a young, unestablished artist get from an exhibition like Serrano's? That the more promiscuous and offensive your art can be, the better its chance of succeeding. They're all scrambling for recognition in an atmosphere in which the last thing that matters is artistic excellence.' Leo drained his glass. He gestured to Melissa's. 'Another?'

She shook her head. 'You go ahead.'

Leo bought himself another drink and the argument continued. Melissa was careful to keep her end of it easy and good-humoured, and after a while it became jokey and idle, Leo's earlier vehemence dwindling away.

'I'm finding it very smoky in here,' remarked Melissa. 'I don't think I can take much more of it.'

'You're right,' replied Leo. 'It's getting too noisy as well. I think I'll have to be getting back.'

Outside, the cold October air struck Leo, filling his lungs and making him realise that he was rather drunk. He felt pleasantly high, in a way which he needed to feel more and more these days. The argument with Melissa had left him with a spurious feeling of camaraderie. He suddenly had no wish to be alone. The pub, the warmth of Melissa's company, all at once seemed like a haven of safety.

'Shall we share a cab?' Leo asked. 'We live in the same direction, as I recall.' He pulled up the collar of his coat, realising he was very slightly unsteady on his feet.

In the half-darkness of the street Melissa smiled. 'Why not?'

They spoke little on the way back, but as the cab drew up to Melissa's door, she said, 'Why don't you come in for coffee? It's not particularly late.'

Leo thought momentarily of the darkness of his own flat, the sense of emptiness that awaited him, the uncertainty of the hours until Joshua came home. He couldn't face it. Sometimes, without Joshua there, he hated the place. Besides, he was drunk, and it was better to be drunk in company than alone. He could have some coffee, chat for a while, then get a cab back. That way the hours until Joshua's return would be shortened. 'I'd like to. Thank you.' The words did not come out as coherently as he had intended.

On the pavement he stood fumbling for some moments in his pockets until he found money to pay the cab.

Leo didn't take much stock of his surroundings as he came into Melissa's flat, except to notice that the front door opened straight into a large, low-ceilinged living-room. Gratefully he shrugged off his overcoat and sat down heavily on a sofa, loosening his tie.

'Coffee, or another drink?' asked Melissa, moving around the room, switching on a series of lamps, so that the light was muted and intimate.

Leo stifled a yawn. What the hell . . . 'Scotch, if you have it. Just a small one, please.'

Melissa was careful to keep it small. She didn't want Leo passing out on her. That wouldn't exactly serve her purposes.

'Here.' She handed him his drink. Leo raised it to her in a sloppy toast and sipped. He was aware that she had put on some music, unfamiliar, but pleasantly gentle. He leaned back and closed his eyes.

'I'll be back in a moment,' said Melissa and left the room.

Leo lay back on the sofa, his thoughts ebbing and flowing tipsily, his mind now numb to any depressing thoughts. Roused out of something approaching a light sleep, he became aware that Melissa had sat down next to him on the sofa. He opened his eyes, shaking his head a little to clear it.

He stared at the glass in his hand. 'Perhaps coffee would have been a better idea,' he murmured, then turned to glance at Melissa. She was sitting quite close to him and he noticed that she had untied her blonde hair, so that it fell over her shoulders, and that she had changed into something loose and flowing, a robe of some kind. His mind was too slow to make much of these details, beyond observing them. He had begun to wonder, in a fumbling way, what time it was, when he felt a soft hand laid against his cheek. Melissa gently turned his face towards hers and he drunkenly registered her faint smile as she leaned over to kiss him. He closed his eyes and let her kiss him, because he felt too inert to do anything else, and because it was rather pleasant. Her touch felt kind and healing, and he did not think beyond this, but began to kiss her back in instinctive response. Melissa guided his hand inside her robe and he felt the touch of her naked breast with only vague surprise. Slowly he took his mouth away from hers, feeling as though he were standing outside himself, watching himself take up a role like an actor, and with both hands slid the robe from her shoulders. For a few seconds he gazed at her nakedness, at the low light burnishing her breasts, and ran thoughtful fingers over her skin, the hardness of her nipples, making her shiver with pleasure. Then he lifted his eyes to her face. Drunk as he was, he scrutinised her soft, hungry features with detachment. For Leo, sex had always been in a realm of its own, an art beyond emotion, the pleasures of the body removed to a level that was almost clinical. There was a practised sensuality about this situation, a calculation in the manner in which she offered herself to him, which he found irresistibly erotic. He lowered his mouth to one of her breasts, pushing her gently back against the cushions, aware that he was, in spite of the amount he had drunk, hard and aroused. It would be as dispassionate and enjoyable a sexual consummation as any other, performed with neither love nor meaning, but for the pure pleasure of the moment. He had known many such encounters in the past, with men and women, and at least this one might give him brief respite from his feelings of isolation and weakness.

Just as his hand traced its way down across her body, parting her legs, the delicacy of the moment suddenly erupted into a fever, on Melissa's part, of urgent, hungry action. She pushed herself up from the cushions and threw herself against Leo, moaning, pressing her mouth to his, her hands tearing at his shirt, then at the waistband of his trousers. The sudden disturbance of the equilibrium took Leo completely by surprise. As she thrust him back on to the sofa, her breath hot and panting, her limbs threshing against his, the absurdity of the whole thing suddenly welled up in his mind through the fog of whisky and he began to laugh. He couldn't help himself. He pulled his mouth away from her hectic, insistent kisses to let the laughter escape, feeling his body grow weak. Jesus Christ, thought Leo, I'm being raped. She was unfastening his shirt buttons with shaking fingers and, still laughing, he pushed her away, having to do it quite roughly in order to move her. Melissa, still gasping, sat back, strands of hair sticking to her damp face and lips, staring at Leo uncomprehendingly. Awareness of his helpless laughter dawned upon her. It had come to all this, she had been so close to having him, and he just lay there, holding his shirt together, giggling. She dragged her robe across her naked body, pushing her hair back from her face.

Leo put up a shaky, apologetic hand as if to ward her off. 'I'm sorry.' He managed to get the words out through bursts of unstoppable laughter, his chest heaving with the effort. He hadn't had a fit of hysterical laughter like this for ages. It must be the alcohol. He tried again to speak. 'Please. I'm sorry. I don't know what came over me.' This made him snigger again. If only she hadn't thrown herself on him like that. He glanced down and became aware that the glass of Scotch she had given him had got spilled in the mêlée, soaking one leg of his trousers and part of the sofa. This at least enabled him to stop laughing. 'Oh, God, I'm sorry. Your sofa. Here, I'll get a cloth.' Leo tried to rise, but failed. Melissa, mortified, was about to get up, but Leo managed clumsily to detain her, one hand on her wrist. 'I'm drunk, I'm afraid. This has been unforgivable. I'm truly, truly sorry.' The words slurred and he felt that he might start laughing again at any moment. All he wanted to do was get out of this place, before she raked her nails across his face and spat at him. It looked as though that was exactly what she felt like doing. He looked round hazily for his jacket and stood up.

'I'm sorry. I'd better be going.'

Melissa said nothing. She watched as Leo made his way to the door, listened as his unsteady footsteps died away on the stairs. Then she got up and closed the door and stood there for a long while, wondering what had gone wrong, until at last her humiliation found vent in a weeping, uncomprehending rage.

The flat was in darkness when Joshua let himself in around two o'clock. He saw a glow of light from Leo's room and put his head round the door, expecting to find Leo sitting up in bed and reading, waiting for him. But Leo's figure lay sprawled across the bed covers, still dressed. Even from the doorway Joshua could smell the reek of whisky. He wondered for a moment whether he should try to rouse Leo, help him out of his clothes and into bed. Then he decided he couldn't be bothered. Yawning, he closed the door and went off to his own room.

Chapter twelve

On Saturday Leo drove to Bath to pick up Oliver. He felt ill and dispirited. Since the morning two days ago when he had woken up fully dressed and hung-over, Leo's self-esteem seemed to have hit an all-time low. Joshua had said nothing, but no words were required to make Leo feel any more abject than he already did. He told himself he would have to cut down on his drinking. Incidents like the one with Melissa were too awful to risk repeating. He could hardly believe that it had happened. Loving Joshua as he did, how could he have gone near that woman?

As he drove, Leo contemplated the destructive changes which had occurred in his life. If only things could become more settled between himself and Joshua, if only he could be sure that his love was completely returned, that there was certainty and permanence in their relationship, then the insecurity might vanish, and he could run his life as smoothly and confidently as before. But Joshua was unread-able. He was there, he took Leo's gifts and favours, and he returned his affection in a remote fashion, but he said nothing of love. Neither in word nor gesture did he make Leo feel wanted and safe. The reverse was true of Leo. He tried hard – too hard, probably – to bind Joshua to him.

Charles's house came into view among the trees, and Leo turned into the driveway and parked his car.

'How are you?' asked Rachel, when she opened the door. 'You look rather tired.' Her concern was genuine. She had never seen Leo look so tired and careworn.

'Work is a little stressful,' he replied abruptly.

Rachel went to fetch Oliver's belongings and watched as Leo strapped Oliver into his car seat. They drove off and Rachel stood on the driveway gazing after them. She wondered if the boy whose voice she had heard on the phone had anything to do with Leo's altered appearance. She felt no guilt at what she had told the welfare officers who had called on Thursday – Oliver was too important – but she didn't like the idea of Leo suffering emotionally. Even if he had done much to deserve something of his own medicine.

Leo took Oliver back to Stanton, where Oliver played happily with his toys. Leo noticed that Oliver was picking up new words very quickly and that it was possible now to conduct a certain kind of baby dialogue. His heart expanded with love as he listened to the staccato questions Oliver asked about his toys, holding up items and seeking confirmation of their colour or purpose. He marvelled at the frankness of the child, his unquestioning warmth and trust. He began to wonder whether he wasn't mad to jeopardise his chances of custody by having Joshua live with him.

After lunch Leo chopped up some potatoes and apples, and he and Oliver took them down the road to a field where some horses grazed. As he stood by the fence, handing Oliver chunks of apple to feed to the horses, Leo felt a distinct lightening and strengthening of his spirits. Being with Oliver calmed him, gave him a new and clear perspective. He gazed out across the field. Perhaps it would be better if Joshua moved out altogether. Maybe then some balance could be achieved and some dignity restored to his life. Leaving aside the question of Oliver, possibly sharing his home and life so openly was doing the relationship no good. As things stood, Joshua in residence was Joshua in complete control. He had everything he wanted. He took Leo, his money, his flat, his possessions, his pictures, his food and his drink, entirely for granted. If those things became occasional rewards and treats, instead of a way of life, Joshua might become more grateful, more willing to earn Leo's time and affection.

Leo glanced down and smiled at Oliver, who was laughing in delight at the feeling of the horse's whiskery soft lips against his hand as he fed it. Did he have the strength of will to alter the *status quo*? The thought of the flat empty of Joshua, devoid of his presence and belongings, struck Leo with a desolate pang. And then there would be the uncertainty of arranging to meet him. Maybe everything which existed between them would change and ultimately die . . . He was afraid. He was so afraid. Yet something had to be done. He had to find a way to end the destructive pattern which had taken hold of his life.

In the flat in Belgravia Joshua was growing bored and restless. He'd been fairly offhand with Leo before Leo had left to go to Bath – he hated it when Leo drank too much – but now he wished Leo were still here. He quite liked weekends with Leo, who always found amusing new things to show him or places to take him. Okay, the pace was generally a bit slow, but there was something relaxing about that. It felt to Joshua like he was being looked after.

Now he idled around the flat, pausing to gaze down from the drawing-room window at the silent garden in the square, wondering how to fill the hours until Leo got back the next day. He thought of driving around a bit in his new car, but the idea of Saturday traffic in Chelsea was a turn-off. Besides, he had nowhere to go. He flung himself on the sofa and folded his hands behind his head, wondering what Leo was doing. He was with his kid, Oliver. Leo had said he was just a toddler. Kids were quite good at that age. They could talk a bit, kick a ball, you could do stuff with them. Leo was probably having fun. Joshua's thoughts wandered to the room which Leo had set aside for Oliver's visits. There hadn't been any so far. Would the kid be coming to stay at weekends? Joshua pondered this. That might be quite a laugh, really. He and Leo would have to do things with him. Joshua thought he might like that. When he was younger, he'd always wanted a little brother. God, thought Joshua, that way of thinking turned Leo into his father and that was definitely perverted. Would he be around long enough, anyway, to meet Leo's kid? There were days when everything seemed okay, when this place, all the things Leo bought him and did for him, seemed like all he wanted.

But there were other days – and quite a lot of them recently – when it felt like he was burning up inside, like he wanted to break free of the middle-aged domestic serenity and kindness, and just go out somewhere and breathe in rawer, dirtier air. It was practically a physical thing, like his brain and limbs were twitching against the order and harmony of Leo's world. Those were the times when he got out and saw his mates. That did some good. But then it was back to Belgravia and Leo, with all his love and need. Sometimes Joshua felt like it would stifle him, all that affection. And the fear that underlay it. Joshua was always aware of Leo's fear. No, this definitely wasn't a long-term thing, whatever Leo might want. Even the money, all the material things which had seemed really great at first, couldn't compensate for the kind of freedom he wanted. They made life better, but in a way they set him apart from his friends. Sure, they all liked the fact that he had a car and a bit of money now, but they could use those things against you, too, when they wanted to. He'd noticed the occasional snide remarks.

He was still lying on the sofa, thinking, when the phone rang. Joshua immediately assumed it would be Leo, missing him, wanting to talk to him, to hear his voice. He often rang up in the day just for that. Joshua didn't mind, even though he'd imagined at first that it was Leo's way of checking up on him, but he actually thought it was a bit soft.

But it wasn't Leo. It was Damien.

'Hi, mate. How's things?' asked Joshua.

'Slow. Not much happening. Wondered if you fancied a few beers tonight, see if we can find a party somewhere. Or does the old queen want you to stay in and watch telly with him?'

'Fuck off,' said Joshua amiably. 'He's not here. He's gone off to see his kid and he won't be back till tomorrow.'

'Yeah? Well, that's useful, now. Why don't I get some of the lads together, find some girls and come round to yours for a bit of a party?'

'No way,' said Joshua. 'Sorry.'

'Oh, come on, Josh. I'm not talking anything major. Just a few people. We'll look after everything. I mean, come on, it's Saturday night, your old bloke's out of town, what harm can it do?'

Joshua hesitated. He'd promised Leo that he would ask him before he had friends over, but he wasn't here to ask. Joshua didn't have his number in the country. Anyway, he lived here as much as Leo. That was one of the things that got him down about this set-up – everything was meant to be a partnership, but Leo made the rules. Sod the rules. If this was meant to be his home as much as Leo's, then surely he could have a few mates in. Like Damien said, they'd make sure it didn't get out of hand. 'Oh, all right, then. But not a lot, okay? And no slags.'

'Yeah, yeah, don't worry.'

'And bring your own booze. I don't want all Leo's stuff getting drunk.'

'Don't worry, man. We'll see you about nine.'

After Damien's phone call, Joshua didn't allow any regret or fear to touch his mind. He kept telling himself that he was entitled to have people round to the flat. It would be all right. Joshua would make sure they did no damage, didn't make too much noise or stay too late, and he would get up first thing and tidy the place up. When he got back tomorrow, Leo would be none the wiser.

The buzzer sounded a little after nine, and when he opened the door and saw his friends, plus assorted girls, crowding the landing outside Leo's flat, Joshua felt his first misgivings. He didn't want that old trout from downstairs complaining to Leo. 'Get in quick and shut up!' he hissed, then stood back to let everyone in. There couldn't be more than twenty people, but as they swarmed through Leo's flat, into the drawing-room and kitchen, they seemed like a lot more. Still, they were here now and he'd just have to hope for the best.

After he'd had a couple of drinks, Joshua's nervousness disappeared. Everyone seemed to be behaving themselves, more or less, and the music wasn't too loud. A girl came over from the other side of the room, a spliff in her hand. Joshua had noticed her earlier when they'd all come in. He'd seen her occasionally when he'd been out clubbing, but he'd never had the chance to speak to her. She was really, really nice, he thought, with black hair that was cut quite short, a funny, small face with eyes that made you look back at her a lot. She was using them now, smiling at him in a way that really turned him on. She handed him the spliff and he took it, inhaling the warm smoke and letting it pool deep inside him. He loved the taste of that first drag, the way it sort of warmed and softened your limbs, leaving a faint giddiness.

'I'm Katie,' she said.

'Hi. I'm –'

'You're Joshua. Of course I know who you are. Anyway, I've seen you around.'

He nodded. 'I've noticed you, too.' They gazed at one another for a moment.

'Well,' said Katie, 'since that's the formal introduction over . . .' Gently she put one hand to the back of his neck and drew him towards her. Joshua realised he hadn't kissed a girl in weeks. The sensuality of it was instantly and fiercely arousing. After a moment she drew away and he looked directly into her eyes. The pupils were black, huge. He could read the desire in them and knew that she could sense his own.

'If this is your place, you must have a bedroom somewhere,' said the girl softly. 'Why don't you show me it?'

The directness of this mildly astonished Joshua, just as her kiss had, but it wasn't an offer he was about to pass up. He glanced round at the others in the low light of the room. Everyone was occupied, talking, drinking, putting on music. Nothing looked like it would get out of hand. And if he didn't take the chance now, he never would, not with the life he and Leo lived. The thought of Leo crossed his mind in a small, guilty flash, but he dismissed it. This was just a one-off, another thing he need never know anything about. And he'd make sure he took precautions, so there would be nothing to worry about. He took Katie by the hand, giving her back the joint. 'Come on,' he said.

Leo returned Oliver punctually at half past seven, declined Charles's offer of a drink and headed back to Stanton. The house seemed bleak and empty without Oliver. Why the hell couldn't Rachel have been reasonable and let the boy stay, for once? It was going to happen sooner or later. The fire which Leo had lit earlier, and in front of which Oliver had played contentedly with his toys, had burned down to a dismal heap of faintly glowing ash, too far gone to rekindle. Leo tidied away the toys and wandered into the kitchen. There was very little food in the fridge, just the remains of lunch. Time with Oliver had been too precious to waste in a supermarket, and they had just picked up a few bits and pieces in the village. The thought of cheese and biscuits for supper wasn't exactly tempting. The full bottle of whisky in the cupboard, however, was. Leo took it out and stared at it. Did he really want to be here? Sunday morning with no papers, the prospect of waiting for the village shop to open so that he could buy something for lunch, eating it on his own, then heading back to London with the rest of the weekend traffic . . . It was depressing. How much pleasanter it would be to go back to Belgravia now, be with Joshua, and on Sunday morning wander out to some quiet London restaurant with Joshua and the Sunday papers, and while away the time over brunch and a glass or two of wine.

Abruptly Leo put the whisky back in the cupboard. He put his things together, switched off the lights, locked up, got into the car and headed back to London.

'Damien says you live here with some older bloke. What's that all about, then?' Katie lay on Joshua's bed and smiled up at him, stroking the side of his face.

Joshua reached across and picked the remains of a joint out of the ashtray. He drew on it deeply for a few seconds, then blew out the smoke and handed it to her. 'He's a friend. That's all. I don't really feel like talking about him.' Joshua lowered his head to kiss her.

From the other room came the insistent reverberation of music, and the sound of voices laughing and talking. In the kitchen there was a sudden crash, followed by laughter, and Joshua sat up. He buttoned up his shirt and went through to the kitchen, where a group of young men and women were variously sitting and standing around, drinking. The surfaces of the kitchen were littered with beer cans and bottles, and the air was heavy with cigarette smoke.

'Come on, Les,' said Joshua in a tone of mild reproach to one of his friends, who was crouched down trying to scoop the remains of one of Leo's glasses on to a newspaper. Joshua went to the cupboard and took out a dustpan and brush, and handed them to Les. 'Try not to make too much mess.' He glanced round. 'Who put that grill on?'

'I'm only making myself some toast,' said a girl, burrowing in Leo's fridge for some bread.

Joshua sighed and went back to his room, closing the door, hoping Leo's neighbours weren't going to complain. They hadn't said anything so far.

*

As soon as he came through the front door Leo heard the noise. It took a moment for him to realise that it was coming from his flat. He stood in the carpeted hallway, remembering the last time that this had happened. He tried to stay calm, but could feel his pulse rising along with a low tide of anger. It was his own fault, trusting Joshua to look after the place while he went away for a day. He fingered his keys, trying to work out how he should play this. For a weak, lunatic moment he even thought of going away quietly and letting them get on with it. Just at that moment the door of one of the ground-floor apartments opened and a woman stepped out. Mrs Gresham. Leo had encountered her only a few times; she was a severe old creature who drove an ancient Daimler and walked her Tibetan terrier every afternoon in the garden square. She looked surprised to see Leo standing there.

'Mr Davies – I was just on my way up to speak to you. Really, the noise . . .' She gestured with a thin hand in the direction of Leo's apartment.

'I know. I must apologise. I've been out, you see, and I had no idea. I have a young friend staying and I'm afraid he's let things get a little out of hand.'

'We have had the constant tramping of feet on the stair, the buzzer going, the door slamming . . . It's really not what we expect, Mr Davies, in a building of this character,' went on Mrs Gresham, warming to her theme.

'Yes, yes, I quite understand,' said Leo, turning in the direction of the stairs.

'I have to say,' Mrs Gresham called after him, 'that it's not the first time we have been disturbed in this way. And in the daytime as well. I have spoken to the other residents about it, you know.'

'Yes. I'm sorry. I'll go and do something about it immediately. I promise it won't happen again.'

Leo escaped upstairs, took a deep breath and went straight into the flat. It seemed to be full of people. They were

213

sprawled in the hallway, lounging in doorways, and spilling in and out of the kitchen. Stepping over legs, he glanced into the drawing-room, which was in semi-darkness. The noise that came from it rivalled that of a small night-club. How many friends had Joshua invited round? And the music – the pounding, insistent, senseless music. He accosted a passing black youth. 'Have you seen Joshua?'

The boy stared at Leo. 'No, man. He was around somewhere, but I ain't seen him for a while. Sorry.' He shrugged and went off, a large glass of Leo's best Polish vodka in his hand.

Leo scanned the faces in the kitchen, all of whom looked back curiously at the silver-haired middle-aged man in his well-cut casual clothes who had suddenly appeared. Joshua wasn't among them. On his way to Joshua's room, Leo stopped outside his own bedroom. He opened the door a little way and saw the figures on the bed, then closed it. He tried hard to suppress the anger he felt, but it was impossible. He had spoken to Joshua about this. He wanted to be told if any of Joshua's friends were coming round, he wanted the numbers kept down, and the music. Above all, they were to leave the liquor alone and to respect Leo's possessions. But as soon as Leo was out of sight, or so Joshua thought, he had broken each and every promise. He had apparently invited every friend and acquaintance he possessed to come round and do as they liked with Leo's flat, and had then left them all to get on with it.

About to open Joshua's door, Leo hesitated and knocked. What in the name of God am I doing? he wondered. But he couldn't help himself. Even under the present circumstances, good manners prevailed. There was no answer. Leo heard the sound of a girl's voice and knocked again, a little louder. After a few seconds Joshua came to the door, naked to the waist, fastening his trousers. He stared in shock at Leo. Leo glanced past Joshua at the girl on the bed and felt his heart

214

begin to thud thickly, unpleasantly. He tried to keep his voice from shaking as he spoke.

'I want you,' he said quietly to Joshua, who still stood immobile in the doorway, 'to get all of these people out of here within the next ten minutes.'

It was a few seconds before Joshua spoke. 'No,' he replied, recovering his self-possession. 'I don't see why I should.' His expression was sullen and defensive, but also wary.

Leo was lost for words. He thought something within him might explode. He closed his eyes briefly, willing himself to relax. 'Joshua,' he said, his tone deliberately even, 'I don't want them here. This is my flat, and they have no place here. And you won't either, if you don't get them out of here. They are your guests and you will ask them to leave.'

'No,' said Joshua again and tried to close the door on Leo. Leo pushed back and they struggled on either side for a few seconds before Leo's strength prevailed and the door flew back open, sending Joshua sprawling back against the bed. The girl sat there, staring, Joshua's shirt clutched against her nakedness. Leo, panting with the exertion, turned and went through to the drawing-room. He switched the lights on briskly, one after another, and crossed the room to turn the music off, stumbling over people on the floor. *Déjà vu*, thought Leo, as he flicked the music centre off. The noise of conversation died away instantly.

He addressed the silent room. 'Despite what Joshua may have told you to the contrary, you are not welcome here. The party is over. This is my flat, and I want you all to leave. Now. Please.'

A murmur rose, then some laughter. People got up from armchairs, sofas, the floor, and began to move towards the doorway. Leo was surprised at their docility. Following them to the doorway, Leo saw a couple emerge from his bedroom. He turned and went back into the drawing-room. Joshua appeared in the doorway, pulling on his shirt, watching as

215

his friends drifted out, not responding to their bantering remarks.

Leo surveyed the empty, smoky room. Someone had spilt a glass of red wine on the arm of a sofa and on the floor. The glass lay where it had fallen, unbroken on the carpet next to the stain. Among the glasses on the mantel, someone had left a cigarette to smoulder unnoticed, burning a long groove in the polished wood. Apart from the general mess of cans and a few plates on the floor, that appeared to be the extent of the damage. Nothing that he couldn't throw some money at and have put right within a few days. He felt his heart rate gradually drop, a sense of proportion return. There couldn't have been more than fifteen people in the room and another six or so in the kitchen. The illusion of a full-blown party, crowded with people, throbbing with deafening music, had been transitory. Still, the sense of violation was inescapable. The couple in his bedroom, the contents of his drinks cabinet plundered and, he guessed, a large amount of his wine gone. And Joshua's barefaced, amoral indifference, while he busied himself with that girl in his room. That was the worst part for Leo. To be faced with a truth which he had known and failed to acknowledge. That Joshua didn't care for him in the slightest, had absolutely no sense of morality, or fidelity. Yet he, in that stupid escapade with Melissa, was hardly any better. They were both wretched.

He glanced up, met Joshua's hostile gaze and felt, with something that was almost panic, a sudden, familiar urge to pacify, to apologise. Instead, he turned and picked up a bottle of Scotch, still three-quarters full, from the top of the drinks cabinet. He took out a glass and, with a wry smile, poured himself a couple of inches and drank it back, while Joshua watched.

'I'm surprised they left anything at all,' said Leo, with a calmness which he did not feel, as he set down the glass. He had no idea what Joshua would do or say next. After that futile little shoving match in Joshua's bedroom, he doubted if the worst had blown over. Still, he would try to defuse it, to play the situation down. The drink, after two days of abstinence, shot through his system like fire.

'You meant what you said in there, didn't you?' said Joshua, his voice shaking slightly – whether from anger or agitation Leo did not know. 'I don't have a place here, do I? Not really. This just proves it.' He swallowed and his voice grew harder 'You know what, Leo? I'm sick of all this. Moving in here was the biggest mistake of my life. All that crap about sharing everything. When it comes down to it, you want it all on your terms, don't you? You give me money, presents, fuck me when you want to, and think I should be happy. You must be mad.'

Leo said nothing. He watched as Joshua buttoned up his shirt, his eyes fastened on that heart-breaking hollow between Joshua's throat and breastbone. He tried to regain the lucidity of thought which had come to him earlier that day, when he had been feeding the horses with Oliver. Feeling in need of another drink, he poured more whisky into the glass. If he was going to ask Joshua to go, this was the moment.

But he couldn't do it. He could not stand there, looking at Joshua, and ask him to leave. He might never see him again. In the end, he was too much in love for anything but another compromise. His need of Joshua was so utter that he couldn't face losing him. Patiently he began his familiar litany. 'Look, it's a question of trust, Joshua. I want this to be your home, as much as mine, but in the end there have to be ground rules. We've talked –'

'Oh, forget it, Leo.' Joshua's voice sounded suddenly weary. It was this which shocked Leo most. The complete lack of antagonism, the sudden, unmistakable sound of someone who didn't care any more. 'I don't need this bullshit. I don't need the car, the clothes, the money or you.' He paused, looking directly at Leo, and said in a voice that was almost light with relief, 'I'm off.'

Leo stood motionless as Joshua left the room. He waited for his feet to move, to feel himself cross the room, go after him. But he didn't. A few moments later Joshua returned, carrying a canvas holdall hastily stuffed with a few belongings. He set it down in the doorway as he pulled on his jacket, the one Leo had bought him just a few weeks earlier. He fished in the pocket, pulled out his car keys and the keys to Leo's flat, and chucked them down on a side table. 'Tell Chay I'm sorry about the job. I'll see you around.'

It was done. It all happened so fast, so easily. There was nothing about Joshua's behaviour to suggest that he wanted Leo to remonstrate with him, or plead with him to stay. Perhaps if there had been, Leo would have said or done something. As it was, he just stood with his glass of whisky in his hand and let Joshua go. Heard the door close. Then the door downstairs. The light sound of Joshua's footsteps in the street. In his mind's eye, Leo could see him crossing at the corner, heading – where? Sloane Square tube, probably. Maybe to find a taxi. And then? Oh, Joshua had lots of friends. Girls as well as boys. Leo did the only thing he could think of to thaw the numbing pain which was already closing coldly round his heart. He picked up the bottle of Scotch and poured some more, wondering how he was going to live now.

'Hullo,' said Anthony, bumping into David in the doorway to the clerks' room. 'I'm just off to tea. Coming?'

'Yes, in a minute. Let me get rid of these.' David dropped some papers in a tray and joined Anthony. They crossed Caper Court together. The sky above the Temple was mild and blue, and the distant roar of the Fleet Street traffic competed only slightly with the tapping drift of leaves as they fell, one by one, from the autumn trees. Anthony breathed in the chilly air, conscious of how well he felt, how perfect everything seemed to be. He had just won an important case, his bank balance was looking healthy enough for him to think about buying a new car, and Camilla would be back this evening. The only flaw was his regret and guilt over Sarah. Regret? Well, that wouldn't be quite true. He had gone into it with his eyes wide open. Sarah had her own wonderful way of putting things, of making you feel that it was all just harmless fun. It was a seductive line of thinking – that if no one knew, then no one would be hurt. Only it didn't quite work out that way. He had slept with someone else while Camilla was away and however much he might tell himself that it had been purely physical, that there had been no element of emotional betrayal, the fact was that he had deceived the person he was supposed to be in love with. Quite deliberately and calculatingly. Sarah had told him that their brief fling would have no consequences, and he had gone along with that. But everything had consequences. He knew that. He was afraid of what they might be, in this case. In his heart he knew that damage had been done, even if Camilla never found out, and was fearful of what it might turn out to be.

David's voice interrupted his train of thought. 'Sorry, David. I was miles away. What did you say?'

'I said, Roderick told me this morning that the chambers in New Square have fallen through. Some planning set have got them. I believe a few strings were pulled with the Estates Committee.'

'Really? I thought it was all done and dusted. Mind you, I'm not exactly sorry,' remarked Anthony, as they went into the warmth of the common room. 'I'd rather stay in the Temple. Still, I don't suppose it ends there. We have to expand, so it's just a question of finding somewhere else. No doubt Jeremy's already on the case.'

Anthony noticed Leo sitting in a corner by himself. He had a newspaper on his lap, but was staring distractedly out of the window, a cup of untasted tea at his elbow. Anthony and David bought their tea and joined him.

'You're looking rather gloomy, old man,' said David, as he

sat down. 'Practice collapsing?' It was a joke which David always made to Leo, whose reputation and considerable earnings had been a source of envy to David ever since he had joined 5 Caper Court ten years ago.

'I shouldn't wonder,' replied Leo. Although he smiled, Anthony saw that the expression in Leo's eyes was hard and bitter, as though a nerve had been touched. He had noticed that Leo looked pretty awful these days. He seemed dog-tired, and his manner had lost its usual polish and sharpness. He even needed a haircut. Anthony longed to be able to help, to reach out with his mind and divine the source of Leo's problems but, in the swings of intimacy and remoteness which characterised their relationship, Anthony knew that Leo was, at this moment, unreachable, a million miles away.

Still, he made an effort and said, 'David just told me something that'll cheer you up – unless you've already heard.'

The pause before Leo registered this and responded was slightly too long. 'What's that?'

'We won't be moving to New Square after all. Some other set has taken up the lease.'

A little life came into Leo's face. He drank some of his tea. 'Really? Christ, it's about time I heard some good news.' That was something, at any rate. His life might be falling apart, but at least it could happen in the peace and security of the one home he had ever known. The brief flash of animation died away in his heart. He turned away and fastened his gaze on the plane trees lining the end of King's Bench Walk, and let his thoughts drift painfully back to Joshua, heedless of the conversation around him.

Five minutes later the arrival of Michael Gibbon broke Leo's maudlin train of thought. 'Leo,' he said in surprise, setting down his tea, 'I thought you had a summons before the Master at three?'

Leo glanced at his watch. It was five past. He rose hastily, the pages of his paper spilling to the floor. 'Bloody Felicity,' he muttered. 'She didn't say anything. Thanks,' he added to Michael, and went out abruptly.

'I don't know why he blames Felicity,' remarked Michael as he sat down. 'He mentioned it to me himself earlier this morning.'

'Leo's seemed a bit off lately, if you ask me,' said David. 'Not his usual self. Perhaps it's this divorce business. I hear he's having trouble over custody of his son.'

'Yes, it's all rather sad,' agreed Michael. 'Not that I ever thought of Leo as the marrying kind, but she seemed a very nice girl. What was her name?'

'Rachel,' said Anthony.

'Rachel, that's right.' Michael sipped his tea, then said, 'Tell me, David, what's the news on that unseaworthiness case of yours? I think I may have a very similar point coming up . . .'

Anthony let his thoughts wander as Michael and David conversed. Whatever Leo's problems were, Anthony didn't think they were to do with Rachel and Oliver. Though he might be wrong. He reflected briefly on Rachel, remembering, almost with bemusement, how much in love with her he had once been. That pale, slender beauty, her hesitancy, the haunted expression in her dark eyes. A complete contrast to Camilla. She was warm and immediate, hiding nothing. Anthony thought of her with affection and, as he did so, experienced again that sensation of slight fear. It happened every time he thought about her and it wasn't very pleasant. Perhaps it was just guilt. Okay, he shouldn't have done what he did, but Sarah wasn't going to say anything. When he saw Camilla tonight, he could put the whole damned thing behind him and forget about it.

'Mr Davies – a word, if I may.' Mr Justice Gardner's voice was courteous, but distinctly cold. Leo stayed where he was, while the other parties to the hearing filed out of the judge's chambers. The door closed.

'Mr Davies, you are well aware of the necessity for punctuality in these matters. The lists are very full and we must avoid time-wasting at all costs. I must say, I was most surprised to find you late for the summons this afternoon. It is, if you will permit me to say so, out of character.' He paused, then added, 'As was the distinctly offhand manner in which you offered your apologies at the start of the hearing. I expect a higher standard from members of the Bar, particularly from Her Majesty's counsel.'

'Please accept my apologies once again, my Lord,' said Leo stiffly. 'Particularly if I failed to express them with sufficient conviction earlier.'

Mr Justice Gardner stiffened slightly, but he decided to ignore any implicit insolence in Leo's reply. Like most of the members of the High Court bench, he had a high regard for Leo and it vexed him that he should have to have any occasion to reprimand him. There was something incongruous about it. But he had undoubtedly arrived fifteen minutes late without any sufficient explanation, the curtest of apologies, and everyone had been inconvenienced. It could hardly go unremarked. 'Very well. I trust you won't let it happen in future.'

Accepting this as his dismissal, Leo left the room. Some part of him knew that he should care more about this dent to his pride, but it seemed these days as though all his senses were muffled by the weight of unhappiness which lay about him. Only three days since Joshua had gone and it seemed like an eternity of hell. He could think about nothing else, cursing himself for letting him go, reliving over and over those brief minutes in which he had let Joshua walk out of his life for ever, without even telling him that he loved him.

He walked slowly back to chambers, and when he reached Caper Court he paused to lean against the stone wall of the archway, suddenly aware of the loveliness of the day. But even its beauty, the light on the soft stone walls, the colour of the trees in their last leaf, wearied and sickened him. He felt tired, both in his body and spirit. He was sleeping badly and drinking too much. Each day he promised himself that he wouldn't drink that evening, but each evening it was the same. What else was there? He didn't have the heart to get in touch with friends, or try to get out. Whatever dismal kind of life he had been leading before Joshua, it was nothing compared with this wretchedness.

Well, he would have to make an effort. He was badly out of condition. He would start by having a game of squash this evening, possibly with Anthony, if he wasn't busy. They hadn't spoken much for several weeks. Leo had been too bound up in Joshua to make room for anyone else. That was what love did to you.

Going into chambers he met Jeremy Vine coming out of the clerks' room in his shirt-sleeves.

'I suppose you heard about the New Square place falling through, did you?' said Jeremy. He was cross, and when Jeremy was cross, he spoke even more loudly and moved even more aggressively than usual.

'I did, as a matter of fact,' said Leo. 'What a pity.'

'Hm. Don't pretend you're not pleased.'

'I can't say I really relished the thought of Lincoln's Inn, Jeremy. What have you got lined up for us next? Gray's Inn? I hear the rents are nice and low.'

'Don't tempt me,' said Jeremy. 'I might just think about it.' He gave Leo a searching look. 'Am I right in thinking you're growing your hair long, Leo? Must be something to do with middle-aged insecurity. Doesn't suit you.' Smirking, he turned and bounded heavily upstairs.

'Mr Davies?' Felicity called over to him.

'Yes?'

'I've got a call for you. Miss Draper.'

Leo glanced across to the waiting room and saw that it was empty. 'I'll take it down here,' he said.

Leo closed the door of the waiting room and picked up the phone. 'Alison?'

'Hello, Leo. Just to let you know that the court welfare officers have confirmed the Friday appointment. Is that still convenient? They'll come round about half-two – it should only take an hour or so.'

'Fine,' said Leo. Well, he thought as he put down the phone, now that Joshua was gone there was nothing to indicate to the welfare officers that he did not lead the most blameless of lives. Joshua's room remained just as it had been on the night he had walked out, a token of Leo's faint hope that he might still come back, but the few possessions he had left behind could easily be tidied away.

Leo sighed, then went upstairs to Anthony's room, knocked, and put his head round the door. 'Wondered if you were free for a game of squash this evening?'

'Can't, I'm afraid. I'm seeing Camilla.' Anthony was genuinely sorry to have to say no. He was worried about Leo and would have welcomed the chance to have a talk with him. 'Maybe tomorrow night?'

'I don't know. I'll have to see. Maybe.' Leo closed the door and went to his room. With an effort of will, he sank himself into some work. He sat there, combing through books, writing up notes for an opinion, while dusk and eventually evening fell over Caper Court. At last he looked up from the pool of light on his desk, gazing into the shadows at the far side of the room, and realised that he had been working for several hours in a kind of oblivion, free from pain or emotion. The building was silent. Everyone had long since gone. Leo stood up and stretched, feeling the anaesthetic of drudgery wear off, and the familiar misery settle once more on his mind and heart. He walked to the window and looked out over Caper Court. All the windows in the buildings were in darkness, except for his own, and a faint light which glowed behind Desmond Broadhurst's curtains. Poor old boy. He was due another visit. But Leo had not the heart for company. He had nothing to say to the world. Perhaps it was a good thing that Anthony was seeing Camilla this evening.

He could get on with his life without having to share Leo's troubles. It seemed as though the closeness which had once existed between them had vanished like so much mist. Another ache crept into Leo's heart at this thought.

Glancing at his watch, Leo saw that it was past nine. He collected his papers, put on his jacket, switched off the light and left the building. He was so tired that he drove home almost mindlessly, hardly hearing the music which he had put on, not even thinking, consciously, of Joshua.

He parked his car and walked round from the mews, slowing his footsteps as the windows of his flat came into view. He glanced up, letting his heart tighten in wild and faint anticipation. Not really anticipation at all. Just a kind of hopeless fantasy. One in which the long windows stood not in uncurtained darkness, but were lit from within, the curtains drawn. In this fantasy it was only five days ago, and he still had time and the chance to make everything right with Joshua. The fantasy died before it had even begun.

The flat was silent. Leo put on a few lights and poured himself a drink, careful to make it a small one. Then he went into the kitchen and stared listlessly at the contents of the fridge. He made himself a ham sandwich and took it, with his drink, into his study. There he switched on his computer, and took off his jacket and loosened his tie as he waited for the computer to boot into life. Without sitting down, still chewing his sandwich, he went into his e-mail. Five new messages, more than usual. He clicked on the first one and watched as it filled the screen. He read the first words listlessly, without really comprehending them. Then the content of what he was reading dawned on him. He swallowed, put down his sandwich and read it again from the beginning. It was invective, as obscene and puerile as might possibly be imagined. It went on, an outpouring of filth, for several sentences. Shock made his flesh tingle, his heart begin to hammer. Jesus. He had never received anything like this in his life before. It brought with it a sense of violation that was almost physical.

Without pausing to consider, he leaned down and clicked on the 'delete' button. When the screen asked him if he was really sure he wanted to delete this item, it came across to Leo as a kind of sneering innuendo, as though the machine itself were looking slyly up at him. Angrily he clicked 'yes' and the words vanished from the screen. He felt an instant sense of relief, although the shock of what he had read had not left him. Messages two, three, four and five still waited. He hesitated for several long seconds before clicking on the second. Its contents were similar to the first, but worse. Mechanically he deleted it and went to the third, fully expecting the screen to fill with obscenities and abuse once more. It was a message from a friend, a female lawyer in New York, telling him that she was coming to London on business at the end of November and to keep the twenty-seventh free. It was cheery and brisk, and ended snappily with the word 'Bye!', but because of the vile force of the last two e-mails, it read at first to Leo like a coded message, in which obscenity and insult surely lay buried. He had to read it several times before it gradually took on the form of an innocuous, friendly transmission.

He sat down now, picked up his glass and swallowed its contents. He felt better after a few seconds, as the whisky did its work. He was reluctant to click on to the last two messages. He sat for a long while, thinking it all over. He had no idea who could have done such a thing. Who would want to? What enemies did he have? His mind moved reluctantly, inevitably, to Joshua. No. If Joshua had thought of him since he left, it had been negligently, unregretfully. He didn't care enough. Leo half smiled as he remembered trying to show Joshua, largely unsuccessfully, how to perform basic tasks on the computer. The memory had a sweet pain attached. To do this kind of thing was beyond Joshua in every sense.

In an instant Leo regretted deleting the earlier messages. If

the two remaining ones were mere mundane correspondence, then he had lost the possibility of identifying the
sender. He had been too shocked to look for clues, to
references which might point to an individual. After a few
moments Leo put out his hand, hesitated, then went into the
fourth of the messages. More filth, this time of a threatening,
sickeningly sexual kind. Trying with difficulty to ignore the
content, Leo read it through three times, but could find
nothing to tie it in to anyone he knew. Perhaps it was just
random. One heard of such things. Unsolicited material
turned up on screens every day, all over the world. But Leo
wasn't on the Internet. This had come from someone who
knew his e-mail address. Knew his name. He clicked on to
the fifth message and what he read there made his gorge rise.
As soon as he saw Oliver's name, and read what was
written, he got up, went to the bathroom, and was briefly
and violently sick. With trembling hands he went to the
basin and splashed water over his face, then dried it. He
stood for a while, hands on the side of the basin, waiting for
the trembling to go away, the taste to leave his mouth. He
tried to erase what he had read from his mind, but that was
the worst of words. Once they were in there, they could not
easily be dislodged. Whoever had written these messages
knew that. They had found a way into his mind. From now
on, he would be unable to switch on his computer and look
at his e-mail, for fear of finding more messages like those of
this evening.

After a while he went through to his study and, not
looking at the screen, managed to delete the message and
close down the system. Then he went through to the
drawing-room and poured himself another drink, this time a
large one, which he swiftly followed with another. The
whisky had the desired effect of dulling his senses, putting
everything which he had just experienced at a kind of
remove. And inevitably, it brought back thoughts of Joshua.
Leo got up and went through to Joshua's room. He had done

this every evening since Joshua had left. He gazed around. The cleaning lady had made the bed and tidily arranged what was left of Joshua's belongings. The easel still stood in the corner by the window. Leo went over to the bed and pulled back the cover, picked up a pillow and held it to his face, breathing in what was left of the scent of his lover. Then with a groan he chucked it down and went back through to the drawing-room. Tears stung the backs of his eyes. You maudlin, bloody drunk, he told himself. No more whisky. Then again ...

As he poured out an unsteady measure, the phone began to ring. Leo picked it up and said hello. He listened to the silence. Then he clicked the phone off and put it back on the handset. He stood, nursing his drink, staring at the phone. When it rang again, he picked it up and this time said nothing. And listened to nothing. He curbed his urge to shout and swear at whoever was at the other end, at whoever had come into his mind and his life with such violent stealth that evening, and put the phone down once more. He switched on the answerphone, finished his whisky and went to bed. There he fell into a sweating and unpleasant sleep, one from which he half woke several times in the night, to hear the insistent beep beep of the phone, before the machine clicked on to record the black silence at the other end.

Chapter thirteen

Leo left chambers just before lunch-time on Friday. 'I'll be at home for the next few hours,' he told Felicity. 'If it's anything urgent you can reach me there.'

'All right, Mr Davies. By the way, I had Bernard Pannick's clerk on a few minutes ago, wanting to know about your skeleton argument in that ship finance case. I said I hadn't seen it being typed up.' Felicity's manner was tentative. She didn't like having to chase Leo up on cases. He was usually on top of everything, but recently she'd had to do it more and more. 'The hearing's on Monday.'

Leo let out a sigh of exasperation. 'Yes, Felicity, I know when the bloody –' He stopped. No point in taking it out on Felicity. He could only blame himself for forgetting to do the damn thing. He'd meant to do it two weeks ago, but had kept putting it off. Still, he could put something together later in the afternoon and still get it in on time. 'Don't worry,' he said pacifically. 'I'll get it sorted out.'

'Okay.' Felicity lowered her voice slightly. 'By the way, I was wondering if I could have a word with you, when you've got a free moment. It's something personal.' A nervous lump rose in her throat. She'd been letting the days go by, saying nothing to the members of chambers about her pregnancy, but she would have to do it soon. Leo seemed to be the most approachable; she knew him best, even if his manner with her did blow hot and cold at times.

Leo was not so bound up in his own affairs that he couldn't see, from the expression in Felicity's eyes, that this 'something', whatever it was, was important to her. He glanced at his watch. It was only ten to one. Plenty of time to get home and tidy the place up. 'What about now? We can go into the waiting room.'

They went in and Leo closed the door. Felicity sat down on the edge of one of the armchairs, while he leaned against a bookcase and folded his arms, waiting for her to begin.

'The thing is, Mr Davies, I'm going to have to leave chambers in a few months. Probably for good. I'm going to have a baby.'

There was a pause, then Leo smiled and said, 'Congratulations.' Seeing her face, he added, 'No need to look so glum about it. It has its up sides.'

Felicity looked up at Leo. He could be a right bastard sometimes, when things weren't going right, and lately he'd been a complete misery, but when he smiled that smile of his and looked at you with those eyes – a hard blue sometimes, but not at the moment – she liked him best out of the whole bunch. She felt tears brimming up.

'I know. I mean –' She sniffed and, to Leo's astonishment and amusement, plucked a tissue from the depths of her cleavage. 'Don't think I'm not happy about it. I am, I suppose. It's just that Vince and I hadn't exactly planned it . . .' She wiped her eyes, dabbing carefully to stop her mascara running. 'It's not really come at the best of times. I was just beginning to feel I was getting good at my job and things . . .'

'You are. You're very good,' said Leo. 'But look, it's not the end of the world. We'll keep your job open for you. Henry can muddle through. He's done it in the past. You'll be back before you know it.'

Felicity shrugged. 'Maybe, but I doubt it. Vince doesn't hold much with working mothers. The trouble is, he doesn't know how much this job means to me.' She looked up at Leo confidingly. 'I even thought about – you know, not having it. Just so that I could stay on here.'

Leo felt a sudden chill as he recalled trying to persuade

Rachel to have an abortion when she was pregnant with Oliver. 'Don't. You mustn't think about that.' Felicity was taken aback by the abruptness of his tone. Then he smiled again. 'You'll be fine. As I said, it isn't the end of the world. I'll speak to the other members of chambers. Your job will still be here if you want to come back. And knowing you, Felicity, I think that if you want it badly enough, you will.' Felicity nodded. She looked sad and unconvinced. 'When's the baby due?' added Leo, as he turned to open the door.

Felicity got up. 'May next year. May the fifteenth.'

'Plenty of time for you to talk Vince round. Lots of mothers work these days, you know. Rachel does.'

Yeah, thought Felicity, but she's not living with someone whose best hope of a job is still two years away. She smiled and said, 'Thanks for listening.'

'Any time.'

Leo left chambers and Felicity went back to her work, trying to think of new arguments to persuade Vince out of his steadfastly reactionary position.

Leo found that he was strangely nervous at the prospect of the imminent visit of the welfare officers. He put away the few odds and ends of Joshua's that might indicate ownership of his room, dismantled the easel, and stacked away the canvases and paints. He went through to the room which, ever since he had taken the flat, had been earmarked for Oliver. It was bright and airy, facing the south of the building, with a cot in one corner, a chest of drawers, a cupboard full of toys and some picture books on a shelf. Leo had even put up two large posters, one of Postman Pat and Jess, and another of Thomas The Tank Engine. He remembered the day he had put them up, balanced on a chair, Joshua laughing as he handed the adhesive up to him. Joshua, Joshua . . .

As he went back through to the drawing-room to wait, Leo found himself reflecting upon the occasion when Rachel had rung the flat and Joshua had answered. What had she made of that? He had never asked her, too fearful of the idea that she might have said something prejudicial when the welfare people had visited her. That was madness. If she *had* said something, then he ought to know, ought to be prepared for anything they might say today.

Hastily he rang Nichols & Co. and asked to speak to her. 'Rachel, look, I've got these welfare people coming round shortly. I need to know what you said to them when they came to visit you.'

'Said to them?'

'About me.'

'What about you?' Rachel felt edgy and faintly guilty. The tone in which Leo spoke brought home to her just how much this business of regular access to Oliver meant to him. It was something to which she managed to harden her mind most of the time.

'Don't prevaricate, Rachel. You know what I'm talking about. I know that you spoke to Joshua last time you called the flat.'

'Oh – Joshua, is it? So you like their names to be pretty as well as their faces.' She spoke from a sense of bitterness which had never left her, not since the day when she had found out that Leo had never really loved her, not as she had loved him, burning with a need for him that persisted even now, despite Charles, despite everything. She despised herself for speaking as she did, but couldn't help it.

There was a pause, then Leo said in a tired voice, 'He doesn't live here, if that's what you'd been thinking. Not any more.'

'Well, that's something you'll have to explain to the welfare officers. As far as I was concerned, Leo, when I talked to them, I felt they needed to know what kind of person you are, the sort of life to which Oliver might be exposed.'

'So you did say something?'

232

'What did you expect, Leo? It's the truth, isn't it? You've had young men flitting in and out of your life and your bed ever since I've known you. Even when we were married,' she added bitterly. 'Why should anyone think you're likely to change now? I don't want Oliver seeing all that, knowing what you do.'

You bitch, thought Leo. When he spoke his voice was cold with fury. 'This isn't about morality – don't you understand that, you stupid woman? You're lying to yourself and to me, and to everyone else, if you think that. I *love* Oliver. I am as I am, but I wouldn't let anything about it affect or hurt my son. You know that – Christ, you *know* that, but you just won't admit it.'

He slammed the phone down, and automatically and unthinkingly snatched a small crystal tumbler from the drinks cabinet and reached for the Scotch. Then he realised what he was doing and put them both back. He sat there, letting his anger die away.

Joshua passed through the ticket barrier and came out of Sloane Square tube station into the chilly October air. He turned right into Cliveden Place and headed towards Eaton Gate at a brisk walk. Then after a few moments his pace slackened and he came to a halt, leaning against some railings. He still didn't think he had any clear idea of what he was going to do or say when he got to Leo's. There was a lot he'd missed over the past few days. A sleeping bag on Les's floor didn't exactly compare with the comfort of his bedroom in the Belgravia flat and the last of his money was running out. Still, he had a job starting next week – places always seemed to be on the look-out for good-looking waiters with enough charm and experience – and the up side was that he had his independence back. He did miss Leo a bit, but it was a relief to be free of the pressure of all that affection, no longer to be the focus of someone's desires and expectations. He couldn't live with that any more. Much as he liked Leo, he knew he could never become what Leo wanted him to be. Joshua pushed himself away from the railings and started to walk again. All that stuff about his paintings, maybe getting him an exhibition. Could Leo have done that for him? Maybe. Then again, maybe Leo had hoped it would be a way of making him stay, by promising things . . . Leaving Leo had also had something to do with Katie, that girl at the party. He'd really wanted her, wanted her in a way that being with Leo couldn't compare with. Not any man. That had started out as a way of making money and look what it had turned into. No, he wasn't going back to that. He was glad he'd left. But Leo had been really good to him, really generous, and he was grateful for that. He just hoped that he could pick up his things without any fuss and they could part amicably.

The sound of the buzzer to the flat made Leo jump. When the welfare officers announced themselves through the intercom, he pressed the button for the downstairs entrance and stood waiting for them at the open door of his flat. There were two of them, a woman in her mid-thirties, plump, short-haired, dressed in leggings and a long beige anorak, scruffier than Leo had expected, and carrying a clipboard and notebook. With her was a nondescript, unsmiling young man whose handshake was damp and flabby.

The woman, who was clearly in charge, introduced herself as Mrs Jenkins, and her colleague as Mr Purser. Young Mr Purser glanced round the interior of Leo's drawing-room with a melancholy eye, as though he didn't quite approve of what he saw. Mrs Jenkins, smiling benignly, began to ask Leo questions about his work. They made a tour of inspection of the flat, Mrs Jenkins nodding and making notes, Leo accompanying them diffidently, feeling somewhat humiliated by this scrutiny. When they returned to the living-room, Mrs Jenkins glanced round at Leo's collection of modern art and at the ceiling-high bookshelves and remarked, 'It's certainly a very grand place, Mr Davies. Quite palatial.' She said this in such a way as to make Leo feel it might have been better for him if he'd lived in a modest little semi. 'No garden, though, of course.'

'There is a garden,' said Leo. 'It's a communal garden, in the square. Only the residents have access. Oliver could play there.' He went to the window with Mrs Jenkins while Mr Purser stared glumly at a shelf full of plays and poetry books. 'Or there are the local parks, of course,' added Leo. He looked down with Mrs Jenkins at the garden in the centre of the square, then felt his heart rise sharply in his chest. Joshua was walking across the square, unmistakably coming in the direction of the flat. He reached the pavement and disappeared into the doorway below.

'Would you excuse me for a moment?' muttered Leo, as the buzzer sounded. He went quickly into the hallway and pressed the intercom. 'Come up.'

He heard the door open below and the sound of Joshua's feet on the stairs. The sight of him almost overpowered Leo. All the misery of the last several days seemed to come to a head in raw emotion. It was the worst possible situation in which to encounter Joshua, with all that he felt and wanted to say to him. His throat felt stopped with love and longing.

'How did you know I was here?' was all Leo could think to ask.

'I rang your chambers.' Joshua stood in the doorway, his fists rammed into the pockets of his jacket. Leo could not read the expression on his face, which wore its customary blank beauty. The only sense he could make of the situation was that Joshua had come back, that there was something still to be said and some future for them. He hoped and prayed, inwardly, that this was so, more fervently than he had ever done about anything in his life. He was suddenly horribly conscious of Mrs Jenkins and Mr Purser in the room behind him, waiting, listening, and wished Joshua had picked any other time but now.

'Look –' He put out a hand and laid it on Joshua's arm;

Joshua let it rest there, hardly seeming to notice. 'This is not a good time. There are some people here. Some welfare officers. It's all about Oliver. You know, I told you.' He hesitated, then said, 'But look, come in, anyway. They must be just about finished.'

Joshua stepped into the hallway. 'That's all right,' he said. 'I've only come to pick up the rest of my stuff.' The complete lack of concern in his manner struck Leo like a blow.

Joshua started up the hallway towards his room, but Leo put out a hand to stop him. 'Don't,' he said quickly. 'Don't. Listen, wait until these people are gone. It'll only take a few minutes. Go into the kitchen and make yourself a cup of coffee or something. We need to talk.'

'No we don't,' replied Joshua, gently shaking off Leo's hand. 'I just want my things. I told you before, this was all a mistake.'

'No, no – you have to listen.' Leo's voice was low and urgent. He glanced towards the half-shut door of the drawing-room.

'No, Leo,' said Joshua firmly. He went to his room, Leo following.

Once inside Joshua's room, Leo shut the door and leaned against it, watching as Joshua began to take the remainder of his things from drawers and cupboards, putting them into the rucksack he had brought when he had first moved in. Leo had no idea what to say or do, was only filled with the knowledge that he could not let Joshua go, that things could and must be set right between them. Anguish filled him with speechless panic and he tried desperately to summon up the right words, the ones which would work. He could feel himself shaking. He watched as Joshua stacked up his three canvases.

'Joshua, this doesn't have to happen,' he said at last, trying to keep his voice calm. 'I overreacted last time. I can see that. But since you left it's been unspeakable. I can't work, I can't sleep –'

'I'm sorry, Leo. I really am.' Joshua stuffed odds and ends into the rucksack, then straightened up. The expression on his face was one of genuine regret and Leo felt a faint hope, until Joshua went on, 'But the fact is, the whole set-up is false. I've been feeling like a real hypocrite these past couple of weeks. You want something from me that I can't give you. And the longer it goes on, me taking things from you, presents and money and everything, the worse it will be in the end. I've thought it all out. I don't want to belong to anybody.'

He moved towards the door, then stopped when he saw that Leo did not intend to move.

'Please, Joshua,' said Leo, 'it doesn't have to be that way. I want you to have freedom. I do. We can arrange it any way you like. Everything on your terms. I don't care. I just can't bear you to go. I love you, damn it.' Leo's voice cracked on these last words, and he felt all the weakness and unhappiness of his desperation rise to the surface in tears.

Joshua shook his head. 'That's it, you see, Leo. I really like you. I do, honestly. You've been great to me, and we've had some good times. I don't want you to think I'm not fond of you. But –' He stopped and searched for words. 'But it was never going anywhere. Not where you wanted it to.' He put out a hand to the doorknob. 'Look, I've got to go. Please.'

Leo stepped away from the door and, as Joshua opened it he swallowed hard, regaining control of himself. 'Joshua, just listen. I don't care if it has no future. I just need you to stay now. Just until these people have gone. I have things to say to you.' Joshua shook his head and went into the hallway with his rucksack. Leo's voice rose as he went after him, heedless of the couple in the drawing-room. 'I have important things to say! You can't just go like this, without giving me some kind of chance!'

At that moment Mrs Jenkins opened the drawing-room door and looked out. She still wore a smile, a tentative one. 'Mr Davies, do you think we –'

Leo turned to her in rage, tears reddening his eyes. 'Will you damn well shut up? I have something to sort out here!' He turned back to Joshua. 'Joshua, wait – leave me a number or something. This isn't the right time, I know, but we can talk later.'

Joshua turned round, glanced in embarrassment at Mrs Jenkins and Mr Purser standing in the doorway, and looked directly at Leo. 'There's no point. I'm sorry if I picked a bad time. I just needed my things.' He moved to the front door, Leo following him.

'Joshua!' Leo's voice was anguished, desperate. 'Joshua, for God's sake wait!' He tried to catch the sleeve of Joshua's jacket as Joshua opened the door, but Joshua shook him off again, went out quickly and closed the door behind him, while Leo called after him, 'Please! Please! Joshua, I love you! Oh, God . . .'

Leo turned away from the door and went down the hall and into the kitchen, ignoring the two figures in the doorway of the drawing-room. He closed the kitchen door, leaned over the sink and took several deep breaths, blinking away his tears. Then he splashed his face with water and dried it. The emotional outburst of the last few minutes had left him spent, shaking. He began to realise the implications of what he had just done. Those two people had witnessed every-thing, could draw only one conclusion. Taking a minute or two to collect himself, Leo went back through to the drawing-room to salvage what he could of the situation.

Mrs Jenkins and Mr Purser were now by the window, talking in low voices. They had clearly gone over there to watch Joshua's departure. They stopped talking as Leo came into the room. Then Mrs Jenkins, clutching her clipboard against her anorak, came across the room, her smile quite gone now.

Before Leo could say anything, she spoke. Her voice was quiet and regretful. 'Mr Davies, you know that the purpose of this visit here today is to ascertain that this would be a fit and proper place for your son to stay on a regular basis. We all have domestic upsets in our lives – believe me, I do appreciate that. Nobody's perfect. But what you must understand is that your wife – your ex-wife, I should say – did raise certain questions regarding your life-style when we went to see her.' Mrs Jenkins paused, plainly a little embarrassed. 'She mentioned, for instance, that you regularly entertain young men and she is concerned that this might create circumstances where the environment is not one in which she would be happy for Oliver to stay. You understand my meaning?'

Leo turned away. He went over to a silver box lying on a table and took out a small cigar. He felt drained, dead. Nothing mattered. He lit the cigar and blew out the smoke. 'What you mean is that the unfortunate little scene which you witnessed a few moments ago has reinforced your prejudices.' His voice was flat.

'Now, Mr Davies, I don't like it when you use that word. This has nothing to do with your sexual orientation. It's not our policy to let matters of that kind influence our thinking. What we're concerned with is a stable, calm environment for your son.'

Leo lifted his head and looked her in the eye. 'I love my son. My emotional life is a bit of a mess. I accept that. But I would never let him it harm him, or touch him. You have to believe that. It has to be kept separate.' Mrs Jenkins let out a little sigh, dropped her eyes and said nothing. 'You have to write up your report. Fine. You have to say what you saw. But please accept that if Oliver came to stay with me, I would make sure that everything was as peaceful and stable as anyone could want.'

There was a silence, then Mrs Jenkins, her tentative smile returning, said, 'I think we've seen everything we need to. We'll make out our report and submit it to the court in due course. Thank you for your time.'

She and the silent Mr Purser left the room, Leo followi

them. He saw them out without a word, then went back into the drawing-room and picked up his cigar from the ashtray. It was as though his mind and body were entirely devoid of life. He had never felt emptier. He looked at his watch and saw that it was half past three. The idea of going back to chambers was beyond him. He poured himself a large drink, sat down and finished his cigar. The afternoon light outside faded to early dusk, and Leo carried on drinking, letting his unhappy thoughts chase themselves more and more slowly round his mind as the whisky took hold. He kept on playing out a little fantasy in which Joshua came back, regretting what had happened and telling Leo that he had been right, and that he loved him and would stay. Even though he knew that all hope was now utterly gone, dead, he let the fantasy thread through his mind, filling the silence with imagined words, until at last he was sitting in complete darkness, with his bottle and his glass.

Later that evening, Camilla and Anthony were sprawled comfortably together on the sofa in Anthony's flat, Camilla's legs resting across Anthony's lap. The remains of a meal lay scattered on the coffee table.

Anthony yawned, then put out a hand to stroke Camilla's hair. 'Shall I put on some music? It seems dreadfully quiet.'

Camilla sipped her wine and studied him curiously. 'That's something I've noticed about you since I got back.'

'What?'

'This sudden need to fill silences. When you're not talking non-stop, you're doing something else to compensate.' She gave a little smile.

'I just thought it would be nice to have some music, that's all.' Anthony moved her legs gently aside and got up. He went over to the CD player and absently flipped through the discs. Had he been behaving differently since she'd got back? Certainly the knowledge of what he had done seemed to be instantly with him, colouring everything he did and said.

240

He slipped in a CD and glanced back to where Camilla lay on the sofa. He felt an urgent need to bridge the distance which his own guilt seemed to have created. The smooth balance of perfect trust and affection which had existed before she went away had been destroyed. It was something he had never contemplated in those lost, erotic nights spent with Sarah. Not that he had contemplated much beyond the satisfaction of his own lust. Perhaps the only way to destroy the feeling was to stifle it, smother it, by bringing Camilla closer to him, so that then it wouldn't matter.

He went back and sat down, drawing Camilla's legs on to his lap again and stroking her feet. 'Did you do any thinking while you were away?'

'Thinking? What about?'

'Us. You moving in here.'

Camilla set her glass down on the low table, as though preparing for something. 'I suppose so. I mean, I suppose I thought about it a bit. But everything I said before I went away still stands, Anthony. I want to find somewhere of my own. We see so much of one another in chambers, I think it's important that we have our own space.'

'To do what? What are you going to do with this new space? See other people?' He felt detached, wondering at his own brusqueness.

Camilla looked at him in amazement. 'What makes you say that?' She reached out a hand and touched his face. 'I'm so lucky. We have something so special. But you must remember what it was like when you first got started. You have a feeling of independence. You want a place of your very own, a life that doesn't belong to other people.'

'In other words, what we have may be special, but it's just not special enough. Look, you say you want independence. What can that mean, if it doesn't mean that you want to put distance between us? I don't understand.'

Camilla gave a little laugh of exasperation and took his hand away. 'Anthony, are you being deliberately obtuse' you want to talk about distance, well, ever since I got back you've been –' She hesitated. 'You've been odd. Like there's something on your mind.' There was a silence as they gazed at one another. 'Is there?'

Anthony felt vulnerable, confused. He wanted so badly to make everything whole again, to put it back the way it had been. He told himself that he loved Camilla. With her he felt a completeness, a sense of safety and warmth. But even at this moment he knew that he could think about Sarah, the things they had done, the smoky sound of her laugh and the touch of her fingers, and feel longing. If, in one brief absence from Camilla, he could give in so easily to the idle temptation of someone like Sarah, what might not happen in the future? Perhaps he wanted Camilla to move in so that it would lessen the risk of anything like it happening again. Loving her as he did, he couldn't even trust himself with other women. Miserably he leaned his head back, sighing, and closed his eyes.

Should he tell her? The thought swam around in his mind in lazy circles with the music. If he did, then the weight of guilt and the fear of her finding out would all be lifted. He could tell her how sorry he was, make amends . . . No, he couldn't tell her. Nothing was that simple. To know he had betrayed her trust while she was away would hurt her so much that it would badly damage things, if not destroy them. He would just have to let it be, hope that things would adjust, that his guilt would lessen.

He opened his eyes and looked at her. 'No, there's nothing on my mind. I just wish you'd think again about being with me.'

'I've done enough thinking. Let's just leave it, shall we?' replied Camilla gently. 'Don't spoil the evening.' And she leaned forward to kiss him.

woke on Monday morning a little before nine. He had, at no sense of its being morning, or indeed any particular

242

day. He was conscious only of grey light from the window. The curtains were open. It was only the angle of the light which gradually brought home a rough realisation of what time of day it must be. He could hardly move his head from the pillow. A pressure like a tight band of steel bound fast against his skull enveloped it. Not pain, but a remorseless tightening sensation. His limbs felt cold and his tongue seemed to have swollen to the roof of his mouth. Shivering, he put out a hand and drew the duvet up around him, realising as he did so that he was still partially dressed, having managed to divest himself only of his trousers the night before.

The night before. He could remember little of it, except as a dark, empty remnant, the end of a grey day spent drinking himself back into oblivion. Saturday? Saturday came back to him in very gradual, crepuscular recollections. He had a memory of being in Earl's Court, looking for Joshua, walking round the streets. How had he got there? He must have been drunk then, or somewhat, though he had no recollections of anything he had done on Saturday morning. He couldn't even recall waking up. He must have gone by train, though again he recalled nothing of the journey. He remembered going back, though, on the tube, and going to the off-licence to buy more whisky. Then nothing. Back to Sunday, grey and lost.

He put up a hand to his chin and felt the three-day stubble. He had, he realised, been on what was known as a bender. Never in his life had he done such a thing. Perhaps he was lucky he could remember anything at all. As though seeing himself through several layers of smoky glass, he remembered dimly that his sole aim and preoccupation for the past two days had been to stay in a state of partial oblivion. Well, he had succeeded and this was the result. Jesus Christ . . . He drew his knees up almost to his chin and lay there, curled up, stiff with self-hatred and disgust, his face screwed as though to shut out the thought of himself. Moisture seeped

243

between his eyelids, not so much tears as a rheumy, exhausted watering. He could smell the rank scent of whisky from his very pores. It came very slowly and dimly to him that it was the start of the week. He tried to grasp hold of this, to gain some sense of the day's significance. To do this, he had to put himself back to Friday and work through it from the very beginning.

Realisation, clarity, came to him with pain, a sudden, throbbing bolt of pain that seemed to lance his brain. If this was Monday morning, he had a hearing at ten o'clock in the High Court. The ship repair case. He turned to look at the clock and saw, thankfully, that he had an hour in hand. Then, as he heaved himself out of bed and put his bare feet on the floor, Leo realised with a thrill of horror that he hadn't put in his skeleton argument. Of all procedural oversights, this was one of the most unpardonable. He showered, shaved and dressed in a kind of hideous, waking dream. His cuff-links were impossible. His hands shook so violently that he couldn't begin to thread the links through. With a curse, he went through to the drawing-room. The whisky bottle, uncapped, stood on the mantelpiece. Leo lifted it to his mouth and took two swift swallows, then sat down in a chair, closing his eyes. After a few minutes he held out his hands. They still trembled, but only slightly. He went back to his room and managed to fumble the cuff-links in and knot his tie.

In the bathroom he cleaned his teeth twice again and searched in the bathroom cabinet for some breath freshener. The whisky had made him feel better, clearer, though he knew this was illusory. By lunch-time he would feel like death. The few brief hours till then were almost beyond contemplation. He could think of nothing he would say or do in court to cover his omission. It did not for one second cross his mind to call chambers with some excuse, and simply not show up in court. It was not a thing Leo had ever done. Work was duty, and duty was something one automatically fulfilled, even if one had cocked it up quite monumentally.

He gathered together his belongings and drove in, knowing that he shouldn't, but knowing, too, that it was too late to take the train. Not that he could have faced a crowded commuter train even if he had had hours to spare. His head was beginning to throb violently as he parked his car in the Temple, and he wondered, as he walked up King's Bench Walk, whether he wasn't about to be sick there and then on the cobbles. He had forgotten his overcoat and the cold of late October made him shiver uncontrollably again as he walked, fighting against the rising of his gorge.

In chambers he went to David's room. David wasn't in yet and Leo fished around in a drawer where he knew David kept some Alka-Seltzer. He fetched a glass of water from the kitchen and dissolved four of the tablets, then drank it. He picked up his robing bag and made his way to the Royal Courts of Justice. Once robed, he had to make a quick detour to the lavatory to throw up the whisky and the Alka-Seltzer. They swam in the pan in an unpleasantly yellow, foamy mixture. Thereafter, everything he did and said seemed to Leo to be surreal, detached.

The judge hearing the case that day was Mr Justice Aston, a stony-faced and humourless man, who had once been Leo's leader some years ago in an unfortunate case which they had lost, for which Aston had largely blamed Leo. Now he stared down from the bench at Leo, who endeavoured to make his excuses and apologies, two things which he loathed doing.

'Really, Mr Davies, this is a most appalling waste of the court's time and a gross discourtesy to all the individuals involved. I find it quite inexcusable that someone in your position should come to court today without adequate preparation. I have no alternative but to stand this case out of the lists.' He glared down through his spectacles. Leo felt a horribly queasy rocking in his stomach and wondered if he was going to have to flee the court room to throw up again. Mr Justice Aston went on, 'Given the circumstances, Mr Davies, can you give the court any reason why you should not bear the costs of today's wasted exercise yourself?' Leo muttered words to the effect that he couldn't. 'Very well, the costs today will be borne personally by you.'

It was all Leo could do to offer his apologies to Bernard Pannick, who uttered a few curt words and walked away. Leo went slowly back to the robing room, his footsteps echoing on the stone flags. In his heart he did not think he had ever felt so wretched and alone. He went into the robing room and took off his wig. Above all, he was conscious, despite his nausea, of a craving, now familiar, for a drink to ease the depression he felt. He knew, with a kind of detached clarity, that the chemistry of his body had been altered over the past few weeks and that this was the reason for the feeling. But even that dispassionate knowledge did not alter his longing for a couple of large Scotches to make him feel better.

He stuffed his gown, wig and bands into his bag and went back to chambers. The costs of today's futile exercise could be anything in the region of ten to twenty thousand, he reckoned. He would settle it out of his own funds as swiftly as he could, rather than let it come out of his chambers' insurance. In that way, the other members of chambers might not come to hear of what had happened, though he doubted it.

In the clerks' room Felicity was busy with some accounts, when Leo came in. She glanced up and smiled. 'Everything all right, Mr Davies?' she enquired innocently.

'No, everything is not bloody all right. Why didn't you remind me last week that I hadn't put in my argument in that ship repair case? I'm incredibly busy at the moment and it's up to you to make sure that I'm on top of things. I have just spent a very embarrassing half-hour in court trying to explain myself.'

Felicity stared at him. 'But I did remind you. I told you at the beginning of the week, and then I reminded you again on Friday.'

'Not to my recollection, Felicity,' retorted Leo. His tone was still angry, but a small misgiving sprang up in his mind. Through the hellish haze that was the past few days, he couldn't really recall the events of Friday. Had she said something? Still, he couldn't remember her mentioning it at the beginning of the week, so he clung to that. 'You're my clerk and you're there to remind me about these things. Don't let it happen again.'

She watched him go upstairs, incredulous. How could he say that? It had been bad enough having to go out of her way to remind him, without him blaming it all on her. Smarting with the injustice of it, she went off to have a moan to Henry.

On the way upstairs, Leo met Jeremy. 'Hello, Leo.' Jeremy glanced more closely at Leo's red eyes and pallid face. 'You look as though you had a bit of a heavy weekend.' Leo muttered something by way of reply and was about to go into his room when Jeremy continued, 'By the way, I think I've found new chambers for us.'

Leo looked at him indifferently. All he wanted to do was to lie down somewhere and think about absolutely nothing at all. With an effort he responded, 'Have you? Where?'

'In Sussex Street.'

'Sussex Street? But that's out of the Inns of Court.' This new idea of Jeremy's seemed to Leo to be even more unattractive than Lincoln's Inn.

'Well, yes, but there are advantages. The rent's lower, for a start, and there are probably all kinds of things we can do in a building of that kind which we couldn't do in the Temple. Air-conditioning, central heating, lifts.'

Leo said wearily, 'I don't like the idea, Jeremy. It's too much of a break with tradition. It's really not us.'

'Face facts, Leo. There are eighteen of us now and we need to expand. I'm not interested in tradition. I'm concerned with moving ahead, modernising things. I'm going to set out these proposals at the next chambers meeting. If you've got a better idea, you'll have to come up with it by then.' He clumped off downstairs, then stopped and turned. 'By the way – perhaps you haven't heard.'

'What?'

'Cameron. He died last night.' Jeremy turned and carried on downstairs.

Leo went into his room and closed the door. He felt very, very unwell. He sat down heavily in his chair and glanced round the room. Everything was as it always was – the books, the pictures, the neat rows of briefs, the view from the window. At this moment it all meant absolutely nothing to him. How typical of Jeremy, to put the news of Cameron's death in second place to his wretched proposals for moving chambers. He looked at the briefs ranged in a row, the work which awaited him. The thought of taking one down and looking at it was utterly beyond him. Not just at that moment, hung-over and tired, but at any given moment in the near future. The idea of being himself, of being a barrister, of being someone on whom others depended and of whom they thought highly, was a stark impossibility. He felt as though he didn't want to be anything to anyone ever again. As he understood the truth of this, he wondered fleetingly whether he might not be having some kind of breakdown. He didn't think so, but, then, he didn't know what one of those felt like. The only thing he wanted was to feel Joshua's arms around him, to have that comfort, that love. His need was entirely childlike. Beyond that, he cared about nothing.

Slowly Leo stood up. He left his room, closing the door behind him, and went downstairs.

Felicity was talking to Henry in the clerks' room. They both glanced up as Leo came in, instantly silenced by his appearance, which was dreadful, tired, aged and red-eyed.

'Felicity,' said Leo, 'I think I should apologise for what I

said earlier. I've probably only myself to blame. Anyway –'
he stopped, looked absently around, then went on with an
effort of concentration '– I think I have to have some time to
myself. Things have been going rather badly lately. I shan't
be in for the next two or three weeks.'

And with that he turned and went out, leaving Henry and
Felicity staring after him in astonishment and dismay.

Chapter fourteen

'Gone? Gone where?'

'I dunno,' said Felicity in exasperation. She looked squarely at Anthony. 'He said he needed some time to himself and that he wouldn't be in for a few weeks. That was it.'

'You're joking.'

'I wish I was. He's dropped me and Henry right in it. I've spent all morning on the phone to solicitors, trying to bluff my way out of things. There are some things that won't wait – in fact, there's an arbitration next week that Freshfields want you to take over. I'm trying to juggle your diary around to fit it in. All the solicitors are mad as hell. Whoever said clerks spend their entire lives spinning a load of bullshit was right. Pardon my French.' She shook her head and sighed. 'Mr Davies certainly isn't doing himself any favours. Some of his work might even have to go out of chambers, and you know how Henry feels about that.' She made a throat-cutting gesture and raised her eyebrows meaning-fully.

'But when was this?' asked Anthony.

'Yesterday morning, after he came back from court. I thought you'd've heard by now.'

Anthony went up to his room, digesting this information. That Leo should just walk out of chambers, leaving weeks of carefully arranged work – arbitrations, conferences, court hearings – up in the air was extraordinary, entirely out of character. Clearly there was something wrong. The last time he had spoken to Leo was when Leo had asked him for a game of squash last week. Anthony realised with a pang that Leo must have been in need of someone to talk to then, and he had turned him down, possibly when he had needed Anthony most. He'd been aware that Leo hadn't been himself recently but had been too preoccupied with his own affairs to do or say anything to help. Too busy screwing Sarah every night, then bemoaning his weak character and nursing his conscience ever since Camilla's return. God, how he detested himself of late.

Anthony picked up the phone and dialled Leo's number in Belgravia, and listened as the phone at the other end rang a few times, then clicked into Leo's answering machine. He hesitated, thought of leaving a message, but put the phone down. If Leo had problems, maybe he had gone away to sort them out. He had a house in Oxfordshire somewhere. The memory of going there with Leo to spend the night after a chambers cricket match surprised Anthony with an ache of tenderness. How infatuated he had been with Leo in those days, how much he had wanted to be able to respond to him. Perhaps he should have. Perhaps he wouldn't have made such a God-awful mess of his relationships if he had just let Leo be the focus of his life. He thrust the thought aside. That was all history. The point was that Leo was in trouble and he, Anthony, had neglected his friendship. He sighed. Had Leo gone to ground in his house in the country? Even if he had, Anthony didn't have the phone number and didn't think he could find the house if he tried. He couldn't even remember the name of the village. He would just have to keep ringing his flat throughout the day and, if he couldn't reach him, he'd go round there tonight. Other than that, there was nothing anyone could do but wait and see. For how long, Anthony had no idea, but he knew that if Leo let too many weeks go by, people – clients, solicitors – would grow impatient, his reputation would inevitably suffer and his practice would begin gradually, but steadily, to crumble away.

That evening after work Anthony and Camilla went for a drink with David.

'I told Sarah to join us later,' said David, bringing drinks over to the table. 'She's presently slogging away digging up authorities for a hearing tomorrow.'

'Slave-driver,' remarked Anthony. 'Still, I don't think I'd much enjoy having a pupil. I imagine it simply makes more work for you.'

'Initially, yes,' said David. 'But Sarah's actually very useful. Got off to something of a sticky start, but she's pretty sharp.'

'Oh, yes, she's that, all right,' murmured Anthony. Conscious of Camilla's eyes on him, he tried to move the subject away from Sarah. 'So, what do you make of Leo's disappearing act?'

'I couldn't believe it when Michael told me,' said David. 'I know he's had a pretty rough year, what with his divorce and so on, but I never thought of Leo as the kind of man just to drop everything like that. I mean, I've known him for ten years now, and he's always put his work first. It's just not like him to land everyone in it like that. Henry's going mad.' David shook his head. 'I must say, I never thought Leo could behave so selfishly, whatever problems he might have in his personal life.' David glanced at a group of people who had just come into the pub. 'Ah, there's John Wright. I'm just going to have a word with him. Back in a minute.'

When he was gone, Camilla murmured, 'In my experience, Leo's capable of behaving extremely selfishly.'

Anthony glanced at her. 'What do you mean?' He felt a prickle of resentment. What understanding could Camilla possibly have of Leo's character, given the limited dealings she had had with him?

Camilla, catching the sharpness in Anthony's voice, thought for a moment, then said, 'You remember I told you last February that I had the feeling that certain people in chambers might not altogether approve of the fact that I was seeing you, that we should cool things until I'd got my tenancy?'

Anthony nodded. 'What's that got to do with anything?'

'It was Leo who suggested that might be the case. But it was just a bluff. He wanted to split us up. In fact, he even went so far as to take me out to dinner and spell it out for me. Stop seeing Anthony, or I might make life difficult for you. He didn't say it in those words, of course, but the meaning was pretty clear.' She took a sip of her drink. 'He was jealous. He thought it might be an effective way of ending things between us. Don't you think that's pretty selfish behaviour?'

Anthony said nothing for a few moments. That Leo should go to such lengths to wreck things between himself and Camilla seemed astonishing, but at the same time it explained much about his behaviour since last Easter, when Camilla had got her tenancy and Anthony had started seeing her again. That must have been fairly galling for Leo. But what had he hoped to gain by such manoeuvres? This thought found voice. 'I don't see why he would do such a thing,' said Anthony.

'Don't you? Then you're pretty short-sighted. He's very close to you –'

'Was.'

'All right – was. And I think he regards your time and affection as his special property. He's never liked me.'

Anthony sighed. 'I suppose you're right. Okay, we're all capable of being selfish when it comes down to it. But I don't think Leo just upped and left through motives of selfishness.'

'Well, it's hardly considerate behaviour, is it? Poor old Henry and Felicity have to cope with the fall-out, and the rest of us suffer, too.'

Anthony stared at her. He realised that it was all black and white to Camilla, that she was too young and callous to understand the complexities and difficulties of someone like Leo. The confidence she had gained over the past year, he saw, had brought with it a touch of arrogance. He felt suddenly protective of Leo, in the face of her lack of concern for Leo's well-being. 'Well, we can't all be as brave and assured as you, can we?' he replied.

At that moment David came back to the table, Sarah in his wake. She shrugged off her coat and sat down, while David went to get her a drink.

'Nice to see you two together again. You must have missed one another.' Sarah smiled enigmatically and glanced at Anthony. 'Did the weeks seem terribly long?'

'Oh, spare us,' said Anthony. It was all very well, he realised, to agree that things stopped as soon as Camilla came back, but he was unable to behave with Sarah's cool composure. This guilt thing, he told himself, was out of control.

'Still, I'm sure you did your best to keep busy.' She glanced up as David set her drink down on the table. 'Thanks.'

'So,' said David, sitting down and turning to Anthony, 'you said earlier you'd been trying Leo's flat all day. No luck?'

Anthony shook his head. 'I'm going to go round after this. Not that I expect to find him there. I rather think he's gone to his place in the country.'

Sarah glanced from Anthony to David in surprise. 'What's this about Leo?'

'Didn't you know? He's just dropped everything, told Felicity and Henry he was going away for a few weeks.' David sipped his pint. 'Seems he has a few problems that need sorting out.'

Anthony noticed Sarah's troubled expression and remarked, 'Why are you looking so worried? It's nothing to you.' He couldn't help the slight brutality of his tone, a kind of revenge for her mischievous remark of a few moments ago.

Sarah turned and stared coldly at Anthony. He was

reminded suddenly of the unpredictability of her temper. 'Dear Anthony, you must think you have a monopoly on concern for Leo. For your information, I probably know him far better than you ever will. Don't look so surprised. We go back a long way. I regard him as a friend, and at least we've always treated one another with honesty. That's not exactly your speciality when it comes to relationships, is it?' She glanced at Camilla, then took a swallow of her drink and stood up, preparing to put on her coat. 'I don't feel like staying, somehow.' And she left.

'Phew!' said David. 'I'm not quite sure I understood what that was all about. I didn't know she and Leo were more than passing acquaintances. Well, well. Other people's lives, eh?'

Anthony said nothing for a few seconds, trying to fathom the implication of what Sarah had said. A strange quiet fell over the group. Anthony drained the remains of his pint and said at last, 'If I'm going round to Leo's, I'd better not leave it too late.'

'I'll come with you,' said Camilla.

They left David sitting alone at the table, slightly baffled. Clearly there was much that went on in chambers of which he knew absolutely nothing.

Anthony and Camilla walked in preoccupied silence along Fleet Street. It was drizzling and all the taxis which flashed past them were taken, their 'for hire' signs unlit. At the corner of Waterloo Bridge they stopped and waited.

'What was Sarah getting at in the pub?' asked Camilla suddenly.

Anthony, lost in his ruminations over Leo and Sarah, turned to glance at her. 'What do you mean?'

'About honesty in relationships not being your speciality. Why did she say it in that particular way?'

Anthony suddenly felt everything come to a head, his anxiety about Leo, his guilty conscience, his exasperation with Camilla's arrogance over Leo's problems – that and impossibility of finding a taxi-cab in the rain. 'It doesn't matter,' he muttered. He spoke incautiously, knowing as he did so that it would have been better and easier just to fob her off with some explanation concerning the time that he and Sarah had been seeing one another. But something – perhaps weariness at the concealment, or self-disgust – tempted him to let it all come out now. Then it could be dealt with. If she loved him enough, she would forgive him. Everyone made mistakes.

'What doesn't matter?' She looked at him, her eyes large and fearful. 'It's got something to do with the way you've been behaving recently, hasn't it? Something happened while I was away and you haven't told me.'

He turned to her. 'Yes, it did and I wish to God it never had. It meant absolutely nothing and I'm truly sorry about it. You've got to believe me.' He hesitated. 'I slept with Sarah. It was after a drinks thing in chambers. I suppose I'd had too much to drink, but beyond that I've got no excuses.' Already he was lying, he realised. By making it sound as though it had happened just once, he was hoping to lessen the crime, mitigate the effects. He waited, helplessly, his eyes on her face. 'I'm truly sorry.' She looked away, her expression unreadable. A taxi with its yellow light on came towards them and Anthony automatically lifted his hand. The cab drew up by the kerb. 'I'm glad you know now, in a way. It meant absolutely nothing and I've been feeling guilty as hell. Please, come on. We can talk in the taxi.' He opened the door, waiting for her to get in.

But Camilla remained motionless on the pavement. Then she shook her head. 'I can't come with you to Leo's. I'm going home.' She turned and walked quickly away through the rain, almost breaking into a run. Anthony called after her, his hand still on the handle of the taxi door.

The cabbie slid down his window and leaned over. 'Come ᵑ, mate! You getting in, or what?'

Anthony hesitated, watching her hurrying off down Fleet

Street. Maybe it would be better to let her go, talk to her later. It was done now. He got into the cab and gave the driver Leo's address.

When they reached the square in Belgravia, Anthony asked the cabbie to wait. He got out, glancing up at the darkened windows, and went up the few steps to the front door, where he pressed the bell. There was no answer. He waited for a few minutes, then rang again. At last he turned and went back down the steps to the cab.

He took the taxi home, had something to eat, and after an hour or so rang Camilla. She sounded weary, but at least she was prepared to talk to him. Reproach, he thought, was a good sign, the first step towards forgiving him.

'I can't believe that you would do something like that, take advantage of the fact that I was away and sleep with someone else.' On her way home, after leaving Anthony standing by the taxi, Camilla had resolved that she would end things between them. Hurt and anger had been uppermost. It seemed that what Anthony had done was unforgivable. Now, hearing his voice, she felt a fatal reluctance to let it all go, just like that.

'I told you. It was a mistake, a really stupid thing to have done, and I've been regretting it ever since it happened. It meant nothing. We'd had a lot to drink, and you know how Sarah can be –'

'Oh, please, Anthony! Don't try to blame it on Sarah! Credit me with a little sense.'

'No, no, you're right. I mean, I'm just trying to explain how it happened. I'm so, so sorry. What else can I say?'

'Anthony.' She sighed miserably. 'You sound as though you're apologising for breaking a window, or something. We're talking about trust here. About feelings. What you've done changes things.'

'It mustn't. You mustn't let it. That's the last thing I want. That is what I'm afraid of more than anything else. Please. I love you. I'm asking you to forgive me.'

Camilla didn't speak for a few minutes. Then at last she said, 'I don't know. I'm feeling very tired and upset, and a bit confused. What you've done has really hurt me. I don't think you realise that.'

'I do. Of course I do.'

'Well, anyway, I've got a lot on tomorrow, so I'm going to bed early.'

'Will I see you tomorrow evening?'

'I don't know. Let's just leave it for now, shall we?'

It wasn't entirely satisfactory, thought Anthony when he hung up. But he had a feeling that, with a little time, it could be made all right again. Okay, so he hadn't been entirely honest with her. But how could he possibly tell her the whole truth? She might overlook one single act of infidelity, but a whole series, night after night? He doubted it. And he didn't blame her. He could look back on his brief fling with Sarah and know it was unforgivable, but on the other hand he knew exactly why he had done it. Because Sarah had been there, on offer. Not that it was any excuse. He just had a weak character where sex was concerned. He sat pondering the deep and contradictory mysteries of sexuality and morality for some time.

A week later, Charles announced that he was going to Romania to film some footage for his latest documentary.

'How long will you be gone?' asked Rachel.

'Only a couple of weeks. Though why an entire television crew has to be transported all the way to the foothills of the Transylvanian Alps just to film me talking about the formation of the anti-Ottoman coalition is beyond me. I could as well do it from the bottom of our back garden. Still –' he embraced Rachel and kissed her nose '– tell me you'll miss me.'

'I shall.' It was true. She felt a hollow pang at the thought of being without his steady, loving, cheerful company even for a couple of weeks. The whole custody business seemed to keep her nerves in a constant brittle state and Charles was important to her sanity. She wanted it all settled, finished, so that she could sort out her contradictory feelings about Leo, relegate him to his proper place in her life. Then she would feel that she and Charles and Oliver were a safe unit. 'Oliver will miss you most, I suspect. He has you around all day.'

'I'll bring him back a Vlad the Impaler doll. I'll bet the shops in Bucharest are bursting with them.'

Rachel laughed helplessly. 'Don't you dare!' She hugged him. 'When do you leave?'

'Tomorrow afternoon. I wish I could take you with me.' He paused, then looked suddenly inspired. 'In fact, why don't you come? I'll bet if we slip apple-cheeked Margaret a serious wad of money she'd be prepared to move in for the duration. Then Oliver would be regularly fed and watered, and all would be hunky-dory. What do you think?' The idea was growing in attraction at top speed in Charles's mind. Oliver took up so much of Rachel's time and attention when she was at home – which, given her work, was not as much as Charles would like. He longed to have her to himself, without all the responsibilities and distractions that Oliver involved. Sometimes just having a sustained conversation seemed like hard work with Oliver around. He was, without question, the number one man in Rachel's life, a position which Charles very much wanted to occupy, even if only for two weeks.

But Charles could tell from her expression that she didn't feel the same enthusiasm as he did for the idea. 'Oh, Charles, it's a lovely idea . . . But two weeks is a long time. I couldn't just leave Oliver. He'd miss me dreadfully. He's too little to understand, and he might think I was never coming back, or something awful like that.'

'Well, a week then,' urged Charles, feeling the impetus slipping away. 'One week's not long.'

'It would be to him. And there's my work, you know. It not that easy just to drop things.'

'What if you were suddenly taken ill, or something? You'd have to drop it then. And the world wouldn't come to an end because of it. Someone else would hold the fort. Come on – live a little. Come with me. Just for a few days. We could have a great time, just the two of us.'

The last five words were the wrong ones. Although Rachel trusted Charles's affection for Oliver, she harboured a subconscious feeling that he might prefer it if Oliver did not exist. It made her react defensively, as she did now, grabbing at an excuse. 'Charles, it's not that easy. Frankly, I don't think I have any holiday time left, not after the three weeks I took over the summer and the time that I want to take off at Christmas.' She made a rueful face. 'I'm sorry, darling. It's a nice idea, but for all those reasons, I really don't see that it's possible.'

Charles sighed. He was fighting a losing battle here. It happened whenever he suggested that they should spend some time away from Oliver, even if it was just dinner together in Bath. Rachel was always reluctant. And on the odd occasions when they were apart from the child – such as the times when Leo took him for the day – she was on edge, constantly thinking about him, waiting for the hours to pass until she was with him again. Charles had to admit to himself that he very strongly hoped that the court would decide in Leo's favour in the matter of contact with Oliver. Not just for Oliver's sake, or for Leo's, but for his own.

'Okay,' he said with a rueful smile. 'It was just a thought.'

The week after Charles's departure went by in a humdrum fashion. Rachel made sure that she left work promptly every night so that she would be home in time to bath Oliver and read to him before he went to bed. Margaret, the nanny from the village, had to come in earlier than usual in the mornings ɔ be there when Rachel went to work. Often Oliver was still ˩eep when she left.

ᴳuy Fawkes Night fell in the middle of that first week, and

Rachel wheeled Oliver in his push-chair down to the village green to watch the fireworks in the evening and wished that Charles could be there. She realised then, as she stood watching the rockets explode into crystalline stars against the black night, how much she loved and relied upon Charles as a part of her peace and order and security. He was her bedrock. The feelings she had for Leo were something much darker, to do with pain and rejection, and experiences she did not care to revisit. Still he persisted in her thoughts, and in her love, despite every effort she made to excise him.

Thoughts of Leo were still in her mind next morning at work and, when the switchboard put through a call from him, the coincidence of it startled her. 'Leo,' she said, 'I was just thinking about you.'

'Were you?' His voice sounded tired.

He said nothing more, and after a pause she asked, 'Are you all right? You sound a bit low.'

'Yes – no – I'm fine. I just wondered if I could see Oliver this weekend, maybe on Saturday. If that's all right with you. And Charles, of course.'

'Well, the thing is, Charles is away at the moment, and –' She stopped, realising that she was letting herself be panicked by the idea of being on her own for a day at the weekend. Absurd. Unhealthy. 'Still,' she went on, 'I don't suppose that makes any difference. Yes, if you like. Saturday's fine.' She could get a few chores done while Oliver was away, things which always got slowed down when he was around, and perhaps go into Bath to do some shopping. It would fill in the time. Better than Sunday, when the hours would just drag. 'What time will you pick him up?'

'About ten. I'll have him back by six.'

There was an odd lifelessness in Leo's voice, as though some subtle strength had faded from his personality. The change left Rachel at a loss. All their recent exchanges had been charged, often vitriolic, but there had always been lif in them.

'That's fine. I'll have his things ready.' She hesitated. 'Leo, are you sure you're all right? You don't sound yourself.'

'Yes,' snapped Leo. 'I'm absolutely fine. Just tired.'

That was marginally better, to hear him get tetchy. 'Okay, okay. I'll see you on Saturday, then. Bye.'

Leo said nothing, just hung up. Rachel put the phone down slowly. She thought of Leo coming to fetch Oliver on Saturday, of seeing him on her own, without Charles there. Charles's presence always kept the atmosphere nice and even. Without him there, Leo might take the opportunity to go on the offensive. She hoped not. She didn't think she could stand that. If the temperature rose, she might find herself giving way to feelings she hardly wished to acknowledge. She just wanted relations with Leo to stay neutral and safe. And then she realised that the thought of seeing him on her own made her a little afraid. Afraid and excited.

'Good heavens!' said Rachel. Then she laughed, putting her hand to her mouth. 'I didn't realise you were growing a beard.'

'I'm not,' said Leo. 'I just can't be bothered to shave.' He stood in the doorway on Saturday morning in his battered leather jacket and old trousers, his shirt unbuttoned at the neck. After the initial shock of his week-old beard, Rachel realised that his hair was longer too. That, and the contrasting darkness of his beard, made him look younger and slightly sinister. His appearance sat at odds with his air of weary carelessness.

Oliver toddled towards Leo and clung to his trouser leg, waiting to be picked up. Leo hoisted him up to his shoulder and Oliver laughed and passed a small, fat hand over the dark bristles of Leo's beard.

'What do your clients think?' asked Rachel, folding her ~ms.

'I haven't got any,' replied Leo indifferently. He kissed

Oliver and smiled at him. It was a smile solely for Oliver, clearly unrelated to anything else in life.

'What do you mean?' asked Rachel.

Leo turned to look at her again, as though seeing her properly for the first time. 'I'm having a few days off. That's all.' He spoke calmly, as if in reassurance.

Rachel was still puzzled. 'Your clerk can't be very happy about that. Or was it planned?'

To this Leo made no answer, but wandered towards the kitchen table, Oliver still in his arms, and picked up the bag of Oliver's belongings. 'Six all right?' he asked.

'Yes,' replied Rachel, 'that's fine.'

'Come on, mate, let's hit the road,' said Leo to Oliver. He walked to the door, then turned. 'Where is Charles, by the way?'

'He's in Romania, filming.'

Leo nodded, then walked out to the car. Rachel stood in the doorway and watched them drive away. It was only when they were out of sight that it occurred to her that never for one moment had there been the slightest suggestion of tension or animosity between them. Whatever apprehension she might have had about betraying her perplexed feelings for him had been entirely unfounded. There had been simply nothing to which to respond. In fact, he had arrived and departed in what she could only think of as a kind of emotional vacuum. She thought about it for a while, about his altered appearance and manner, and wondered if she should have let Oliver go with him. Telling herself this was absurd, she went back into the house and set about filling the emptiness with domestic activity.

She had got a mere half an hour's work done when the phone rang. The voice at the other end was a woman's, one Rachel did not recognise.

'Is that Rachel Davies?' asked the voice uncertainly.

'Yes.'

For a few seconds there was nothing but concern

elderly breathing, then the woman went on, 'My name's Mrs Munby. I'm a neighbour of your mother's.'

'Oh ... Mrs Munby.' Rachel's gathering recollection of a taciturn, large-bosomed woman from the house next door to her mother's was almost instantly replaced with a sense of foreboding. 'What's wrong?' she asked. 'Is my mother all right?'

'Well, that's why I'm calling. They took her into the hospital this morning, about half an hour ago. St Mary's. I went outside when I saw the ambulance, and the ambulance people said did I know who her nearest relative was, and I said, well, she has a daughter, and I had a look in your mother's address book and found your number. They said would I call you, and I said I would.'

'What's wrong with her?' Rachel felt oppressed by a sense of guilt and dread.

'I don't know, to be honest, dear, but I think it must be her heart. I thought I'd better find out how she was before I called you, but when I spoke to the hospital all they would say was that you should get there as soon as you could. I'm sorry to be the bearer of bad tidings.' She waited, breathing stertorously, for Rachel to speak.

Rachel managed to keep her voice calm. 'Thank you for calling me, Mrs Munby. I'll go to the hospital straight away.'

'Is there anything you want me to do? I've locked the house up for her, taken the keys and so forth.'

'No, no, thanks. You've been very kind. I might call round later, depending on how my mother is. Goodbye.'

Rachel hung up and glanced at her watch; her immediate thoughts were for Oliver. Damn, Leo wouldn't be at Stanton yet. She could try his mobile ... But when she tried, the maddeningly sweet voice of a female automaton informed her that the mobile phone she was ringing was switched off. When she called the house at Stanton and tried to leave a message, the phone at the other end merely rang and rang. d Leo suddenly taken against modern technology? Rachel wondered, as she replaced the receiver. Anyway, she would just have to go to her mother and try Leo later. She grabbed her coat and her keys, locked up the house and hurried to the car.

'So, baby boy, where shall it be?' murmured Leo as he drove, glancing at Oliver in the car seat next to him. 'South America? France? Where can we bury ourselves out of sight? Just think of all the people Daddy knows, all the lawyers and the business men and the wheelers and dealers . . . do you think they'd help us?' Oliver glanced up at his father, following the sound of the words with brief wonder, then became absorbed once more in the little plastic plane he was playing with. 'But what would I do with you? What kind of a time would we have, and what would become of us both?' Leo sighed, turning off the motorway on to the road to Stanton. 'And what would your poor mother do if I were to spirit you off somewhere? Go demented, no doubt, and turn into a hysterical wreck for the rest of her life. I couldn't do that to old Charles, now could I? No, nor to Mummy, I suppose. So we'll all go on as we are . . .'

He carried on talking all the way to the house, unaware that he was doing so, his mind flitting from thought to thought, unable to fix on anything. He did not care to think much at the moment. At least he would have Oliver for company today, something to focus on, a reason for living. Each day seemed painfully empty of such reasons.

Rachel drove the fifteen miles to Bath, forcing herself to think about her mother, something which she usually avoided doing. The weight of guilt was heavy. She thought about the woman her mother had been when Rachel was a little girl – slim, pretty, fairly quiet, but cheerful and affectionate in an absent-minded kind of way. She remembered murmurings among her aunts about her mother having had 'a difficu￼ time' when Rachel was born, so Rachel had always suppos￼

this to be the reason why her mother had had no more children. Rachel, even then, had felt herself in some vague way responsible for making her mother suffer – though how, she did not know. But the mother of her childhood had been transformed by the events of Rachel's adolescence. Even as she drove, Rachel found herself physically flinching at the recollection of her mother's tearful anger, the shouting, the blame, when Rachel had finally summoned up the courage to tell a teacher at school about what her father had been doing to her. Then the awful blackness of that time, being disbelieved, then believed, her father going to prison and out of her life for ever. She had never wanted that.

Rachel found her face wet with tears as she took herself back to the pain and difficulty of those days, about which she so rarely thought and never spoke. She had told no one except Leo. Oh, God, Leo ... How much he had helped, how much he had done to restore her faith and her belief in people – and then how utterly he had undone all that with his lies and deceit. She wiped the tears quickly away, but still they came, blurring her vision. She could look back now, she realised, and understand why her mother had been so angry, why she had blamed Rachel for everything that had happened, rather than her husband. She could trace now, in her memory of all the things her mother had called her, the tracks of her mother's own shame and guilt. Had she known what was happening and ignored it? Rachel had always wondered about that. It had not been a question she could ask. After her father had gone to jail, the lines of communication went dead between Rachel and her mother. Oh, they had an outward relationship, they spoke of mundane matters, life went drearily on, her mother still made her packed lunch every day, ironed her school blouses, saw to it that Rachel was fed and clothed. But from that time, Rachel had been alone.

Why, she wondered now as she drove, had she clung to pathetic remnants of their relationship? When she had left home to go to university, she could have cut her ties, left her mother behind her. After all, she didn't feel her mother wanted her any more, or regarded her as anything more than a reminder of shameful events, but somehow Rachel had never managed to do it. She still sent birthday and Christmas cards, she still made the occasional – very occasional – visit with Oliver. Not that her mother seemed to welcome these visits, or ever acknowledged the cards. So why did she do it? Why did she send out these forlorn little signals? Was she waiting for forgiveness? Possibly. Like every child who is the victim, but still feels itself to be the perpetrator, the culprit, she was constantly apologising. That was why she was driving to the hospital now.

When she arrived, Rachel was shown to the coronary care unit, where her mother lay in bed, oddly small and insignificant among the paraphernalia of monitors and drips and bedside equipment. She was unconscious, but Rachel could see the slight rise and fall of her thin chest as she breathed, and a little blip ran with bright regularity across the monitor screen.

'The doctor knows you're here. He'll be along in a minute,' said a nurse.

Rachel sat down at the bedside and stared at her mother, not sure what to feel or do. Her mother's hand, with a patch of white tape holding the drip in place, lay on the bedspread, and Rachel felt she should touch it, hold it. But she had no wish to. She couldn't remember how long it was since she had touched her mother. So she sat gazing at her mother's face, trying to think about nothing.

The doctor came after twenty minutes.

'Your mother has had a massive heart attack,' he told her. 'She's very unstable, I'm afraid.'

'So – so what is likely to happen?'

'Well, we're doing everything we can, but the chances of stabilising her aren't very good, I have to tell you. There is a risk that she may have another heart attack within the next twenty-four to forty-eight hours.'

Rachel nodded. 'I see. Can I stay with her?'

'Of course. There's a relatives' rest room just down the corridor, where you can make tea and coffee.'

They spoke for a few more minutes, then he left. Rachel looked at her watch. It was half past eleven. She gazed helplessly at her mother, wishing she felt more, guilty that she did not. She must stay, that much she knew. However little life her mother had left, it was all eternity to her. She might wake up and, if she did, she would be frightened. Rachel couldn't leave her alone.

She sat there for several long hours. Occasionally her mother stirred, and once she seemed to mutter something, but it was indistinct. The little pulse of light blipped over and over on the screen. Twice Rachel went to make tea in the rest area, and in the middle of the afternoon she purchased a sandwich from a vending machine. At five o'clock she realised that she would have to ring Leo. She took her mobile phone from her handbag, then hesitated. Wasn't there something about not using mobile phones in hospitals, in case they interfered with the equipment? She went in search of a pay phone and rang the house at Stanton, and was relieved when Leo replied. She explained what had happened and where she was.

'The thing is, I can't leave her. The doctor seems to think she might not last the night out. Oliver will have to stay with you. He's got no pyjamas, but I did put a change of clothes in with his things – Oh, has he? Well, he'll just have to make do with those tomorrow. How many nappies have you got? . . . I suppose he can do without cleaning his teeth for one night . . . Can I speak to him for a minute?' Leo put Oliver on the phone and Rachel talked to him, finding comfort in his incoherent bubbles of noise. Then she spoke to Leo again. 'I feel so guilty, Leo. Something in me just wants all this to hurry up. How can I feel like that? It's her *life*, after all. But I just can't help this awful feeling of impatience. And pity, I suppose. Anyway, look after Oliver for me. I'll call you again when – well, if anything changes.'

Rachel hung up and wandered back to her mother's room. On the way she passed the hospital shop and paused, wondering if it would be some awful betrayal to buy something to read, just to relieve the tedium of the hours. She bought a paperback, went back to the coronary care unit, and sat and read, and waited.

Chapter fifteen

'You shouldn't go out. It's getting too dark,' said Felicity, glancing out of the window at the gathering dusk.

l 'Well, cabbies have to drive in the bleeding dark, don't they?' Vince pulled on his jacket and took the bike keys from a shelf. 'How am I ever going to get this knowledge done unless I put in the hours?'

'You could have gone out earlier, when it was daylight, 'stead of sitting around watching television.'

'Yeah, well, that was an important match, that was.'

'And you've been drinking.'

'Couple of cans doesn't count as drinkin', Fliss. Anyway, I'll be back later. Then we can have a take-away.'

'All right,' sighed Felicity. 'Take care.'

Vince went out of the flat and down the two flights of stairs to the street. He fetched his bike from the lock-up where he kept it two streets away and sped off, his list of routes clipped to the board in front of him.

It was only when he reached Shaftesbury Avenue that it occurred to Vince that perhaps half past five on a Saturday evening wasn't the best time to be navigating and memorising a route from the National Gallery to Wembley Stadium. The traffic was infuriatingly slow as he wove his way round buses and between lines of cars. He slewed left into a side street, almost running into a little knot of pedestrians blocking his way. Vince revved and swore at them, and they fell back. He was about to head off up the street when suddenly he felt someone kick the back of his bike, not once, but twice, and shout a few obscenities at him. Vince stopped and looked round at two youths who were eyeing him aggressively. Stepping off the bike, he walked back to them.

'You kick my bike? You –' He jabbed one of the youths in the chest with the fingers of one hand. 'You fucking kicked my bike, didn't you?'

'What if I did? You're asking for it, you are. You own the road, or what? Me and my mate was walking there.'

The youth's mate was looking uncertainly at Vince, sizing him up, hoping there wasn't going to be trouble. Vince and the youth began pushing and shoving, swearing at one another. A few pedestrians slowed down to witness the altercation. After that, everything moved very suddenly. Vince hit the youth, who tried to punch him back but only managed to connect with Vince's helmet, and the next thing the boy was on the ground. Still enraged, Vince swung a foot at his head and kicked the youth viciously so that he fell back, his head hitting the side of the pavement with a sickening crunch. The blood that flowed astonished even Vince. The boy's mate launched himself at Vince, but some people had already grabbed Vince, pinning his arms behind him to restrain him and a man was kneeling beside the youth on the pavement, shouting for someone to get an ambulance. The next ten minutes, for Vince, were a blur of people and voices and flashing police lights. He watched the boy he had kicked being stretchered into an ambulance and was aware of two policemen talking to excited witnesses from the crowd.

One of the policemen turned to where Vince was still being held by onlookers. 'Come on, son,' he said, taking Vince by the elbow and leading him towards the police car.

'Hold on – what about my bike? That's my bike there. I can't just leave it!'

'We'll take care of it, don't you worry,' replied the policeman, glancing at Vince's bike and noticing the board marked out with the city routes. 'Doing the knowledge, are you? I'm afraid you've damaged your chances there a bit.' He shook his head in mock sympathy.

'What you on about?' Vince tried to shake off the policeman's grip as he got into the back of the car.

'You go down on a charge of GBH, son, and I'm afraid the Public Carriage Office have to be informed. Then that's that. They don't like their cabbies to have records for violent crime, do they? And you can see their point.'

Vince said nothing, feeling his insides shrivelling into a small, nerveless ball. He threw one last glance at his bike lying by the side of the road as the police car drove off.

Rachel sat with her mother throughout the night. She tried to read, but found herself constantly glancing at the monitors, then at every slight rise and fall of her mother's chest. Towards morning she dozed in the chair, and woke up with a stiff back and a headache. She went to the rest area to make herself some coffee and stood at the window watching the grey light filtering across the roof-tops, listening to the sounds of the hospital preparing for the day. She wondered whether Oliver was awake and whether Leo had taken him into bed with him, the way he used to when he was a tiny baby, when it had been the three of them.

She went back slowly to the coronary care unit, then stopped in the doorway. A group of people were standing round her mother's bed. She could tell from their voices and movements that an urgent moment had just passed. She glanced at the dead monitor screen, then walked in.

The doctor who had spoken to her earlier turned to her. 'I'm sorry, Mrs Davies. Your mother had another attack. It was very sudden. We couldn't resuscitate her.'

Rachel nodded at the doctor, her face expressionless. She felt totally blank. Then she sat down next to the bed where her mother lay and suddenly, in the tiredness which overwhelmed her, she found she could do what was expected of her, and wept.

*

Half an hour later she drove to the street where her mother lived, a row of modest terraced houses with tiny front gardens, and rang the bell of Mrs Munby's house. Mrs Munby came to the door in dressing-gown and hairnet. Rachel apologised for disturbing her so early and told her the news of her mother's death. After much tut-tutting and sympathy, Mrs Munby handed over Mrs Dean's keys, and Rachel went next door and let herself into the house. In the little living-room a copy of the *Radio Times* still lay open on the arm of a chair and a cigarette, presumably her mother's last, had burned itself out in a brass ashtray in a long and perfect cylinder of grey ash. The dishes from her mother's evening meal still sat in the sink in the kitchen. Rachel washed them, dried them and put them away. She could bear to do no more for the moment, she decided. Were there things to do, like cancelling milk and papers, and so on? Perhaps, but her tired mind couldn't face the thought of them right now. She went into the hallway, sat down on the stairs, and took out her phone to call Leo and tell him she would be with him and Oliver in a couple of hours.

By the time she reached Stanton, the early November sun had burned away the mist, leaving a perfect autumn day, soundless, bright and beautiful. Rachel parked her car on the gravel driveway and sat for a moment, looking at the house, remembering the first time she had come here, the haven it had been. She had been so much in love with Leo that anything of his possessed a special enchantment, but even without him she would have loved this place. She got out of the car and went to the front door, hesitated for a moment, then turned and walked round to the back door. She came into the kitchen and found a scene of domestic tranquillity: Oliver sitting in his high-chair eating toast and butter, Leo cooking breakfast.

He glanced up as she came in, mildly startled. 'I didn't hear your car.'

Rachel went over to Oliver, who put up small buttery

hands as she bent to kiss him. He grabbed a hank of her hair. 'Ow! Oliver!' She laughed and gently disengaged his hands from her hair. She turned to Leo. 'How has it been?'

'Terrific. Having him for the night was a real bonus. We've had a great time – haven't we, Oliver?'

By way of reply Oliver carefully dropped his toast on to the floor, leaning over the table of his high-chair to watch it fall.

'You look worn out,' said Leo, glancing at Rachel. 'There's some coffee on. Would you like a cup?'

She nodded and took off her coat, then sat down at the kitchen table. She saw that Leo was frying bacon and eggs, and suddenly felt ravenously hungry. 'I'd love some breakfast, too, if it isn't too much trouble.'

'Okay.' Leo poured her some coffee and put some toast on. He brought two plates over and sat down, and they ate. Rachel talked for a little while about her night at the hospital, then fell silent. She sipped her coffee and looked thoughtfully at Leo.

'I still can't get used to that beard.'

'It's a little itchy. I may shave it off. I think Oliver likes it, though.' Leo stretched out a hand to Oliver, who grabbed it and kicked manfully in his high-chair. Leo lifted the boy out and sat him on his lap.

Rachel gazed at the two of them, then asked quietly, 'What's been going on?'

'Mmm?'

'The beard, the way you look, the way you – Oh, I don't know. Something's happened. I could tell when you came to pick him up, all that stuff about having a few days off.' Leo said nothing, clapping Oliver's pudgy hands together between his own, his blue eyes distant and thoughtful. 'Has it anything to do with that boy who answered the phone at your flat? I've forgotten his name.'

Joshua. The word formed itself in Leo's mind, but he couldn't say it. He replied with an effort, 'A little. He left. I didn't want him to. But he left.' Rachel was conscious of the pain it still gave her to know he could love other men, but not her. 'And I've just become rather – rather disenchanted with life in general.' He gave a bleak smile. 'I came down here to get away from myself.'

Rachel cupped her chin in her hands. 'I don't know what you mean.'

'To get away from me. Leo Davies, the barrister who lives in Belgravia, who has such a wonderfully successful legal practice and a whole host of distinguished clients and friends, and who seduces young men on the quiet, and who completely managed to screw up his application for access to his own son as a result.' He shook his head. 'It was like some bizarre comedy sketch. There I was, doing my best to impress these two nerds from social services, or wherever they breed these people, trying to convince them that I lead a blameless life and that Oliver couldn't wish for a better place to stay on his weekends off, when my ex-lover came to the door. To collect his belongings.' Oliver wriggled down from Leo's knee and began to busy himself with his toys on the kitchen floor. Rachel noticed the whiteness of Leo's knuckles as he clasped his hands together. 'It was my last chance, you see. Or I thought it was. I begged him to stay. I utterly abased myself. And these welfare people watched it all.' He smiled a thin smile. 'Which I should think just about completely buggers up my chances, wouldn't you say?' Leo stood up. 'More coffee?'

Rachel had no idea what to say. She watched as Leo poured coffee into her cup, then was suddenly aware of her mind taking a sharp dip, of blackness coating her vision for a few seconds. She wondered if she was about to faint. 'Leo,' she said, 'I think I need to lie down.' She closed her eyes.

'Are you all right?'

She opened her eyes and shook her head to clear it. 'Just utterly exhausted. I haven't slept all night.'

'Go up and have a nap. Oliver and I have things to do.

275

We'll go and get the papers, then after lunch I'll take him for a walk. There are some horses down the road that he likes to feed.'

'All right. Thanks.' Rachel rose and went upstairs. She paused on the landing. Through the open door she could see Leo's enormous bed, the one that she had always refused to sleep in, rumpled and unmade, Oliver's toy elephant lying on the covers. She went in, kicked off her shoes, got into bed and pulled up the covers. Breathing in the smell of Leo, she fell asleep in minutes.

The sound of Oliver crying woke Rachel some hours later. She blinked, uncertain where she was at first. She glanced at her watch and saw that it was almost four o'clock. The light outside was fading. She'd been asleep for nearly six hours. She got out of bed and went downstairs.

Oliver was sitting at the bottom of the stairs, screaming, while Leo knelt in front of him and tugged at his wellingtons.

'What's the matter?' asked Rachel. She leaned past Oliver to her bag on the end of the banisters and fished in it for a hairbrush.

'I can't persuade him that he should take off his muddy wellingtons when he comes into the house,' said Leo in exasperation. 'There.' He got the second boot off, and stood up with them in his hand. Oliver lay back on the stairs and roared. 'Cry away, my man. These are going to the back door.'

'What's the problem with a little mud?' asked Rachel, shrugging.

'A little mud? They're covered in cow shit.' He glanced up at Rachel as he crossed the hall and thought, fleetingly, how beautiful she always managed to look, even when she'd just woken up.

Rachel put down the hairbrush and picked up Oliver, then padded barefoot into the drawing-room with him. She sat down on a sofa, cuddling him. The room was cosy, a large fire burning in the grate, the Sunday papers scattered in a heap on the floor near Oliver's toys.

Leo came into the room and switched on a couple of lamps, drawing the curtains against the gathering dusk. He began to tidy up the papers. 'What about a drink?' he asked Rachel.

'Thanks. I think I'll have a small brandy. It's that kind of day. And I feel like something revivifying.' She yawned and kissed the top of Oliver's head. He snuffled away the last of his tears and began to suck his thumb.

'Aren't you having one?' she asked, as Leo handed her a glass.

He shook his head and sat down in an armchair opposite. 'I've rather been punishing the stuff in the last few weeks. Thought it was about time I gave it a rest.'

Silence fell. A log in the grate slipped, loosing a little shower of crackling sparks.

Rachel felt the warmth of the brandy lifting her spirits. A memory of the hospital came to her and she pushed it aside. She didn't want to think of her mother now. That would come later. 'This is good,' she remarked after a while.

'The brandy? Yes, it's rather rare stuff. Some client –'

'No,' she said quickly. 'I meant being here. Just the three of us. You and me and Oliver.' A sudden sense of the importance of this moment touched Rachel, a realisation that this was the last chance she would ever have to try and salvage what was left of their relationship. Mad and hopeless though she knew it to be, she had to speak. 'If we could be together like this all the time, you wouldn't have to worry about access to Oliver, and all that business. The person you are, the one you described earlier – you don't have to be like that, you know.'

'Don't I?' Leo gazed at the fire.

'I still love you. In spite of everything, I find I do. I could help you, whatever the trouble is. I really think I could.'

He turned to look at her. She sat like a Madonna, absently

277

stroking Oliver's hair, her beautiful eyes fixed on Leo's face. He saw that Oliver had fallen asleep, his small face slack against Rachel's body. 'What about Charles?'

Rachel bent her head. 'I'm not saying that I don't love Charles. I do. He's kind and very supportive, and he looks after me. Of course I love him. But if it meant that you and Oliver and I could be together –'

'It's not possible,' said Leo suddenly. 'For any number of reasons.' He sighed, glancing away from Rachel, not wanting to see that look on her face, that look of humility and patience and hope. 'First of all, I've done you far too much damage already. I don't know if it's some sort of pattern programmed into you, but you mustn't keep coming back for more pain and rejection. That's what would happen. I don't want to sound brutal, but you know it's true. I tried to tell you before we got married. You've found it all out for yourself. Why should you want to come back for more?'

'I love you. And I love Oliver.'

'You hate me. You must. What if I were to tell you that if Joshua were to walk through that door right now, I'd go to him? Without hesitation, without thought, I'd go to him.' Rachel said nothing. 'There are other reasons why it's not possible. You need a family. You've just lost your mother. Don't you think that might have something to do with the way you're feeling? I can't give you any of that. Tell me, how often do you see Charles's sister and her family?'

'Quite often. Oliver sometimes plays with Lottie, Charles's niece. She's three.'

'And Charles has grown-up children. I remember you telling me that you get on well with them.'

'Yes.'

'That's a family, Rachel. Charles can give you something I never could. He can give you and Oliver security and love. It's what you need, now more than ever. Not more uncertainty and deception and unhappiness. Because that's what you're asking for in me.'

Rachel was silent for a moment, beaten down by Leo's arguments. Then she lifted her eyes and looked at him curiously. 'You don't think much of yourself, do you?'

'No,' replied Leo, 'I don't. In many respects I think I'm a failure. The one thing I wanted to succeed at – being a father to Oliver – looks like eluding me, too.' He sighed and stood up. 'I'll go and put Oliver's things together. You should be heading back before it gets too late.'

He left the room. Rachel sat gazing at the fire, cradling Oliver's small, inert body, knowing that it was the last time she would ever offer herself to Leo. Certain things between them had been dead for a long time, if they had ever been alive in the first place. She saw that now, suddenly and clearly, and she wished with all her might that Charles were not away.

On Monday, Felicity recounted her woes of the weekend to Henry. 'They've charged Vince with GBH. The bloke he did over is still in hospital and he's critical. Oh, God, Henry,' she groaned, 'why does he always have to mess it up? Every bloody time, he screws it up. If he goes down, that's the end of his chances of getting his black cab licence. And then what's he going to do? I had my hopes pinned on him getting his knowledge. Now what chance has he got of making a living? He's good for eff-all, is Vince.'

Jeremy strode into the clerks' room. 'Why didn't anybody tell me that hearing date had been changed? Everything's going to hell around here. First Leo walks out, I get landed with half his work –' He grabbed a brief out of the basket. 'I've been waiting for this! Why didn't you tell me it had come in? And why can't you start chasing up some of my fee notes? I've got a tax bill the size of a third world country's debt. I don't know how you two run things. Place is a madhouse.' He strode out again, and Felicity and Henry snorted with laughter.

'You should be glad you're leaving,' observed Henry. 'I sometimes wonder why I stay.'

'Oh, Henry! Don't remind me. How do you think it's going to be when I'm out of a job, with a new baby, and Vince has got no work?'

'True,' agreed Henry miserably, wishing that there were a way of making his fantasy – the one in which Felicity left Vince because she found herself deeply in love with Henry and couldn't live without him – a reality. Some chance. It seemed Felicity would stick with her beloved Vince, no matter what. 'Don't worry. It'll all work out,' he said mournfully.

Camilla came downstairs. 'I'm just going over to Crown Office Row. I'll only be ten minutes. If John Sharples calls, tell him I'll call him back.'

'Okay,' said Henry.

Camilla crossed Caper Court in the autumn sunshine, brooding on Anthony. The hurt of his casual betrayal of her while she was away had lessened over the last few days, but it had left in its wake a new understanding of the kind of person Anthony was, or was capable of being. She still felt as much for him as she had ever done, so much so that she was prepared to forgive him and let things go on as before, but she realised that the incident had brought about a certain shift in the balance of their relationship. An element of trust had gone. Anthony kept saying how sorry he was, in a way that rather puzzled Camilla, as though it was something everyone did now and again, as though he had a right to be forgiven.

Sarah was crossing Fountain Court when she saw Camilla coming out of Caper Court. She quickened her stride so that the two of them fell into step walking down Middle Temple Lane.

'Hi,' said Sarah with a smile. 'Off to a con?'

Camilla marvelled at her falseness. How could she be so friendly after what she had done? No doubt she imagined that it was a safe little secret between herself and Anthony. That would explain her wonderfully smug smile. Sarah liked to be in the ascendant, behaving in that cool, knowing fashion which had so intimidated Camilla when they had been students at Oxford together.

'No, I'm dropping some papers off,' replied Camilla, her manner chilly.

'I'm just off to the library.' They turned the corner into Crown Office Row, walking in silence. 'Everything all right between you and Anthony?' asked Sarah, with an air of interested innocence.

Camilla stopped and turned to look at her. 'Why do you ask? You really seem unduly interested in how things are between myself and Anthony. It may interest you to know that whatever damage you tried to do while I was away hasn't had much effect. I know exactly what happened.'

Sarah flicked her blonde hair back from her shoulders. So Anthony had felt obliged to confess, had he? She had calculated that his simple conscience would eventually get the better of him. But how much had he really told Camilla? Not everything, clearly. Sarah's smile broadened. 'Do you? You must be remarkably forgiving, in that case. It was really a rather strenuous two weeks. He couldn't leave me alone for a single night. I was worn out by the end, quite glad to see you back.'

Camilla was dumbstruck, totally taken aback by the outrageousness of what Sarah had said.

Sarah looked at Camilla with an expression of feigned concern. 'Oh, I haven't said the wrong thing, have I? I can be so indiscreet. It's a dreadful failing.'

Camilla struggled against the helpless, angry tears that came to her eyes. 'You are a complete bitch. The worst I've ever known. I don't believe anything you say, Sarah. No one in their right mind would. You're a scheming, conniving trouble-maker.' Her voice shook as she tried to control it, wishing that she could match Sarah's composure. But how could she? If what Sarah said was true, then Anthony had deceived her utterly, had made a complete mockery of her and of their relationship.

Sarah shrugged. 'Don't believe me. Believe Anthony if you like. You've got your wonderful, loving relationship to preserve, after all. But take it from me, darling, you'd be much better off just treating him as a casual lay. That's what I do.' She glanced at her watch. 'Must rush.' She walked off, leaving Camilla standing, speechless, her heart raw, on the pavement of Crown Office Row.

Lunching with Anthony in a Chancery Lane wine bar, Chay was expressing concern at Leo's sudden mysterious disappearance.

'Not exactly the most convenient time for him to do a runner, particularly as he's a member of the acquisitions committee. We've reached a critical point in putting together the core collection. You haven't any idea at all where he's gone, or when he'll be back?'

Anthony shrugged. 'My guess is that he's gone off to his country retreat to sort himself out. I've been there, but I can't for the life of me remember where it is exactly. Somewhere in deepest Oxfordshire. No one in chambers knows either, and the clerks don't have a phone number.'

'Oh, well.' Chay pushed away the remains of his vegetarian quiche. 'We can manage without him, but it's an inconvenience. He was in the middle of arranging for the purchase of some important sculptures. Strange – he seemed such a stable kind of guy to me. Very straight.'

Anthony gave a wry smile. 'Looks can be deceptive. Beneath the pin-stripes he's a bit screwed up, I'm afraid. Well, he is at the moment.' Anthony stared reflectively at his plate, then glanced up and signalled to a passing waiter for the bill. 'Actually, I've just had a thought. His ex-wife will have his number in the country. Damn. Why didn't I think of that before?' Anthony was astonished that he should have overlooked Rachel as a means of getting in touch with Leo. 'Tell you what, I'll see if I can get hold of him through her and find out what's going on.'

'I'd be grateful. I particularly don't want the acquisition of the Anthony Caro sculpture to fall through.' The waiter placed the bill in front of Chay, who looked at it, then slid it across to Anthony. 'Sorry I've only got enough cash for a taxi.'

With a sigh, Anthony took a credit card from his wallet. No matter how many millions Chay was now worth, clearly the habits formed over a lifetime of living in squats and hippy communes died very hard.

On his way back to his room, Anthony knocked on the door of the room Camilla shared with Gerald, the newest junior tenant, and put his head round. He was pleased to see that Gerald was still out. Camilla was at her desk, apparently absorbed in what she was writing, her head propped on one hand.

'Hi,' said Anthony, closing the door behind him. 'I was hoping to see you at lunch-time, but my father called in and I had to take him to lunch. Do you know, he never pays for a meal? I still have to –'

'Anthony, go away,' said Camilla, without looking up.

Anthony stopped a foot away from her desk, surprised by her tone. 'Sorry,' he said, faintly offended. 'I didn't realise you were too busy to chat.'

Camilla looked up. 'We have nothing, absolutely nothing to chat about. Leave me alone.'

Anthony was struck by the miserable, stony look in her eyes. His mind faltered, filling suddenly with guilt. Until he knew exactly what was wrong, he had no choice but to make his response defensive, tentative. 'Come on,' he said mildly, 'I thought we'd sorted things out. What I did was stupid and impulsive. I hoped you'd forgiven me –'

'You are unbelievable.' Camilla laid down her pen. 'You

still intend to stick to that lie, despite the fact that you might have known that Sarah would tell me everything sooner or later. How can you?' She sounded genuinely bewildered. 'How can you conduct a two-week affair with someone while I'm away, then lie about it, pretend it was a one-night stand, and still say you love me and that you want me to move in with you? I thought I knew you so well. I'm a complete idiot. No doubt that's what you were counting on.'

Anthony tried to interrupt, bleakly aware that the entire house of cards was coming down around his ears. 'It might as well have been just one night, for all that it mattered. Oh, God, I never wanted this to happen. I can't explain to you why –'

'I don't want you to explain anything. I only want to know one thing.' She paused, gazing at Anthony. 'Did you make love to her every night while I was away?'

There was a brief silence, in which Anthony felt swamped by horrible and complete humiliation. 'That's not the point. The point is that it's you –'

'Did you?'

'Yes. Almost. But it meant nothing, it was something I couldn't help –'

'Anthony, do go away. It's finished,' Camilla said with weary unhappiness, picking up her pen.

He hesitated, watching her begin to write calmly, aware of his own sudden desperation, his mind scrabbling in a futile way for a means of salvaging the situation. He began to speak, but she interrupted him.

'Go away.'

He tried again, this time raising his voice a little in frustration, but at that moment Gerald came in, bearing sandwiches and a cup of coffee, and Anthony stopped in angry embarrassment. Realising he had no choice but to leave, he went back to his own room and closed the door. He stood by the window, hands in pockets, staring down at the courtyard, his mind bleak and wretched. There was no way

284

back now. If Sarah had let Camilla know the extent of what had happened, then he couldn't see how it could ever be put right. He had taken a perfect and genuine love, and utterly destroyed it. Had it been a risk he wanted to run? he wondered. Did he possess some deep, subconscious urge to bugger up every relationship that was halfway good? He thought of the way Camilla had looked at him and almost groaned aloud. All the qualities he loved most in her were the very ones which made it certain that she would not forgive him. He knew that. He sat down at his desk and gazed inertly at the papers which were spread out before him. It was finished. The one relationship for which he had had real hopes, and he had brought about its end.

For a while he did nothing, just sat contemplating the destructive extent of his behaviour. Although he could happily have wrung Sarah's neck, he knew that her part in this was minimal. It was all his own doing. Sluggishly he tried to force his mind to think of other things, and remembered his conversation at lunch-time with Chay. Slowly he pulled his address book from the drawer, looked up Rachel's work number and rang her. At least it was something to take his mind off all that had just happened.

'Rachel? It's Anthony.'

'Oh, Anthony – hello.' Rachel sounded mildly surprised. 'How are you?'

'Fine,' he lied. 'Listen, I'll tell you why I'm ringing. I don't know if you know, but Leo has more or less disappeared from the face of the planet. Everyone's rather worried about him and we can't raise him at his London flat –'

'He's at Stanton,' cut in Rachel. 'I saw him over the weekend.'

'Stanton? That's his place near Oxford?' Anthony was relieved at the news.

'Yes. He said he was taking some time off. He seemed – well, a bit overwrought. As though things have got on top of him. His personal life and so on.'

That boy, thought Anthony. The one Leo had mentioned, the one he was so happy about. God, he might have known. He felt an unreasoning anger. 'Did he say anything about when he was coming back?'

'No. I only went there because he was looking after Oliver for me. My mother died at the weekend, you see. It was very sudden. Actually, you're lucky you caught me. I just came in to tidy up some loose ends. I have to take some time off, see to the funeral, go through her things ...' Rachel's voice trailed off.

'I'm really sorry.' Anthony allowed a respectful little pause, then said, 'Could you give me Leo's phone number there and some idea of where the house is? I think someone from chambers should try and have a word with him. He's left us in a bit of a jam, as you can imagine.'

'Yes, I can. Hold on a minute.' After a few seconds Rachel gave Anthony the phone number and directions to the house. Anthony thanked her and was about to hang up when Rachel said, 'By the way, can I ask you something? It's about Leo. I just wondered if he'd said anything about his application in respect of Oliver. You know, the access business. I thought if he'd mentioned it to anyone, it would be to you. He's very close to you. I'm worried that it may have contributed to – well, to his problems.'

Anthony hesitated. 'It might have. He has mentioned it in passing. I know that Oliver means the world to him and the past few months have been very tough – well, they must have been tough on both of you.'

'Yes ...' Rachel sighed. 'Anyway, I just wondered.'

'Right. Look, thanks for your help. Bye.'

Anthony hung up, fingering the piece of paper on which he'd jotted down Leo's address and number. His hand moved to the phone again, hesitating. He stood up, folding the piece of paper and slipping it into his pocket, and went downstairs.

'Henry, I'm taking the rest of the afternoon off. I'll see you tomorrow.'

'Right ho.'

Anthony took a taxi back to Kensington, studied his road map briefly, then set off in his car for Oxford.

Leo's Aston Martin sat on the broad gravel driveway in front of the house. Anthony parked and got out, relieved to see that Leo was there. He knocked, waited for a while, then knocked again. Perhaps he was wrong. Perhaps Leo had gone off somewhere. He had a picture of him, trudging the fields and roads at dusk, trying to exorcise whatever demons were tormenting him. But as he was about to turn away, Leo opened the door. Anthony was as much surprised by Leo's altered appearance as Rachel had been.

'Hi,' said Anthony a little uncertainly. 'I thought I'd look you up. We've all been worried about you.'

'We?' Leo's expression was blank, almost dismissive. He didn't look as though he was glad to see Anthony.

'You know – everyone in chambers.' Anthony still stood on the doorstep, wondering if Leo was going to turn him away.

But after a few moments Leo sighed and said, 'Come in.'

Anthony closed the door behind him and followed Leo into the drawing-room, where the fire was burning low. A book lay open, face down, on the sofa where Leo had been lying reading. Leo picked it up and closed it, then sat down with it on his lap. He looked up at Anthony. 'Sit down.'

Anthony sat in the armchair opposite. There was a silence. 'So,' said Anthony, 'what have you been up to since you left?'

It was a few seconds before Leo spoke. 'I suppose you could call it a re-evaluation.' His tone was flat. Anthony didn't think he had ever seen so spiritless a Leo in all the time he had known him. He found it disturbing.

'A re-evaluation?'

'Of everything. Myself, my life. What I am, what I'm not, what I should be.'

Anthony nodded thoughtfully. There was another silence, then he said, 'Actually, I pretty much liked you the way you were.'

For a second something quickened in Leo's expression. 'Did you? That's kind of you, Anthony. But things are not the same. Please don't think you can just pop down here and try to sort me out. You know nothing about how things have been with me recently. In fact, we haven't actually been very close for a while, have we? You've been busy with Camilla –'

'That's finished,' said Anthony quickly. He stood up abruptly and paced round the room. Leo sat in silence, watching him. 'I did something bloody stupid and it's over. Anyway, that's not the point. I'm here to talk about you. To help, if I can.'

'I rather think I may be beyond help. At any rate, the kind you're able to offer.'

The remoteness of Leo's manner caused Anthony to feel an instant's anger and unhappiness. 'Why don't you let me try? You're behaving as though I'm an unwelcome guest that you can't wait to see the back of. The way you're talking, this distant manner of yours –' He stopped, looking down at Leo, suddenly filled with the recollection of all that they had once meant to one another. The time in this room when Leo had kissed him, and held him. That had been so precious. Whose fault was it if distance had grown up between them? He hesitated, then sat down next to Leo and laid his hand upon his arm. 'Tell me. Just tell me everything, and then see if I can help,' said Anthony gently. 'I haven't forgotten, and neither have you.' Their eyes met, and an instantaneous current of feeling passed between them. Anthony was startled by its intensity, filled with sudden longing and affection. 'I still love you,' he said, not in the least surprised at how easily the words came.

Leo leaned back, closed his eyes, then moved his arm so

that his hand clasped Anthony's. Something seemed to loosen within him, a kind of emotional release. Then he began to tell him about Joshua and all that had happened.

When he had finished, Leo opened his eyes and stared blankly ahead. 'What do you do about love? It takes hold of you and makes you utterly powerless. Perhaps I give in to it too easily.' He turned and looked at Anthony. 'Do you think I give in to it too easily?' He searched in Anthony's brown eyes for an answer. Anthony said nothing. 'Why couldn't it have been you? Why not someone kind, with no mercenary motives, that I can be on equal terms with?' asked Leo thoughtfully. 'Why?'

'Because – because I didn't let it happen,' said Anthony quietly. 'If I had, it would probably all have ended just the way it did with Joshua.' There was a brief silence. 'Perhaps we were lucky,' went on Anthony. 'I'm still here. One way or another, I always will be. You should be asking why it couldn't have been Rachel. I've never understood that.'

'Oh, Rachel,' groaned Leo. 'Everything was wrong there from the beginning. My fault. My motives. Everything we do comes back on us. She tried. She really tried. But I can't give her what she wants. I couldn't even tell her about Joshua. She wouldn't understand. Wouldn't want to. It was hard enough keeping up a brave front with her when she came to fetch Oliver.' He laughed ruefully. 'Oliver seems to be the only person I don't have to pretend with, and that's because he's too little to care. But I've made a complete balls-up where he's concerned, of course.' He passed a hand across his face, rubbing at his beard. 'Another thing that hasn't helped,' he added, 'is that I started to get some rather unpleasant e-mails. In fact, that adjective doesn't begin to describe how vile they were.'

'At chambers?'

Leo shook his head. 'At home.' He reflected for a moment. 'Do you know, they actually frightened me. I've never received anonymous messages before.'

'Who do you think sent them?'

'I've no idea. Someone who plainly dislikes me. That covers a fairly broad sweep.'

'What about Joshua?' ventured Anthony.

'No,' said Leo thoughtfully. 'I don't think Joshua disliked me. And he wasn't that kind of person. Joshua was – was far too . . .' He stopped and sighed, a look of pain creasing his features.

'The point is,' said Anthony gently, 'what are you going to do? You can't just hide away down here for ever. Two weeks is a long time in anyone's politics, and your practice is going to suffer if you stay away much longer.' He paused, wondering if this was a wise thing to say. Given Leo's frame of mind, it was possible that he didn't want to give work any thoughts at present. He added tentatively, 'There's the museum as well. Chay's a bit worried about the Anthony Caro sculpture.'

Leo sighed. 'Oh, he's no need to worry about that. That's all tied up.' He glanced at Anthony. 'When's the next trustees meeting?'

'Wednesday. I think Chay would like you to be there. Things are coming together now and he's getting rather nervy. Besides,' added Anthony, 'there's also a chambers meeting on Friday. Jeremy's going to try and bulldoze through his proposals for moving to Sussex Street. You don't want to lose your say in that.'

Leo pondered this. 'No,' he said. 'You're right. When I came down here I didn't care if I never saw chambers again. But it's just about all there is, in the long run. That, and Oliver.' He stared at the carpet, musing. 'I suppose a couple of weeks away has helped me to come to terms with things. Nursing one's wounds in solitude is ultimately extremely boring. And I rather think that work has become a habit which is impossible to break. I keep thinking about it, about cases.' He glanced at Anthony, a slight smile betraying some of his old animation. 'Believe it or not, throughout my hermit-like existence of the past two weeks I have found myself wondering if it might not be a good idea to serve some interrogatories on the other side in that salvage case, just to upset Sinclair's. What do you think?'

Chapter sixteen

'You'll be pleased to know that I tracked Leo down,' Anthony announced to Henry the following morning. 'Well, that's something. I'd be even more pleased if I knew when he was going to show his face again.'

'Quite soon, I think.' He glanced at Felicity and smiled. 'Congratulations, by the way – David told me on the way in. When's the baby due?'

'May,' replied Felicity.

'Sorry you'll be leaving us, though. Is that for me? Thanks.' Anthony took his mail and went upstairs. Outside his room he bumped into Sarah.

'Good morning,' she said amiably.

'Possibly for you,' replied Anthony coldly. 'Tell me – is it something pathological, this desire to interfere in other people's lives, to ruin relationships?'

Sarah smiled. 'Oh dear, has your past caught up with you?'

At that moment Anthony could hear Roderick's footsteps descending the stairs. He'd by no means finished saying all he wanted to say to Sarah. He opened the door of his room and gestured to her to go in.

He closed the door and turned to her. 'Why did you have to tell her? What earthly good has it done any of us?'

Sarah sighed. 'You don't get it, do you? It's not her finding out that's messed things up. It's you. And if it hadn't happened now, it would have happened sooner or later. Face it. I've probably done you a favour. Just think how it would have been if she were to find out about you six or seven years from now, perhaps with a jolly little baby or two around. Now, that really would be an unhappy situation. As it is, she knows the kind of person you are, and she can go off and find someone who really is stable and considerate and faithful, and all those other boring things.'

'What would you know about the kind of person I am?' demanded Anthony, smarting none the less from the painful truth of this.

'Put it this way – you may dress and sound and behave like all the other drips in this and every other set of chambers in the Temple, and you may want to lead a nice conventional life, but you just can't handle it. You have this ideal, this cosy, safe relationship that you want to construct with someone, so that you can hide away from reality. Do you think if we hadn't got it together a few weeks ago that you and Camilla would have lived happily ever after? If it hadn't been me, there would have been someone else. You'll never be satisfied, Anthony, because you don't really know what you want. You just think you do. Or you think you know what you *ought* to want. You're like Leo, living a lie. Only at least Leo woke up to the fact a year or so ago. When are you going to?' Anthony said nothing. 'Anyway, I've got work to do. Can't keep dear David waiting.' She left, closing the door behind her.

Anthony turned and walked slowly to the window, his hands in his pockets. Was all that true? Was he destined to go through life trying to find the perfect partner, only to see each and every relationship come to nothing through his own perfidy and weakness? He tried to trace the evolution of his feelings for Camilla. He had liked her, he had enjoyed the safe acceptance that he found in her. It had been easy to make himself fall in love with her. Was that what he had done? Made himself? He remembered the first time he had made love to her and realised that there had been a sense of completion about it, as though he had taken another satisfactory step on some then unspecified road. The road to the right relationship. Certainly he had wanted her but, as he had discovered, he wanted most attractive young women, in a random, automatic sort of way. And asking her to move in with him – had that just been an attempt to parcel it all up neatly? It was hard to tell how much was genuine, and how much manufactured. He felt pain at having lost Camilla, but less than he had imagined. Surely if he really had been in love with her, the loss would have been devastating, crippling?

He stood moodily by the window, looking down, and suddenly a familiar figure came through the archway and across Caper Court. Leo was walking rapidly towards chambers, his cashmere coat slung carelessly over his shoulders, looking for all the world as though nothing had ever happened to disturb the tranquillity of his life. He had shaved, Anthony noticed, though he hadn't yet had his hair cut, its silver fringe an inch or so over his collar. He saw Leo stop to chat with another barrister crossing the court, their breath making little smoky plumes in the cold air as they talked. As he stood at the window watching him, Anthony was struck by the force of his affection for the man. He had always taken Leo's presence for granted, even in those times when they were not close. The sound of his voice, his rapid step on the stair, the sight of his smile – Anthony realised that they were part of his own security. Leo and the other barrister parted company, and Leo's figure disappeared from sight below. Anthony thought about what Sarah had said. Were he and Leo alike? Perhaps. He recalled the feelings he had once had for Leo, and wondered whether he hadn't found more pleasure and intellectual stimulation in Leo's company than that of any woman. Not just intellectual. There had been a time when he had thought that he and Leo could be more than just friends. But at what cost? His tenancy, almost certainly. He could not imagine how things would have been. Besides, he had been young and too afraid, too confused by his feelings. Perhaps Sarah was right.

Perhaps he was lying to himself, trying to construct safe, conventional relationships that were ultimately doomed to disaster. Leo was probably the one person with whom he was happiest. But Leo now had his struggles, his own problems to contend with. That visit to Stanton, although it had helped Leo to some degree, had shown Anthony just how isolated Leo really was. With a sigh Anthony sat down at his desk to work.

Felicity and Henry looked up as Leo came into the clerks' room, shrugging off his coat. Felicity thought he looked better than he had when he left, though he still had dark hollows beneath his eyes.

'Good morning. I hope you managed to keep my practice afloat while I was away?'

Felicity caught Henry's stony look and said brightly, 'Yeah, we muddled through, Mr Davies. There's quite a lot of stuff here for you, though. And your diary'll need sorting out. We weren't certain when you'd be back.'

Henry waited to see if Leo would take this cue for an apology, but Leo merely put out a hand for his mail and said, 'Thanks. Pop up in half an hour and we'll go through it.'

'Bloody cheek,' muttered Henry, when Leo was out of earshot. 'You'd think he could at least say sorry, all the trouble he's put us to.'

'You know what he's like. No excuses, no apologies. I'm just glad he's back.'

In his room Leo leafed through his mail. He paused at one letter, a small, oblong envelope with his name written on it in meticulous script, obviously hand-delivered. He tore it open and read through the contents. It was from Desmond Broadhurst, letting Leo know that he was going to be leaving the Temple by Christmas to live with his daughter in Lincoln, and would Leo care to come to a small drinks party he was throwing on December the eleventh. Leo read the letter thoughtfully, then folded it up. An astonishing yet rather obvious idea had just occurred to him. He sat thinking for a few moments, then stood up and walked to the window, and looked across to Desmond's top-floor flat. Was there any reason why it couldn't be done? In his mind he mapped out the plan of the rooms on the floor above. The room at the end, where Desmond's flat adjoined number 5, was occupied by Roderick, so he'd have to move out while the work was done. But it was possible. There were eight good-sized rooms in Desmond's flat. Leo tapped his chin thoughtfully and smiled.

Felicity climbed wearily up the flight of stairs to the flat. It had been a long day, made longer by having had to field all the little jokes and congratulations in chambers, now that the news of her pregnancy had gradually got around. The kind things everyone said only brought home more forcefully to her the fact that she would be leaving in a few months to face a future that suddenly seemed frightening in its uncertainty. She reached the front door, wondering whether Vince would be in. She almost hoped he wouldn't be. Since the events of Saturday evening, everything was suddenly horribly, starkly changed. Vince had retreated into a state of angry depression. He seemed more concerned about the idea that he might not be able to get his black cab licence now than about the condition of the youth with whom he'd had the fight. Felicity sometimes wondered whether Vince properly appreciated what would happen if the boy died. The thought tormented her every waking moment and each day she would come back home, half expecting to discover that Vince had been carted off by the police again to face a more serious charge than GBH. When she tried to discuss it with Vince, he simply clammed up, refused to speak.

The sound of the television as she opened the front door told her that Vince was in. She glanced into the kitchen as she passed it and saw the empty cans by the sink. Her heart sank. The one thing she didn't need was for Vince to start drinking. But it was inevitable, she supposed. It was his way of coping.

She went into the living-room and found Vince stretched out on the sofa, watching television, the pages of *Sporting Life* scattered about and a half-drunk bottle of vodka on the floor next to the sofa. He looked up when Felicity came in, but said nothing, merely reached for the bottle and took a swig.

'Oh, Vince . . .' sighed Felicity. 'This isn't going to do any good. Have you just been sat in here all day?'

'Course I bloody have,' replied Vince. 'What else is there for me to do? What do you suggest, eh?'

'Don't have a go at me,' said Felicity, taking off her shoes and rubbing at her toes. 'I just think you'd be better off getting out, instead of lying around here feeling sorry for yourself and getting pissed. That's not going to help.'

'Oh, yeah? Go out and do what, exactly?' Vince glared at her. 'You know what that pig said. My chances of doing my knowledge are knackered now.'

'You don't know that. Not yet. You might not go down on that GBH charge. You can't tell. So why don't you just carry on doing your routes? Then at least you're not wasting your time –'

'Oh, do me a favour!' Vince suddenly shouted, swinging his feet off the sofa. 'Of course I'm gonna go down! Aren't you the one who's been going on about this bloke dying, an' all? Then I'm gonna go down fucking big time, aren't I? And you tell me I ought to be out on the bike, like I've got nothing to worry about!' He grabbed his boots and pulled them on. 'Okay, lady, if that's what you want me to do, I'll do it. I'll pretend that everything's hunky-dory. Anything to get away from you goin' on at me.'

He got up and picked his jacket off the back of a chair.

'Vince, don't be stupid,' said Felicity in alarm, getting up and following him as he strode to the front door. 'You've been drinking all afternoon. Don't go and make it all worse.' Vince picked up his cycle helmet in the hallway, ignoring her, then opened the front door. Felicity, in her bare feet, followed him out on to the landing, grabbing at the sleeve of his jacket.

He stopped on the top step and turned to her, his eyes angry and drunk. 'I'm doing what you want, Fliss. All right?' He shook his sleeve free of her grasp and started down the stairs. Felicity reached out to pull him back, but he had moved away too quickly. Her hand clutched at air and she stumbled forward, missing her footing, and fell. An agonising pain shot through her knee as it made contact with the concrete steps and she tumbled past Vince, grabbing for the banister and missing. It seemed absurd to her that she kept on falling, as if for ever. Then a searing light touched her vision for a second as her head hit the stairs and she was unconscious, sprawled at the bottom of the flight of steps.

Henry learned about Felicity's accident from Roderick the following morning. 'How is she? What happened?' he asked in alarm.

'She's not too bad. It was quite a tumble, as far as I can gather. She's cracked a bone in her knee and – well, very sadly, she's lost the baby.'

'Oh, God . . .' muttered Henry. His mind reached out to Felicity, filled with pity and unhappiness.

'Anyway, she's going to be away for some time. I don't think we can expect her back until after Christmas, at the earliest.'

'No, of course not.'

'Think you can cope?'

'Probably not,' sighed Henry. 'But don't worry – you'll be the first to know.'

Henry went about his work in miserable distraction. He would go and see her that evening, take her something. She liked those glossy magazines, *Tatler* and *Vogue*. He'd pick up a couple on the way, and some chocolates. But how useless and trivial such things would appear in the light of her loss.

Some flowers? No, there was something too celebratory about flowers. Maybe he should take nothing. It was ironic, really, to think that when she had first found out she was pregnant she had wanted to get rid of the baby. And now that she had come round to being happy and accepting it, this should happen. Poor Felicity. Still. A sudden realisation came to Henry and with it a little surge of happiness that made him feel quite guilty. Felicity wouldn't be leaving chambers after all. There was that. So one of Felicity's worries had been wiped out, in a cruel way. Henry sighed. Perhaps it was wrong of him, but given that Vince's chances of earning a living for Felicity and the baby had vanished overnight, he couldn't help thinking that, in some ways, it was all for the best. He really couldn't.

At the end of the day, just as he was about to leave, Rachel rang Leo. 'I just wanted to thank you for looking after Oliver on Saturday night.'

'He's my son,' replied Leo. 'You don't need to thank me.'

'No ... Well, anyway ... I suppose the real reason I'm ringing is to say that you can drop the application for access in respect of Oliver.'

'What do you mean?'

'I mean there's no need. If you want him every other weekend you can have him.'

There was silence for a moment. Then Leo said slowly, 'You do know that because of what happened when the welfare officers came round, I'd probably have been unsuccessful anyway, don't you?'

'Yes. And I said some things to them which might not have helped, if we're being honest. But I've done a good deal of thinking since Sunday and I think Oliver needs you just as much as he needs me.'

'Thank you,' said Leo, his voice light with relief and happiness. 'Really, thank you.'

When she put the phone down, Rachel felt lifted by the

fact of having made the decision, but was conscious of a sense of loss, too. Still, Oliver would only be away for one night every two weeks, she told herself. And perhaps she had been unfair on Charles recently, by not taking him into account in all this. Maybe he did need more of her love and attention than she'd been prepared to give him. An idea suddenly came to her. Tomorrow was the day of her mother's funeral and after that ordeal was over there were four more days until Charles got home on Sunday. She had told Nichols & Co. that she wouldn't be back until next week. Why shouldn't she just leave Margaret in charge of Oliver, and fly out to spend the last couple of days with Charles? She would have to start getting used to being away from Oliver for brief spells, after all. It would be good for all of them, all three of them. With a smile she picked up the phone to enquire about flights to Romania.

Leo came downstairs. He dropped a brief on Henry's desk and glanced at his gloomy face. 'Thinking about Felicity?' he asked.

'Yes. I'm going along to see how she is once I've finished here.'

'Good idea,' said Leo. 'Give her my best. I'm very glad I talked her into taking out private health cover a few months ago. You never know when something rotten is going to happen.' He slung his scarf around his neck, about to leave, then paused. 'By the way,' he added, 'I'm sorry if I rather dropped you in it over the past couple of weeks.'

'That's all right,' replied Henry quickly. 'We all need a bit of time off now and again.'

'Yes . . .' Leo paused. 'Rather interestingly, I stopped shaving while I was away. It's only the second time in my life I've ever done that. Grown a beard, I mean. It was amusing while it lasted, but I'm rather glad to be rid of it. Facial hair's a bit of a transitory novelty, don't you think?'

Henry flushed slightly. Was Leo having a go at him? All

right, he knew his moustache hadn't been the success he'd hoped, but still . . . He resisted the temptation to put his hand up to his mouth. 'You could be right, Mr Davies,' he replied stiffly.

'Night.'

'Night.'

When he had finished, Henry went into the little down-stairs lavatory and stared at his face. Then he went back to the clerks' room and fished out Felicity's nail scissors from her drawer, and the electric razor he kept in his own desk, and went back to the mirror. Carefully he clipped away most of the length of the moustache, then shaved off the bristles. He stared at the result. Better. Much better. In fact, it was a real relief to be without it. He gave himself a smile, rinsed the hairs out of the wash-basin and went off to lock up.

Melissa wrapped herself in a long towelling bathrobe after her shower and lay down on the bed. She closed her eyes and drew her hands idly, sensuously across her body and thought of Leo. Sexual fantasy had taken on a whole new dimension where he was concerned. It had been astonishing to discover how pure loathing failed to eclipse desire, but, in fact, ignited new and stranger passions. Passions which needed to be satisfied in their own ways. The very creation of those e-mails had been in itself a voluptuous and pleasurably obscene act, and sending them, envisaging Leo's repulsion and fear on receiving them, had been deliciously vindictive. There was something almost sexual in the participatory nature of it, sharing in her imagination his reactions, probing his vulnerability, reaching to the very core of him. She shivered with pleasure as she thought of it and the movements of her fingers quickened. That was the black and secret pleasure of it – reaching him, touching him. A very intimate revenge. The phone calls, the sound of his voice, at first assured and then slightly hesitant, talking into the void, while she remained silent at the other end, had been particularly satisfying, but she would make no more of those. They were too risky.

After a moment she sighed and drew her robe together. She opened her eyes. In an hour she would see him. The fact that she still wanted him after the memory of that disastrous evening together no longer surprised her. It was desire of a very different flavour, after all. What she now felt, this mixture of lust and hatred, made her previous infatuation seem quite innocuous – almost innocent. These new feelings were lubricious, intoxicating. She gave a little shudder of pleasure at the thought that she had yet to explore all the different and decadent ways in which she could torment him and satisfy her cravings. She rose from the bed with a smile and began to dress herself in readiness, trembling like a girl at the prospect of seeing him again.

Leo drove to Shoreditch. Anthony had said the meeting was at seven, and that he would come along later after he had finished what he suspected would be a lengthy con at 4 Essex Court.

Work on the museum had progressed considerably since Leo's last visit. The renovations were now complete and the whole place had an exciting, airy feel to it, a showplace just waiting for its exhibits. It looked as though Chay's hopes of having the opening around Christmas would be realised. He walked through the empty, echoing galleries to the meeting room and found everyone already there. Chay gave his customary peace sign greeting and came over. 'Glad you're here. I was a bit worried you might not make it. Anthony said you'd been away.'

'I took a couple of weeks off, that's all. I hope Anthony reassured you about the sculpture. It's on its way from Paris, plus a few other rather interesting items. I'm afraid I didn't have time to run them past the rest of the committee, but I don't think you'll be disappointed.'

Leo took his place at the table and said good evening to the rest of the trustees, meeting Melissa's cool gaze with a faint nervousness. He didn't care to remember the embarrassment of that last encounter. The sole resulting benefit, he hoped, was that she was probably now disinclined to continue her amatory pursuit of him.

The meeting got under way. Chay ran through the list of works which had been accumulated over the past months, and there was discussion as to where and how they would be exhibited. Leo made a few contributions, but mainly listened. He was conscious of Melissa studying him covertly. 'So now, finally, we come to the matter of the open space,' announced Chay. 'I'm pleased to say that Melissa's come up with some very exciting plans. I'll let her tell you all about them.'

Melissa smiled and glanced round the table. 'I don't really deserve any credit. That belongs to the people who have come up with the ideas. They're a women's collective called Beaver – well, it's actually spelt with a "u" at the end, and it stands for "beautification of the environment and visual urban regeneration". Their field of work is urban environmental projects, with a particular focus on bringing rural values to inner-city sites, utilising their essential drabness to accentuate the textual contrasts of city and countryside.'

'Lovely, but I wish you'd get to the point, Melissa,' interrupted Derek Harvey dryly. 'What exactly is going to go into the open space?'

'I was about to tell you, Derek,' replied Melissa tartly. 'As I say, the idea is to juxtapose nature and the urban setting. What they've done so far is to break up the ground and turf it. Unfortunately it's dark now, and there isn't an awful lot to see, as it's still at the formative stage. Now, when the turf has grown – and unfortunately some of it seems to have died, but then, it's not the optimum time of year to start this kind of project – anyway, when it's grown, the idea is that it will be long and lush, giving the feel of a country meadow, but it's the anarchic context which will give it its real impact. And in

303

this meadow area the women are going to build a sheep pen, and in the pen will be sheep, cropping the grass. Around the green area they're going to erect a series of television monitors, on which will be shown – and this, I think, is one of the most exciting aspects of the whole thing – continuous film of rolling countryside. In addition, they're planning the use of reflective material to mirror the urban decay that surrounds the museum and heighten the contrast.'

Derek, chin on hand, stared at her. 'Who's going to look after the sheep? An inner-city shepherd?'

Melissa accepted the suggestion with serious thoughtfulness. 'That could be a rather good idea. It would add the perfect touch of irony, wouldn't it? Anyway, to continue. The sheep pen will be moved around the green site, so that different parts are cropped. The idea is to create a kind of grass sculpture. And the sheep will be belled, so that their movement and sound will produce a symphonic, gentle contrast to the basic environment. I'm in the process of getting a costs breakdown from the collective, and I'll let you all have details as soon as they're ready.'

Derek shook his head, too bemused to pass the remotest criticism. The others shifted slightly in their chairs and a few sighed.

'Well, I like it,' said Chay. 'It's organic, interactive, totally visual. Just what we need. It's naturally a pity that it won't be operative when the museum opens, but in the nature of open-space projects, it takes the right weather, and so on.' He smiled round at the assembled trustees. 'I take it we're all in favour of going ahead?'

'I think we should look at the costs breakdown first,' said Tony Gear. 'Make sure that it's realistic.' There was a murmur of agreement.

'Yes – yes, I suppose that's right,' said Chay. 'In any event, I think that just about concludes the business for this evening.'

People rose from their chairs. 'Personally,' murmured

Derek to Leo, 'I think that woman is totally bonkers.' He hitched his shabby raincoat round his shoulders. 'My one hope is that a few of her sheep fall foul of the local organic urban Rottweilers. Beaver, my arse.' He moved off.

Leo slipped on his coat and headed for the door, hoping to avoid any contact with Melissa. But she waylaid him, laying a thin, insistent hand upon his sleeve. His heart sank as their eyes met. He had so hoped that their drunken evening together would be the end of it. But her lips were forming a smile.

'Don't you think you've behaved in a rather ungentlemanly way?' The smile was one of steel, almost a leer. 'The least I expected was a phone call.'

There was something so disturbing about her expression, and about the unwarranted pressure of her fingers on his arm, that Leo was moved to rudeness. 'A phone call? Why on earth should I phone you?'

The distaste in his voice made her shrink, but she managed a light shrug. 'Well, we'd both had a little too much to drink, but it had been an enjoyable evening in its way – hadn't it? And it could have been even more enjoyable.' She felt her hatred slacken. Here, in his presence, his flesh beneath her hand, she was still willing to have him on ordinary terms, without malice. Her voice was low and breathy. 'I thought you might see that, under other circumstances, we could have been very good together. Very good. I thought you might still want that.'

Leo stared at her, aware of mild revulsion. There was something oddly disjointed about her features, as though their expression might fragment with the force of whatever emotions bubbled within her. Perhaps Derek was right – perhaps she was mildly unhinged. He regretted now ever having given her a lift home that first night. He shook his arm free. 'Melissa, let us be clear about one thing. That evening was a mistake. There are no circumstances, apart from these trustee meetings, when I would ever wish to see

305

you. Forgive my bluntness, but I want there to be no future misunderstandings.' Turning to go, he added, 'And if you feel an apology is due for my behaviour that evening, please accept one.'

He reached the door and collided with Anthony coming in.

'Have I missed the entire meeting?' asked Anthony. 'I thought Henry Runcimore was never going to shut up.'

'I'm afraid so,' replied Leo. 'Not to worry. Let's go for a drink and I'll fill you in on the important bits, especially the open-space project. You'll like that.'

Melissa stood by the table, the fingers which had held Leo's arm opening and closing. What a mistake he had made. He had had a chance, and he had thrown it away in ignorance. He deserved everything that might happen. The thought of exacting her revenge now spread like fire through her mind with a sensual, anticipatory warmth.

Cautiously Henry pushed open the door of the hospital room and put his head round. The room was lit only by a small lamp by the bed, where Felicity lay, eyes closed. She opened them and saw Henry, who smiled.

'How are you?' he asked, sitting down in a chair next to the bed.

'Bloody awful,' sighed Felicity. She looked pale, her eyes weary with dejection.

'I'm really sorry about the baby,' said Henry, and put a hand over hers.

'Ow!' said Felicity. 'That's my bad wrist. I must have bashed it when I fell down, along with every other bit of me. Here, have the other.' She slipped her other hand into Henry's and he stroked it. To his alarm, he saw large tears suddenly well up in Felicity's eyes, and her shoulders began to shake.

'Hey, come on, it'll be all right,' he said soothingly, and

tried clumsily to pat her shoulder. It wasn't really possible to give her a hug from the chair.

'Oh, Henry,' said Felicity through her weeping, 'it's like the worst time ever. I can't believe how wrong everything's going. It's not just losing the baby. My mum was in a couple of hours ago. That boy that Vince was in the fight with. He died.'

'Oh, God,' said Henry. 'Oh, God.'

'And they've got Vince in custody. They reckon he'll be charged with murder.'

'No,' said Henry. 'From what you've told me, Vince didn't murder anyone. Don't worry. That's just what the police have to charge him with. The CPS will bring it down.'

'It doesn't matter,' sobbed Felicity. 'He'll go to prison. I know he will. And it's partly my fault. I was going on at him, that's why he went out on the bike –'

'It's not your fault,' interrupted Henry. 'It's just all a horrible piece of bad luck.'

'Yeah,' sniffed Felicity. She leaned back against the pillows. 'But I can't help feeling responsible, in a way.'

'You mustn't worry,' said Henry. 'The thing to do is to get better, and then see how you can help Vince.' He paused, stroking her hand, wishing he had the nerve just to put his arms around her. She looked so vulnerable, so pretty. 'Everyone in chambers sends their love.'

Felicity smiled through her tears. 'That's nice. In fact, it's the only good thing about all this. At least I've still got you lot.'

'That's right.'

She looked more closely at Henry. 'You've shaved it off. I've only just noticed.'

'Mmm. I got a bit bored with it.'

'I'm glad,' said Felicity. 'I really liked you better without it.'

Anthony went home that night, his heart and mind full of

307

Leo. It was the first time in many months that they had spent time alone together, apart from the Sunday when Anthony had gone to Stanton. Then relations had been tentative, still balanced on the uncertainties of Leo's state of mind. This evening, however, he had seemed to be recovering something of his old self. Leo had told him about Rachel's decision, and it had only dawned on Anthony then, listening to him, just how much Oliver meant to Leo. Having never seen Oliver, Anthony had always had difficulty in imagining how he fitted into Leo's life. From the very first time he had met him, Leo had been to Anthony a most singular creature, a man who purposely kept his life devoid of ties and emotional responsibilities. It was hard to think of him as a father. Clearly, however, it was now one of the most important aspects of Leo's existence. Anthony felt a fleeting sense of envy, that this small being should occupy so vast a space in Leo's life and heart. He had held such a place once.

He pondered these things as he strolled from the station to his flat. This evening had brought home to him how pleasurable it had all once been. Listening to Leo talk about Joshua had created again the atmosphere of intimacy which had once existed between them. He had found himself experiencing a touch of jealousy as Leo described the intensity of his feelings for the boy, but he was glad that Leo seemed to have recovered sufficiently to talk about the affair with some detachment. As he let himself into his darkened flat, Anthony realised that he hadn't thought about Camilla once during the hours he had spent with Leo.

The following afternoon Anthony sat at his desk, deeply absorbed in work, when Leo knocked and put his head round the door. Anthony looked up and experienced that odd tipping sensation in his heart at the sight of him, something he associated with his early days at Caper Court. It was only because of the dream he had had the night before, he told himself. Its vestiges still clung there, like a veil across his thoughts. It was a long time since he had dreamed about Leo.

'Chambers meeting. Had you forgotten?'

Anthony glanced at his watch and saw with surprise that it was four o'clock. 'No. I just lost track of time. Hold on.' He slipped on his jacket, and together he and Leo made their way upstairs to Cameron's room, where the other tenants were assembling. In the weeks since Cameron's death his personal belongings had been taken away by his widow, but the big man's character and personality still seemed to pervade the room. The matter of his successor was the first item on the agenda, and it was agreed as a matter of course that Roderick, who had been acting head of chambers, should take over the position permanently.

Then, after a few minor matters of chambers' expenditure had been dealt with, Jeremy raised the question of moving chambers to Sussex Street. With his customary confidence he recited the advantages of the move, the low rent, the additional prestige which state-of-the-art technology and facilities would bring to chambers, and the rest listened with a dull sense of inevitability. Leo glanced around at them. He caught Anthony's eye and gave him a brief, secretive smile.

'The fact is, if we look around for suitable premises within the Temple, we could wait for ever and there's no guarantee that we'd secure the kind of terms we want. We need to expand, and quickly, and this seems to me the perfect option. I think it's an unarguable case,' concluded Jeremy.

With a little thrill of affection Anthony caught Leo's smile. Leo glanced at Jeremy and remarked mildly, 'Surely, Jeremy, you've been at the Bar long enough to know that there's no such thing as an unarguable case.'

'Arguable or not, Leo, the fact is that this is the best we can do. And there's no point in sentimentalising about the Temple, and tradition, and all that nonsense. I, for one, am fed up with the limitations of the place. There is no viable alternative.'

'But there is,' said Leo. He got up and walked to the window, holding the attention of the others. He glanced out, then turned to them. 'In two weeks' time Desmond Broadhurst will be vacating his flat on the top floor of 7 Caper Court. He's lived there for years. The flat has eight good-sized rooms, a kitchen and a bathroom. It's perfect for our requirements. I've spoken to the Estates Committee about it and, subject to negotiations, they're agreeable in principle to our taking it over as an annexe.' There was a murmur of interest among the other barristers. 'The advantages are obvious. We are spared the upheaval of complete removal, the additional rent we would have to pay remains on favourable terms, and we are still within the Temple. Now, Jeremy may fret under the yoke of tradition, but I for one can do without air-conditioning and windows I can't open.' Jeremy tried to bluster an interruption, but Leo carried on. 'It also means that we are spared the tiresome business of drawing up a constitution, giving cross-indemnities and so forth. Those are aspects of Jeremy's proposals which he hasn't so far mentioned – or, perhaps, thought of.' He paused, looking round. 'So, I propose that we expand by taking over Desmond's flat, rather than moving lock, stock and barrel out of the Temple.'

Leo strolled back to his seat and sat down. Roderick looked round at the other members of chambers, his expression pleased and unmistakably relieved. 'Well, I think we can take a vote on it, can't we? Those in favour of expanding chambers to occupy the top floor of number seven, please raise your hands.'

Everybody raised their hands except Jeremy. Then he, too, shrugged and raised his hand. Much as he disliked being bested by Leo, he couldn't object. Even he knew that it was a provident solution.

'Excellent,' said Roderick. He looked at Leo. 'I take it that you'll be able to get more details in due course from the

Estates Committee so that we can discuss them at the next chambers meeting?'

'Of course.' Leo thrust his hands into his pockets and tipped his seat back, smiling in a way that Anthony hadn't seen for a long time.

Leo drove home that night with a feeling of mild satisfaction, and enormous relief at the knowledge that the threat of leaving the Temple had been removed. With luck, he thought, as he walked from the garage to the flat, he could see out the rest of his days in Caper Court. Maybe that was a melancholy notion, beginning and ending one's days in the same place. But to Leo it had a certain comfort. He went upstairs and let himself into the dark flat. He instantly felt a pang of longing for the days, not so long ago, when it would have been bright and welcoming, Joshua in the kitchen, or loafing around listening to music. Now it was silent. He felt himself beginning to tremble, the feelings within him give way. No, he couldn't let that happen again. This was where he had to live for the present. There was nowhere else that he could sensibly go. He snapped on some lights and went into the drawing-room, poured himself a drink and sat down. The effort of holding together the pieces of his life, of presenting a sane façade to the world, was taxing. Day by day it got a little better, but Leo knew he still had a long way to go until he recovered from the events of the past few months. If he ever did.

At least he had the comfort of knowing that Oliver would be with him regularly. Thank God Rachel had given in. If she hadn't, the court would almost certainly have rejected his application and that might just have finished him off. God knows what he'd have done then. One could only take so much of one's world falling to pieces. Now, with the knowledge that he would see Oliver every other week and that chambers would be staying put, he felt a tenuous hope. The pain of losing Joshua didn't diminish – there were still moments, wild and futile, when Leo felt as though he could willingly throw everything in and go and find him, try to bring him back. He had never loved anyone with such passion in his life. Still, to have known that depth of feeling, to have tasted the heaven and the hell of it, was perhaps not wasted. Work lessened the torment. He shouldn't have spent so much time away. Leo drank some more of his whisky, leaned his head back and closed his eyes.

It was because he was thinking of Joshua that the sound of the buzzer to the flat made him jump with a sense of *déjà vu*. It ebbed away quickly. It couldn't be Joshua. It never would be again. He went to the intercom.

'Hello?'

'Leo? It's me, Sarah. Let me in – I'm freezing.' He could almost hear the shiver in her voice.

Mildly surprised, Leo pressed the buzzer and opened the door, then went back into the drawing-room and sat down.

He heard the front door close, then she appeared in the doorway, dressed in a full-length black coat, her blonde hair tucked into the collar.

'Hi,' she said. 'I was in the neighbourhood, so I thought I'd drop by and see you.'

'How very sociable of you. Help yourself to a drink.' He realised that he felt quite grateful for the sight of her.

'Thanks.' She took off her coat and poured herself a Scotch, wandering round the room with it, glancing at books and paintings. 'It's all very tasteful, Leo. And quite clinical, if I may say.' She sipped her drink. 'Not like Stanton.'

'Which do you prefer?' Leo flipped open the silver box on the little table next to his chair and took out a cigar. Seeing this, Sarah picked up a heavy silver lighter from the mantelpiece and came across with it. She snapped it open and bent slightly to light his cigar. He murmured his thanks and watched her as she recrossed the room to put it back, taking in the lines of her black-stockinged thighs. Did she really get away with wearing skirts that short to chambers?

he wondered. No doubt David enjoyed it too much to say anything.

'I prefer Stanton,' said Sarah, sitting down opposite him and crossing her legs. 'But then, I know it, don't I? I have certain – memories.'

Leo smiled and drew on his cigar. 'Your life must consist of a rich and varied assortment of memories.'

'Mmm. Some are more amusing than others.' She sighed. 'To be honest with you, I get a little weary of it all. Men. Different men. In the end, they're all much alike. Not you, though.'

'No?'

'No.' She studied him as she sipped her drink. 'I hear you managed to persuade the rest of chambers not to move to Sussex Street.'

'They didn't need much persuading. I simply came up with a better idea.'

'You always do.'

'Tell me, dearest Sarah, why exactly are you here? Not that it isn't lovely to see you, but with you there's usually an agenda.'

She shrugged. 'None. I was bored.' She fingered her glass. 'And, to be honest, I've been worried about you.'

Leo let out a short burst of laughter. 'Worried? You?'

'Don't laugh. I *was* worried when you were away. I knew you must be at Stanton. I almost went down to see you.'

He saw that she was sincere. 'Well, that was sweet of you. But I think I'm over the worst,' he lied.

'Are you?' She got up from her armchair and came over to him. She knelt down, setting her glass on the carpet, and folded her arms across his knee and rested her chin on them. There was something unguarded about the move which rather touched him. 'I thought you might be feeling rather lonely. Or bored.'

'Both. Potentially.' He raised his cigar to his lips but she put up a hand and took it lightly from him, then crushed it into an ashtray.

'In which case, since I was rather feeling that way, I thought we might keep one another company.' She ran a hand slowly along the length of his thigh.

He smiled down at her, enjoying her practised flirtatiousness, the hidden depths of her glance. She always had been the most marvellous tease.

'Come here.' He drew her up so that she was kneeling between his legs. 'Since you're in the neighbourhood,' he murmured, 'I don't see why not.' And he kissed her, glad of the familiarity, the unthreatening, easy acceptance of their mutual desires. If anyone understood him, Sarah did.

Anthony parked his car on the north side of the square and sat there for a moment. He had done enough thinking. After the chambers meeting he had gone back to his room, and for two hours he had wrestled with his thoughts, searching his feelings, questioning his motives over and over again. He had told himself that it was simply a reaction to Camilla's rejection, and an over-reaction at that. Then he had tried to persuade himself that he was fantasising, creating an illusory ideal of a relationship founded on mere hope, without any substance. But he could not ignore it. It had grown on him all day. He had known last night, as they sat and talked, and he watched the lines of Leo's face, the cadence of his voice. He wanted to be with the man, to be part of his life, on whatever terms. If he didn't take this step now, he never would. It was all unknown, untested. But at least he knew what he felt.

He pulled his key from the ignition, got out and locked the car. Then, turning up the collar of his coat, trembling a little with the cold and the force of his own hopes and emotions, he crossed the deserted square, went up the steps, and pressed the bell of Leo's flat.